Risk of Harm

Risk of Harm

Lucie Whitehouse

4th ESTATE · London

4th Estate
An imprint of HarperCollins*Publishers*
1 London Bridge Street
London SE1 9GF

www.4thEstate.co.uk

HarperCollins*Publishers*
1st Floor, Watermarque Building, Ringsend Road
Dublin 4, Ireland

First published in Great Britain in 2021 by 4th Estate

1

A catalogue record for this book is available from the British Library

ISBN 978-0-00-826904-3

This novel is entirely a work of fiction. The names, characters and incidents
portrayed in it are the work of the author's imagination. Any resemblance to actual
persons, living or dead, events or localities is entirely coincidental.

Typeset in Minion Pro by Palimpsest Book Production Ltd, Falkirk, Stirlingshire

Printed and Bound in the UK using
100% Renewable Electricity at CPI Group (UK) Ltd

MIX
Paper from
responsible sources
FSC
www.fsc.org **FSC® C007454**

This book is produced from independently certified FSC™ paper
to ensure responsible forest management.

For more information visit: www.harpercollins.co.uk/green

For Suzy and Paul
&
Millie and Andrew,
safe harbours in the storm

Chapter One

Robin could feel bracelets of sweat round the suit's elasticated cuffs. It was early but the air was already humid and her heart was thudding from the physical effort. Ahead, Rafferty, the scene manager, was hacking through the undergrowth as if they were up the Amazon rather than ten minutes from Birmingham city centre. She and Malia followed in silence, focused on staying upright and alive. Loose electrical cables, open lift shafts, fallen beams – if you were looking for an untimely death, this place was the jackpot.

The old Gisborne works, relic of British industry, shuttered in the Nineties according to Google. Until then, they'd made bicycle parts and evidently on a major scale: the grey cube on the aerial map filled the entire depth of the block. This one workshop alone was the size of an ice rink, stretching away between graffitied iron pillars like a ruined Victorian greenhouse.

The roof *had* been glass but it crunched underfoot now, glinting among the sea of rubbish that surrounded them in all directions: traffic cones, a rusted-out fire extinguisher, plastic bags. Nettles and elder sprouted from every crevice, and the air stank of petrochemicals and decay. It was a steampunk garden, so far post the apocalypse that even the zombies had moved on.

'It's a young woman, Rob,' Samir had said on the phone. 'I want you to take this one.'

Rafferty tripped suddenly and fell forward with a shout. When they reached him, he was picking himself up but one of his gloves was torn and bloody. He looked shaken and they saw why: a foot away gaped a huge square-mouthed hole in the ground, its dank sides falling away towards the gleam of stagnant water twenty feet below. There was no warning at all – no tape, no sign. The fall would have killed him.

He put a second glove over the top to contain the bleeding and they went on, chastened, through vandalized steel doors to a slightly smaller space. The glass roof was intact here but so moss-covered that light penetrated only in patches. A mangled Venetian blind reared from the junk like the ribcage of a futuristic beast.

At the far end, SOCOs moved through the half-light, spectral in their white suits.

Without them, Robin thought, she'd never have seen her. There was no clearing in the junk, no sign that this spot had been chosen with any care – except maybe that it was away from the doors and anyone who happened to traipse through. If no one had, she might have lain undiscovered for weeks. Months.

One of the white suits stood and raised a hand: Olly Faulkner, the pathologist. As they neared him, Robin saw a length of dark carpet at his feet. The victim was on her side, her back to them, the only parts of her visible at first a pair of blood-soaked white cotton plimsolls protruding from one end of the carpet and her hair spilling from the other, thick and shiny chestnut brown, incongruously clean amid the squalor. Robin's stomach turned over; she hoped it hadn't registered on her face.

The girl wasn't wrapped or rolled in the carpet – nothing so effortful – just lying on one half, the other pulled roughly over her. Maybe *that* was why her killer had chosen this spot to dump her: the carpet had already been here, a happy bit of luck.

Olly Faulkner was Robin's favourite of the two pathologists they dealt with regularly. About fifty, with collar-length blond-grey hair swept straight back from his forehead and wide-set eyes over a broad-bridged nose, he was known in Homicide as Aslan, and not only for his looks. The people he saw were beyond appreciating it but he treated them as gently as if they'd turned up in A&E, talking to them as he worked. 'It's like he thinks they can still hear him,' Robin had overheard a uniform snarking on one of her early cases with West Midlands. '*I* can still hear you,' she'd said.

'Robin, Malia. Good to see you.'

'How are you, Olly?'

'Not bad. Unlovely location, though, even by our usual standards, and this is a terrible thing.'

Robin was trying not to inhale too deeply but the butcher's-shop tang in the air was inescapable. The carpet, she realized, *wasn't* dark, or hadn't been – its nylon backing was pale. It was soaked, completely saturated. Jesus.

When she looked up, Olly was watching her. 'The only comfort,' he said, 'is that with this degree of blood loss, as you know, she would have lost consciousness quickly. Come to this side, you'll see her better.'

She and Malia picked their way over to him. He motioned to one of the SOCOs to take the opposite corner and they lifted the carpet gingerly away.

Robin knew it wasn't Lennie – of course it wasn't, she'd left her at the kitchen table, messing around on her laptop – but she was still holding her breath. When she saw the girl's face, an involuntary sound escaped her.

She *was* young – so young. Older than Len but only a little: eighteen, maybe, twenty or twenty-one at most. She was white – paper-white now – her forehead high and lineless, her nose Roman with a saddle of freckles. Her bloodless, chapped lips revealed front teeth that were gently ridged like Len's had been when they first came through.

Robin crouched, glad to hide her face. Not *her* baby but someone's. She'd been borne and looked after, fed, clothed, and then, as if none of that mattered, killed and dumped here amongst the rubbish.

Her clothes were as soaked as the carpet – the T-shirt could have been white or pale blue or green because every visible inch was sodden. The weight of the blood pulled it sideways but she could see that the material was slashed in several places, long gashes, a couple of which revealed the mouths of puckering wounds.

'A knife?' she said, eyes still down.

'I should think so,' said Olly. 'Look.'

The woman's left hand rested on her thigh but her right arm was trapped under her body, hand palm-up on the filthy carpet. The fingers weren't curled as Robin would have expected, but slack. Blood obscured what would have been obvious otherwise: the palm was bisected from the base of the index finger almost to the wrist by a cut that had severed the tendons. Another cut, parallel, had sliced the insides of her fingers between the first and second knuckle.

'She grabbed it? Tried to stop it?'

'It looks like it, yes.'

'But only once?'

He tipped his head to one side. 'Maybe because she lost

4

consciousness so quickly? It wasn't tooth-and-claw – as far as I can see so far, there are no other defensive injuries. But her killer was strong, too. Look.' With a gloved finger, he moved the fabric of her T-shirt aside. 'The blade cut a groove in the bone here, probably elsewhere, too. It *could* have been a woman, if she was young and very strong, in a passion, but much more likely a man, I think.'

Robin looked at her nails: cut short, unpolished and undamaged. They might get lucky, the blood trapped underneath might belong to the killer, but she wouldn't hold out much hope.

'Time frame?'

'Hard to be precise at this stage, with the various temperature factors in here – the damp and the concrete floor would lower her temp but she was wrapped in the carpet so . . . For now, let's say after midnight, before six.'

'Was she killed here?' asked Malia.

Olly braced his hands on his thighs and stood, unfolding his body with the care of someone with long-time lower-back issues. 'I'd say yes. There's no sign of any inconsistent *livor* and though the carpet's done a good job of soaking up the blood, there's some on the leaves of this elder over here, and here, for starters. That's more Rafferty's territory than mine, though.'

Robin turned to him. 'What do we have on ID?'

Rafferty shook his head. 'Nothing. No bag, no purse, no phone, empty pockets. We've done a very preliminary search of the immediate area but it'll take a while to do it thoroughly.'

There was an understatement. 'How about her prints?' Response carried mobile readers.

Another head-shake. 'She's not in the system.'

'The guy who found her is an "urban explorer",' Rafferty told them, scorn barely concealed. 'Came to nose about and take pretentious pictures of the decay. He got in the other side, Warwick Street, he said, there's an open door. Ton of homeless back there, all together in one room.'

'How many?'

'Twenty-five, thirty, maybe? We're keeping them there.'

'Can we get through from here?'

'Yeah. After this bit, it's easier, actually – there's a corridor with a roof on, much less plant-growth.'

They followed him back the way they'd come, silent at first. Birds darted over their heads, their song mocking: this was their place; humans were finished here and nature was taking it back.

Knifed to death, then dumped in this hell-scape. Robin felt a surge of outrage. What had she done – what could anyone ever do – to deserve that?

But what was worse? That or being knifed and left to die on the pavement yards from your own front door?

Because if you'd been killed in Birmingham last night, those had been your options. When Samir had called, she'd told him Webster was on. 'I know,' he said, 'but he's already in Erdington.'

'What's in Erdington?'

'The *other* new case. Kieran Clarke, aged sixteen. Stabbed and left to bleed out on the street thirty feet from where his parents were watching television.' They'd both been quiet for a moment then he'd given a deep sigh. 'Two in a night.'

Back in February, barely four months ago, three teenagers had been stabbed to death in the city in twelve days. There'd been public outcry, quite rightly, but while it had been exceptional, it wasn't *that* exceptional: so far this year, they'd been averaging a murder a week. Any lingering idea Robin may have had that she'd left the Met for a sleepy backwater had been well and truly shut down: last year, their rate *per capita* had been higher than London's, the *Sun* had even run a piece about it, 'The Wild West Midlands'. And things had gone downhill since, big time: homicides on their patch were up 70 per cent.

Knives. Knives the great equalizer, democratic weapon of choice: you didn't need money or underworld connections to buy a knife; you could get one at Tesco with your weekly shop or nick one from your mum. It was an arms race, out of control. Street gangs had knives, kids took knives to school to protect themselves, then more kids tooled up to protect *them*selves – more and more all the time. Last year, seven hundred children had had knife injuries, some of them still in primary school. In February, after the three deaths, the Commissioner had called the situation a national emergency and begged the government for more money. In some areas, desperate residents were starting to patrol their own neighbourhoods at night.

'It's bad,' Samir told her when he'd asked her to apply for the job. 'Really bad. We've lost more than two thousand officers since 2010 – officers, not support staff. We're radically under-funded across the board and we're losing control. There's just not enough manpower to deal with a city this size.'

'You're really selling it to me,' she'd said, dry.

'It's why I need you,' he'd replied with no edge at all.

Up ahead now, Rafferty had stopped. When they caught up, he took them through a single doorway into a small room, perhaps an office once, where a pair of foetid mattresses lay at right angles to one another, some soiled heavyweight material, maybe old curtains, piled where they met.

'The urban explorer said he heard them in here,' Rafferty said. 'He shouted when he found her and heard running. He thinks they went through there then out the front on to Bradford Street.'

'Men?'

'He wasn't sure. He didn't see them.'

'Great.' Robin crouched to look at an area on the floor that had been used for fires. She held her hand over it but it hadn't been used last night. The ashes were cold.

If the workshops at the front were post-apocalyptic, the loading bay at the back was a vision of hell, a huddled mass of human misery in shades of black and grey and yellow. The scant natural light came from a ring of low windows just beneath the roof; it reached ten feet down and then petered out, as if losing heart. In the gloom below, human beings were arrayed on three levels: several in the loading bay itself; more on this raised ground level; and, like battery hens, in wooden storage bays against the wall.

The air was rank, every flavour of bodily emission mixed with damp and mould, oil, the sickly-sweet smell of stale alcohol. Stepping forward, Robin stumbled on an empty can and sent it skittering across the concrete floor, shockingly loud. A colourless face emerged from a pile of cardboard and blankets, eyes wide, hair in patches. It lisped some unintelligible words – a woman, Robin realized – and subsided. In the far corner, a man muttered to himself, arms wrapped tight around his knees.

'I've seen more reliable witnesses,' Malia said, her dismay visible even through the gloom.

'Also,' Rafferty said, and Robin heard apology, 'the CCTV.'

'What about it?'

'There's not going to be a ton, sorry, at least not in the immediate vicinity. None of the cameras on this place are working.'

'Vandalized?'

'Hard to say, could be wear-and-tear. The place has been out of business for twenty years. From the look of it, a lot of them bit the dust then.'

*

By the time they made it back to the street, twenty or more members of the public were clustered at the cordon, voices low but excited at this interruption of violence into a Sunday morning. Several filmed on their phones as they stood by the Forensics van to take off their suits and filthy shoe covers. 'Lovely day for a murder,' Malia muttered.

A couple kept filming as they walked to the car so Robin waited until they were round the corner before calling Varan at the station. She asked him to pull up the recent missing-from-homes and dictated the witness appeals for the social media accounts. 'We need to find out who she is ASAP,' she said, 'and make sure her people are told decently. I can't have them finding out on bloody Twitter.'

She hung up and they waited for the lights in silence. On the pavement, a man swung a carrier bag like a metronome: *tick tock*. She imagined a time-bomb, the hand grenade about to fly through the family's front door. They'd never truly recover.

'You all right?' Malia asked quietly.

'Me? Fine.' She looked across. 'Why?'

'First girl we've had since . . .'

So she'd noticed. Or – a sudden thought – had Samir rung her, asked her to keep an eye on her? No, paranoid, of course not; he'd never undermine her like that in the eyes of a junior officer. She was asking because she was Malia – perceptive. Astute.

And she'd been there that terrifying night sixteen months ago when Robin had faced the possibility – the likelihood – that her own daughter's life would end like the girl's today, that she'd never see Lennie alive again.

The darkest point of a dark, dark time. Within twenty-four hours of Robin being forced to move back to Birmingham, her best friend, Corinna, had been murdered here, her body found

9

in her burned-out house. For her killer, that hadn't been enough: Corinna had deprived him of what he believed was rightfully his, so he'd taken a substitute: Lennie. A rapist, a multiple murderer, he'd snatched her from outside her new school, driven her away to a remote farm building. The chances of Lennie surviving – surviving unharmed, untouched – had been so small. Even now, Robin couldn't think about it without feeling immediately nauseous.

Samir had headed the rescue team, and he'd posted Malia with her, allowing Robin to see her gift for unobtrusive empathy for the first time. Now she was the first person Robin called whenever a case came in. She'd been sure she'd never find as good a fit as Gid, her DS back at the Met, but she'd been wrong about that.

A light-skinned black woman with yoga-teacher poise, Malia was the acknowledged babe of Homicide. Even in crime-scene gear with an elastic ring round her face, she managed not to look entirely ridiculous, a feat no one else pulled off. Out of the gear, she was lovely-looking, and chic, too. Slim black trousers today, the cuffs of her pale shirt turned back twice – *Detection by Ralph Lauren*. Last year, while Robin's own life was orbiting the plughole at warp speed, it had felt pointed – *This could have been you if you'd managed to keep your act together* – but now she just made her feel a bit dishevelled and graceless which, frankly, was not beyond her usual realm of experience.

'I was thinking about it,' she told her now, the sick feeling turning her stomach. 'How close she came. How easily it could have been her.'

The lights changed and they moved off. 'Lennie's everything to me,' she'd told Samir that night at the hospital, trying to express her gratitude, her giddy sense of vertigo at the chasm that had yawned at her feet. He'd nodded. 'I know.'

He'd never said so – of course, he wouldn't – but to anyone, like Malia, who cared enough to think, it would be clear that he'd been protecting her. In the year since Robin had joined West Midlands and he'd been her boss, there'd been three cases involving women under thirty and Samir had given them all to other people.

It looked like the grace period was over now.

Chapter Two

'Why the hell would she go in there?' Robin asked. 'In broad daylight, let alone at night.' She made a right turn and had to stop almost immediately for an old man crossing the road at a glacial pace.

'She was forced?' said Malia. 'Physically carried? Even if one person did the stabbing, they might not have been acting alone.'

'No obvious bruising, though. Maybe she went in willingly with *one* other person – looking for somewhere to have sex?'

Malia looked sceptical. 'If she was turned on by end-times scenarios.'

'Or to do drugs.' There was no evidence of long-term use, according to Olly, but they'd need the labs for anything recent, and it would be days before they got those. 'I don't think she was living rough.'

'No, and if she turns out to have been working, I'll be surprised but we'll see if the local teams know her. What if she was one of these urban explorers as well?'

'Interesting. And if she died towards the end of Faulkner's time frame, she *wouldn't* have gone in at night, would she? What time was sunrise?'

Malia checked her phone. 'Four forty-four.'

'Right. Either way, the house-to-house is going to be patchy at best – industrial and office space, Saturday night, early Sunday morning.'

They'd had a look at Bradford Street while they'd waited for Rafferty to come and get them. It was pretty typical of Deritend, inner-city Birmingham mid-regeneration. The premises next door to Gisborne's had been derelict, too, but the Victorian red-brick factory directly opposite had been redeveloped as an office complex, all wrought-iron gates and inner courtyard with topiary planters. Whatever had originally occupied the plot next door but one had been bulldozed and replaced with a snazzy new Asian banqueting hall.

'They might have had an event last night – it's wedding season, graduation time, more or less. We could also get lucky with people on their way home from a night out.' Not so much on Warwick Street, maybe, but Bradford was a thoroughfare to and from the city centre.

The phone rang through the Bluetooth suddenly, making them both jump. Sara Kettleborough, the chief crime reporter at the *Birmingham Post*. Robin answered.

'Robin? I've just seen you on Twitter. The girl in Deritend – you're SIO?'

The phone rang again as she indicated into the station car park.

'Where are you?' Samir said.

'Pulling in now.'

'Could you come straight to my office? Assistant Chief Constable Kilmartin's with me.'

Kilmartin – on a Sunday morning? Was the golf course closed?

'On my way.'

Climbing the stairs, she did a mental run-through of what

13

they had so far. When it came to Kilmartin, she liked to be iron-clad. Aside from her interactions with the homicidal, there'd only been two or three times in her life when she'd felt a deep-tissue repulsion towards a person, a vestigial lizard-brain shudder. It was chemical, she'd concluded, molecular level, which was not to say that some of his elective behaviours weren't also repellent. He hadn't noticeably gained weight in the time she'd known him but every pair of trousers she'd ever seen him in was too tight; walking behind him down the corridor, you'd be treated to the full outline of a pair of budgie-smugglers. Was it a security thing or was he getting a kick out of it? A question she never wanted answered.

Samir's office was on the corridor between the two largest incident rooms, buffered from the hoi polloi by the small ante-room occupied during the week by his PA, Rhona. She wasn't in today so Robin knocked on the inner door herself.

Most of the senior officers she'd worked with over the years, men and women, kept their offices like operating theatres, presumably to communicate either that they'd reached a plain beyond the need for paper or that even this was only a pit stop on the relentless march to the top, no point settling in. Samir's, by contrast, had undeniable human touches; despite the feature-lessness of the room's shell, at certain times of day, when the light was soft, it bordered on hospitable-looking. There were two plush eau-de-nil bucket chairs for visitors, a cluster of plants on the shelf and a bamboo tray with a coffee pot and cups. His in-tray contained real, live paperwork and she knew from taking a stealthy look one day when he'd stepped out for a minute that the pair of Perspex frames on the desk corner held photographs of his wife, Liz, with Harry and Leila, one fairly recent, the other from when the children were younger, about five and three. Her eyes had lingered on the newer one, Liz sitting with her arms round the children on the steps of a church in Italy or Spain, probably, an azure wooden door behind them, all three of them in shorts and sandals, Liz slim-shouldered in an olive vest top, slightly pink in the cheeks. She was grinning soft-eyed at the camera, wisps of brown hair escaping from a loose topknot.

Head of Force Homicide. At the start of last year, it had felt like a cosmic joke. Of course she'd known what he was doing – over the years, she'd had to employ top-level fieldcraft to avoid him at conferences – but after thirteen years of evading him while she was making a success of her life, they'd come face to face when she'd blown it all sky-high. Of course.

Even after a year of seeing him most days, though, she still had moments like this, when she looked at him and instead of the Samir nearing forty, she saw his eighteen or nineteen-year-old avatar, skin lineless, hair still completely black, none of the hatching round the eyes or silver over the ears. He'd been six foot one by the time he was fifteen, lean from cross-country running then, more solid now but still a runner, pounding pavements and parks before work, and in his navy suit and tie, the white shirt, it was easy to remember him as he'd looked in his sixth-form uniform when they'd gone to his house after school. His parents were both hospital doctors, they'd worked late, and so they'd spent hours lying on his bed listening to music, talking, kissing. She'd been the first person he'd ever slept with.

He was standing behind his chair, hands resting on the back, no doubt because Kilmartin was standing, too, posing his bantamweight frame in front of the long window, hands wide on the sill, upper body manspreading at the focal point of the room. She'd wondered before whether he'd actually studied how to do it, *Physical Dominance for Men of Slender Means, a two-week online course.* Compared to Samir, he was a slip of a thing.

'DCI Lyons,' he said in his reedy voice. 'Take a seat.' He gestured towards the chairs.

'No.' She wasn't going to give him the height advantage; they were at eye level now. Samir flashed her a look. 'I'd prefer to stand. Thank you, sir,' she added, slightly too late.

Another gesture, faintly courtly, as if to say, against my better judgement but as you wish. 'I hear Superintendent Jafferi has given you the Deritend case. The girl.'

'Yes, sir.'

Robin glanced at him again – *See, I can play the game* – but Samir was watching Kilmartin with an expression of deliberate focus.

'Now, as we're all well aware, we're working in straitened circumstances across the board but we need to be completely on top of this. Dead girls are media catnip, as you know, especially if they're photogenic . . .'

There was a questioning rise at the end that Robin pretended not to hear. She was dead, for Christ's sake; could they leave whether she was hot or not out of it for a couple of hours?

'It's very hard for people to imagine,' he went on, 'a wife or a daughter . . .'

Oh, *wives and daughters*. 'Absolutely,' she said.

'What have you got so far? Who's the pathologist?'

'Oliver Faulkner.'

'Hm. Does he think it was sexual?'

'To be confirmed, but it doesn't look like it. She was fully dressed, her clothes weren't disturbed or damaged.'

Kilmartin pursed his lips. 'That's something.'

'He's going to prioritize the PM tomorrow.'

'Good. Obviously, you'll talk to DI Webster this morning about the boy in Erdington, see if they're connected?'

'Yes, sir.'

He let go of the windowsill and paced a little, affecting interest in Samir's potted peace lily. He reached out a hand to touch a leaf then seemed to think better of it. 'I'm wondering,' he said, back still turned, 'whether you should be the public face of this one, Samir.'

'Why?' Robin said, before she could stop herself.

'Why?' This time Kilmartin did touch the leaf, rubbing it speculatively between his thumb and forefingers as it were a piece of cloth whose quality he was assessing. 'As I said, I think it's got the potential to blow up, PR-wise, and I want to be totally sure we're putting our best foot forward.'

'You don't think I'm our best foot.' She was conscious of Samir glaring now, and ignored him.

Kilmartin turned, giving her a cold-eyed smile. 'You're not our most senior foot. As Head of Force Homicide, DCS Jafferi has the advantage of rank, and I think the public would find it reassuring to know this was being handled from the top.'

DCS Jafferi also has the advantage of a pair of balls, which is what you'd find reassuring.

'Clearly we need to do what's best for everyone here,' Samir said, letting go of the back of his chair and doing some pacing of his own. 'My team as well as the public. So let's keep that in mind as an option. But I'm confident DCI Lyons will do an excellent job, as she has done across the board since she joined us. We know she's a first-class investigator, which is why I wanted her on this case.'

'And indeed the force, am I right?' Another reptilian smile.

Was he alluding to their past – was that possible? Thanks to Corinna, it was known in Homicide that she and Samir had gone out years ago but he'd told her Kilmartin wasn't aware. When she'd badgered him about it at drinks before Christmas, he'd finally

17

said that the ACC's animus towards her – he hadn't denied it existed – was about what he saw as West Midlands taking the Met's cast-offs, especially a cast-off who'd been dragged through the tabloids only months beforehand.

'Yes,' Samir said now, decisive. 'Exactly why I wanted her on the force.'

'So, DCI Lyons, a nice quick solve is in order.' Kilmartin paused, giving her the same assessing look he'd given the plant. 'Let's see if DCS Jafferi's faith in you is warranted.'

'Wives and daughters,' she said as she watched him exit the building directly below. He was evidently doing some Trump-level hair manipulation; from an aerial view, he was much balder than he looked face to face. 'Does it help them imagine that women are relevant in some way, or is it a chattels thing?'

'Don't.'

She heard Samir sit down and turned to look at him. 'What?'

'Let it into your head. He's an old chauvinist, he's never going to change, and if you let him get to you and get lippy, it'll be you who gets torched.'

'Back in your box, Lyons, in other words.'

'In other words. For your own sake.'

'Yes, Most Senior Foot. Christ, Samir, how do you do it, being so bloody *political* all the time.'

An upward flick of the eyebrows. 'What was the scene like?'

'Something out of J. G. Ballard. Totally porous, a forensics nightmare, lived in by a ton of homeless people, minimal CCTV coverage.'

'Excellent.'

Kilmartin's BMW slid silently out of the car park. 'And even though he *was* stating the bloody obvious, he's right about the media attention,' she said with a sigh. 'And she probably *was*

18

photogenic before she was murdered and dumped in a sea of trash in a bit of foetid carpet.'

She felt it again, the glow behind her ribs. It went without saying that she'd put everything she had into 'a nice quick solve' but it would be for the victim and her family, nothing to do with Kilmartin tossing down his pathetic gauntlet.

Chapter Three

Her last Major Incident Team in London had been based off Putney High Street in an office building in dire need of renovation, and the team had complained non-stop: it was old; it was cramped; on summer afternoons, it reached volcanic temperatures. 'I've spent cooler weeks on the Costa Brava,' Gid used to announce, struggling to make himself heard over the aerodrome roar of the desk fans. Robin had loved it. The closeness heightened the drama: the sound of phones and computer keys bounced off the walls and low ceiling like they were in *All the President's Men*.

Force Homicide's purpose-built offices were spacious, decently appointed and about as architecturally interesting as a car dealership on a trading estate. They'd been built in the Eighties or early Nineties on the site of an old toy factory – Police! A toy factory! The jokes! – in a style Robin thought of as Late-Twentieth-Century Call Centre, bog-standard red-brick girt with characterless strips of windows. For a week after she'd accepted the job here, she'd felt panicked: the Midlands had won, she'd been sucked back in by everything she'd tried so hard to escape. *You can take the girl out of the provinces . . .*

Corinna's voice, still talking in her ear as if nothing had happened.

When she walked into the incident room these days, however, all she noticed were the similarities, the same smells of printer toner and coffee mingled with body-spray heat-hazing off the younger bucks, the same chatter of keyboards and phones. And today, there was the same unmistakable new-case edge on the air. For now, everything was pristine, immaculate, the possibility of getting every detail right unsullied by hour upon hour of recalcitrant witnesses and dry-eyed computer-gawping, runs of eighteen-hour days and 'bab van dinners. This was the golden hour – for now, it could still be the perfect case, a boxed example in the next edition of the Blackstone's handbook.

DC Varan Patel was already at his desk. The day Corinna died, he'd come with Malia to interview Robin and even through the fog of disbelief and horror, she'd registered that he looked about fifteen years old. He was twenty-nine, she knew now, though if she sent him undercover in A-level History, she doubted anyone would rumble him; when the chubby older guard teased him for his skinniness, it was always along the lines of 'Isn't your mum feeding you, Varan? A growing boy?' She was increasingly fond of him; he was sharp and precise with a tendency to workaholism that, as his guv'nor, she appreciated.

'Two calls from families with missing girls already,' he told her, standing. 'Their voices, all that hope and fear mixed together.' He shuddered. 'They heard about it from public posts but I've put ours up now, so we'll get more any minute.'

'What about the two?'

He shook his head. 'One was too old, the other was Chinese. The first pictures have just come in from the SOCOs.'

He handed them to her, still warm from the printer. There she was, exactly as they'd left her, but the distancing had already begun, the start of the process by which she would slip away. The photos had reduced her to two dimensions, turning her into something they could fix to their board, a butterfly on a collector's pin. By this afternoon, she'd have been removed from the real world forever, no longer a person but evidence, part of Rafferty's crime scene, labelled and stored in a mortuary drawer.

Once they had an ID, they'd ask her family for as many photographs as possible, plaster them all over the board. It was something Robin had picked up years ago, when Corinna's dad had been dying of his alcoholism. One of his nurses had urged the family to bring in photographs that showed Trevor as he had been: a family man (of sorts, for a handful of years), a good-looking, funny man, anyway, until it had all gone pear-shaped. The point, she'd said, was to remind the medical staff that, however bad the condition of the patient, they'd once been out in the world like everyone else, a human being with friends and family, favourite foods, vanities, quirks, insecurities. It was true for their murder victims, too, and part of her job, as Robin saw it, was to make sure no one forgot it.

'What about the missing-from-homes?' she asked Varan.

'We're on it. Nothing yet.'

'Right,' she turned to Malia. 'We need to put a marker on the PNC and we also need to be up on HOLMES straight away. We're going to get this right and we're going to be *seen* to get it right.'

'I've found a Flickr account for Jonathan Quinton, guv,' Varan said.

'Great – show us?'

He had it open onscreen. She and Malia stood behind him to look.

'It looks like he actually *is* an urban explorer at least,' he said, clicking from a picture of an abandoned needle factory in

Redditch to a dilapidated room with an ornate fireplace, empty except for a single dining chair on bare boards at the centre, fabric seat torn.

'Looks like somewhere you'd be interrogated by a military junta,' she said.

'Halesowen, apparently. The account's nearly four years old, created in October 2015, and he's been in all sorts of creepy places. There's a network of them on here, these "explorers", all commenting on each other's posts.'

'Could you make a list of them? Also, everywhere he's been – let's cross-check and see if there's been anything at the others.' She pointed at the screen. 'RusInUrbex? That's his handle?'

Varan grinned. 'Think he wants people to know he went to the grammar school?'

'Did he?'

'Three years above me. He was a smug git back then, too.'

'I wasn't even supposed to be there. I mean, I know I wasn't at all, trespassing on private property and . . .' He stopped before digging himself any deeper. 'What I mean is, I normally go with my mate but his shifts changed last minute. He's a doctor.' He offered this up hopefully, as if it might somehow be mitigating.

Indiana Jones seemed to have been Jonathan Quinton's wardrobe inspiration for his outing this morning: he wore a khaki shirt with the top two buttons undone, the sleeves rolled to reveal tanned, lightly muscled forearms. A leather jacket and backpack lay on the sofa-seat next to him, along with a large professional-looking camera. His petulant expression was more miscreant in the headmaster's office than Raider of the Lost Ark, however, and his dark hair trod a careful line between cool and business-appropriate.

'What do *you* do, Mr Quinton?'

'I'm a financial adviser. A small company in town, wealth management for private clients.' He looked at her and – unbelievable – she saw self-pity in his eyes. 'This is going to live with me forever.'

'Where were you planning to go originally?' said Malia gently.

Robin watched his expression soften as he turned to her. 'West Bromwich,' he said. 'Most of what's in town's been done now.'

'Done?'

'Discovered already – photographed to death.' Robin raised an eyebrow at the choice of phrase and he had the grace to look embarrassed. 'Part of urbex is finding places people haven't been yet. That's why it's called exploring – once everyone's tramped through, it's just a wreck. But if you're first . . .'

'You've done a fair bit of it, then?'

'I like it. There's not that many places left to discover in the world, are there, but standing somewhere abandoned, seeing into lives that are gone – it's . . . nostalgic.'

'Elegiac?' said Malia.

He stared at her as if she'd seen into his soul. 'Yeah.'

'So if you knew Gisborne's was "done",' Robin said, 'why *did* you go there?'

'I'd been looking forward to the trip with my mate, we haven't done one for a bit, and I'd got everything ready. I'd heard about it online, people saying that it was nearly done, and I was gutted I missed the old Co-op furniture factory so . . .'

'Tell us what happened,' Malia said. 'From the beginning.' She was laying it on thick; Robin half-expected her to put a comforting hand on his arm. Quinton was lapping it up.

'I'd hoped to be there earlier than I was – really early, for the light quality? I'd read about an open security door on Warwick Street so I knew I could get in safely.'

'Read where?' Robin said.

'An urbex site.'

'So that information's online?' she said. Great – at this rate, she'd turn out to be the only person in Birmingham who hadn't known. 'We'll need the name of the site.'

He nodded. 'Once I was in there, I just followed my nose. For what it's worth, I only took five or six pictures, I normally get way more. Also, there were a lot of homeless in one of the rooms at the back. I tend to move on quite fast if that's the case.'

'Why?' She couldn't resist.

'It's . . . awkward. It's like, I don't know . . .'

'Like you're a misery tourist? I mean, it could be interpreted like that, couldn't it? Tramping through someone's ruined business – the loss of a lot of people's livelihoods? Disturbing people who're really struggling? And some of those people are a bit frightening, aren't they? The ones with mental-health issues?'

'On your way through,' Malia said, steering things back around, 'did you feel like anyone else was there?'

'Only when I found her. That's when I heard them – the people who ran. I think I shouted when I realized she was dead, disturbed them.'

'How many did you hear?'

'Two, I think – two sets of feet. Scuffling, though – I'm not sure.'

'Did you hear their voices? Did they say anything to each other?'

'No.' He looked at Malia. 'I should have gone after them, shouldn't I?' *Because I would, you know, I'm that sort of guy. I'd chase down the villains in the Temple of Doom.*

'You did the right thing,' she said. 'It could have been dangerous.'

He looked a bit sick. 'I thought she was asleep at first.'

'In there?' said Robin.

'Only from a few yards away, when I first caught sight of her – her feet and hair. She was wrapped in that carpet; I thought maybe she was homeless.'

'Did you touch her at all, Mr Quinton?'

'What?' He looked outraged.

'I mean, to see if she was warm? Breathing?'

'No. I knew she was dead as soon as I got close. That paleness . . . My mum died three years ago – I know what it looks like.'

'So we won't find any trace of your DNA on her body?'

'*No*. Jesus.'

'Did you take any photos? Anything . . . elegiac?'

He gave her a disgusted look.

'The homeless people off Warwick Street – would any of them recognise you? Could they confirm, for example, that you entered the building alone? Or that all you had with you was your stuff there?'

'What?' He surged from his seat, upending his tea. 'What are you saying?'

When they got back upstairs, Varan was on the phone. Seeing them, he held up a hand.

'ID?' Robin mouthed.

He shook his head as he put the phone down. 'Rafferty. Two things. First: he's got a witness who saw two men jumping out of a window on Bradford Street earlier.'

'Good. What time?'

'A couple of minutes before eight.'

'Score one, Jonathan Quinton,' said Malia.

'Second: the shafts you saw in the workshop floor, like the one he nearly fell down – he said you'd know what he was talking about – they used to have conveyor belts on, to bring stuff up

26

from storage underneath. There's a whole other floor down there, he said, rooms linked by corridors, all connected.'

'So people could get from place to place in the factory down there, too, unseen, then pop up one of these shafts?'

'Yes.'

Robin sighed inwardly. 'Right. Who's the witness?'

'A woman called Kate Coombs, she's an artist, does graphic novels. Her studio's in the offices across the road.'

'Early for a Sunday.'

'She's got a deadline so she's at her drawing table round the clock, she told Rafferty, and it's right in front of the window. She saw them jump out and when Response turned up minutes later, she thought it might be relevant. Being an artist, she said this would be better than her verbal description.'

He reached for his mouse and clicked on an email attachment that opened a pastel sketch of two men both in evident need of showers, barbers and a month's worth of decent meals. 'This one's in his mid-twenties, apparently,' he pointed to a man drawn with mousy, shoulder-length hair and a round, open face with high cheekbones. Ratty dirty-blond beard, navy beanie, a filthy khaki combat jacket and black scarf. The second man was taller, narrower across the shoulders, and his open blue and green plaid shirt was belted like a kimono with what looked like a tie or a pyjama cord. His hair was either short or tucked up under his black baseball cap but his facial hair had a touch of red in it. 'He's older, late thirties, maybe early forties.'

'If she only saw them jump out of a window and leg it, it's very detailed.'

'She's seen them coming and going quite a bit over the past few weeks; she thinks they've been living there.'

'The mattresses,' said Robin, glancing at Malia.

'They're using, aren't they?' she said. 'Got to be. If our victim's an urban explorer, too, maybe she had an expensive camera on her. Maybe they nicked it and everything else she had on her – jewellery, phone?'

'Wouldn't they just have threatened her in that case, though? Two men, one girl? Why kill her? And right where they're living?'

'If they're using, they might have been totally off their heads.'

The first time Robin had seen DI Simon Webster, he'd been on TV appealing for witnesses outside Corinna's burned-out house. He was stocky, ruddy-cheeked, and he'd been wearing a green wax jacket which, no matter how many suits she'd seen him in since, had indelibly cast him as a bumbling Farmer Giles figure in her mind and therefore – and especially given the lack of immediate progress – unfit for running Corinna's investigation.

Their rocky start had been mutual and not only because, in the end, she'd been the one to discover who'd killed Corinna, but because she'd then been hired to fill the DCI vacancy that Webster had been angling for, despite having been a person of interest in his case only months earlier. How to make friends and influence people, eh?

She found him in the incident room across the corridor, standing in front of his investigation board. 'How are you, Simon?'

He shrugged. 'Well, you know. Some of them get to you more than others, don't they? Sixteen years old, and it's all over for him.' He had two sons in their early teens, Robin knew.

Kieran Clarke's name was written at the top of the board in red block capitals, underlined twice. Directly underneath was a headshot printed out at A4 size. A school portrait, Clarke in a royal blue V-neck sweater, shirt and tie against a hazy neutral background. He was sitting at an angle to the camera, posed as if in the act of turning towards it, his expression an awkward compromise between the smile without which he knew he'd get hell from his mum and the moody wide-eyed teenager-sulk that he needed to retain any cred in front of his mates. His hair was close-cropped, his eyes big and brown with curling lashes.

In the scene pictures, he lay on his back in front of a low brick wall. He'd tried to support himself on it, she guessed, but ultimately ran out of strength. One showed a trail of blood-drops the size of two-pence pieces, one after another, thick and fast; another picture detailed partial handprints on the top bar of a white gate.

'Hand over hand,' said Webster. 'Trying to get himself home.'

For a moment, neither of them spoke.

Robin broke the silence. 'What have you got?'

'Two separate witnesses who overheard raised voices and looked out their windows, saw two black lads of a similar age hoofing it down the street.'

'A similar age – teenagers?'

'Witnesses went to early twenties, max, but they thought younger.'

'Did he know them?'

'Unclear as yet. The witnesses only heard shouting, not the words. His parents are devastated, obviously – the mother's had to be sedated. He was a good lad, by all accounts so far – neighbours, his class teacher. No trace of him in the system. We're talking to his friends now, see if he was into any trouble that hasn't come to light.' He sighed. 'What about you?'

'A pair of men seen and heard fleeing the scene after the window for time of death but ours are older, and white. Apart from that, not much.' The only dubious upside of which was not having to feel embarrassed now. She'd never meant to circumvent Webster or show him up, all she'd cared about was finding Corinna's killer, but the awkwardness lingered.

'Have you got an ID yet?' he asked.

She shook her head. 'No. What time was this?'

'Call was ten seventeen, and it was pretty immediate: our witnesses rang in one after the other.'

'Faulkner's saying between midnight and six this morning for ours so if they *are* connected, Kieran was first.'

She handed him copies of the SOCOs' photos and watched as he looked through them, the dark hairs between his eyebrows bristling as they pulled closer together. 'Crying bloody shame,' he said when he reached the last one. 'Effing knives – it's never going to end, is it?'

'Will you show them to Kieran's friends and family, see if any of them know her?'

'Course. We'll let you know.'

'Likewise, when we find out who our girl is. Are you doing *Midlands Today*, by the way?'

He nodded. 'About to go and do my bit any minute. You?'

'Yep. Going to look good, isn't it, back-to-back murders?'

Chapter Four

By half past ten, the incident room had thinned out, the team pushing off one by one for a night's sleep before tomorrow's early start. In a circle of light at her desk, Robin looked at what she'd just written. Over the years, she'd developed the habit of getting down everything they had at the end of the day, a five- or ten-minute stream-of-consciousness jumble of notes and images that occasionally turned up a connection or shook something loose in her brain. Today, the writing barely covered half a page, and the only semi-interesting idea she'd had was that while Kieran Clarke was killed in the open, their girl had died out of sight. His killers hadn't made any attempt to hide his body; hers had made a half-baked effort to cover her with the carpet.

Her segment on *Midlands Today* had aired shortly after seven and, as they'd hoped, the phones had started ringing almost immediately. They'd shown Kate Coombs's sketch of the men leaving Gisborne's and had three new calls from people who said they'd seen them coming and going over the past month or six weeks. No one who'd called in so far had seen Jonathan Quinton enter the building, however, or anyone else.

31

But more disappointingly, they had nothing new on an ID. She'd given it her best, emphasizing that any information would be handled in complete confidence, and she'd had high hopes. Not everyone combed social media or had Google alerts set up but TV reached a different audience, an older, parental one. There'd been tens of calls, some of them from hundreds of miles away – Liverpool, Devon, Scotland – as friends and relatives of families with missing girls passed on the news, but none of them were her.

They needed an ID. Webster's segment had followed hers and with a name and pictures, it had been much more compelling. Kieran Clarke was a human being; for the public so far, their girl was a cypher.

As she logged out of her computer, her mobile rang. Samir.

'Hi.' He paused, apparently listening. 'Are you still at work?'

'Leaving now.' In the background at his end, she heard Liz telling Harry to turn his light off, it was school tomorrow, *And no torch or I'll take the batteries out again,* followed by a laugh.

'Anything to report?' he asked.

'Not really. Honestly, I'm disappointed by what the TV's brought in.'

'Well, let's keep our fingers crossed for the morning – maybe someone'll be having a sleepless night. Gives people a bit more time to notice she's gone, too – colleague not at work, room-mate not back from a weekend away.'

They'd thought she might be a student, living away from home, perhaps that was why her family hadn't noticed yet, but they'd contacted all five of the universities in Birmingham, plus Coventry, Warwick and Leicester, and none were missing any female students. 'And we'll have the e-fit later tomorrow.' They'd put out a description of what she was wearing but it had hardly felt worth it. When the list came in from the SOCOs, it had said

Gap jeans, Gap T-shirt, plain white bra and knickers, unlabelled. It was all totally basic, there were probably twenty thousand people with the same stuff.

'How about the homeless at the back?' he asked.

'Malia's team finished talking to them. A lot of them are past being useful; the rest say they didn't see anyone last night.'

'Hi Robin.' Liz's voice in the background again, much closer now. They weren't on speakerphone; she must have been listening.

'Hi Liz,' she called, hearing a clink, as if Liz had reached over Samir's shoulder to clear glasses away. Perhaps that was exactly what had happened because Samir said, 'Right, I'd better let you go home, it's late.'

'Yeah. See you in the morning.'

As she stepped outside, Robin stopped to fill her lungs with fresh air. There were still streaks of turquoise in the sky, it was only a couple of weeks until the longest day, but the air was crisp, spring not summer, and the dew gave it a damp, new-rain-on-tarmac scent. She looked beyond the railings to the houses across the road, three of which were dark already, two showing lights only in upstairs windows. Aside from the police station, Rose Road was residential, two terraces of increasingly primped-up Victorian cottages facing off from behind lines of mid-range cars. Over there, they'd been having cosy evenings watching *Grantchester* in their PJs; on this side, they'd been poring over pictures of dead people. The juxtaposition of the civic and domestic was very Birmingham, though. Boundaries seemed to blur here in a way they didn't in London.

She headed for her car, feeling for the key, but as she turned the corner of the building, she heard footsteps. She turned, expecting one of the night shift – new information in, she was needed back upstairs – but instead saw something moving in the deep shadow round the cars along the fence. Not something – someone. Hand tightening round the key, she glanced towards the gates and saw they'd been left open again. For God's sake.

'I've seen you,' she said, voice echoing. 'Come out.'

A moment later, a tall figure stepped into the moat of flood-light around the station itself. A man, late forties or early fifties, with broad shoulders and a large head of tufty silver-grey hair. Jeans and a jumper, no jacket. Lace-up shoes.

She squinted: did she know him? No – and yet he looked familiar. She'd definitely seen him before.

'What are you doing in here? This is police property.'

'DCI Lyons?' He took a couple of steps closer and Robin put her hand up, *Stop*.

'Have we met?'

'No.' His voice was deep, with a local accent. 'You're running the investigation in Deritend. The girl's body found this morning.'

'That's right.' Was he an ex-con? Not one of hers, she'd recognize anyone she'd put away, but maybe she'd seen his picture.

'I've been busy all day,' he said, 'I volunteer at a place in Coventry on Sunday, and I only heard the news a couple of hours ago. I came straight away and your car was here,' he pointed towards it, 'so I waited for you. I thought you'd have to go home sooner or later.'

Robin gripped the keys harder, moved two of them between her fingers. Her car – what the hell? 'I'm sorry, what's going on here?'

'I'm Martin Engel.'

He said it as if Robin would know immediately who he was. She frowned – she *did* know the name but . . . Ah – suddenly the picture clarified. Martin Engel – Victoria Engel's father.

Four or five summers ago, aged fifteen, Victoria Engel had

gone shopping in the city centre on a Saturday afternoon. She'd bought a dress at H&M and said goodbye to her friends before heading to the bus stop. She'd never been seen or heard from again. Robin hadn't been in Birmingham at the time but the case was flagged at the Met, too, and it would have been hard to avoid even if you weren't police. Victoria's picture was splashed across the papers for weeks, and Martin Engel had done everything he could to keep it in the public eye since: daytime TV, interviews in the *Daily Mail* and women's magazines, *Five years on: tragic dad won't give up hope for his daughter*. He'd set up a website with artist's impressions of what Victoria might look like now, a little older, with different hair; talked about how she would have been finishing her A-levels, leaving school, starting university.

Engel, Robin thought now, could do parallel pictures of his own. Five years ago, he'd been good-looking, with gym muscles and a tan – the family had recently taken a beach holiday some-where hot, she remembered. When he didn't fade from view within the generally accepted time frame, however, some in the court of public opinion insinuated that he was trying to leverage his daughter's disappearance to get himself unrelated media gigs. Another wave of commentary followed when his wife left him: who could blame her? Who could live with someone who refused to move on, who wouldn't try to make any sort of a life again? And, of course, there'd been people who'd thought maybe Martin Engel knew more than he was admitting about his daughter's disappearance.

Whatever the truth, he was no longer the man he had been. The gym-muscle was gone, the jeans were too big, and his hair needed a cut. His face was most changed, though, pale and prematurely aged: he looked as if he were being eroded from the inside out.

'Martin, it isn't Victoria,' she said gently. 'My team's been through all the local missing-from-homes from the past ten years, including Victoria. It's not her.'

'You've seen her picture? You know what she looks like?'

'Yes.'

His body seemed to sag as the news sunk in, his head dipping towards his chest, but then, suddenly, he swung his face up until he was looking at the sky, as if offering thanks. *Thank you for not taking her, for letting me go on.*

'Mr Engel,' Robin asked, 'how do you know my car?'

'I follow you.'

'I'm sorry?'

'In the news. On social media. I saw videos of you in the car tonight when I searched for the story on Twitter, you and your sergeant outside the factory this morning.' A prickle ran down Robin's arms – how did he know Malia was her sergeant? – but he didn't register her unease. 'You've been in Birmingham for about a year. You were in London before, with the Met. You're good, aren't you?'

'I'm a decent detective, if that's what you mean.'

He gave a small snort. 'It's not, don't give me that self-deprecating bullshit.' Real vehemence, apparently out of nowhere. 'You give a toss, that's what I'm talking about. You give a toss what happens to people. That guy in London, the one who got you in trouble – you wouldn't charge him because you didn't think he'd done it. And you were right.'

'Look,' she said, 'you shouldn't have approached me like this – half ten at night, waiting in the dark. You should have called the incident room, the number's all over our social media.'

He shook his head. 'I needed to see you. Face to face. If it wasn't her, you wouldn't have seen me, would you?'

He had a point.

36

'I need you to help me find my daughter.'

'Mr Engel, this is completely . . . Apart from anything else, I'm a homicide detective and it's not a homicide case – there's never been any evidence, has there, that Victoria—'

He cut her off. 'I'm not saying she's dead. I'm asking you to *find* her.'

She got him off the premises but he was still standing on the pavement as she pulled out, still watching when she took a final glance in her rear-view mirror before turning the corner. Maybe it was accidental, a chance intersection of the pool of streetlight and the disappointment that stopped his feet moving any further, but to Robin, the scene looked calculated, a symbol of intent: *I will not stand down.* It was unnerving. But anyone would have been unnerved, she thought, annoyed at herself for letting him disturb her peace of mind. And at least having stayed there, it'd be harder for him to follow her in the car. Even so, she was glad she wasn't going directly home.

Since she and Lennie moved out, her parents had started having family dinners at Dunnington Road on Sunday. Eighteen months ago, Robin would have assumed her mother, Christine, was doing it to show her up: here's what *you* should be doing, providing Lennie with a proper family life, everyone back to the Fifties and conventional gender roles, enough of this female breadwinner nonsense. These days – God, she was mature – some of the heat had gone out of their relationship and she understood that her mother had been sad when Lennie moved out, especially as before that, when they'd lived in London, she'd only seen her a couple of times a year. The suppers were her way of making sure she saw her granddaughter at least once a week, though, as it had turned out, she saw her a lot more than that.

Robin suspected her mother had another motive, too, though: a hope that by bringing them together regularly, she could gradually effect some sort of truce between Robin and her brother. It was the ultimate triumph of hope over experience: Luke had loathed her from the day she was born. Robin still had the scar on her foot from when, aged two and a half and jealous of the attention she was getting, he'd sunk his teeth into her. Her childhood had been filled with sly kicks and pinches and 'accidents', and then, as she'd only found out last year, as a parting shot before she left home, a lie so cruel it still shocked her.

She followed her dad into the sitting room and stooped to drop a kiss on Lennie's shiny hair. 'Sorry I'm so late, lovely.'

'S'okay.'

She perched on the arm of the sofa. The windows were closed – her mother felt the cold like no one else – and the air was hot and over-breathed. The furniture alone filled the narrow room to near-capacity, let alone people actually *using* the furniture, and now even the triangles of space between armchair and sofa, sofa and door were occupied by a multi-coloured Fisher Price bouncer and a rainbow basket of stackable hoops, rubber blocks and stuffed toys. Space aside, it was an improvement – and the threat of imminent bodily harm had driven the Spode figurine of an Edwardian lady into exile from the mantelpiece, too, Robin hoped for a good long time.

Luke lolled in her parents' seashell-shaped armchair like a pound-shop Neptune, Natalie, his wife, an adoring sea nymph on the rug at his feet.

'You're here late, too,' Robin said to them.

'Yeah, nice to see you as well,' said Luke.

Natalie made an agonized face and flapped her hands – *Ssssh* – before springing to her feet and cartoon-tiptoeing the three steps across the room to shut the glass doors. For all the good

38

it would do – there were speakers that transmitted sound less effectively than her parents' house.

'Jack's finally gone to sleep,' she whispered to Robin, going back to her spot. 'He hasn't slept properly all weekend and he'll wake up and need feeding again as soon as we move him. It's so late but to sit down for a couple of minutes and actually finish a glass of wine . . .'

Robin nodded. 'Oh, I remember.' Not that she'd had wine then unless someone had brought it over. She and Corinna had run to occasional Singha beers from the corner shop.

'What?' said her dad, Dennis, from the sofa. 'You were never like that, were you, Lennie? You never gave your mother a hard time?'

Lennie rolled her eyes. 'No, Grandpa, of course not.'

'How's he otherwise?' Robin asked.

'Brilliant.' Natalie smiled. 'Gorgeous.'

Both she and Luke were madly in love with him. They'd tried for years to have a baby and Nat had had several miscarriages – to say he'd been wanted was the understatement of a decade. And he *was* gorgeous. At dinner a couple of weeks ago, he'd been sitting up independently for the first time, legs frogged, chunky little back rod-straight. He'd looked around at them all, mouth an O of wonder and showmanship, *Check this out!* His brown hair was still wispy and baby-fine, just like Lennie's had been at six months.

Having him had chilled Natalie out significantly. Even as a teenager, when she and Luke had first got together, she'd been wound very tightly, ferret-like in going after any perceived slight or encroachment on her territory, but there'd been a couple of occasions lately where she'd made vaguely self-deprecatory comments. The first time it happened, Robin assumed she'd misheard. She'd always been a diet zealot – 'Must be like shagging a geometry kit,' Corinna said once when they were at school – but it seemed extreme thinness was no longer a priority, and the stone or so of baby-weight she'd held on to so far suited her. She looked warmer.

'How's it going, Robin, love?' her dad asked, settling back in his spot at the other end of the sofa, tummy filling out his jumper. 'Are you making any progress?'

'Not a lot.'

'We watched you on the news,' her mother said. 'We thought you did very well.'

Robin wished she could do a better job of masking her surprise – *Who knew you were so competent?* – but she was trying. 'Thanks, Mum.'

'What a nightmare,' her dad said. 'That poor girl. And her family.' He shook his head.

For a moment, the air shimmered with memories of that horrendous night sixteen months earlier. This room was where they'd waited for news about Lennie, sick with fear.

'Do you think they're connected, these two cases?' said her mother.

'I don't know. Different parts of town, different gender, different race – I don't want to presume anything but I think it's unlikely, to be honest. They're similar in age but my girl's a few years older, which matters in your teens, doesn't it? Kieran Clarke was . . .'

Luke muttered something Robin didn't catch. She saw Natalie give him a hard stare.

'What was that, Luke?' she said.

'Nothing.' A tiny pause. 'I said it's gangs, isn't it, all these knives? These black kids in gangs, the Burger Bar Boys, Johnson Crew, whatever. Drill videos – they boast about it, what they're going to do, how they're going to do it . . .'

'Kieran Clarke was in the middle of his GCSEs. Why do you think he was in a gang? Did Webster say so on the news?'

'No, he didn't,' said her mother, missing the point. 'Was he?'

'No, Mum. Luke assumes that because he was black.'

'Bollocks!'

'Language,' said Dennis wearily.

'What? She's putting words in my mouth – I never . . .'

'You did, actually,' Natalie said. 'You said gangs – black kids in gangs.'

'Oh, don't *you* start.'

'I'm not *starting* – you said it. You did.'

Surprised, Robin and Lennie glanced at one another. Natalie never took issue with Luke in front of other people.

'Let's not any of us start,' Dennis said, standing. 'It's gone eleven, Monday tomorrow. Speaking of GCSEs, Robin, get this girl of yours home and into bed.'

'Have you eaten?' her mother asked. 'I know what you're like when you're at work all hours.'

'I'm going to have some toast when I get home.'

'Oh, for heaven's sake. I've made you up a box of roast chicken. Take it for lunch tomorrow. You'll get ill.'

'What?' Luke said, indignant. 'I thought *we* were having the chicken for lunch tomorrow.'

'I've made us some fresh soup. I've got a doctor's appointment first thing but I'll bring it round with me after that. I thought we'd take Jack to see the ducks in the afternoon.'

Even if it had been logistically possible at the time, Robin wouldn't have wanted her mother's help with Lennie but she still felt a pang at how much she helped with Jack. As the lower wage-earner, Luke had resigned from the phone shop in Solihull to look after him but since Natalie had gone back to work, her mum was round there every day. She shopped, she did their

41

washing and ironing, and apparently she made Luke's lunch as well.

'Doctor's appointment, Gran?' Lennie asked as they followed her into the kitchen.

'Just a check-up, love. They're on at me about my cholesterol. Here.' She handed her a rectangular tin painted with tulips.

'What's in there?' Robin asked.

'A lemon drizzle. I know you don't have time for baking when you've got a new case. I thought Lennie would like it for after school.'

They'd had their own place for nine months now but as she put her key in the lock, Robin experienced a moment of deep appreciation nonetheless. Living with her parents had grown easier over the eight months they'd been there – nothing like a crisis to put things into perspective – but it had been a glorious day when she'd signed the lease on The House on Mary Street, as the family always called it. Their own front door, their own sitting room where they watched what they wanted on TV, delivered from her dad's Meg Ryan double bills, Luke's frequent unannounced incursions and her mother's relentless meal-provision. Day after day, week after week, the dinners rolled from the kitchen, nutritionally balanced, painstakingly prepared and delicious, and utterly stifling to any notion of spontaneity between the hours of six and eight p.m. daily. Drunk on liberty, she and Lennie had eaten beans on toast for three nights in a row when they'd moved here – rock'n'roll – and they had accounts at both the Indian and Lebanese down the road. She *never* baked.

Mary Street was long, bisecting Balsall Heath and running more and more steeply uphill as it extended away from the city centre. After fifteen years in London, one of the things she'd found most depressing when she'd come back was the flatness of Hall Green. Birmingham was built on a plateau but from her parents' house you couldn't see anything taller than two storeys. Stunted was the word that had come to mind then; at her lowest, the acres of uninterrupted sky overhead had felt threatening, like something might come swooping down out of them, and so the hill was one of the reasons she'd chosen the house: elevation, literal and spiritual. Plus which, from the other side of the road, the rise gave a view of the city centre: the Bull Ring, the spike of St Martin's. She'd never want to live in the centre but she needed to feel in touch with it. *In suburbia, too many people can hear you scream.*

The house was an Edwardian terraced worker's cottage, one bay window on the ground floor, two dormers upstairs, all three in need of painting. Inside, though, the kitchen had been recently refitted, and the staircase – which had been on the point of collapse when he'd bought the house, their landlord told them, explaining the lingering smell of sawdust on the air – had been replaced, too, along with the windows at the back.

The house had come unfurnished so what furniture there was was Robin's own, a fact that still gave her a pathetic sense of personal satisfaction. In London, she'd always rented furnished flats so that, other than a couple of lamps, Lennie's single bed and the small amount of kitchen stuff she'd accumulated over the years, she'd owned embarrassingly little for a woman of thirty-seven. When she'd signed the tenancy agreement, however, she'd taken out a small loan and bought furniture from eBay and junk shops plus new sheets and towels, three new rugs, plates and glasses and mugs. It was all quite civilized.

Len ran upstairs straight away to put her pyjamas on and Robin went to the kitchen to put the kettle on. A cup of tea before bed was Lennie's new thing – cups of tea at any time of day, actually. She and her new friends were forever huddling

round the kettle, wrapped in long cardigans like a gang of preternaturally smooth-skinned old ladies at a WI tea-urn.

The boards creaked overhead. Len's bedroom was at the back
of the house, overlooking the tiny outside space. She'd left a gap
in the curtains and a bar of yellow light lay across the decked
area and up the back wall. They'd moved in September, too late
to use the garden much before it got cold last year, but she had
visions of reading out there this summer, Saturday breakfasts,
lunches with Len and her friends. A couple of weeks ago, she'd
bought a little barbecue and she could see it hovering in the
shadow outside the double doors, a friendly red UFO.

Len reappeared in her vest top and baggy striped pyjama
trousers tied with burgundy ribbon. Fifteen going on twenty-five
but, without the mascara she seemed to think Robin couldn't
see, also entirely recognizable as the five- and six-year-old she'd
been what sometimes felt like decades ago, sometimes about a
fortnight.

The same age as Victoria Engel when she'd vanished without
a trace.

'What?' Len said.

'Nothing. Just thinking how lovely you are.'

She rolled her eyes. 'Right.'

'What? You are.'

'You're *somewhat* biased.'

'Doesn't mean it's not true.'

Len shook her head in pretend despair, squeezed her teabag
against the edge of her mug then carried it over to the bin.
'Mum, you'll be late again tomorrow, won't you? Is it okay if I
go over to Asha's with Niamh? We need to finish our project.'

And, the unspoken subtext, *I won't have to sit alone in the
house after dark.*

44

Chapter Five

Robin handed a cup into the car, retrieved her own from the roof and lowered herself into the passenger seat. She pulled the door shut quietly then glanced around the circle of sleepy semis outside. No sign that she'd drawn attention to herself: good.

Maggie already had the paper bag open. 'Pain au chocolat?' she said, at Attenborough-in-the-bushes volume, peering in. 'How did you know?'

'Wild guess,' she murmured. It was still only quarter to seven but as usual Maggie was fully made-up and rattling with silver jewellery, her black hair backcombed and doubtless crisp to the touch. Bar a marginally lighter hand with the eyeliner, it was the full Alice Cooper. She spent her days hanging round suburbs and industrial estates but if ever an Eighties hair band needed a last-minute stand-in, she was ready. Even now, Robin found it bizarre that Maggie was one of her mother's best friends. Talk about the odd couple.

'How're things?' she asked. 'How's Richard?'

'Oh, you know,' Maggie shrugged. She swallowed her mouthful then said, 'Your ma hasn't told you?'

'Told me what?'

'Well, it's fine, everything's fine. You know we're moving in together, or I'm moving in with him, to be accurate?'

'Yes, I knew that bit.'

'He's furious with me because I won't sell my house until I know I can do it – live with someone again, I mean, after all this time.' Maggie had been divorced since Robin was a teenager.

'Doesn't sound unreasonable to me.'

'Well, we're birds of a feather like that, aren't we, you and me, too used to calling our own shots. He says it shows a lack of faith. *I* say, it's bloody miraculous I'm even considering the idea and he should think himself lucky.' She started one of her fox-bark laughs then remembered she was supposed to be inconspicuous. 'Anyway,' she said quietly. 'We'll see. He's being melodramatic, that's all.'

Robin nodded towards the window. 'Who's your date here?'

'Scummy little benefit fraudster at number seven.' Bangles chiming, Maggie tore off another bite of pastry. 'On the sick with an alleged shoulder injury for thirteen months,' she said, chewing, 'while working full-time cash-in-hand for his mate's plastering business. You can feast eyes on him yourself in a minute: the mate'll be along to pick him up.'

Cul-de-sacs at dawn was how Maggie had described her private investigation work when she'd offered Robin a job eighteen months earlier. 'Pictures of people up bright and early, suited, booted and slinging their briefcase/toolbox in the back of the car/van, delete as applicable, are of the essence.' As it turned out, *she* hadn't been entirely honest about her job, either, however, and while most of her closest friends still believed she only did benefits and insurance work, on Robin's first day, Maggie had had to confess to her own side gig, albeit mostly unpaid, working to help women in jeopardy. Their first – and last – case together had been a missing woman.

'This poor girl in Deritend, is it?' she asked now, sipping her coffee.

'I wondered if you'd heard anything on the vine. Anyone you know of gone AWOL?' Most of Maggie's side work came via the police but there were other avenues for people who wanted to stay low-profile.

'No, I'd have been in touch.'

Robin nodded. 'I know. I wanted to show you a couple of photographs, though, just in case. I couldn't email them for obvious reasons.'

She brought them up on her phone. The first was a full-face shot. Lying on her back, make-up-free face drained of colour and framed by her hair, the girl looked not so much old-fashioned as hundreds of years out of time. Robin imagined her suddenly as a poor novice dead of plague, awaiting burial at some chilly fifteenth-century convent. In the second picture, her eyes had been opened to show their colour, irises muddy green, rings of amber round the pupils like sun flares. Her nose was probably bigger than she might have wanted, the kind of nose you grew into, that made you look characterful rather than pretty. Maybe she'd moaned about it but by her thirties and forties she might have appreciated it. She'd never get the chance now.

Maggie looked at the pictures for some time. 'No, I've never seen her,' she said at last.

'Sure?'

'Definite.' She handed back the phone. 'But she does remind me of someone.'

'Who?'

'I can't think. No one relevant. Probably some D-list celeb from one of those reality shows, *Big Brother* or *Has-Beens-on-Ice* or what have you.'

'Really? I think she looks old-fashioned.'

'Yeah, I can see that, too.'

They fell silent as a front door opened on Robin's side of the close. A man in his thirties stepped out, locked it behind him then walked to a silver hatchback. He hadn't noticed them.

'How're things otherwise?' Maggie asked as he pulled off. 'Len all right?'

'I think so. Her Easter grade card was great, Mum probably told you.'

'She didn't – the academics are more your line, I think. She says Len had her friends over to Dunnington Road for dinner a week or ten days ago, you all made pizza?'

'Yeah, Asha and Niamh, her new besties. They're good girls – sparky. Quite hilarious, actually, some of the banter.'

Maggie glanced at the rear-view mirror. 'Incoming.'

Passing alongside now was a Ford Transit, its side painted with the details and logo of Philip Ramsey, 'Master Plaster'. It looped the cul-de-sac and came back, facing them now, to hover in a space at the opposite kerb a couple of cars behind. The height of the cab gave them a clear view of the driver. Maggie's phone was ready on her knee, camera app open, and she picked it up and took bursts of photos as a skinny bloke in paint-flecked jeans and a Whitesnake T-shirt loped down the path from one of the houses and swung himself easily up into the passenger seat. A few words to the driver and they were away.

Robin waited until they rounded the corner. 'Whitesnake – blast from the past.'

'The past? Do you mind?'

'Maggie, different note, have you ever come across Martin Engel?'

She turned, surprised at the change of direction, then narrowed her eyes. 'Martin Engel – is that the one with the missing daughter – Vivian, is it? No – Victoria, of course it's Victoria. The dad who's still in the papers from time to time?'

'He turned up at the nick late last night – he was waiting for me in the car park when I left. Lying in wait's probably more accurate.' A sense-memory, the knuckleduster keys cool between her fingers.

'For you specifically?'

'He'd heard about the girl in Deritend and he knew I was SIO. He knew all about me – the case in London, which station I'm at, my car.'

Maggie frowned. 'I don't like that. Did he think the Deritend girl might be her?'

'So he said but, given how involved he's been in her case over the years, he must have known we'd have gone back through the records straight away. She's probably the highest-profile misper on our patch.' Of course he must, she'd realized, lying in bed, cogs turning. 'I don't think that was really why he came. He pretty much admitted he'd been keeping an eye on me for a while; I think this was just his way in.'

'You should tell someone. Waiting for you in the dark – and he knows your car?' Maggie shook her head. 'God, don't tell your mother, will you? She'll freak out. Do you think he's unhinged – *been* unhinged by it all? You could hardly blame him.'

'Dunno. He's definitely . . . intense.' But if things had gone the other way with Lennie, or if she'd vanished without a trace, she'd be the same. She'd turn over every blade of grass in Europe.

'Tell someone. Tell Samir.'

Robin half-nodded, non-committal. 'I'll handle it. Really, I wanted to ask if *you'd* had any dealings with him? On the other side of your business.'

'No. He'd have gone with someone higher-falutin' than me, if he went the PI route.'

49

Which, again, he must have done, Robin thought, given how much else he'd thrown behind it.

'Don't get involved,' warned Maggie. 'You've got enough on your plate and he's already overstepped. Leave it.'

'Yeah.' She shook her cup: empty bar a last mouthful. 'Okay, I'd better get going.'

'That's me, too. Drop you at your car?'

'No, don't worry, it's only round the corner.'

'Well, thanks for the breakfast. And keep me posted.'

Robin started walking, raising her hand as Maggie passed, feeling an odd sense of loss as her car disappeared from view. Things were better between them now, the mess she'd made of working for her receding into history, but once you'd lost someone's confidence, she didn't know if you ever totally got it back. Not that it was stopping her from trying. She'd wanted to ask about the dead girl, of course, but she'd also wanted to show her how assiduous she was, how on it. She knew Maggie missed police work so here she was bringing her titbits, too, dropping tasty morsels of information at her feet. Pathetic.

Lennie had still been asleep when she left so she got out her phone to ring her. Before she could bring up her number, however, it buzzed.

'Morning, boss,' Malia said. 'I've just had a call. A woman rang Crimestoppers – she saw the two guys from the sketch heading into a soup kitchen in Bordesley Street. Uniforms are on their way and I'm heading straight over.'

Robin mapped a mental route. 'I'm only a few minutes away. I'll meet you there.'

Like many of its neighbours in Digbeth, Bordesley Street was a mix of the few Victorian red-brick factories that had survived the war and a jumble of modern builds, a lot thrown up in the

Fifties and Sixties, some slightly better ones in the Nineties. Behind a chain-link fence, a large 'Overflow Car Park' – overflow from what? – occupied what Robin guessed was an old bombsite, undeveloped since. The squad car was parked down the street outside a large plumbing wholesalers.

'Didn't want the smell of bacon putting people off their breakfast,' said one of the officers. 'There's two doors, front and side, we've got them both from here.'

'Okay. Bring the car up now, then wait. If it is who we're looking for, we'll need you to take them to Harborne.'

The Good Hope Kitchen occupied what had once been a workshop or a garage, a flat-roofed single-storey building with narrow reinforced windows at the outer edges and an isolated central doorway probably put in when a rolling grille was taken out. The pebble-dash was recently whitewashed, though, and a Plexiglas case displayed a bright patchwork of flyers for LGBTQ groups, social events for pensioners, AA and confidential HIV testing. She glanced at a card giving 'Kitchen Hours': 7.00 until 9.00 for breakfast, lunch daily from 12.00.

More flyers covered the walls of a narrow entryway that smelled of toast and frying onions. Beyond was a square room dominated by three long picnic-style tables at which thirty or forty people were seated, some talking, in groups, others pointedly alone. One man seemed to be bodily protecting his plate, hunched with an arm curled around it.

Despite the plain clothes, they were identified as police within seconds and watched the awareness spread through the group, conversation dying away. Alerted by the quiet, a woman in a yellow T-shirt at the hatch halted, serving spoon in mid-air.

Even if they hadn't been looking for him, the younger of two men at the end of the centre table had flagged himself as worth questioning in connection with *something*: the panic on his face as he looked for the exit was vaudeville-worthy. The sketch had got him just right, filthy combat jacket and black scarf, the face that was somehow round and thin at the same time. His jacket might once have fitted him or it might have belonged to someone twice the size.

The other man's likeness hadn't been quite as good. The hatching had made him look older but he was in his mid-thirties at most, even allowing for lifestyle. He was still easily recognizable, however, in the same green and blue plaid shirt belted with what did in fact look like a tie, the black baseball cap with a fraying peak. His straggling facial hair was red.

In front of them were half-eaten plates of scrambled egg, plastic knives and forks abandoned. Robin watched the older one lean forward, hand feeling for the backpack at his feet.

'Can I help you?' Another woman in a yellow T-shirt approached from her position by a giant toaster on a side table. She was in her late twenties, with a shiny hennaed bob and a small silver ring through her left nostril. A yellow lanyard hung round her neck: *Annika, Morning Front of House.* On her T-shirt, the letters of Good Hope were printed in an elongated font to look like rays around a rising sun.

They showed her ID. Malia's posture, full meerkat, told Robin that she'd seen the hand on the bag, too, the tension in the two men's bodies. The older one had a finger on the other's forearm now: *Wait, wait.*

'We'd like to talk to a couple of your patrons over there, please,' she said. 'We're—'

Now. With surprising agility, the men spun on the bench, freed their legs, and surged back between the tables towards the rear door. She and Malia lunged after them but there were too many people, none of them fast-moving, and before they were even halfway across the room, the younger man had his hands on the bar of the fire door and they were out, away. Running footsteps up the alley to the street but then came shouts – 'Oi' – scuffling, and noisy complaints.

When they reached them, the uniforms had both men on the pavement, arms behind their backs. The older man's bag, strap torn, lay at the kerb.

'We haven't bleeding done anything,' he yelled, cheek against the tarmac. 'We're only having breakfast.'

Chapter Six

Malia led the interviews, Varan in with her. Robin watched from upstairs, one eye on the monitor, the other on her brimming inbox. Two of her cases from last year were about to go to trial, and the volume of CPS email was doing her head in.

The elder of the two men was Stuart Granger, known as Stewpot. At thirty-seven, he'd been living rough on and off for six years after the break-up of a long-term relationship, punctuating stretches on the street with stints in hostels and, for a while, he said, tears welling, at the flat of a friend who'd OD'd. Now he kept himself going by panhandling outside the Rag Market and a couple of other spots round the Bull Ring. At close range, his beard was visibly matted, and inhaling too deeply through the nose was a mistake Robin had only made once in his company. When Malia asked him to identify himself for the tape, however, he'd leaned forward and enunciated his name as if he were recording a professional voicemail message.

'Why did you run this morning, Stuart?' Malia asked him.

'Because you're police.' Robin watched as his fingers moved to a loose thread on his cap-peak. He pulled on it, dipping his head momentarily, hiding his eyes. 'Because I've already got two cautions and I can't afford a fine.'

'Cautions for what?'

Stewpot's look said, *Come on, you already know*. 'I had some smack on me, didn't I? In my bag.'

'What about yesterday? A witness says she saw you and Martin jumping out of a window and running from the old Gisborne works on Bradford Street.'

He scratched his forearm savagely. 'We thought it was police then, too.'

'It?'

'A shout – this bloke shouting.'

'Had you seen police entering the building? Vehicles outside?'

'No.'

'Other people live there, yes? But your mind still went straight to police?'

He shook his head, as if he regretted being put in this position. 'Because we knew she was there.'

'Who?'

'The dead girl. We found her.'

Malia let his words hang, leaving a vacuum. When he didn't fill it, she asked, 'Was she dead when you found her, Stuart?'

'Yes.' Emphatic. '*Yes*.' Even remotely, Robin could see that his forehead was shining with sweat. 'We went back there, into that room, and we saw her. Wrapped up in the carpet, only her feet and hair sticking out.'

'Did you know her? Or recognise her?'

'No. First time either of us seen her.'

'What did you do when you found her?'

'Nothing. We didn't get it straight away, for a start – we were still a bit . . . out of it. It was only when we got closer, with the torch . . . I touched her hand and she was cold.'

55

'Is that something you do often – roam the factory in the dark? It's not easy to navigate in broad daylight, all that junk and weeds, gaping holes in the ground . . .'

'It wasn't dark. We went to get wood. There's a pile of old pallets back there – we've been breaking them up to burn. Martin was shivering so I got up and he wanted to come with me. He gets like that – paranoid. Doesn't like being left on his tod.'

'Hot yesterday, for a fire.'

Stewpot scratched again. 'We were coming down. And you're never hot at dawn if you're sleeping rough. Even with a roof, it's cold. Damp – gets in your bones.'

'We didn't see evidence that a fire had been lit that morning.'

He nodded. 'Because it wasn't – we *didn't* light it. When we saw her, we scarpered, didn't we? Back to our room, tried to work out what to do.'

'Hm. Did it occur to you to call the police – or ask someone else to? You found a dead woman and you just went back to your room?'

'It did *occur* to us. But we didn't do it straight away because we needed to think. We knew this would happen – you'd come and be all over the place, we'd lose our spot. And you'd pull us in, like you have done.'

'Only for questioning. You're not under arrest.'

'Yet.'

'Why would we arrest you if you haven't done anything?'

'Because we live there and she was in the room next door. Because we're junkies. Because she was a pretty girl and . . .'

'You don't get many opportunities in that direction these days?'

'Did I ever?' He gave a funny half-smile and for a moment Robin wondered. Somewhere under the grime and the ratty beard was a kind face, she thought suddenly.

'You didn't touch her at all?'

'Only the hand, like I said.'

'And you didn't take anything from the body? Purse? Phone? Because when we found her, there was nothing on her at all. You didn't take anything so you could score?'

'Steal from a dead girl? We're not bleedin' animals.'

'I know,' she said, mollifying. 'But you've got an expensive habit, Stuart, and no visible source of income.'

'I told you, I beg.'

'What we care about here is finding out who killed her. If anything was taken from the body, it could help us do that, and . . .'

'I. Didn't. Take. Anything.'

'What about Martin?'

'He'd never.'

'How long have you known him?'

'Don't know exactly. Three years, maybe? Something like that.'

'How did you meet?'

'Random. On the street. But we got on so we started moving round together, became friends. It's better not to be on your own. We look after each other, keep an eye out.'

'How long after you found her did you hear the shout?'

'I don't know.' He shook his head. 'A while – an hour? I don't know. Like I said, we'd been using, we'd been on the nod all night, so . . .' He rubbed his top lip with the back of his index finger.

'On the nod?' said Varan.

'Drifting in and out. Smack, innit.'

'Do you have anything to do with the group of rough sleepers at the back of the building?' Malia asked.

'Not really. We keep to ourselves. Sometimes if we've been to the soup kitchen and they've got sandwiches or whatnot, we'll bring some back for them.'

'Do they ever come over to you?'

'Once or twice when we were first there. Not since.'

'How long have you been living there?'

'A couple of months, probably. Easter-ish.' Another half-smile. 'We didn't get each other an egg or anything, in case you're wondering. We see the stuff in the shops – it's like a calendar, isn't it? Easter, Christmas, Halloween . . .'

'Where did you sleep last night, given that you couldn't go back there?'

'Up town. I've got a mate in the underpass through by Moor Street. Curly. He'll be there this afternoon if you want to check.'

Malia squared her papers. 'Is there anything else you think we should know? Anyone been hanging round lately? Anything unusual caught your eye?'

Stewpot was shaking his head then stopped, something appearing to dawn on him. 'Actually, there *has* been this bloke. We've seen him two or three times – in that room.'

'Who is he?'

'Don't know. He ran away.'

'Right . . .' *Here we go* – Robin heard it in Malia's voice as she thought it herself.

'He comes at night, that's when we've seen him. I followed him once and saw him going back down the shaft with some of our wood under his arm. He legged it when he saw me – started running. Don't know for sure but I think he's living in the place next door.'

'What shaft?'

'There's these sort of, like, sloping ramps into the basement? A couple of them you can walk down – the slope's gentle enough. I saw this bloke and I went down later to see what was going on, if he was living down there or what. I didn't know where he'd gone but then I found this hole through to the place next door.'

*

Between the two interviews, Robin called Rafferty at the site and by the time Malia and Varan had talked to Martin, he'd phoned back to confirm: yes, there was a walkable shaft two workshops back from where the body had been found and, further through the warren, a hole knocked through Gisborne's outside wall, apparently from the other side in.

'Is it new?' Malia asked.

'Not brand-new. At least a year or so, Rafferty's guessing, going by water stains, fungal growth, etc.' She spun a biro between her fingers. 'That the hole exists doesn't mean this other guy does, obviously.'

'No, but I think they *are* telling us the truth. The fact their descriptions don't quite match – now we're looking for a man who's either Indian or Pakistani, according to Martin, or "Middle Eastern", according to Stewpot, wearing either a navy anorak or a black one, early thirties or late thirties . . .'

'Yeah, and if they'd cooked him up, I think Stewpot would have been quicker off the mark in telling us, too,' Robin said. 'He doesn't seem that calculating.'

On the desk, her phone buzzed. *Mum, do u mind if I stay over at Asha's tonight?*

If okay with A's mum, she quickly replied, *okay w me.*

Thanks!

Malia perched on the filing cabinet. 'What shall we do with them?'

The question Robin had been weighing. They could charge Stewpot with both possession and intent to supply – the amount in the backpack, though small, had been enough for two – but the longer she'd watched the second interview, the more reluctant she'd felt. Martin was clearly vulnerable; she guessed he'd been abused in the past. He'd grown up in care, and Stewpot, though only eleven years older, was a father figure to him. 'He looks out for me, you know?' Martin had said, eyes wide as a bush baby's. 'Makes sure I get food and clean works. Without him, I'd probably be dead by now.'

The problem was, with no fixed address and the unreliability of addicts, however well-intentioned, there was no guarantee they'd find them again if they needed to. On the other hand, they were already going into withdrawal, and the pain would get worse and worse.

'When they've done their statements, let's give them some food,' she said. 'Rafferty and his crew are going over the place next door now. I'll get in touch with the soup kitchen and see if we can leave messages there. As long as Stewpot and Martin agree to check in there, let's let them go.'

A rap on the open door: Niall, one of the DCs. 'Sorry, guv.'

'What's up?'

'I just saw DI Webster and he said to tell you they've got a solve on Kieran Clarke.'

'Really? Who?'

'A classmate. His girlfriend had been flirting with Kieran, and he'd had enough. They brought him in this morning, and he's broken down and confessed.'

'A classmate? So he's sixteen as well?'

'Didn't mean to kill him, apparently. It was supposed to be a warning.'

Chapter Seven

It was after five when Robin got back to the car, the post mortem had taken all afternoon. As SIO, she always attended but sometimes, in simpler cases, she saw the beginning then deputized to Malia, who updated her on anything significant. Today, she'd stayed to the very end, watching from the observation booth so the team could reach her by phone. Part of it was the fading hope that Olly Faulkner would discover something useful but she'd known she'd stay as soon as the woman was lifted from the bag and laid on the table. She'd looked so alone, so starkly, absolutely alone; she couldn't leave her.

They'd been contacted by thirty or forty families now so where the hell was hers? Where was *her* mother or sister or boyfriend? Who had loved *her*?

The body had changed since yesterday. She was less medieval novice now than discoloured marble tomb effigy, her skin turned waxy yellow. She looked smaller, too, perhaps 80 per cent of her original size, as if, without her spirit, her body was losing the power to occupy physical space. She was disappearing. *Don't go yet,* Robin had urged her. *Help me. Tell me how you ended up here, murdered before your life really started.*

She'd tried to imagine what that life had been like but they had so bloody little to go on. Where had *she* been at that age then, she'd asked herself. Her first or second year at university, probably. God – the idea had sent a chill down her arms. The way she'd lived then, she could easily have ended up the same way.

She'd arrived at university a complete wreck. Five days before she started, a week after they'd got back from seven months backpacking together, Samir had summarily dumped her, no explanation except he didn't feel the same any more. She knew the truth now but at the time, she'd been completely sideswiped. It had felt more like a bereavement than a dumping.

On top of that, it had ripped a jagged hole through her self-esteem, and that hadn't been entirely sea-worthy to begin with. She'd always been confident in her abilities – she'd done well academically; she knew she was bright – but undercutting her faith in herself in almost every other area was the message of her brother's life-long attitude towards her: you're hateful, despicable, a waste of space. 'Who'd ever want to be with *you*?' Luke had sneered regularly when she'd started liking boys. Until he dumped her, she hadn't realized how much her relationship with Samir had done to counter that.

In her first term at UCL, she'd pursued a punishing schedule of academic work to distract herself – lectures; the library; essays twice as long as they had to be. Then, after Christmas, when the first wave of grief began to pass, it had been Operation Oblivion: *Watch this, Samir! You're not the only one who can move on!* She'd gone from near-recluse to party animal in the space of a week. Her liver hurt to remember how much she'd drunk.

And the blokes, because that was really the point of it. *See, Samir?* He *likes me* – he's *flirting with me.* He *wants to sleep with me so I can't be* that *repellent.* And then, most of those mornings, the cold gathering of the clothes off durable halls carpet, the walk of shame and then bravado in the face of the ribbings down the bar before doing it all over again.

But it hadn't been solely fellow students and the cosy, regulated confines of the university. All of London had been her oyster. Pubs, bars, clubs, any sparkly-eyed stranger with a good line in banter, and no one had felt like a stranger after five or six drinks. Her friends homed in on unthreatening boys who turned out to have been at school with their older brothers but she'd been drawn to men with an edge, a suggestion of darkness far beyond her friends' comfort zones. She'd wondered since if, at her most nihilistic, she'd been testing providence.

One morning she'd woken up in a flat on the tenth floor of a block in Woolwich next to a shaven-headed man whose back was tattooed from shoulder to shoulder with an eagle. She had no memory of the tattoo, and she'd never been to Woolwich before – barely heard of it until she'd sneaked out and asked where she was at the nearest corner shop (of course, her phone had been out of battery). She'd remembered the night before in snatches as the day developed: she'd met him in a club, he'd been with a group of friends. She didn't know any of them, she'd never seen them before, but she'd got into a car with three of them and driven across London without a second thought. Anything could have happened. They could have raped and killed her, dumped her body at the side of the road.

But the worst of her judgement had always involved booze, and as Olly had told her, there was no alcohol in their girl's stomach. And while she'd died in the small hours of a Sunday morning, she wasn't dressed for a Saturday night.

Her phone rang through the Bluetooth, pulling her out of the thought.

'Guess who's just called me,' Malia challenged.

Robin considered. 'Jonathan Quinton.'

'Oh,' she said, deflated. 'Well, remind me not to bother wrapping *your* Christmas present.'

'Sorry. What did he want?' She could guess.

'Ask me out for a drink,' Malia confirmed. 'What do you reckon? Trying to involve himself in the investigation?'

'Could be. You said yes, of course?'

'Of course. Who wouldn't want to go out with a dude who found a dead body and thought it was a pick-up opportunity? How was the last bit of the PM?'

'Olly's narrowed the time of death. Between one and four a.m., he says now.'

'Well, that's something. Anything helpful on ID?'

'Zero. No numbered surgical devices or secret tattoos; no visible injuries apart from the stab wounds; no signs of surgery or disease or long-term drug use, no scars, no birthmarks.'

'Not so much as a filling, actually,' Olly had said, a gloved finger in her mouth. 'A missing point on this back molar here, bottom right, and that's it.'

'Recent?'

'Maybe but not new, new. There's a little bit of staining – coffee, I'd guess.'

'You know,' Robin said to Malia now, the thought forming as she spoke, 'maybe the blankness is relevant. The point, even. No tattoos, no drugs, no alcohol, no scars – fair enough. No phone, no purse, nothing in her pockets – all of that could have been taken. But there's nothing about her *clothes* that was anything but bog-standard.'

'And no make-up,' said Malia.

'Yes, right. Maybe she did have jewellery and it was stolen with the purse and phone, but, as you say, no make-up. And her ears weren't pierced. Even her hair's been left long, no particular style.' She thought of Lennie, her tubes of Rimmel mascara and eyeliner, the hot-brush she'd wanted for her birthday.

'And at that age, girls are experimenting – not only girls – trying different looks, trying to work out who they are. Committing crimes against fashion – I know I did. But she's . . . basic. Not even, in *that* sense.'

'If so, then why?'

'Given what's happened, maybe she was hiding from someone. Trying to stay low-profile?'

'Or maybe someone *else* wanted her low-profile.' Robin thought of Lennie again. She saw men looking at her and she wanted to smack them, demand to know how old they thought she was. 'Over-protective parents,' she said, 'keeping her on a tight rein? She was pretty – she'd attract attention. Maybe they didn't want that.'

She'd called Good Hope before the post mortem but she hadn't got through. One of the support staff had emailed as she'd left the morgue to say that the director had returned her call but when she'd tried again, the line had been busy. She was five minutes from Bordesley Street and the rush-hour traffic was creeping, a couple of cars getting through at each change of the lights. When she reached the turn, she took it.

The kitchen didn't do dinner, she remembered, but through the narrow open window at the front, she could hear voices inside, a man and a woman. When she rang the bell, the man came to the door. He was in his late forties, she guessed, though he had less grey round the ears than Samir who was ten years younger. He was quite handsome, actually, in a hippie way that normally didn't do much for her. As far as she was concerned, no one over the age of twenty-one needed to wear leather brace-lets, but the arms they were on were tanned and muscled to the right extent, the T-shirt clinging to his biceps without bulging. His eyes were a warm brown, thickly lashed.

She introduced herself and told him she was looking for Daniel Reid.

'You've found him.'

'Thanks for calling earlier,' Robin said. 'Sorry I missed you.'

'Well, you've got a bit on your plate, I imagine.' His voice was middle class, no regional accent. 'Come in.'

She followed him down the long passage to the main room where Annika, Morning Front of House, was sitting at one of the long tables with two mugs. She looked none too thrilled to see her again, and Robin wondered if she was interrupting something.

'We're just having a cup of tea,' Reid said. 'Would you like one?'

'I'm fine – thank you, though. You probably heard that we were here this morning looking for Stuart and Martin?'

'Annika told me, yes.'

'They're still at the station and I want to let them go but it's problematic because they've got no fixed address or phones. I wanted to ask if we could leave messages for them here if we need to get in touch again.'

He nodded, seeming to think. 'I want to say yes,' he said after a few seconds, 'I *will* say yes – obviously we want to do everything we can—'

'But . . . ?'

'It's a difficult situation. It's not a problem as far as *we're* concerned, the team, but for our clientele . . . We work hard to let people know they can trust us and they're welcome, whoever they are, whatever their circumstances. Life's tough for all of them, but some in particular . . . Well, clearly I don't have to tell *you* that addiction can lead to criminal behaviour. I don't

66

want people who need us to be put off because they think we've got a hotline to the police.'

'It's a message or two, not a hotline.'

'Something like this morning, people getting hauled off during breakfast . . .'

'Stuart and Martin weren't "hauled off", Mr Reid. They weren't arrested. The only reason we had to stop them physically was because they made a run for it.' She took a breath. 'The work you do is very important, I don't dispute that, but they're witnesses in a murder enquiry.' And still pretty much the *only* witnesses. 'You can imagine why we couldn't ring ahead this morning and also why I'm keen to release them now – we've had them all day.'

'They'll be in withdrawal,' he said.

'Exactly. So . . .'

'We'll pass on messages as soon as we see them.'

'Great. Thank you. We'll ask them to check in regularly so you might see them more often.'

'That's fine, we like Stew and Martin. If I can – Annika and I were talking about it before you arrived,' he looked over at her. 'We'd like to say that we really doubt they had anything to do with it. They're a bit lost in life – Martin in particular's had a very hard time – but they're gentle souls. They've taken food from here to give to the other homeless at Gisborne's a couple of times – portable things, you know, if one of the sandwich chains donates their short-dated stock, for example. Neither of them could do this.'

'Unfortunately,' Robin said, 'in my experience, given the wrong set of circumstances, anyone can do anything.'

Half man, half chair was the gag about DC Les Hargreaves in Homicide; he didn't so much sit down at the beginning of a shift as become one with his rolling chair and part from it as infrequently as possible thereafter, darting around the place at right angles, stomach nestled between the tops of his thighs like a super-sized Easter egg. His head was huge, too, round, bald and fleshy, with three parallel rolls of fat that appeared at the base of his skull whenever his head declined more than a couple of degrees from a vertical axis.

Les was known universally as Tarka or Tark. She'd asked about it the first time they'd had real drinks, the night they'd got their first solve as a team. (That had been a knife crime, too, a pensioner found dead in his chair, killed for the forty-two pounds he'd had saved in an old marmalade pot.) Eventually Tark had admitted to breaking down and sobbing at the end of *Tarka the Otter*. 'His niece had to cuddle him better,' Varan had grinned. 'She's six.'

When it came to CCTV, however, Tarka was king, his capacity for remaining alert during hours of mind-numbing footage almost super-human, and at around four o'clock that afternoon, if they'd been in the same room, Robin might have been tempted to kiss him.

He'd called her at the morgue. 'As you know,' he said, 'we're playing a pretty hard-going game of Sudoku with what we've got so far, tape-wise. There's not many squares filled in – as well as all the broken cameras, two or three of the businesses along Warwick Street are being slow to hand theirs over, for whatever reason.' He paused for effect. *Get on with it, Tark*, she'd barely refrained from saying but all she'd been doing otherwise was waiting for Olly's next move, so she'd bitten her tongue and allowed him his glory-building suspense.

'*But*,' he'd said, 'this afternoon we got tapes from the office building directly across the road on Bradford Street – you know, where the cartoonist is, Kate Coombs.'

'And the camera on the eastern corner,' Robin told the semi-circle assembled in front of the board now, 'gave Tark this guy.' She pointed to a grainy black-and-white still of a man in a baseball cap and dark anorak crouched on the sill of an open window. 'Four thirty-seven yesterday morning, which is shortly after Dr Faulkner's narrowed window for time of death.'

She glanced at Samir, who'd slipped in at the back of the room and perched on a desk-edge, long legs extended in front of him. 'Based on what Stewpot and Martin told us, Rafferty's team found an access point to the disused works *next door* to Gisborne's and also evidence that someone's been living or at least spending significant time there recently. Stuart and Martin said the man they saw had been coming over to get firewood and that would make sense.' She indicated a photograph of what looked like a manhole cover propped off the floor on bricks, the remnants of a fire on top.

'This is on the first floor. The building's in much better condition all round than Gisborne's. It's only been empty two years and the roof's still on, which makes a huge difference, of course. All the orthodox ways in – gates, doors – are padlocked and most of the windows are still intact – we can see him opening this one.'

She pointed at a cluster of three pictures further down. 'What's striking is how organized this is, especially compared with where Martin and Stuart were living. It's rough, sure, but it's far from chaotic. This big pile of cardboard here has a blanket that was actually folded; there's a torch and a stash of tinned food. The best-before date on this milk here is today.'

A murmur from those who'd come in from outside and hadn't already heard.

'Kate Coombs says she thinks she's seen him before but only once, Tuesday or Wednesday last week, she couldn't say which, in the early evening, around seven o'clock, on her way back from getting some fish and chips.'

'The fact that his things are still there is interesting. Given our presence in the area since yesterday, he might be lying low, intending to collect them later. We've had guys outside since the victim was found so we're confident he hasn't come in from Bradford Street and, unlike Gisborne's, this building doesn't stretch back to Warwick Street – there's another factory directly behind it and that one's in use. So, no rear access.'

'He could just have abandoned the stuff, couldn't he?' said Tarka. 'None of it's valuable or that personal-looking.'

'Yes, though you'd think that was risky, forensics-wise. Torch, cans – hard to think of better surfaces for prints. On the other hand, he may have been counting on us not finding it – different premises. Maybe he thought killing her in the other building – or near Stuart and Martin – would be subterfuge enough. Or, despite the apparent order of his set-up, he might have acted impulsively and been forced to scramble. *Not all snivelling little crims are Professor Moriarty*, as Kilmartin had pointedly declared in her hearing at least three times.

Robin looked around, making sure she had everyone's attention. 'So, potential progress, but unfortunately, as we're all aware, we're nearing the forty-eight-hour mark. We need to find this guy ASAP.' She tapped the board with the end of her biro. 'Now, Stuart and Martin's initial descriptions didn't completely match but based both on what Coombs says and the tins, it looks like he's Indian or Pakistani rather than "Middle Eastern" – mango in syrup, curry potato, lentil dumplings. The brand's Sohna. CCTV aside, our best line of enquiry now is finding out where he bought this food. We need to track down local stockists and talk to them all, no stone unturned. We'll also do another round of house-to-house with this picture.' She pointed to the still.

70

'Right, ID. We're still totally empty-handed: the autopsy told us nothing we didn't already know on that front. At this point – forty-eight hours – we're required to register the case with Missing Persons so they can get it up on their database.' She glanced at Varan, who nodded, *On it.* 'We could use a photo from the scene but my feeling is that, for sensitivity, we should use the e-fit for now. It's just come in and, as you can see, it's good – anyone who knew her would recognize her.'

'We put a marker up on the computer straight away yesterday, young woman's body found, but we'll do a PNC broadcast, too, now. We'll start with West and East Midlands, London and South East, then, if there's nothing in twelve hours, we'll broaden it to all-forces.'

Samir was watching her with his usual complete focus and she met his eye. 'One last thing,' she said, 'an idea that DS Thomas and I have discussed. Clearly, we've got very few clues about our victim across the board. That might be pure chance but let's bear in mind the possibility that it's deliberate. The lack of personal items might have been an after-the-event clean-up, but her whole look – hair, clothes, no make-up – was pretty much a blank slate. Was this how she presented herself normally? And if so, was it what *she* wanted? Or someone else? In either case, why? Because if it *was* deliberate, it was successful – she's anonymous. But she *is* someone – was – and somebody *else* knows who.'

Samir closed her office door behind him. Robin braced herself, expecting complaints from Kilmartin at the lack of progress, but instead he gestured at her computer. 'Can I? Something I want to show you.'

Behind her desk, he tapped about a bit then motioned for her to come and look. Moving close enough to see properly, she caught his scent, washing powder and the Old Spice deodorant he'd always worn and that she'd mocked him for back then even though she'd secretly liked it. She felt a sudden weird pang. Bloody nostalgia, she thought, forever ready to take a pop if you let your guard down for a second.

Facebook, the profile circle in the top left showing the silhouette of a man super-imposed over the flag of St George, a loudhailer to his lips. The banner along the top was a Union Jack, the words 'For Queen and Country' stamped in red across them slantwise like 'Fragile' on a box. Samir scrolled past Photos – she caught a glimpse of a lion-and-unicorn tattoo, evidently brand-new, and what looked like mugshots of two black men – to Videos.

The 'Play' arrow hovered above the head of a man sitting at a table. A Venetian blind in the window to his right was open but the slats were angled so that he was cast in a strange underwater light. He was about forty, with brown hair cut close to his scalp, beard trimmed to a similar length. Pale green eyes under eyebrows that arched up towards the outer corners, faunish and intelligent. He did a lot of weights, that was evident: his shoulders were wide and padded with muscle, and there were visible cords in his neck. The gym-bunny thing was never her bag, she was actively suspicious of anyone with a six-pack who wasn't a professional athlete, but taken as a whole, she had to admit he wasn't unattractive.

Samir dragged the cursor to the three-minute mark then hit play. '. . . again and again and again.' The man's voice was Brummie, and surprisingly deep given his age, almost gravelly. 'At every level. We're being ignored. We're being cheated. Look at our health service. Look at the benefits system – immigrant families given houses straight away while British people are shunted from bedsit to bedsit for years, sharing HMOs with foreigners, people who *don't even speak English*. And that's if they're lucky – there are good British people, *useful working men*, living their lives on the street.'

He pulled back, allowing his unseen audience a moment to drink that in. Then he gathered a breath and leaned forward, equal parts menacing and confidential. 'I'm asking why,' he stabbed the desk, 'exactly *why*, won't our police – West Midlands Police – prioritize British people? White British people, from the British families who have lived in this country – whose work has *built* this country – the place where the rest of the world now thinks they can come for an easy ride?'

'This week, here in Birmingham, a black kid was killed. Guess what I've heard? That's right, the police have arrested his killer. Today, the very next day, he's behind bars, done and dusted, justice will be served. But on the same night, across town, a lovely-looking white girl was *also* killed, her body dumped in one of our derelict factories – derelict because jobs have been shipped overseas to India, China, Bangladesh, anywhere but bloody here, eh? Have the police got her killer? Have they fuck – never mind *him*, they don't even know who *she* is.'

Samir leaned in and tapped to stop it.

'Great,' Robin said, moving to the other side of the desk. 'So now the bloody BNP are sticking their oar in, too?'

'His name's Ben Tyrell. I had a tip-off from Cyber earlier.'

'They're watching him?'

He tipped his head from side to side. 'Not really, they've got bigger fish to fry. Keeping an eye, that's all. He's clever, they said, knows where the line is and never steps over it. They just thought we should know we're on his radar.'

Chapter Eight

The dashboard said 12 degrees as she drove home, surprisingly cool for the second week in June, even at this time of night. She opened the window and let some air swirl in. Her eyes were scratchy and she could feel the day layered on her skin, frying onions at the soup kitchen and the chemical tang of the morgue overlaid with hours of artificial light at the station. Sometimes she imagined it falling from the ceiling like dust, particulate and mildly toxic.

She was tired but her mental synapses were snapping away like a pinball table. There was no chance she'd be able to sleep yet but, as luck would have it, that wasn't the plan.

Lennie being at Asha's for the night was good for two reasons, the more important being that she'd certainly had a much better evening than she would have done sitting alone waiting for her to come home. Asha had an older brother, Austin, and the three of them hung out together, listened to music. Austin played guitar and was trying to get her to sing, which Robin liked. Len had a good voice, she'd been in the school choir back in London, but she didn't use it now.

The second reason was more selfish.

When she reached Mary Street, she parked the car, locked it and walked down the road towards the Mercedes estate on the other side. He'd come from the top end of the street, evidently, and when she dropped into the passenger seat, the windscreen framed the view of the city centre, the quicksilver gleam of the Selfridges building, the cylindrical Rotunda speckled with lights like a cob of Indian corn. The car was warm and the cracked-leather seat shaped itself round her rear end like an old padded glove.

'All right?' said Kev, smile in his voice. 'Long day.'

'Yours, too.'

'Mine was only a client dinner, though. Known Greg for years, more of a friend than anything now. How about you? I heard you got someone for that lad in Erdington.'

'Webster did. Much slower progress on mine, unfortunately.'

'You'll get there. Nice surprise to get a text on a Monday, though – unusual, Len away on a school night.'

'Might happen a bit if things carry on like this. She doesn't want me to know it bothers her, but she doesn't like being alone in the house after dark. Plus, of course, it's way more fun at Asha's.'

He nodded. 'Well, anything I can do to help, pick her up, drop her off, say the word. I'm up late, out early, as you know.' He gestured towards the windscreen. 'Nice, this view of the city, isn't it, all the lights twinkling.'

'Yeah, it's quite pretty. In the dark.'

He rolled his eyes, mock-despairing. 'Watch it, that's my home town you're dissing.'

'Mine, too.'

'Oh, really, Judas? Thought the cock had already crowed three times – my mistake.'

'Yes, all right. I've plighted my troth to West Midlands Police, haven't I? That not enough evidence of home-town commitment for you?'

'Only rented your house.'

'No choice: years of personal-finance mismanagement.' Plus the early days, when she'd earned a lot less and it had been a struggle just to keep them going. Once she'd paid the rent and Lennie's babysitting, she'd have been better off on benefits, but that had never been the plan.

'Well, time will tell – once a Londoner, always a Londoner, I reckon, adoptive or otherwise. It's a state of mind. Mum and Dad said to say hello, by the way. I was round at theirs last night, we saw you on the telly.'

'They don't know about this, do they?' Suddenly she wondered. Kev was very close to his parents.

'Nah, 'course not. Good Catholic boy like me?' In the glow of streetlight, she saw him grin. 'All they know is that we're back in touch.'

A tortoiseshell cat slunk across the road and disappeared into the shadows under the row of parked cars opposite. 'Are you finished with Birmingham appreciation for the night?' Robin asked. 'Shall we go in?'

'Before we do . . .' He reached across and slid a huge hand behind her head, turning her to face him. He grinned again and leaned in. Sweetly, she noticed, he closed his eyes before his mouth met hers.

Kevin Young, sexy kisser – those were the words that had gone through her head the first time it happened. She still couldn't entirely remember how the kiss had actually come about – large quantities of alcohol had been involved, of course. It had been the anniversary of Corinna's funeral and the three of them, she, Kev and Samir, had gone for a drink. After Samir had gone home to Liz and the kids for dinner, she and Kev had stayed and got smashed.

She might not remember how it happened but she definitely

remembered how it felt. She'd never fancied Kev back when they were teenagers, she'd been with Samir, and Kev had carried a hopeless torch for Corinna, but the kiss had made her see him in a whole different light. Soft at first, then more urgent, that hand behind her head. When he'd pulled away for a moment, his eyes had stayed on her, full of desire. A chemical, physical rush – of course, it had been over a year since she'd split up with Adrian and there'd been no one since but even so . . . Within two minutes, they'd been in a cab on the way to his place, like teenagers on the back seat, one part of her laughing at the ridiculousness of it – Kevin Young! – the other part asking how much longer could it take to Bourneville, for God's sake?

But when they'd reached his bedroom, she'd stopped. Even with all Sasha's personal things gone, it was so clearly a room designed by a woman. The Liberty print curtains and cushions on the bed, the tall lamps on the bedside tables, the glass bowl on the chest of drawers – there was no way Kev had chosen them and yet he'd kept it all: it had been three years since Sasha had walked out. As he'd unbuttoned her shirt, large fingers surprisingly deft, Robin had been filled with a sudden pathos for him, this bear-like man left alone in the house where he'd once lived with his wife and daughters.

He'd felt the shift in tenor, but misinterpreted it. 'You all right?' he said. 'Is it Samir?'

'Samir?' She'd pulled back, looked at him. 'What? It's been fifteen years – eighteen.' She'd caught him by the belt and tugged him in. 'Get over here.'

And yet it was as if by saying his name, Kev *had* summoned Samir, not the one whom they'd seen that night but the eighteen-year-old whose clothes had lain on his bedroom floor in a tangled heap with hers on those sixth-form afternoons, the one she'd shared beds and sleeping-bags with in any number of campsites and hostels across Europe and southern Africa. The idea that she would ever have done this then, slept with one of their friends . . . But that time was gone – long gone – and this was now. Kev was a divorcé and she was a single mother, neither of them had anyone else. If they wanted to be friends with benefits, who was it hurting?

Chapter Nine

Day Three was her first thought when she woke up. From here, the enquiry would get substantially harder. Witnesses' memories would blur, and the team would start to grow frustrated and tired. The public outrage would continue for a few more days and then, failing progress, their girl would fade from view. It was human nature, the lure of the shiny new object, the disillusionment when things proved difficult. Within a week, two, if they were lucky, there'd be another murder in the city, another story for people to get angry about, and their girl would slide into oblivion. Robin thought of Martin Engel, the monumental work it must have taken to keep Victoria alive in people's minds as long as he had. The list of the forgotten was infinitely longer.

She looked at the clock – 5.53 – and then at Kev's head on the other pillow, the dark hair tapering at the base of his skull. He was asleep, of course, like anyone sensible would be at this hour, his ribcage gently rising and falling. She was reluctant to wake him – before six; it seemed inhospitable – but would it be weird to slip out and leave him sleeping? No, he'd be all right with it, surely; he'd understand. And he knew his way around the house, knew where the coffee was if he wanted one before he went.

She wondered if she should put the sheets in the machine before she went to work, though. Enjoyable as they were, these get-togethers, she didn't need Lennie to know about them, and she was like a sniffer dog, always had been. 'Have you been to the pub, Mum? Who was smoking?' Once she'd come home after attending a scene with a body stashed in an airing cupboard and Len had physically recoiled. And she'd commented on Kev's aftershave before. Not, of course, that that put her in any kind of minority.

Her phone rang on the bedside table and she grabbed it. At this hour, it could only be work – had the duty team got something? But the screen said *Natalie*. Why the hell would Natalie be calling?

'Robin?' She sounded breathless. 'Have you heard from Luke?'

'No. Should I have?' He hadn't rung her in twenty years.

'You've got to help me.' Panic now, unmistakable.

'What's going on? Is it Mum and Dad?'

'No! He's gone nuts.'

'What – who has?'

'Luke! We had a row. Last night. I lost my cool and told him I wanted a trial separation and he . . . went mental.'

Robin was momentarily lost for words. Separation – them? They'd been together since they were sixteen, they were fused at a molecular level. 'What do you mean "went mental"? Are you all right? Is he there?'

'No. He stormed out twenty minutes ago.'

She felt a surge of frustration. Bloody Luke, months from his fortieth but still behaving like a toddler denied the big Lego. 'Look,' she said, 'don't worry about it. You know what he's like. You said something you didn't mean in the heat of the moment and he's flounced off to make you feel bad – Luke classic.'

'No, you don't understand – he's off his face! He's been up all night drinking, he's had at least half a bottle of Jack Daniels, and he's taken the car – he's driving.'

Shit. And that explained why Natalie had called *her*.

She pictured him careening drunkenly through town, an accident bound to happen. If it hadn't already. What if he killed himself? Or someone else? God, he was so fucking selfish, it took her breath away. 'Okay, Nat, listen,' she said. 'Call him and if he doesn't answer, keep trying. When you get him, make him tell you where he is.'

'Then what?'

'I'm going to go and find him. Tell him you can talk it all over but not like this. He has to stop, wait for me then come home and sober up. Ring me back as soon as you can – I'll get in the car.'

When she ended the call, Kev was awake and looking at her. 'What's going on?'

She picked her trousers off the back of the chair and shoved her feet in as she explained.

'Bloody hell.' He threw the duvet off and swung out of bed. 'I'll come with you.'

'Kev, I'm police, I don't need . . .'

'Don't be daft. Chuck me my shirt.' He caught it and pulled it on.

'Seriously, I'm fine, you really don't have to . . .'

'He's driving, right? Off his face?'

'Yes.'

'At the very least you'll need someone to drive his car back then, won't you?' *Checkmate.* 'Come on, let's go.'

'I'm heading for Stratford Road,' Robin said. 'Pure guesswork but if he's as drunk as she says, he probably couldn't cross town without being stopped. I think he'll have headed out.'

'Has he done this before, then?'

'No.' But actually, she wouldn't know if he had. She was the last person Luke or Natalie ever confided in, and her parents wouldn't tell her, either. Their mother would protect him – *'From your judgement, Robin. You're so hard on him'* – and Dennis never volunteered anything that might be inflammatory; their relationship was enough of a bonfire.

'Not that I know of,' she amended.

'How about Natalie – the separating thing? Is that normal for them? Do they fight like that?'

'I don't know.'

From the corner of her eye, she could see Kev's knee jiggling. 'How old's their boy now?'

'Six months.'

The phone rang through the Bluetooth, making them both jump.

'I spoke to him.' The voice from the dashboard shook. 'He's out in the country somewhere near a pub called the Durham Ox – he can see it. Or saw it – I don't know, he wasn't making total sense . . .'

Robin glanced at Kev, *Could you . . . ?* but he was typing it into Google already.

'Is he still in the car, Nat?' she asked.

'I don't know.'

'Is he moving? Is he still driving?'

'I don't know!'

Kevin tapped his phone and a map loaded. He nodded at the dashboard: *Can I?*

'Natalie,' he said, 'Kevin Young here, I'm an old mate of Robin's from back in the day, don't know if you remember. I'm with her in the car, bit of moral support. I've got the Ox – it's in Shrewley, all right? Little village, and we're not far off – Rob guessed he'd come out this way so we're heading in the right direction – ten minutes, fifteen, not long. Have you got anyone with you?'

'Only Jack. He's in the kitchen, in his highchair. I'm trying not to cry, it upsets him, but . . .'

'Where's your mum?' said Robin. 'Can she come over?'

'She's in Gran Canaria, on holiday. And my brother. They all are.'

Twenty minutes later, Birmingham was behind them and they were speeding on country lanes between fields lush with June grass, hedges and ivy-wrapped trees shivering their leaves in the breeze. Her heart was in her mouth; every time they rounded a corner, she expected to see his car in the ditch or ploughed up against a tree, Luke slumped over the wheel.

A speed camera on the way into Shrewley – she slowed down in the nick of time. The village started as a series of large detached properties set in sizeable gardens but quickly shaded into a jumble of smaller, modern houses crowded against the pavement. Even at thirty-four miles an hour, they were out the other end in a minute. The place was empty, or still asleep, not so much as a dog-walker in evidence.

'Pub should be any moment now.'

'He's probably long gone,' she said, 'that was twenty minutes ago. He could be miles away.' But as they rounded a curve in the road, she saw her brother's silver Ford Focus, apparently undamaged. 'Oh, thank Christ.'

Kev pointed. 'Look.'

Fifty yards ahead, in a gap in the trees, a dark-haired man in jeans and a black fleece – yes, Luke – was sitting on a stretch of brick wall, his back to the road, head bent towards his knees.

Another wall lined the other side of the road, another gap in the trees.

Kev enlarged the map. 'Shit, Rob, it's a railway bridge. He's over the tracks.'

They were thirty feet away. She stamped on the brake before they got any closer, not wanting to startle him into a sudden disastrous movement. Half a bottle of JD – *at least* half a bottle – more than enough to throw his balance off. Her hands gripped the wheel. 'What's he playing at?'

'I dunno. Just . . . take it steady.'

Robin took a fortifying breath, opened her door and got out. Luke had given no sign of hearing the car and he didn't seem to hear her door close, either, unlike the pair of rooks that burst from the top of a tall pine and nearly gave her a heart attack. An uneasy feeling stirred in her stomach – the breeze was gone and the air felt unnaturally still.

She approached slowly, the scratch of her shoes loud on the loose gravel. 'Luke.'

He jumped as if she'd woken him up and she flinched, hand automatically reaching out even though he was too far away. Behind her, she heard Kev get out of the car.

Luke bowed his head further, chin almost touching his chest, then turned. God, his face. Wrecked was the word that came into her head. Drunk, yes, definitely, but more than that. He looked distraught. She made eye contact and the vulnerability she saw shocked her. She'd never seen it in him – he'd never *let* her see. As if he'd read her mind, his face hardened and he turned his back.

She stood completely still. His body seemed to exude a force field: *Don't touch me.* What should she do? She couldn't grab him, she couldn't risk him moving to avoid her.

Luke shifted, put his hands on the wall either side of his body. Holding on or bracing to propel himself forward? His legs dangled. Robin's heart thumped, blood rushing in her ears.

'Come to push me off?' He spoke into the empty space in front of him. 'My just deserts for ruining your life?'

'Don't be daft.'

'Daft. Oh yeah, that's me, isn't it? Daft. Stupid.'

'Mate.' Kev appeared alongside her. He took another step forward. 'Why don't you come down from there? You've had a few, haven't you?'

'Oh, look, it's Kevin Young. The big man. What the fuck are *you* doing here?'

'I want to help. Your wife's beside herself – you're scaring the daylights out of her.'

Luke snorted. 'Couldn't be bothered to come.'

'She had to stay with Jack, she couldn't bring him here,' said Robin. 'She's in a real state, Luke. Come on – come down. Please. It's only an argument – people have them all the time. If anything happened to you, she'd be devastated.'

He was rocking, his body moving back and forth, backlit by the sky. Then, breaking rhythm, he tipped his head forward, looking between his knees and for a split second, she thought he was falling forward, letting go.

'Luke!'

He rocked backwards. 'Fuck off. Leave me alone.'

Robin tried to think: if he was a stranger, what would she do?

'You need to talk to her, Luke,' Kev said, taking another small step closer. 'If you fall off there, you're never going to sort things out, are you?'

Luke swayed. 'You fit to give advice? Your wife left you, didn't she? And what are you doing with this tart so early?'

'Yeah, my wife left me,' Kev's voice was calm. 'Doesn't mean yours will. And my girls still need me, like your boy does. I see them all the time. They're with me three nights a week, every week, holidays, too – they're with me half their lives.'

A snort. 'Half.'

'It's a lot better than nothing, which is what you get if you fall.'

'Who's talking about falling?'

He raised his head. A moment later, Robin heard it, too, a faint beat, getting louder. Nearer. Then she saw what he'd seen first: a train, a yellow-faced grub emerging from the line of low trees at the bend, coming up the track towards them.

'Luke,' she said, and now her own voice was shaking. 'Come down. You can sort this out but not like this – you've had too much to drink, you're not thinking straight.'

He raised his head and looked over his shoulder at her. His eyes shone with a mad exhilaration. His arms stiffened.

The train was two hundred yards away.

'Luke,' she said. 'Please!'

A hundred. Fifty.

She charged forward, arms outstretched. 'Luke!'

The word was swallowed, unheard. The train streamed under the bridge, taking her knees with it. The ground shook, the air filled with diesel and the roar of the engine, so loud she covered her ears, squeezed her eyes shut. *Please.*

When she opened them again, Luke had gone from the wall, the spot where he'd been sitting just a patch of empty sky.

In her horror, it was a second before she registered him hunched into the angle between the wall and the pavement, arms tight round his knees, a foetal ball.

Chapter Ten

When they hauled him to his feet, the fumes on his breath were enough to anaesthetize a horse. Between them, they took almost all his weight as they steered him slowly towards the car. It wasn't cold but he was shivering, and his face was so pale she thought she could see his skull underneath. Kev took off his jacket and helped him into it while she opened the door. He slumped sideways into the passenger seat as if the bones had gone out of his legs.

As she moved to close the door, she heard another car. She looked up and her heart sank.

Warwickshire Police.

The uniform at the wheel had the door open before the engine was off. He was twenty-five or six, spring-loaded, *Show me the fire*. 'Everything all right here?'

'Fine,' she said, positioning herself between him and the door. 'Thank you.'

'We had two calls from the village. A silver Ford Focus driving erratically, then we heard someone was up on the bridge here, appeared to be in distress?'

Robin showed him her badge. 'DCI Robin Lyons, Force

Homicide, West Midlands. I got here a couple of minutes before you.' She nodded backwards. 'He's my brother. He had a row with his wife, he's a bit upset. We'll take him home, get him sorted.'

'PC Harris,' he said, unintimidated. 'What's your brother's name?'

'Luke. Luke Lyons.'

'I'll have a word.' He took a pointed step around her, walked to the open door and crouched. 'How are you doing, Luke? All right?'

Luke made a non-committal noise.

'Can you confirm your name for me? This is your sister and . . . ?' He glanced up at Kev.

'Kevin Young,' Kev said. 'A friend.'

'You've had a few drinks, Luke, haven't you? How did you get here?'

Silence.

Harris looked at Robin, eyebrows up.

'He drove,' she admitted.

'Right. I'm going to have to ask you to take a breath test, sir, okay?' Standing, he made a move towards his car for the machine but Robin put out a hand.

'PC Harris, could I talk to you?'

He gave her a look – *Really?* – but reluctantly followed her a few steps away before planting his feet.

'Look,' she said quietly, 'my brother's in a state, you can see that – your caller said he was in distress.' She looked back and lowered her voice again. 'His wife wants a separation – she told him last night. He's gutted – we've just managed to talk him down off the wall. Obviously he's had a lot to drink, but my point is, a drink-driving charge, now, another big problem? Honestly, I don't know how much more he can take.'

She made eye contact and held it, pulling on the full force of her rank, hating herself for it. Intimidating a junior officer – Jesus. 'He's never done anything like this before – I've never known him get in the car after a drink. Also,' she said, 'he's not actually *in* his car, is he? Or, in fact, anywhere near it. That's his,' she pointed. 'This one's mine.'

Seconds passed but then Harris blinked. 'I'll take a look at it. If there's any sign at all he's hit anything or if we get any reports in later . . .'

'Thank you,' she said.

Kev drove them all back. She'd opened her mouth – hadn't he come to bring Luke's car home? – then stopped. It didn't matter, it could stay where it was, they could pick it up later. She didn't want to be alone with Luke and she didn't trust herself to drive at the moment, either. The keys jangled as she handed them over.

'You all right?' Kev asked quietly.

'Yep,' she said automatically. Then, 'Bit frazzled.'

He put a hand on her shoulder and gave it a squeeze. 'Let's get him back. Where are we going?'

Luke sat mute in the passenger seat, arms wrapped around his body, staring through the windscreen as if he could see the apocalypse on the road ahead. After a couple of minutes, once they were on the main road, Robin got out her phone. Her hands were still shaking as she went to recent calls. She was about to hit 'Natalie' when Luke spun around, eyes blazing.

'Who are you ringing?' he demanded.

'Nat, to let her know you're okay, we're on the way back.'

'Don't.'

'I've got to. She'll be out of her mind.'

'Don't tell her I was on the bridge. Don't you fucking dare.'

'What?'

'I mean it, Robin.' His voice was as steely as she'd ever heard it. 'If you tell her, I'll make sure your big boss finds out what *you* did.'

She stared at him.

'Kilmartin – that's him, isn't it? Assistant Chief Constable? Twisting that guy back there's arm – he wouldn't like that.'

'You're kidding me.'

'Come on, mate,' Kev said. 'That's not fair – she saved you from a potential criminal record.'

'Stay out of it. This is between me and her.' He turned back to Robin. 'I don't care if they charge me with drink-driving, I don't give a toss. But you? If Kilmartin finds out you pulled rank, you're right in the shit.'

In the mirror, Kev nodded infinitesimally: do it for now, sort it out later.

Still she hesitated. 'I can't believe you,' she said eventually. 'You're . . .' She shook her head. 'For *now*. I won't say anything. But this is serious, Luke, regardless of things between us. You can't do that then sweep it under the . . .'

'I'll do what I want – *I* don't take orders from you. Keep your mouth shut and we'll both be fine.' He pointed at the phone in her hand. 'Call her. Call her and tell her we're on our way back. That's it.'

After she spoke to Natalie, whose tears of relief quickly turned into fury, there was silence in the car. Kev didn't try to get Luke to talk or offer advice; instead he opened his window a couple of inches and let the breeze buffet in, white noise.

They reached the turn-off for Luke's house and passed it. He spun around again. 'Where're we going?'

'Mum and Dad's.'

'What?' Aghast. 'No way – you can't. I . . .'

'Not the best idea to let your wife see you like this, is it?' said Kev steadily, 'if you want her to think you're okay. Straighten yourself out a bit, get some sleep, have a shower. Talk to her when you feel better.'

Luke seemed about to remonstrate then stopped. A couple of minutes later, though, as they turned into Dunnington Road, he said, 'What are you going to tell them?'

'I don't know. They're going to need some explanation, aren't they, for you turning up off your face before eight in the morning.' *With me.*

'So tell them Nat and I had a fight. Tell them I was drink-driving. But don't tell them I was on the bridge. And *don't* tell Natalie.' He glared. 'I mean it.'

Her dad closed the kitchen door and ushered them both away from it. 'What's going on, Rob?' he murmured.

Movement overhead, her mother's voice as she shepherded Luke out of the bathroom towards the bedroom they'd shared as children, and which she'd shared with Lennie much more recently than that.

'He had a fight with Natalie,' Robin said quietly. 'A pretty bad one.'

Her dad nodded.

'You're not surprised.' She frowned.

'They've been having problems again lately,' he said. 'Nat's got a lot to deal with, hasn't she, the baby and keeping them going financially and trying to gee Luke up as well.'

'What do you mean, gee him up?'

He looked stricken for a second, realizing he'd made a mistake. 'Dad?'

He sighed. 'Well, he's quite down about being out of work.'

'But he's not "out of work". He left to take care of Jack.'

With the face of a man who knew he'd be in trouble later, he admitted, 'Actually, love, he didn't. They let him go. He asked us not to tell you.'

'Oh, for God's sake – he knew when *I* was fired.' And he'd jeered at every opportunity.

'Well,' her dad said, 'for whatever reason, he wanted to keep it private. He puts on a brave face – especially round you – but it's getting to him more than he lets on. Anyway, how did *you* get involved today? What actually happened?'

'Natalie rang me.' She glanced at Kev. 'She said Luke had nailed half a bottle of Jack Daniels and driven off in a rage. She was scared he'd have an accident.'

'Or get pulled over by the police,' her dad guessed. 'Hence why she rang you. The bloody idiot.' He shook his head. 'He didn't, though?'

'No.'

'Thank God for that.' He turned to Kevin. 'You went with her, young man?'

'Rob rang me.' He looked at her. 'I was in the area so . . .'

'That was good of you. Thank you. Why didn't you call us, though, love?'

'I thought I could handle it,' Robin said.

Kev drove her back, too, Robin shotgun, moll to his gangster. Her car was an Audi, it wasn't small, but he seemed far too big for it. Even with the seat pushed back to its full extent, his thighs skimmed the bottom of the wheel and his hair brushed the roof. They didn't talk but it wasn't an uncomfortable silence, more an exhausted one.

'That was pretty rough,' he said suddenly. 'On the bridge.'

Robin remembered Luke's face when he first turned round, before he shut her out. And afterwards the shock at how close he'd come, how thin the tissue between life and death had stretched. She knew that look; she'd seen it a hundred times at work.

'I've got to tell them,' she said. 'Later today. I'll work out how to say it without saying it – without him suspecting. Tell them how worried I am about him. Honestly, the fact that *I'm* saying it is probably enough for them to know it's serious.'

They'd stopped at a zebra crossing where a woman about her own age was shepherding a little boy on a scooter. Kev waited until they were both safely on the other side. 'What is it between the pair of you?' he asked. 'Why so much aggro?'

'It's always been like it. Even when we were little kids – remember that time he "accidentally" slammed my hand in the door of Dad's car and broke two of my fingers? Or when he threw my packed lunch in the river on that school trip to Stratford?'

'Yeah. I think you had one of my sandwiches after. And my apple.'

'He thinks I'm Dad's favourite, I *know* he's Mum's. He thinks everything I do is some attempt to belittle him and make him look like a failure. He was cock-a-hoop when I was out at the Met and plastered all over the *Evening Standard*, it was like he'd won the EuroMillions.'

'On the bridge,' Kev said casually, eyes back on the road, 'he said something about getting *his* just deserts. For ruining your life.'

She thought about fudging but she was tired of the cover-ups and half-truths, the constant calculation of who knew what. And Kev had been brilliant this morning. Yes, she wanted to tell someone – she wanted to tell *him*. Like Corinna, Kev knew all the players, he would understand why it had cut so deeply.

'Luke didn't ruin my life,' she said. 'He wishes.' She hesitated.

'But what he was talking about . . . It was years ago now, I've never told anyone. I didn't even know myself till I moved back up here.'

'I'm good at keeping things under my hat, as you know.' A wry up-flick of the eyebrows. Kev was totally straight, you could eat your dinner off the accounts book at his scrap-metal business, she wouldn't have tangled with him even this much if you couldn't, but his dad, Morris, who'd run the business before him, had had some interesting connections and he'd done time for fencing back in the day.

'Me and Samir,' she said, 'Luke broke us up.'

'You what?'

'Remember? A few days before I went away to university?'

''Course I do. That whole thing – no one understood it at all. One minute you were off travelling together, joined at the hip, the next you were gone to London on your own, so fast your feet never touched the ground, and he was about as much fun as open-heart surgery. He wouldn't talk about it, expected us just to accept the new world order and move on, no explanation given. So what did he do, then, Luke?'

'Told Samir he'd never be accepted in our family because he was Indian and that if he married me, it'd finish my relationship with my mum and dad, and they'd never accept our children. Samir decided – who'd blame him? – that he couldn't do it.'

'Fuckin' hell. And it wasn't true?'

'My parents loved him. It was only Luke who didn't.'

The phone rang as they made the turn into Mary Street. 'Speak of the Devil,' said Kev, looking at the screen.

'Yeah, and now he's my guv'nor.' She hit the button. 'Morning.'

'Hi. Can you talk?' Samir sounded worried.

'Yes, I'm in the car but Bluetooth so . . .' She glanced at the

94

clock: five past eight, still incriminatingly early. But she had to – it could only be work. 'Kev's with me.'

'Kev?' Audible surprise.

'Hiya, Sam, mate.' The boom of Kev's voice filled the car. 'How're you doing?'

'Okay.' For a moment, he sounded uncertain. 'Look, can you keep this to yourself, Kev? I've had a call, Robin. We've got another case.'

Chapter Eleven

The evidence bag Rafferty handed her held a bloodied scrap of paper that on closer inspection revealed itself to be a debit- or credit-card slip. Almost translucent, it was disintegrating along the fold – Robin guessed it had been through the wash – and most of the writing was lost forever, either faded or blotted out by blood. At the bottom, however, was a visible signature line and underneath that, barely legible when held to the light, a printed name: Ms Lara Meikle.

'There's nothing else,' Rafferty said. 'No bag or phone, no wallet, but she's wearing a denim skirt and that was in the tiny pocket-within-a-pocket bit on the right hip. It's so fragile, I worried it'd fall apart when we took it out.'

'Lara Meikle – have you looked her up? Is that who she is?'

'Unless she's got a twin with an identical tattoo. We did her prints, not in the system, but I put the name into Facebook. Born here in 1996, went to school here, works – worked – for an insurance company in town, and it's definitely her in the photographs.'

'Right.'

Robin gave him the bag back, hoping he didn't notice the

tremor in her hand. Usually she could click between modes pretty much at will – Adrian, her ex in London, said her ability to compartmentalize was very masculine; it hadn't been a compliment – but the events of the morning so far were proving hard to get a lid on. That moment on the bridge, the train thundering closer as Luke leaned forward – how long until that became a fixture in her nightmares?

'Do you think he missed it?' Rafferty said.

'What?'

'The card slip.' He lifted the bag into her eyeline. 'Like the girl at Gisborne's – there's nothing left to identify her by otherwise but maybe this was so soft he didn't feel it through the denim?'

'Let's keep an open mind,' she said. 'The two could be completely unrelated.'

'There's a lot of similarities, though, aren't there? Both young women, both white, both stabbed and . . .'

'How's your hand, Dave?'

He looked confused until he realized she was cutting him off: 'Surprisingly sore.' He showed her a cut across the heel now spidery with stitches. 'Had to get a tetanus jab, too. I'm counting myself lucky, though – if I'd fallen down that hole, I'd be a goner. Keep having flashbacks about it.'

Open mind or not, it was hard to avoid a sense of déjà vu as she followed him to the body. The inner cordon had been set up at the mouth of an alleyway between a chain-link fence that formed the perimeter of the light-engineering works to their left and the corrugated-iron rear wall of the garage next door. The alley itself was about five feet wide and overgrown with the same medley of waste-land favourites as Gisborne's: nettles, elder and brambles, which here were covered in the buds of small white flowers, bizarrely out of place in their rural innocence. Some of the vegetation had been flattened by earlier feet but the brambles reached out to snag the legs of her protective suit over and over again as if vying for her attention. 'Like *Day of the* bloody *Triffids*, isn't it?' Rafferty threw back over his shoulder.

Placing her feet carefully around cigarette butts and crumpled cans, Robin saw several different sets of dog prints dried into the mud and plenty of dog shit – clearly, it was a popular spot among the local canine community – but as they got closer, she noticed a set of large paw prints pointing out of the alley that was first edged, then filled with blood.

Olly Faulkner stood, nodded hello and stepped back against the chain-link fence to let her see.

The first thing that struck her was the blood. So much blood. For the length of several feet, the alley was soaked in it: the ground, the corrugated wall, the clumps of nettles. Arterial bleeding – blood pumping out while her heart was still beating, her life spattering the weeds. Robin imagined the sound like heavy rain. Like the fat drops of Kieran Clark's blood that had warmed the pavement outside his parents' house.

Lara Meikle, if that was her name, lay slantwise across the alley, on her side, her head resting on her arm as if she were only asleep. Asleep among the weeds and dog shit and rusting beer cans.

On the inside of her wrist was a small tattoo of a cartoon crown with five balled spikes.

Her skirt was undisturbed but the cotton of her peasant-style blouse had been torn away to expose her chest and neck. A pair of purple fingerprint bruises bloomed on her jaw. Gingerly, Robin took a step closer and crouched. From what she could tell, she'd been stabbed three times. Two of the wounds were at the base of her neck – had he specifically targeted the jugular or been lucky? Most likely, that was where

98

the blood that covered the wall had come from. The third wound was in the chest, where the knife had pierced the fabric of her grey satin bra. Around her neck were smear marks – had she clutched at the wounds or tried to staunch them? She must have known it was hopeless – she'd have seen the blood spraying between her fingers and known she was dying. Robin remembered Olly on Sunday morning: *The only comfort is that with this degree of blood loss, she would have lost consciousness quickly.*

She stood and stepped back, looking not at the injuries now but the woman herself.

She'd been more of a dresser than their first girl: the denim skirt was black with a shimmer of gold in the weave and ended a couple of inches above the knee; where it wasn't sodden, her peasant blouse was elephant grey. Her hair was dyed a rich Jessica Rabbit magenta and had probably reached the tips of her shoulder blades when she'd been standing; judging by her eyebrows, it was light brown naturally. Her make-up wasn't excessive but against the drained pallor of her skin, it looked super-imposed: black eyeliner with cat's-eye flicks, pale gold eyeshadow, some sort of glimmering stuff on her cheekbones. She'd been pretty but in a more conventional way than the woman at Gisborne's; her nose was small and unremarkable, no one would ever have singled it out for comment.

Born in 1996. She'd been twenty-three.

Moving forward again, Robin indicated the bruises on her jaw. 'Do you think these happened during the attack? He or she grabbed her – tried to hold her?' Bruises could develop after death as blood seeped through ruptured tissue.

'I'd say so, yes,' Olly nodded.

'Any idea yet when that might have been?'

'Between midnight and three or four, I think.'

Robin looked beyond him to Dave Rafferty. 'How far are we from Bradford Street here?'

'Less than half a mile. Ten-minute walk, max.'

When she ducked back under the tape, Varan was talking to Manda Pryce, a stout woman in her mid-forties still wearing the tartan pyjama trousers and sheepskin slippers she'd had on an hour and twenty minutes earlier, she said, when she'd taken the dog out. Leon, a Staffie, had a frame like a muscular coffee table and eyes that simultaneously begged for understanding and threatened murder. Manda Pryce had his chain wrapped around her wrist, presumably to stop him bolting off down the alleyway again. 'He just legged it across the road,' she said, showing the red weal across her palm. 'Pulled the lead right out of my hand.' Leon narrowed his eyes, Putin-style, and Robin thought they were lucky he hadn't eaten the body. The fur on his paws was crisp with dried blood.

The neighbours were out in force, lining the outer cordon and gathered in little knots along the opposite pavement. Those expected at work tore themselves away with regret. Manda was visibly enjoying her new status and had squeezed the upper arms of at least three people who'd approached to 'offer their support'. 'Thanks, love,' she said to one now, nodding gravely. 'It'll take a while to get over, that will. Awful bloody shock.'

'What's your address, Mrs Pryce?' Varan asked, pen poised over his notebook.

Shifting her cigarettes and phone to the other hand, Manda Pryce pointed across the road to one of the three short blocks of flats surrounded by an area of surprisingly vital-looking grass. 'Twenty-seven Drumall Court. That one, fifth floor.'

'Does your flat face this way?'

'Sitting room and kitchen, yeah.'

'Did you see or hear anything last night? Raised voices?'

The woman shook her head, actually disappointed. 'I went to bed early. I had a headache so I took a couple of Nurofen and got in about ten. I listen to audiobooks to help me drift off so even if there was anything, I might not have heard it.'

'And you weren't woken by anything later on? Fighting? Shouting?'

'Not more than usual.'

Varan raised his eyebrows.

'There's a couple of rowdy families in our block, closing time, you know. But no, not last night, nothing. Bedroom's on the other side, though, so again . . .' She shrugged.

Robin headed for her car, scrolling to Malia in her recent calls, but before she could dial, she saw a dark-haired woman jogging towards her up the pavement. Sara Kettleborough from the *Post*. The street was closed to traffic now, she'd had to park round the corner, and by the time she reached Robin, she was breathing hard. She stopped and, for a moment, it looked like she was going to brace her hands against her knees and put her head down.

'God,' she panted, 'I've really got to start eating less and exercising more.'

'Same,' Robin said. 'Next time I leave the office before ten, I'm going to go to the gym and see if my key still works.'

'Yeah, you must be putting in some hours. How are you doing?'

'Honestly? I've had better mornings.'

Robin liked Sara and she'd thought before that they might have been friends if their jobs didn't complicate things. Or if either of them had the time. As well as being the *Post*'s chief crime correspondent, Sara was a single mother to twin fourteen-year-old sons whose hell-raising had already got them expelled from one school and suspended from another. She had the wary look of a woman constantly expecting a phone call that would make her life logistical hell. She was also a good friend of Maggie's, which was both a grade-A character reference and how Robin knew about the boys.

'Thanks for doing the witness appeals,' she said.

'Of course, hope it helps.' Her phone rang in her pocket; Sara declined the call. 'Anyway, you're heading off,' she gestured towards Robin's car, 'and you know what I'm going to ask so I'll cut to the chase.'

'And you know what I'm going to say.'

'Off the record?'

'I can't.'

'I know.' She lowered her voice. 'You know me, though – I'm not going to go whipping up public panic just to generate a bit of clickbait. This is about public safety. Because if there *is* a serial—'

Robin held up a hand. 'Whoa, stop. Don't even think the word.'

'But people need to—'

'We're in the middle of a knife-crime epidemic, you know that: you did a piece on our homicide figures three weeks ago. Without wanting to sound macabre, a lot of people are getting stabbed in this city at the moment.' Three so far this week, in fact. Christ, she realized, three since Saturday night, and it was Tuesday. At this rate, three in twelve days would start looking like something to aim for. 'This is brand-new and we don't have anything to connect the cases as things stand.'

'Come on, Robin, we're, what, four roads over from the Gisborne works here?'

'It's an inner-city area; there's always a . . .'

'The victims are more or less the same age, both stabbed,

102

found two days apart,' she counted the points off on her fingers. 'And,' she gave Robin a knowing look, 'it looks like you're SIO on both. Homicide so stretched that you're the only one available? Webster's got a solve on the Erdington case, hasn't he? He couldn't take this one?'

'What age?'

'The girl at Gisborne's was late teens, early twenties; this one's twenty-two, twenty-three, isn't she?'

'Why do you think that?'

Sara took out her phone. When she unlocked it, Twitter was already open onscreen. @*ThePrycesRight*, Robin read. The profile picture was a headshot of Leon in best weapon-dog mode, eyes like slits, mouth a Joker-esque smile.

Pray u never see what I did this morning. Lovely young girl, 22, 23, stabbed to death, dumped in an alley in a bloodbath. Whoever did this is an ANIMAL, shd be strung up. RIP.

'Be grateful she didn't post a picture,' said Sara.

Unsurprisingly, Malia's first question was the same. 'You think he did both?'

'It's possible. More than possible,' she conceded. 'But at this point, it could still be coincidence, or they are connected but differently. There's no evidence either way. What I do know is that the media will be on it like a ton of bricks. Sara K literally ran to catch me, and even though she'll be sensible about it, it'll get picked up by the nationals.' Kilmartin was going to freak: Lara Meikle *was* photogenic but she had appeal beyond that, too: she was the second. Nothing to sell papers like a pretty young dead woman – except *two* pretty young dead women.

Malia voiced the other issue. 'If it is the same man – three days apart?'

'Yeah, I know.'

Because in that case, where had he come from? Two killings so close together didn't say beginner. Were they coming in at the end of a spree? Were there more, earlier bodies that hadn't yet come to light?

'We've got to find the guy from the Bradford Street CCTV, Malia,' she said. 'Top priority.' She stamped on the brake, coming to a halt inches from the lorry in front.

'I've just got the list of the Sohna stockists, and the team's heading out as we speak.'

'Good. Samir's giving us more people so let's put them all on the ground. Emphasize the positive: if the two *are* connected, we've got a whole new area for house-to-house and with luck, a much better shot at some CCTV. I saw cameras on both sides of the alleyway, and on the flats opposite, and it's right off Gooch Street. There'll be traffic cams, too. Make sure the house-to-house team has the still and the e-fit of the first girl. I'll be on my phone for an hour or so if you need me. Can you let the others know?'

'You won't be at Harborne?'

'I've got Lara Meikle's address, it's round the corner. Niall's going to meet me there.'

Robin caught the pause at the other end. Notifying the family – The Knock – was the job of uniformed officers, not detectives, especially not senior ones. 'On my phone if you need me,' she said again and hung up.

Lara Meikle had lived in a flat on Angelina Street, minutes' walk from where her body had been found. Before she reached it, Robin pulled in and called her parents' number. The phone rang twice before it was picked up, and her mother's murmured 'Hello?' told Robin straight away that Luke was still asleep. 'He was sick after you left – very sick,' she said. 'God knows how much he'd had. Thank God he didn't get stopped, Robin. What if someone had seen him and called it in?'

What indeed. 'Never mind that,' she said, 'what if he'd had an accident? He was incredibly lucky – as were all the people he somehow managed to avoid killing. I mean, drink-driving – of all the stupid, irresponsible . . .'

'He was upset! He wasn't thinking straight. A major blow-out with Natalie like that—'

'It's no excuse. Nat tried to stop him and he wouldn't listen,' Robin snapped. There she went again, their mother, reflexively jumping to Luke's defence, regardless that what he'd done was actually criminal.

But then, she realized, what she'd done – in his defence – was criminal, too. You could fudge it as much as you liked, say all she'd asked for was compassion for a man at the end of his rope, but the truth was, her brother had committed a criminal offence and she'd committed another by strong-arming a junior officer into letting him off.

'Mum, look,' she said, 'I didn't ring to have a go. Things are nuts at work, and what I wanted to say was . . .' She searched for the right words, enough to get the point across – the importance – without triggering retribution. Would he actually do it? He wouldn't phone Kilmartin, no, that was far too dynamic for Luke, he'd be intimidated, but a sly email was easy, especially from a bogus account. 'I'm worried about the state he's in. Very worried. He didn't want me to tell you but . . . I think he's in a bad way. Mentally – psychologically. I think he might be clinically depressed.'

'He is, love.' Her mother's voice dropped again, and the defence was gone. 'That's why I've been round there so much, it's not only helping with Jack. He's been very down.'

For the second time in hours, Robin felt as if her family was a unit from which she was excluded – they were the planet and she was a moon, condemned to orbit them without ever making contact. 'Why didn't you tell me?' she said, hating the plaintive note in her voice. For God's sake, why get upset about it now? It was hardly new. And anyway, hadn't she wanted it? Hadn't she hightailed it out of here years ago in part to be free of it?

'He didn't want me to tell you,' her mother said. 'You know what he's like where you're concerned. How proud.'

Proud? Of what? What had he ever actually done? It was on the tip of her tongue but she bit it back. 'Anyway,' she said stiffly, 'that's all it was, really, just to say, keep an eye out. I know you do anyway. A close eye.'

'I will do.' A pause. 'Robin?'

'Yes?'

'You . . . well, you have a difficult time, you two, don't you? You always have, for some reason. So, thank you. For going to get him, bringing him home. Thanks for looking out for him.'

Chapter Twelve

There was no answer at Angelina Street. The flat was the upstairs half of a small new build, one of a row of three, and from the front step they could hear the bell ringing inside through an open window overhead. Back in the car, Robin called the station for Lara Meikle's mother's address instead. Then she headed back out into the countryside, the GPS directing her to a patch south-east of the city this time, somewhere between Coventry and Kenilworth.

The house didn't belong to any particular village but, like several they passed, stood on its own at the road's edge, an old farmworker's cottage, she guessed, possibly built for whatever the farm equivalent of a foreman was, given the size. Two windows bordered the road, divided by a front door now apparently out of use and blocked by a row of knee-high pots full of pink and white flowers. Geraniums? Busy Lizzies? Something like that.

She tucked the car as far as possible into the opposite verge and waited for Niall to pull in behind her. He got out as if he was about to face a firing squad.

'I'll tell them,' she said. *I'll be it.*

On the ride over, when there'd been a gap longer than a few seconds between phone calls, she'd asked herself why she'd felt compelled to come, especially when she should be back at the nick. Was it because of what happened to Lennie?

The bolt on the five-barred gate screeched as she pulled it back. The other side of the gate had been covered with a wire mesh whose bottom brushed the gravel and they soon saw why. The screech had alerted a roiling mass of yapping fur that streamed towards them from around the side of the house – seven or eight black and tan puppies, tails aerial-straight as they galloped then launched themselves at them, giant paws hitting their trousers at mid-thigh. Airedales, a whole litter of them.

'Puppies, no! Get down!' A stern voice but edged with humour. A woman of about fifty had appeared from the same direction, sweeping greying curly hair back with her forearm and removing a pair of gardening gloves. 'Push them down,' she called. 'They won't bite, they're ever so friendly.'

'Hello,' she said when she reached them. She folded the gloves one inside the other and wedged them into the back pocket of her grubby fur-covered jeans before fending one of the puppies off by the snout. 'No, Bruno. Sorry, they're eleven weeks, going to their homes in the next few days, most of them. I'll miss them for sure but the energy . . . Stop, Tony.' She raised an eyebrow. 'Named after Tony Soprano, can you believe? Anyway, how can I help?'

The grenade in her hand, pin out. Here she came, the Angel of Death in a black Jigsaw suit jacket. 'Deborah Harper?' she asked.

The woman bent to detach a paw from Niall's trouser-leg. 'Yes, that's me.' The puppies caught sight of a blackbird that had foolishly landed on a patch of lawn and bounded after it, giving her a chance to look at them properly for the first time. Robin saw understanding, then fear fell over her face like a sheet.

'Who? Is it Mum?' she said, all humour gone.

'Your mother? No.'

'Oh, thank God. She's got dementia and she slips out of the house when her carer's not . . .'

'Mrs Harper, I'm DCI Robin Lyons, West Midlands Police. You have a daughter called Lara?'

The woman closed her eyes tight. Almost immediately she started to shake, a whole-body tremor that started in her torso and vibrated down her arms to fists now clenched tightly.

'Is she dead?'

'Is your husband here?'

Eyes still shut, she managed the words, 'In the field.'

'We'll call him,' said Niall, glancing at Robin in dismay.

'Let's go inside. If we leave the puppies, will they be safe out here?'

Stumbling, supported by Niall, the woman took them in through an extension at the back. A brief length of corridor was lined with family photographs; Robin paused briefly to scan them. Deborah Harper had remarried eighteen months earlier, Varan said, and the photos bore that out, the older ones showing two families – two different couples, one with a pair of sons, the other a son and a daughter – but at the middle, where the newer pictures were, the two families merged, one man and woman disappearing, the new couple pictured together and, in others – some evidently from their wedding – surrounded by all their four children. The girl cycled through hair colours – strawberry blonde, a blue streak, brunette – but it was her, no doubt, the same girl Robin had seen in the alley among the weeds and rusting cans.

The kitchen was small, the central space dominated by a round pine table and four matching chairs. Two quilted mats at place-settings opposite each other, one still with a side-plate covered with crumbs and a ringed coffee cup. Deborah Harper headed for it automatically.

'Does Lara have a tattoo?' Robin asked when she was sitting.

Terror. 'One. A little crown – here.' She touched a finger to the inside of her wrist then, gripping the table-edge, she made herself meet her eye. 'Is it her? Is she dead?'

Robin nodded. 'She'll need to be formally identified, of course, but yes, we believe so. I'm so sorry.'

'How?'

The second hand-grenade – no car crash or accidental fall down the stairs but the nightmare, the worst-case scenario.

Deborah Harper's face registered abject horror. For a moment, she appeared frozen but then she took a single ragged breath and shrieked – a preternatural shard of pain that sent ice down Robin's spine.

They'd heard his footsteps on the gravel, the front door wrenched open, but they jumped at Mike Harper's bellowed 'Debbie!' nonetheless. The man from the photographs barrelled into the kitchen like a small-scale bull, plunged to his knees and wrapped his arms around his wife's waist, his face buried in her lap. Deborah's tears dripped on to his jacket, turning the light grey fabric the same elephant colour as the top her daughter was wearing when she died. Niall looked stricken.

Eventually, the first shock receded and the Harpers sat next to each other, swiping at tears with one hand, gripping the other's as if they'd be swept away if either let go. Niall made the first cups of the inevitable river of tea and Robin asked them questions as gently as she could.

Lara, they told her, had just turned twenty-three. She'd been an admin assistant for the insurance company for three years but she'd recently been accepted to start training as a nurse. She'd moved in to the flat on Angelina Street with her boyfriend, David Pearce, a supervisor at a call centre, only a month ago, and the pair of them were like the puppies, Mike Harper said, so bubbly and excited about it all you'd think they hadn't already been together for three years. Pearce, who was twenty-eight, had been suggesting it for a year or so, apparently, and with her nursing place sorted out and her career path clearer, she'd finally felt ready.

'There was no one at the flat when we tried earlier,' Robin said.

'No.' Deborah shook her head. 'He wouldn't be there, or work, either.'

'Do you know where we might find him?'

'Plymouth,' she said, looking at Mike. 'Oh my God, he's going to be – he'll be . . . devastated.'

'Why Plymouth?'

'He's gone to help his dad. He's in hospital there, the Dereford, complications from his diabetes. Dave's gone to sort things a bit for when he comes out, pay some bills, get some food in the fridge. He's good like that. Kind. Practical.'

Robin watched the thought dawn on her.

'Oh no, you couldn't – No, he couldn't. He would never . . . He had nothing to do with this. Nothing.'

'I'm sure you're right. But of course we have to notify him, and talk to him. We'll need to speak to everyone your daughter was close to.'

'Then Dave and Cat – Catherine Rainsford, that's her best friend. They've been best friends since school.' Another pair of silent tears slid down her cheeks.

'When did you last speak to Lara, Debbie?'

'The day before yesterday. She was coming over at the weekend to say goodbye to the puppies before they go.' She freed her hand from her husband's now, propped her elbows on the table and sobbed, shoulders heaving.

Robin looked at Niall. 'Do you have the pictures?'

He opened his file and took out two. When Deborah Harper looked up, he slid them across the table to her, the CCTV still and the e-fit of their first victim.

'Do you recognize either of these people?' Robin asked. 'Have you seen them before?'

The woman blotted her eyes with her cuff and tried to focus. After several seconds, she shook her head.

Mike Harper had leaned in, too. He put two fingers on the edge of the e-fit. 'I've seen this before,' he said, looking up. 'I saw it on the news last night. It's the girl you found in that old factory, isn't it? At the weekend. What's she got to do with Lara?'

'Maybe nothing,' said Robin. 'We don't know yet. But the factory where this girl's body was found is very close to where Lara was found and unless the post mortem finds otherwise in Lara's case, they both died of knife wounds, so we do have to consider the possibility they're connected.'

'Is this him?' Harper said. 'Who did it?'

'Again, we don't know. We're in the very early stages of that enquiry, too. This was taken close to where this woman was found so we need to eliminate him from our enquiries – at this stage, that's all.'

'Did he . . . ? Was Lara . . . ?' Deborah said.

'Sexually assaulted?' Robin finished for her. 'We won't know for sure until the post mortem, but at this stage, there's nothing to suggest that.'

'The other girl . . . ?'

'No.'

Lara's mother closed her eyes.

'Mrs Harper, it can't change anything, I know that, nothing

can bring Lara back, but we will find whoever did this. I'm in charge of the investigation, and I promise you we will find your daughter's killer.'

Back in the car, she checked her messages. In the thirty-two minutes she'd been inside, phone on silent, she'd missed thirteen calls, forty-seven emails and ten texts. She skimmed them all, gave herself a bodily shake as if to get rid of the memory of the scene inside, then rang Malia. She hadn't expected the Harpers to have David Pearce's father's details but, hands fumbling the pages of the old address book, Mike had given them both his phone number and address. 'Apparently they've got to know him quite well,' she told her. 'Family occasions, etc. I think they're those kind of people – hyper-sociable.' The address book had been stuffed – outside of work, Robin doubted she'd ever even met as many people. 'Could you get in touch with Plymouth and ask them to send people round there ASAP? If he's not there – David – ask them to try the hospital. Her best friend's a woman called Cat Rainsford; I'll ping you over her number.'

'Right.'

'Any news your end?'

'A couple of people who saw our Twitter appeal – a woman in the same block as the one who called it in. She heard a scream at about twenty past twelve which she'd thought was kids messing around but now she's not so sure. The other one's a bloke who saw a woman matching Lara's description walking along Gooch Road ten minutes or so after midnight.'

'Alone?'

'Yes, so he said.'

'Okay.' So two hours in, they were already doing much better than they were with the first girl at the same point. And perhaps even now.

'We need to look at her social media right away,' she said. 'Obviously anything untoward but also anything that might connect her to our first girl – did they follow each other? Is she in any of the pictures? Did Lara mention the case?'

'Already on it.'

'Thanks.'

She hung up as another text message arrived. Kath Legge.

What time for dinner tonight? Pete really looking forward to seeing you both!

Oh God, she'd completely forgotten. And there was no way she could go.

Pete was her godson. Corinna's son. Thirteen now, he'd been eleven when Corinna had died and the police had launched a search for his father, Josh, on suspicion of murder. To escape the fire that destroyed their house, Pete had jumped from a skylight, breaking multiple bones including his ribs, one of which had punctured his lung and then became infected. It had been touch-and-go for days; he'd stayed in the children's hospital for five weeks. When he was finally fit enough to leave, he'd moved in with Josh's sister, Kath, and her family in Edgbaston.

The old Pete had been a comedian before he was two – if he discovered a funny face or a noise that made people laugh, he'd repeated it again and again – but that side of him was gone or at least buried deep. Robin *had* seen him smile in the past year – Kath, Gareth and their boys, Al'n'Ed, were busting a gut to make his life as happy as possible – but he was a different child. It wasn't just losing his mother; she and Kath had had to tell him the truth about what had happened and why. They'd done it together. To her surprise, after years of thinking Kath was stern and holier-than-thou, Robin was becoming quite fond of her. They'd been out for drinks together three times now independent of anything to do with the children.

She texted her back and explained.

Can Lennie still come? Kath replied at once. *I could drop her home afterwards?*

She'd like that. Will text her now. Robin paused, embarrassed, then added, *If you're sure about lift home, wd be great. Thank you!*

On the drive back, she rang the people who'd left messages that needed answers and then, between incoming calls, she let her brain idle. She'd always found the car conducive to thought and by the time she arrived in Harborne, she'd answered her own question.

Why had she come? *We will find your daughter's killer* – she hadn't been able to say it to their first victim's family yet and she wanted to. She'd needed to make the promise out loud, to look someone in the eye and make it binding.

Chapter Thirteen

When her desk phone rang, it was Niall. Through the glass Robin made eye contact with him. 'It's Martin Engel on the line, guv. He says you'll know what it's regarding.'

'Thanks, but could you tell . . .' A click – he'd put the bloody phone down. For God's sake.

'DCI Lyons,' she said, trying not to sound too resigned.

'Thanks for taking my call.' Engel, by contrast, sounded hyper. 'I didn't think you would. Look, I've heard about the new girl.'

'Yes. Mr Engel, it's not Victoria. We've got an ID this time and she's—'

'I know. Her name's Lara Meikle.'

Robin frowned: they hadn't released it yet. 'How did you know that?'

'Social media. So, yes, I know it's not Vee but I was thinking: what if it's *the same guy*? Two girls, four streets apart. I've done a lot of research in the past five years and if there's a serial killer at work, it'd be really unusual for him to kill so quickly at the beginning of his career so there'd be other, *earlier* victims. What if Victoria's one of them?'

'Martin,' she said, choosing her words carefully, 'it's very early days in the case – in *both* these cases – and we've got no evidence at all they're connected.'

'But . . .'

'If it turns out they are, and if there's any reason to suspect a connection to Victoria, we'll investigate it to the full extent of our power. We will.'

'I'm just . . .'

'The other day, outside, you told me you follow me. You knew about my case in London; do you also know what happened to my daughter?'

'Yes,' he admitted.

'Then you'll know that I have at least some fraction of understanding of how you must feel. I know it's incredibly hard but can I ask you to sit tight and let us handle it? Victoria isn't forgotten here, I promise you.'

By seven o'clock, the light outside the windows had started to soften. There were hours of it left yet – well, at least two – and in a different life she'd text Kev and suggest they drive out into the country to a beer garden and a pub supper. But this was this life, she'd be here until well after dark, and that was fine by her. More than fine. And she'd had quite enough of the country today.

The extra people Samir had given her brought the team to nearly fifty. Ranged on desks and chairs, they were waiting, all eyes front. She stepped aside so everyone could see the whiteboards. Over the course of the day, now that she needed to be differentiated from Lara Meikle, their first victim had been referred to more and more frequently as the Gisborne Girl, and eventually, to avoid confusion, she'd written it at the top of the wall-mounted board in inverted commas.

Even now, there'd be plenty of space to draw a line down the middle and dedicate the other half of the board to Lara but to

117

reinforce the point that, until further notice, these were two separate cases, she'd had a free-standing board set up alongside.

'Do you want to transfer the Gisborne Girl to the smaller board?' Varan had asked. 'Put Lara up on the wall instead, given that we've got a lot more detail for her?'

Robin had felt a surge of resistance, as if he'd suggested something more than a practical idea. 'No,' she said neutrally. 'Let's keep her where she is.' As she'd walked into her office minutes later, she'd identified the feeling as indignation: no, she wasn't going to let her be moved off the top spot. Lara Meikle had photographs in which she was alive and smiling, magenta-haired; she had multiple witness sightings and a rapidly filling timeline of her final hours. More than that, though, she had her people, the Harpers and her own father, who worked on an oil rig in the North Sea and was making his way home to Birmingham from the north just as David Pearce was coming from Plymouth in the south. Lara's brother, Graeme, had done the formal identification. Give the Gisborne Girl the wall board at least.

Two hours later – yes, she knew she was being over-sensitive, no one was saying the Gisborne Girl was less important – she'd felt vindicated.

'Right,' she said. 'Let's get started. For those of you who've been elsewhere this afternoon, the good news is, we've got a major lead on this guy.' With her pen, she tapped the CCTV still of the man crouched in the window of the works next door to Gisborne's. 'One of the stockists of the Sohna foods is a small shop-cum-newsagent in Sparkbrook, about twenty minutes' walk from Gisborne's. The owner recognized our man, says he's been in there four or five times in the past couple of weeks. He's positive it's him – beyond a doubt.' She looked at Malia, who nodded.

'The shop opens at five, and our man comes in almost straight away. They've spoken. He's Indian, they spoke in Hindi. He always pays in cash so there's no chance of tracing him by bank details *but*,' she held up a finger, 'the owner says that after he leaves the shop, he's picked up by a white Ford Transit across the street at five fifteen. He's seen it happen several times, and one of them was yesterday morning.'

A murmur went round.

'So, *tomorrow* morning, we've got a team lined up and we'll be waiting for him. Let's keep our fingers crossed he hasn't changed his routine as a result of Lara last night. As we know from our surveillance there, he hasn't been back to Bradford Street since Sunday.

'That's the day's progress so far in terms of the Gisborne Girl. We've got no further witness sightings and still nothing on CCTV.' She glanced left, to the prime spot at the front of the circle into which Tark had whirled his chair like something out of *Starlight Express*.

'Afraid not,' he said.

'But,' Robin addressed the room again, indicating the free-standing board, 'as you see, we're doing much better on Lara Meikle. Unsurprisingly, having an ID makes a massive difference. For starters, we know Lara was out last night with her best friend, Cat Rainsford. They met after work at the Shakespeare on Summer Row, close to both their offices, where they both had sausages and mash. They settled up there at 10.32 – Cat had her copy of the receipt; they split the bill – then walked to Southside for a nightcap at the Sunflower Lounge which, she says, they left just before midnight.

'In response to our social media appeals, we have witnesses who saw Lara walking alone on Sherlock Street then Gooch Street between twelve ten and twelve fifteen. Cat is understandably distraught,' she nodded at Jo Kowalska, the young DC who'd talked to her. 'Cat lives in Aston so she got a taxi and she tried to make Lara take one as well but Angelina Street's only a ten or fifteen-minute walk, so Lara said she'd be fine. Especially after being out for dinner and drinks – she was trying to save up a bit for when she started studying.'

It would haunt Cat for years to come, Robin knew. If only she'd put her foot down, insisted on dropping her off or paying for a separate cab herself, her best friend might still be alive. *If only, if only* – so many tipping points in life, so many choices that should be minor, forgettable from one day to the next, but that turn out to be monumental.

'With an ID, we've also been able to request her bank records and search her social media. That work's still ongoing, she was an enthusiastic connecter, four hundred and odd Facebook friends, five hundred Twitter followers, but no red flags so far, no visible nutters *and* – again, so far – no indication that she and the Gisborne Girl knew each other. Which brings us to the obvious question: are they connected?'

She looked around, deliberately meeting certain pairs of eyes.

'The simple answer is, despite all the similarities: we don't know. It certainly looks like they are but for now we proceed as if they're unrelated. We can't afford to import conclusions from one case to the other and muddy the waters. So be careful.

'On which note – the media. I've had calls this afternoon from two of the tabloids. As we're all aware, they love a good-looking young female victim . . .'

'Good-looking young *white* female victim,' Malia corrected her.

'Yes,' Robin nodded, 'unfortunately that's still true. And we've got two of them. So, be on your guard. Beware the honey-trap, the woman clearly out of your league who's suddenly keen to buy your drinks and . . .'

'That's you she's talking about, Niall,' said a voice at the back, getting a laugh.

Phil Howell, doubtless – Robin looked: yep. 'And those of you with obliging dispositions – *not* talking about you here, Phil – please resist the pressure to be helpful. Anyone calls you, refer them to me or the press office. If the media gets involved in a big way, slapping the s-word on homepages and front covers, it'll be a whole new world of pain.'

'Still here?'

'Barely,' said Rhona, retrieving her handbag from her desk drawer. She stood and glanced at the clock over the door. 'Past eight – I'll be in trouble at home.' She laughed, *as if*, then narrowed her eyes. 'You'll be here late, no doubt. Get some sleep tonight, you look tired.'

'Yes, Mum.' Rhona *was* old enough to be her mum – Samir had ordered in a big cake for her sixtieth in March – but she'd probably been looking after people at twelve. Physically, she went against stereotype – skinny, she had no bosom to which to gather anyone – but she exuded calm, and stepping into her little ante-room always knocked a couple of points off Robin's blood pressure. The slight Eighties vibe in here played a part, too, the dated coffee machine with its smoked-glass pot and the vitreous china cups, the rubber plant. Occasionally, when he and Liz, who was a property lawyer, had a childcare shortfall, Samir's daughter, Leila, came and spent the afternoon joining all Rhona's paperclips together. It reminded Robin of visits to her father's office, back through the mists of time.

'Go on in,' Rhona said. 'He's off the phone now.'

'Thanks. Have a good evening.'

'And you. Sleep!'

Robin gave her a salute then rapped a knuckle on Samir's

door. He was standing at the window and turned when he heard her. 'Hi.'

'Everything all right?' She felt her heart rate accelerate again. *Have you got a minute?* his email had said, and the memory of Luke's threat had come roaring back. He'd be long awake by now – what if their mother had told him what she'd said on the phone? She thought she'd been subtle, and of course she hadn't mentioned the bridge, but what if Christine had told him she'd said he was depressed and that was enough? Would there have been time for him to send Kilmartin a poisonous email and then for Kilmartin to contact Samir? Yes. Easily.

'Look at this.' Samir went behind his desk and gestured for her to join him.

When she did, she saw he had Facebook open again. She breathed a silent out-breath. 'Our friends at For Queen and Country?'

'The very same.'

They'd attracted another twelve followers/bottom feeders, she saw, since the first time he'd shown her. Credit where credit was due, though, it looked like whoever ran the page put the effort in, providing their audience with a steady stream of fresh bullshit. She didn't recognize any of the photos, and all the videos in the box at the top looked new, too.

'Can't fault them on that score,' Samir said. 'They work at it. This morning, they linked to stories on the *Daily Mail* and English Defence League sites, and to a band of fellow travellers based on Merseyside. Then I looked a few minutes ago, and saw this.'

The most recent video. It had been posted less than an hour before and under the 'Play' arrow, she could see Ben Tyrell again. The slats of his Venetian blind were open slightly wider today, the sun stronger, allowing a less shadowy view of him. It was a tough face, Robin thought, with its large, misshapen nose and mean lips, but the eyes and the eyebrows with their ironic lift in the outer corners suggested the same knowing intelligence she'd recognized last time. He was no brainless thug. The idea that she'd even fleetingly thought he was attractive made her shudder. She bet he was hot stuff among the local lady-Nazis, though.

Samir clicked and Tyrell came to life, stretching his neck as if limbering up. He joined his hands together on the table and looked directly at the camera, seeking eye contact. 'Friends,' he said, 'thanks for joining me again. If you're one of our growing number of regular visitors, then you know that For Queen and Country is a place you can come to hear straight talk about what's actually going on in this city – no sugar-coating, no liberal crap, just real talk. I set up this page as a place where those of us who know what's what can communicate – a place where we don't need to pussyfoot round the snowflakes and the limp-dick lefties and their PC bollocks. There's been too much pandering by half – it's the reason we're in this bloody mess.

'And when I say bloody, I do mean literally. Never mind the government, never mind Theresa May and her failure to get the Brexit we voted for fair and square *three years ago,* I'm not talking about that today. Today, I'm talking about *real* blood – blood being spilled on the streets of Birmingham *right now*. Shout out to Enoch – you weren't wrong, mate.

'On Monday, I mentioned the two murders that happened in our city on Saturday night. Now, I know you lot know your news, you're switched on, but a quick recap for those of you who've been busy the past couple of days. The two killed on Saturday – separate crimes – were a black kid and a white girl. One of those cases was solved almost straight away, and even if you've been under a rock lately – and frankly who'd blame you?

– I bet you'll know which. Yep, that's right, top marks, it was the black kid. Well done, West Midlands Police, good one – yet again you've prioritized the son of immigrants over the daughter of a British native. Nice.'

He sat back, taking an audible breath through his nose. When he rejoined his hands on the desk, one was a fist in the other, ball and socket.

'Well, those of you who've seen the news today will know that we've moved on to chapter two in this shameful saga. While the kid who killed Kieran Clarke is safely locked up, the killer of the girl found at the old Gisborne works is not only still at large but,' he leaned forward, bringing his face close enough to the camera that Robin could see freckles, 'he has killed again. *He has killed again.* The body of another girl was found this morning. And yes – it's another young *white* girl.

'Now, we all know that West Midlands Police have taken massive budget cuts since austerity. Let's face it, even if they hadn't been whingeing on about it themselves – over and over again – we'd be able to work it out. Friends, the state of things in this city – have you ever seen anything like it? Murders were up *seventy per cent* last year. Let that sink in. Seventy. Per. Cent. Our kids aren't safe to go to school because of knives – fucking McDonald's have got metal detectors on the doors in the city centre. Things are so out of control that the cops have written off twelve thousand burglaries without even trying to investigate. Written off! *"We're sorry someone broke into your house and nicked the telly and the laptop and the PlayStation you earned by hard graft but we're busy."* His police voice was whiny and high, female.

'But we know the context – we're living with it day in, day out. What I want to talk about is this guy – and it *is* a guy – who's preying on our young women. At least the police have got a suspect now, three days later; small mercies, eh?' He reached towards the bottom left-hand corner of the screen, the corner of his desk, and with a rustle like a strong wind heard over the phone, he produced a sheet of paper. Robin knew what it was before he turned it round: their CCTV still of the man leaving the factory.

'Here he is,' Ben Tyrell said, holding it in front of his camera until it came into focus. 'This is the man Homicide are looking for. The description says he's probably in his thirties, and he's Indian or Pakistani. Well, blow me, Indian or Paki – what a bloody surprise.'

He put the picture down. For a moment, he said nothing, just nodded his head, lips pursed, as if gathering himself, a gymnast winding up to the dismount. 'Gents,' he said, '*ladies* and gents, I'm going to leave you with a question. Do you think that when the suspect is Indian or Paki and the Head of Homicide at West Midlands is Indian, too, maybe the cops – cops whose wages come out of taxes that decent people like you and me pay – do you think they tread more gently?'

'Decent people, eh?' Robin said, taking a seat in one of the bucket chairs. She hadn't felt tired when she'd walked in but she did now. 'At least he's got a sense of humour.'

Samir rolled his eyes. 'Blink and you'll miss it.'

'What a . . . knob-jockey.' She said the word purely to make him smile and was pathetically pleased when it did. 'Seriously, though, I see what they mean, Cyber – you told me they said he's careful never to cross a line.'

'Yep, it's not *quite* inciting racial hatred, is it? Not *quite* accusing me of race-based professional misconduct.'

'Though you could be forgiven for thinking either.'

He pulled up his chair and sat down, putting his elbows on the desk and pressing his fingertips against his lips, a posture she'd seen him in hundreds of times over the years. 'The question is,' he said, eyeballing her, 'is he dangerous?'

'What do Cyber say? Any change?'

'No, not really, but they're going to monitor him a bit more closely – I gave my friend there a ring. Either way, it's another fan for the flames of customer dissatisfaction, isn't it, if it does all kick off on these cases. You got calls from London papers today?'

'Two. *Sun* and the *Herald*.'

He nodded. 'If we get this guy tomorrow morning, do you reckon we'll have our man?'

'No way of knowing. At the moment, he was seen leaving shortly after the window for time of death and that's it.'

'There's got to be a good chance, though? I mean, for one thing, how many other people can have been hanging round there in the small hours of the morning?'

Robin snorted slightly. 'Well, you say that but: Stewpot and Martin, the homeless guys we spoke to; the other lot of homeless from the back; CCTV guy; the urban explorer . . . Who knows who else we'd see if we ever got any CCTV from Warwick Street. For a place that's supposed to be abandoned, it's like Piccadilly Circus in there.'

'Say it isn't him, who else is in the frame?'

'To be honest, at the moment, no one.'

'Lara Meikle's partner?'

'We're talking to him first thing tomorrow, he's on a train back from Plymouth as we speak. Obviously, it's possible he went to Plymouth and visited his dad in hospital for the alibi, then drove back to Birmingham again, killed Lara, then drove back to *Plymouth* again in time for the Devon cops to knock on the door this morning – it's a nine or ten-hour round trip, we've timed it out – but by all accounts, they were really happy together, just moved in, and her parents were aghast at the idea. Not, she raised her eyebrows, 'that that means anything.'

'How about the urban explorer?'

'Jonathan Quinton? Again, if we ever got any CCTV from Warwick Street, we'd be in a better position to say. We've got traffic cams from the cross-streets but there isn't one on Gisborne's actual block.'

'Stewpot and Martin?'

'Decent, I reckon. The guy at the soup kitchen said the same.'

Samir took a long breath. 'What about an ID for her?'

'Nada. Nothing relevant from Missing Persons or the local PNC broadcast. We broadened it to all-forces at lunchtime but only dead ends so far.'

'What's *your* thinking?'

She grimaced. 'Frankly? I'm stuck. There's so little to go on. Even our idea about how plainly she was dressed – if the two cases *are* connected, then that's out the window. Not that Lara was tarted to the nines but she wasn't dressed like a ten-year-old.' She leaned back and let the chair take the weight of her upper body. 'Is Kilmartin phoning you on the hour, every hour?'

He shook his head. 'Only every two hours. That'll change, though, if things don't go how we hope tomorrow morning. Don't worry, you're still in his sights.'

'Samir, I've got to tell you something,' Robin said quickly, before she could change her mind. She saw his attention sharpen. 'I did something stupid this morning. Potentially very stupid, if it reaches Kilmartin's ears.'

He closed his eyes. 'Go on, rip off the plaster.'

So she told him the story: the call from Natalie and the mad dash out into the country, heart thumping. Luke on the bridge and the moment she thought he'd gone. The arrival of the police.

He listened, eyes not moving off her for a second. 'And?' he said when she hesitated.

'Well, I couldn't have denied he'd been drinking – the booze was coming off him like a cartoon skunk. So I asked the guy to turn a blind eye.'

Samir put his elbows back on the desk and his face in his hands. 'Asked?'

'Encouraged. With a pinch of emotional blackmail. And a hint of rank-pulling.'

He pulled a face as if he were in pain. 'Why, Robin?'

'He was in distress – extreme distress. I'd just seen him nearly jump off a bridge!'

'He'd come down. You'd got him in the car.'

'But a drink-driving charge on top of everything else that—'

'The least of his worries, in the scheme of things.'

'Well, I wasn't prepared to take the risk. He's my brother.'

He opened his mouth then stopped. Their eyes met. 'Your brother.'

'Yes,' she said, 'my brother.' She stared at him until he looked away. She took a fortifying breath. Sodding, *sodding* Luke – she'd happily throttle him. 'The thing is,' she admitted, 'after I'd done it, he turned on me.'

Samir's eyes were back on her immediately.

'He threatened me. He said if I told Natalie he'd threatened to jump, he'd tell Kilmartin what I'd done.'

'Oh, for fuck's sake! After you'd . . . ? That . . .' He made a face half outrage, half disgust. 'And here was I thinking he'd wreaked enough havoc in our lives.'

He saw her expression and made an exasperated gesture. 'What I mean is, hasn't he already done his damage? Now he has to poleaxe your career as well? And *you* gave him the axe.'

'How was I to know he'd turn round and lodge it between my shoulder blades?'

He said nothing but gave her a look: *Really?*

'Samir, I'm not going to let him ruin my career.'

'I think that decision might be out of your hands at this point, *Robin*.' He paused. 'When I called you this morning,' he said, 'you were with Kev.'

Blood rushed to her face. 'I rang him. I asked him to come with me.'

Raised eyebrows. 'You? Asking for help? Doesn't sound like any Robin Lyons I've met.'

She remembered Kev pulling his shirt on, the way he hadn't taken no for an answer. 'I'm evolving rapidly,' she said, 'adapt or die.' She made a *Ha* face. 'I only needed him to drive Luke's car back.' She felt a guilty pang. *Oh, really, Judas?*

'And did he? Drive Luke's car back?'

Jesus. 'No.'

'I got the call about Lara Meikle before eight,' Samir said, 'and I called you pretty much immediately. You must have already *been* to find Luke by then because you went straight to the scene – early to phone a *friend*, wasn't it?'

'Well, I can see why *you* got promoted to these lofty heights, ace detective.' She waved a hand around his office. 'Kev's always up early, he's told me before. He's at the yard by seven every day.'

'Well, I'm up early, too,' Samir said. 'As you know. As I don't *need* to tell you because you know. So why didn't you call me?'

Chapter Fourteen

Robin turned off the engine and sat for a moment in the dark. The city centre sparkled at the bottom of the hill just as it had last night. Had that really only been twenty-four hours ago? She wished Kev was here now, not for any romantic reason – if romantic was the word to describe their relationship – but for the company. His warm, uncomplicated company. She felt new resentment towards Samir. 'Of course I didn't call you,' she'd told him, 'you were at home in bed with your *wife*. What would *she* think if I started calling you at six o'clock in the morning?'

'She'd think you were calling about work,' he'd said. 'Or maybe because we're *friends*? What about Kev's girls? Where were they?'

'With their *mother*. Oh, for crying out loud,' she'd said, standing up. 'I've got a double murder to solve, Samir, I haven't got time for this.' She'd stalked out, slamming his door behind her. Midway across Rhona's office, she'd experienced the urge to kick something, and only respect for Rhona stopped her. How dare he? He was married – it would be none of his bloody business if she called Kev at two in the morning to go skinny-dipping in Gas Street Basin.

Feeling a rush of warmth towards Kev, she sent him a text: *Thanks again for everything this morning. Really appreciated.*

She shoved her phone in her pocket, undid her seatbelt and reached for the door handle before hesitating again. Lennie would be up – she never went to sleep before she got back. She took a few deep breaths, trying to exhale the frustration, inhale maternal calm. After thirty seconds, she gave up and got out.

Mary Street was silent. Outside the door, she fumbled her key and dropped it on the tiled step, another wave of tiredness hitting her as she stooped to pick it up. As she put it into the lock, however, she felt the back of her neck prickle. She froze, immediately alert, ears straining. Silence still – but the same feeling on her neck: someone watching. She thought of Martin Engel in his pool of streetlight outside the station – lurking in the shadows in the car park. *I follow you.* Had he? She hadn't noticed anyone behind her but then, she hadn't looked.

She pulled her keys out of the door, turned them into the knuckleduster then spun around.

No one – the street was empty. She scanned for movement, a tell-tale twitch of a foot, the flap of a jacket, but there was nothing. Even the breeze that had sprung up again during the afternoon had died away. And yet the same feeling: someone was there.

'Mr Engel?'

Her voice echoed, bouncing off the tarmac and the quiet terraces. Nothing.

Then the tortoiseshell cat they'd seen last night darted out from underneath the neighbour's Mondeo and, without reduction in speed, slipped between the wall and the gate of the house opposite. Robin put her hand on her chest and felt her heart pounding through her shirt. 'Give me strength,' she said out loud, and that echoed, too. She turned the key, opened the door, and locked it firmly behind her.

'Mum?' A querying voice almost immediately from the back bedroom.

'Hi lovely. I'm on my way up – two seconds.'

As usual, Lennie had left all the lights on. In the kitchen, Robin poured a glass of wine from the bottle she'd opened with Kev then carried it upstairs, turning them off as she went.

Len's door was open and she was reading, her knees making a tent of the duvet, a gently steaming mug of tea next to her on the bedside table. The lamp cast a circle in the corner of the room, turning the bed and walls peach-gold, spilling onto the denim rag-rug and the books piled next to the bed. The desk with its laptop, neat pile of notebooks and jam-jar of pens was half-hidden in shadow, redundant now until tomorrow. It looked like a stage set, Robin thought, spotlighted. *THE MOTHER enters stage left. Late. Again . . .*

She dropped her jacket over the back of the desk chair, took a swig of her wine and put it next to the tea. Then she clambered up into the space between Lennie and the wall, her knee finding Len's phone in a wrinkle. She handed it to her then turned on to her back and let her body sink into the bed.

Lennie closed the book and dropped it gently to the floor.

'What have you got there?'

'*The Crucible.* For English.'

'Like it?'

'Yeah, a lot, it's really good.'

'Is it one of your GCSE texts? I thought you were doing *Macbeth.*'

'Ms B gave us things to read around – witches and gender stuff.'

'Nice. I've always been partial to a witch myself.' She'd wanted to be one when she grew up, and over the years, some had said she'd achieved it. She pressed the duvet and watched it puff back up. Her parents had given it to Len for Christmas because she liked the one they had. It was goose-down, about six inches thick but light as air. She'd thought before that it was like parcel padding: Len was tucked in and posted securely to the morning.

'How was dinner?'

'Good.'

'What did you have?'

'Lasagne and garlic bread. Kath made it.'

Rather than buying it in a plastic tray. 'What time did she drop you back?'

'Nine.'

Robin glanced at the alarm clock: 11.07. 'I'm sorry I couldn't come.'

'It's okay. It's not like you ditched us for a better offer, is it?'

Robin paused a moment, trying to work out if there was an edge there. Maybe not intentionally, but "ditched"? On the whole, she'd got off lightly on the working-mother guilt – as a single parent, she'd had to work: who else was going to do it? – but since last year, she'd become hyper-conscious of the strings of long hours.

'Did the same person kill both those girls?' Len asked abruptly.

'We don't know yet, sweetheart.'

'But what do *you* think?'

'I think we'll know more tomorrow. We've got our eye on someone – with a bit of luck, we'll pick him up first thing.' She stopped. No lies to Lennie had always been her rule, and even white lies, whose sole purpose had been sugar-coating, had tripped her up in the past. What she wanted to say was that everything was under control, but that would certainly be a lie, and not a white one.

Lennie reached for her mug, pressing her hands round it as if they were frozen.

133

From Robin's jacket came the sound of a text arriving. 'I'll get it in a moment,' she said. 'I've only got it in me to stand up once more today. Tell me, how was Asha's yesterday?'

'Good.' Len smiled. 'After dinner, we had this epic table-tennis match with Austin.' Their dad had bought them the table and set it up in their garage.

'Did you win?'

'One-all. But it was me and Ash versus him – two on one.'

'He's good, is he?' She tried not to smile. Len had an increasingly virulent strain of mentionitis where Austin was concerned; he was often the answer even when the question was something completely different. She'd met him herself a couple of times when she'd picked Len up from the Appiahs'. He was two years older than the girls, year 12, and he was very tall and slim, apparently shy, slipping round corners like the tortoiseshell cat in his band T-shirts and low-slung jeans, but actually direct and self-possessed when she'd spoken to him. Len had described him once as 'the right kind of geek'. 'He's actually interested in stuff,' she said, 'like music and film and politics – he runs the politics club at school. He doesn't go round slagging things off to make himself look cool. Unlike a lot of people,' she'd added darkly, and Robin had divined that she was alluding to her old friends in London, Carly and Emma.

Her gaze came to rest on the lampshade, one of those paper balls like a full moon. It was one of the few things that had come with the house and it looked old and tatty, she realized, the paper yellowing. A harvest moon. She'd buy a new one when she got a moment and remembered; it was lowering the tone.

When they'd moved in, she'd given Lennie a budget and free rein to design the room how she wanted. A major project ensued, involving hours on Etsy (the denim rag-rug and two framed posters with bold blue and white prints, one each of the London and Birmingham skylines) and eBay (a brushed-steel Anglepoise lamp that to Robin looked like something from a 1950s dentist's office). Miniature potted succulents from Tesco lined the top of the packed bookshelf at the foot of the bed.

It looked good but the room made Robin sad. Having an EQ in the minus numbers, it had taken her a while to understand why. Bar the wicker chair in the far corner occupied by the core contingent of Len's old stuffed animals, Zed and Fred the Teds and Wala, a super-plush koala her parents had given her, there was nothing childish about it. If she'd had the opportunity at the same age, she would have designed something similar (though not half as good) and she recognized it for what it was: all aspiration and self-definition, a vision of the future. In three years' time, Len would be off to university, out of here. Robin quailed to imagine loading the rag-rug and Anglepoise into the car and unpacking them in some room a hundred miles down the motorway, driving off.

A ping as another text arrived and then, five seconds later, another. Len slipped out of bed and patted the jacket until she found the phone. 'Kev,' she said, looking at the screen. 'All three of them.' She frowned.

Shit, what had he put? 'Hey, private!' she said. 'Hand it over.' She grabbed it and skim-read the messages.

Hiya, thanks for the thanks. No problem – any time.

How's your bro – any word?

Did you tell your Ma?

Lennie didn't get back in but perched on the edge, feet still on the rug. 'Why's he asking about Uncle Luke?' she demanded. 'Tell Gran what?'

Christ on a bike. She told the story yet again, this time modifying it to exclude any hint Luke might actually have wanted to fall. 'Kev came with me because I asked him to,' she said, making

135

a display of locking the phone as an excuse to avoid eye contact. 'Partly so he could drive Uncle Luke's car back, partly for some moral support, if I'm honest.'

Lennie hesitated. 'Are you seeing him, Mum?'

'What, Kev?' *No lies to Lennie . . .*

'Why not? You could. He's a nice guy and the two of you have been seeing more and more of each other lately.' She shot her an Olympic-standard bit of side-eye.

'Well, I've got no other mates here, have I?'

For a moment, the memory of Corinna hung between them.

'That's not true,' Lennie said. 'And even if *you* haven't, *he* has.'

Chapter Fifteen

Technically, sunrise had been 4.43 but a little after five o'clock, the sky over Sparkbrook was still a deep royal blue, and Amit Kapoor's shop door cast a long yellow rectangle across the pavement. The street was quiet but at the far end they could see a short length of Stratford Road, where the traffic headed into the city centre was already starting to thicken.

They were tucked in at the kerb about twenty yards back. Kapoor had opened the shop at five on the dot, and they'd watched him load the day's papers into the display cases outside with a degree of self-consciousness probably last witnessed at a school disco. Their fault for telling him to act naturally.

The dashboard clock read 5.05. Beside her, Varan shifted and she guessed he was thinking the same: their guy hadn't come yesterday. Or, at least, he hadn't come into the shop: they'd checked the CCTV. But the tape *had* shown him on Monday, just as Kapoor had described. At two minutes past five, he'd appeared on camera wearing the same baseball cap and dark anorak which, with the closer-range picture, they'd now identified as Adidas. He'd gone to the fridge at the back, where he'd chosen a chocolate milk and a yogurt that he'd brought straight to the counter. A few words with Kapoor, twenty-two seconds in total, and he was gone.

'I hope we're right about the day off,' Varan murmured.

Because unless there was something really wacky going on, they'd discussed at the briefing last night, the van had to be his work, surely, more than likely part of the shadowy off-the-books economy that provided so much of Maggie's surveillance work. Casual day labour on building sites, house-painting, farm work – cash-in-hand, no paperwork, no questions asked. Perfect for someone who wanted to fly beneath the radar for whatever reason.

Movement at the top of the street. They both tensed but it was a young woman in a salwar kameez. She let herself out of a door that opened directly on to the street, locked it behind her, then hitched her handbag on to her shoulder and started walking towards Stratford Road. A car passed on their right, a young couple in the front. *Clunk, clunk* went the manhole cover.

5.08.

'If it *is* the same guy for both,' said Varan under his breath, 'what's he getting out of it? If it's not sexual?'

'We don't know for sure yet that it wasn't with Lara,' Robin muttered back. Olly had scheduled the post mortem for nine o'clock. 'And even if he didn't actually touch them, doesn't mean it wasn't sexually motivated.'

She and Malia had discussed it in her office last night, shortly before Samir's *got-a-minute* email. 'Maybe the violence is his thing,' she'd said. 'The blood excites him? Or maybe he takes their personal belongings as mementoes.' Those were the people who really gave her the creeps, the ones who got their kicks by toying with apparently innocuous items in plain sight, glorying in their secret knowledge. 'Or maybe when we get him, we'll find hundreds of photographs.'

'Or maybe it's *supposed* to be sexual,' Malia had said, 'that's the plan, but he panics for whatever reason and kills them. Maybe that's why two so close together.'

'Tried and failed so tried again.' Which didn't bode well, given the same result the second time around.

'But if it *isn't* sexual, then what?' Malia had asked. 'Revenge? They both crossed him somehow – dumped him, humiliated him? He killed them to punish them? Make himself feel powerful?'

It was all still on the table – a hundred questions, zero answers.

At 5.10 both pavements remained empty. Now she was seriously beginning to doubt he was coming. If Malia was right and the Gisborne Girl and Lara *had* been particular targets, maybe his work here was done and he'd got the hell out of Dodge.

The light on the pavement outside the shop flickered, changed shape. They stiffened again then saw Kapoor looking out. He soon disappeared; Robin imagined the guys inside hissing at him to get back. Well, if their man was a no-show, at least he'd have a story to tell about the day he was part of a police stake-out. Otherwise, it would have been a complete waste of public money. There were eight officers in total, all of them armed – another four were stationed at points down the street, two inside an unmarked van parked further up on the other side. Basically, it was the whole shebang – Kilmartin would throw a fit.

The sun was visible now, throwing its light over their side of the street and evaporating the shadows they'd been relying on to make them less conspicuous. The LED screen of the dashboard clock had switched from luminous green to dull daytime grey. 5.12. 5.13.

And then, in the rear-view mirror, a white Ford Transit van appeared. It was in decent nick, not brand-new but not ancient, either, exactly as Kapoor had described. It swept past them, sounding the manhole cover again, and barrelled on towards

Stratford Road. For a second, she thought it wasn't stopping but then, yards before the end of the street, it swooped in at the kerb and hovered, brake-lights on.

Robin scanned the pavement: still empty. No one else got in the van here, Kapoor said, so either he was mistaken about that or – rightly or wrongly – the van was waiting for their guy.

5.14.

Abruptly, at a level invisible to anyone outside the car, Varan's hand shot across the console to bat her arm. 'Sorry, guv,' he whispered.

A man had turned in at the end of the street – baseball cap, navy anorak. Running. Yes, he was heading for the Ford. The walkie-talkie crackled and almost instantaneously, two of their guys came piling out of the mouth of an alley further up. Another two sprang from the back of the unmarked van.

Their guy reached the Ford, his hand was raised to open the door, but at the sound of their feet, he spun around. Even with the windows closed, they heard his shout of alarm. He spun back again, frantically pulling at the handle which opened just as the officers got to him, causing him to stumble backwards, balance lost. Another shout then they had him on the ground and he disappeared from view.

Varan nodded. 'Gotcha.'

He was in his early thirties, Robin guessed, but his hair was already receding sharply, making his square forehead look very high. The lower half of his face was a similar shape and as a result, his head as a whole had an oddly rectangular appearance. The squareness round the jaw wasn't bone structure but the result of a heaviness in his lower cheeks, like a bulldog. His eyes were bulldog-like, too, pouchy, with two or three rings apiece that looked grey against his skin. Despite the morning chill, his face shone with sweat and his eyes darted this way and that as if he were actually still hoping to escape. She'd seen a few edgy people in her time but he was top ten.

They'd need an approved translator for the interview, that was the law, but Varan spoke Hindi so he'd done the arrest and read the man his rights. As he'd heard what he was being arrested for – or what Robin thought was that bit – a look of horrified incredulity had passed across his face but, asked if he understood, he'd given a single nod. Beyond that, he wouldn't say a word, even his name.

'Do *you* know?' Robin turned to the tall man in jumper and jeans who'd sprung from the Ford's driver's seat. He was white, early twenties, with blond-brown hair and a blithe, boyish face. Given the situation, he was remarkably relaxed. He'd told her his own name, Tom Peterson, without hesitation, and when she'd asked him a minute ago to stop texting, he'd affably dropped his phone into his pocket – 'Right you are' – then waited with no sign of unease at all.

The same could not be said for the two rows of Indian or Pakistani men visible through the open doors of the van. Packed on to wooden benches fitted either side, they looked out of the gloom with wide eyes or else down at the plastic bags and knapsacks held between their feet on the muddy cardboard that covered the floor.

'He's called Dhanesh,' Tom Peterson told her, and the Indian man flinched. 'That's what they call him, anyway. Not sure of his surname, I'm afraid.'

'Does he work for you?'

'For me?' Peterson looked flattered but shook his head. 'No. They're working out at Lissom's Farm, near Evesham. Picking – early strawberries at the moment but up until a couple of weeks ago it was asparagus. Wait, you thought I was some sort of gang-master, didn't you?'

Robin felt an urge to slap the grin off his face. 'Does that

141

strike you as a ridiculous idea, in the circumstances? Or funny in some way?' She indicated the van full of frightened men.

'No, I'm sorry,' he said quickly. 'It's just the idea. A gang-master! I'm more like a bus driver.' A cloud passed over his face as if a thought were only now occurring to him. 'I probably need some sort of special licence for that, don't I?'

'Probably,' she agreed.

'It's a summer gig, that's all, during the holidays – we're at the agricultural college, we haven't quite finished for the year but pretty much, so . . . Andrew Lissom's my best mate's dad and we're both doing it, me and George – he does the south-west lot, I do south-east. We take the vans and come into Brum to pick these guys up in the morning and then we drop them off at night again. There's a massive labour shortage for this kind of work – all the Brexit stuff, you know? You can't get the workers.'

'Do you pick, Mr Peterson?' She couldn't resist.

'No way.' He shook his head again, apparently oblivious. 'Back-breaking. That's why we do the vans, George and me. I mean, yeah, it's an early start, but then basically you're off all day until six when you bring them back. This way, we'll earn a bit of money *and* get to mess around for most of the summer. And we can still be back for the pub at eight.'

'What time do they start?'

'In the fields? Six. Dhanesh here's my last pick-up, then we're off.'

'Six till six – so they're picking for twelve hours a day,' Varan said.

'I know, yeah.' He nodded. 'Like I said, back-breaking.'

They watched Dhanesh get safely into a car bound for Harborne then went to thank Kapoor for his help. Robin picked up copies of the *Sun* and the *Herald* from the piles at the foot of the magazine wall and carried them over to him, feeling in her jacket pocket for her fold of notes. He was buzzing with the excitement, a ball of energy bouncing squash-style round the narrow space behind the counter, waiting for them to go so that he could get on the phone. His wife would be ready to strangle him by the thirtieth time she heard the story.

A basket of soggy-looking plastic-wrapped muffins sat next to the till; Robin picked one up – blueberry, possibly; hard to say – and added it to her pile.

'Do you think it'll be in the papers, all this?' Kapoor asked, gesturing out the window.

'I hope not.' She gave him a warning look. 'At the moment we only need to speak to him. Under no circumstances talk to any journalists, okay? Not a word.'

'But it's in there today,' he said, tapping the cover of the *Herald*. 'About the girls, I mean.'

'Yes, hence my buying it. Not my usual reading matter.'

'Do you think that's really him – the guy who killed them? I mean, if it is, I helped catch a serial killer, didn't I?'

There were no prizes for guessing how he'd reached that conclusion. In the *Sun*, the story took up two thirds of page five, much of the space occupied by the blaring headline:

MIDLANDS MURDER CAPITAL: THREE SLAIN IN FOUR DAYS

'*Slain*?' said Varan. 'With what? Samurai swords?'

'Cutlasses, I expect.' She skimmed the text. Kieran Clarke was in there – they needed him for their headline, after all – but strangely (ha) they hadn't printed his photograph. Instead, they'd used the e-fit of the Gisborne Girl and the most winsome natural-haired photo on Lara Meikle's Facebook page.

The factual but unexciting news that they'd arrested Kieran's classmate was paid lip service but the focus of the piece, of course, was the young white women, their killer (or killers, it grudgingly allowed) at large.

Both girls were killed in the small hours of the morning by repeated and brutal stab wounds to the chest and neck. 'There was blood everywhere,' said Manda Pryce, 47, whose dog, Leon, found Lara Meikle's body in a litter-strewn alleyway opposite her block. 'It was like something out of a horror movie. It's terrible what's happening round here – we're all terrified to go out at night.'

If the looks of the current victims were anything to go by, Robin couldn't help thinking, she doubted Manda had much to worry about.

'The police are too busy for us,' said Graham Lineham, who lives in the same block. 'It's one thing when it's burglaries but murder . . . That poor girl in the factory and now another one right across the road two days later. If there's a killer out there, our womenfolk have to be protected. If they won't do it, we'll have to do it ourselves.'

Womenfolk? What was this, 1640? Her eye snagged on her own name in the paragraph below.

At time of going to press, West Midlands are yet to arrest a SINGLE SUSPECT in connection with EITHER case. Detective Chief Inspector Robin Lyons of Force Homicide, leading both, refused to say whether her team even HAD a suspect in their sights, commenting only that enquiries were 'urgent and ongoing'.

Chapter Sixteen

It was still only half past six when they reached Harborne but Samir's black VW saloon was already there, provoking an echo of last night's annoyance. Why did he think he could get all up in her personal business like that? Her love life – okay, sex life – had had nothing to do with him for eighteen years.

And that was *his* fault. It was all well and good blaming Luke – and yes, of course Luke was to blame – but it might have been nice if he'd had thought to ask *her* whether their relationship would mean her losing her family before he sacked her off as if she'd caught leprosy in one of the grimier youth hostels they'd stayed in (likely not impossible, given the state of some of the bathrooms).

'Everything all right, guv?' Varan asked as they crossed the car park.

'What? Yes, just thinking.' She took a deep breath and tried to put it out of her mind. No time for that today – she'd have to find a way to say sorry for stomping off while also reinforcing the point that it was none of his bloody business, and then they could sweep the whole thing back under the carpet.

When they came through the door to the incident room,

however, he was standing in front of the boards, coffee in hand. 'Morning,' he said.

'Morning, sir,' said Varan.

'You're in early,' Robin said. In his shoes, she'd probably have made some sarky comment about whether she'd heard there was a serial killer on the loose but of course, she thought, even if he wasn't the boss and there weren't other people around, he was better than that. He was irritatingly mature at times.

'I guessed you'd come straight over from Sparkbrook,' he said. 'He's here?'

'Downstairs now.'

'Good. Robin, can we . . . ?' He indicated her office.

He let her go first then followed. All of a sudden she got the fear – he *was* the boss. Yes, they were friends now, in their strange way, but the fact remained, she reported to him in an extremely hierarchical organization, one of whose overlords had the knives out for her. What if he was really pissed off about the Warwickshire cop and he'd decided overnight that it wasn't worth the risk of having her on this?

Or – her stomach dropped – on his team at all.

He closed the door behind him with a quiet firmness that struck her ear like a death knell. Often, if it was only the two of them, he sat on her filing cabinet but he stayed standing. 'You probably haven't had a chance to see the papers yet.'

'I bought a couple in Sparkbrook.' Another pang of alarm – was there a piece she hadn't seen? Something worse? For a moment, she had the wild idea that Luke might have bypassed Kilmartin and gone straight to the media, then told herself not to be ridiculous: as if he had that much initiative.

'Did you see the *Herald*?'

'Yes, I did.' Relief, which she hoped hadn't shown on her face – wildly inappropriate response.

'So the court of public opinion is well and truly in session,' said Samir. 'And I've got a meeting with Kilmartin at eight. What do I tell him?'

'That we have a subject in custody and we'll be questioning him as soon as the translator gets here at nine. Which is also when Olly Faulkner's starting the PM on Lara Meikle – Malia's going to attend, I'm doing the interview.'

'Is it him? What do you think?'

'All I know at the moment is that he's like a cat on a hot tin roof and he's refusing to say a word.'

'Right.'

Was there subtext in the tone, an ironic *Great*? No, maybe not – he seemed to be thinking.

'I wouldn't be surprised,' he said, 'after the piece in the *Herald*, if Kilmartin tells the press office to let people know we've arrested someone.'

She frowned. 'But we don't know what his story is yet. We haven't spoken to him.'

'Optics, optics – he's all about the public face, as you know, and I can guarantee you that little snippet will have ruined his morning. And frankly, with all the anxiety about us losing control, you can see his point. People want proof that we're on it.'

'Will we still look "on it" if it's not him, though?'

'Well, that's the risk. I'll try and hold him off but let's talk again as soon as you've interviewed him. I've got a mound of stuff to do so . . .' He headed for the door then stopped. 'Robin, look, I'm sorry about last night. The Kev thing. It's none of my business.'

'No,' she said. It came out sounding much sharper than she'd intended. She saw it land, and then a flicker of something – what? Annoyance at her apparent failure to accept his gracious apology?

She thought about saying sorry, trying it more softly, but he was already speaking again.

'I think I was. . . surprised,' he said.

Oh, the 'disappointed' approach – Robin felt a flare of defensive anger. 'By what?' she said. Poker face, butter-wouldn't-melt.

'That you'd . . .'

Get together with Kev? Sleep with Kev? For some reason, she couldn't let him say it. 'What?' she interrupted. 'Be good enough friends to ring him early in the morning and ask him to come and help me with Luke?'

He gave her a look she couldn't interpret. 'Yeah.'

They would need Martin and Stewpot to identify the man as the one they'd seen so when she'd calmed down a bit, Robin rang Good Hope. Daniel Reid answered the phone himself, the warm murmur of voices in the background punctuated with the clatter of pans from the kitchen. 'We've just started breakfast,' he told her. 'They're not here yet but if they come in, we'll pass on the message straight away.'

'Thanks.'

'We've heard about the second woman,' Reid said. 'Obviously we want to do whatever we can to help.' He dropped his voice. 'We're worried. Several of the women who come here regularly sleep rough – is there anything we can tell them? Or do to protect them . . .'

'I don't know,' Robin told him. 'We don't want people to panic. We don't know much yet – whether the cases are linked, even. But you could tell them to be careful, to try and stay with groups at night, not alone. Tell them not to take any risks.'

Their man hadn't spoken during processing but among the items found in his backpack – along with a minute capsule wardrobe, a toothbrush and travel-size paste, and £14.32 in cash – was an Indian passport from which they'd learned that his full name was Dhanesh Gupta, he'd been born in Bangalore and he was thirty-two years old. They'd also learned that he was in the UK on a six-month fiancé visa though they hadn't found any official record of a marriage.

When they came into the interview room, he was sitting with his hands in his lap, his head bowed. For a moment Robin thought he was asleep but then he slowly raised his eyes and looked at them. It was as if someone had unplugged him – all the darting, panicky energy they'd seen in Sparkbrook was gone and instead he was resigned. Resigned but still frightened: the room was kept warm deliberately but he'd left his anorak on, zipped all the way up to the chin, a flimsy kind of armour. A sheen of sweat covered his forehead. He'd been offered but refused a solicitor, even when he'd been told it was free.

Sitting next to him at the table was Kunal Singh, top of the list of approved Hindi translators. A neatly dressed man in late middle age, he'd helped on a case they'd had in the autumn. He had a teacherly manner; his striking light brown eyes watched whomever was speaking with such focus it was as if they, rather than his ears, absorbed the words. In the earlier case, he'd calmed their witness down significantly; could he somehow have managed the same thing here in the minute or two before she and Varan had come in?

Varan turned on the tape and did the opening spiel. She asked if Gupta understood the reason for his arrest. Singh asked him in Hindi; Gupta nodded then said 'Yes' in English.

Varan slid the CCTV still across the table towards him.

'Mr Gupta,' Robin said, 'the body of a young woman was discovered at the former Gisborne works on Bradford Street on the morning of Sunday, June ninth, four days ago. The post mortem puts her time of death between one o'clock and four o'clock. This was taken by a camera on the building opposite Gisborne's and it's timestamped 4.37 a.m. as you can see.' She pointed to the bottom right-hand corner. 'We believe the man we see here is you – do you agree with that?'

Gupta's eyes were trained on the image as he listened to the translation. When it finished, he didn't move for three or four seconds but then he turned urgently in his chair, put both hands on Singh's forearm and spoke so fast it sounded as if he was tripping over his words. Varan looked at Robin with an *uh oh, you're not going to like this* expression.

'What's he saying?'

Varan deferred to Singh, who told them, 'Mr Gupta agrees that he is the man in the picture but he says he had nothing to do with the death of the young woman. His situation's compli-cated and he's afraid of the legal consequences, which is why he's so nervous, but he wants to tell you everything.'

Dhanesh Gupta kept his eyes trained on his hands as he told his story. His fingertips, Robin noticed, were dyed strawberry red. He told them that he'd arrived in the UK a month ago – they could check his passport, Singh translated, he had a visa, date-stamped – for a marriage arranged online. At first, all had gone according to plan: he'd been picked up at Heathrow – Terminal Five – by his future father-in-law who welcomed him warmly, and when they reached Birmingham he'd been put up at a cousin's house.

He'd expected to meet his fiancée immediately but her father said she'd had to go away at short notice to fill in for a sick colleague at a conference. Modern women, he'd joked, and assured Gupta she'd be back next week and was looking forward to meeting him.

'I wasn't supposed to know but at night I overheard the cousin and his wife talking in the kitchen,' Kunal Singh translated. 'The girl didn't want an arranged marriage – she was born and brought up in England, she wanted to choose her own husband – but her father and uncle had arranged one in secret. When she found out, she was very upset and she ran away. They were keeping me waiting, hiding the truth from me while they found her.'

Gupta blinked hard. 'Before I came to England,' Singh translated, 'I'd been told that she spoke fluent Hindi, but it wasn't true. She spoke a few words and my English isn't good – we couldn't communicate. She is younger than me, and I am not handsome. I saw it through her eyes – an older man, not good-looking, not even speaking her language well enough to have a conversation. I went to the father and told him that I could not marry her, it would not be fair. We should cancel the arrangement so his daughter could have a different husband. But then he refused to give the money back.'

'What money?' Robin asked.

'We had arranged to pay him thirty-five thousands pounds. That was the price – if we were married, I could live and work in England, eventually have citizenship. But the father said that because *I* said we shouldn't get married, *I* broke the contract so he would keep the money.'

Gupta looked at them, eyes huge, as if they could answer the question for him: how could this have happened? How had he found himself in this situation? Weren't people essentially good? Then, with a rush of words, he swung his hands together above his head.

Robin looked at Singh, who looked pained.

'When I tried to complain,' he translated, 'he said he would hurt me. With a poker from the fireplace. He threatened me.'

Her stomach registered a sensation like a stone sinking

through deep water. He was guileless, she thought. Guileless, and completely credible.

'You said "*We* had arranged"?'

Gupta bowed his head.

'He and his father, he says,' said Singh. There was another flood of words from Gupta. 'My father's brother – my uncle – has four sons, all successful,' Singh translated. 'Two are in India, two are overseas, one in San Francisco working for Apple, one in Germany with Audi. My uncle is always boasting – my son this, my son that. I am my father's only son and I wanted *him* to be able to boast about me, to make him proud. I persuaded him to let me make a marriage in England. I would come here, work hard and be a success. But I failed, and now my father's life savings, thirty-five thousand pounds, are gone. How can I tell him? How do I tell him his son's a failure who lost his money?'

Varan shifted beside her. He believed him, too, Robin thought.

'Mr Gupta, tell us why you were at the factory in the small hours of Sunday morning.'

'I was staying there. Sleeping. After the father threatened me, the cousin told me to leave his house. I stayed at a cheap hotel for a week but I couldn't afford it after that. I slept in parks, on benches, but it was frightening and cold. Raining. Then, walking around, I saw the factories. The big one was no good, the condition was too bad – no roof except for where other people were living already. I was thinking about the tunnels but then I found a way through into the place next door that no one else had found so I moved in. Until the girl was killed and the police came – I came back from work on Sunday and there were police in the street. I was afraid.'

'Why?'

'On my visa, it's forbidden for me to work. I didn't want the

152

police to know. I am working to buy a flight back to India but it is hard to save money. We work every day but we're paid by how many trays we pick and I'm slow. I had to buy a new blanket, I had to leave one at the factory, and after I've bought food . . .'

'How did you find the job, Mr Gupta?'

'One of the other workers,' translated Singh. 'I met him at an Internet café – I go there to email my friend in Bangalore; I needed to tell someone what's happening and he won't tell my father. I heard a man speaking Hindi at this café, talking about work, so I asked him. He told me to meet him early the next day.'

Robin looked at the timestamp on the CCTV picture. 'The van picks you up at five fifteen every day? Even on Sundays?'

Gupta listened to Singh then pointed to himself in the photograph.

'Here,' Singh translated, 'four thirty-seven, I was going to work.'

Chapter Seventeen

She'd forgotten her mother's box of leftover chicken again, though given the four thirty start and the situation in general, it seemed forgivable. By half past two, however, she'd had nothing to eat except the clammy muffin she'd bought from Kapoor, and the incident room was beginning to feel oppressive. If she was going to think clearly, she needed air, food and a change of scene. She chucked her notebook in her bag and told Varan she was going out.

Harborne High Street was a couple of roads away. The area had changed dramatically since her childhood (though, to be fair, in the years she'd been in London, she'd constructed a mental image of the whole of Birmingham existing in a permanent Eighties time-warp, Noddy Holder as local presiding deity/spirit animal). Harborne was distinctly middle class now – there was a Marks & Spencer *and* a Waitrose. Her favourite café occupied a Victorian school building worthy of Coketown but the first time she'd come inside and seen the industrial light fittings and painted boards, she'd thought she'd fallen down a wormhole to Shoreditch.

She chose a small table so no one would join her then got out her notebook. She'd meant to do the brain download in bed last night but she'd fallen asleep with the pen in her hand. Now she wrote 'Dhanesh Gupta' and the sinking feeling flooded back. They were keeping him in custody while they checked his alibi for Lara's murder – he'd been sleeping in the city centre, he said, a few doors down from Marks, so there'd be plenty of CCTV – but she'd bet her life savings (all £462 of them) that he had nothing to do with either case.

Unless his call-centre salary ran to hiring a hit man, hopes that David Pearce was their man were fading, too. His father was more ill than Lara's mother had known and Pearce had stayed with him at the hospital until after ten o'clock. The nurses would be able to confirm it, he'd told Varan; there were cameras in the hospital car park, and he'd stopped at a petrol station to fill up on the way back to his dad's and bought an almond Magnum to cheer himself up. He'd produced a receipt timed 10.42 so he would have had to push the land-speed record to get back to Birmingham in time.

On Saturday night, when the Gisborne Girl had died, he and Lara had been to a house-warming party in Nottingham and stayed over. There'd been about thirty people there, ten of whom could vouch for them staying for the fry-up at eleven the next morning.

And anyway, they'd still to discover any link between the two women.

Robin's phone rang. Malia. 'Just finished,' she said. 'Walking to the car now.'

'Anything interesting?' A half-hearted question; she'd have called straight away if there had been.

'Nothing we didn't know already really,' Malia confirmed. 'Cause of death was stab wounds, probably the lower of the two in the neck most immediately, Olly says, but any of them would have been enough in a couple of minutes, with the blood loss.'

'No sexual assault?'

'No sexual assault.'

Thank God. Though from a forensics standpoint, sexual contact made it infinitely harder for an attacker to leave no trace of himself.

'There was one thing, though,' Malia said. 'Might be nothing but if we're lucky, it might not be. There was a hair on her blouse, stuck in the blood – no one saw it until they took the blouse off. About an inch and a half long, medium brown, probably, though it was soaked so . . .'

'It wasn't hers? In pictures, hers looks that colour naturally.'

'She'd redone the dye recently, though. Olly said her hair's a pretty universal colour, not like when it's natural and lots of different shades.'

'Did it have a root?'

'Yes but it was dead, it didn't have the waxy bit on the bulb.'

Bugger. So it had fallen out naturally, not been pulled out during a struggle. Which was what she'd have guessed, though: the SOCOs hadn't found any hair at the scene and if Lara had yanked it, she'd have got more than a single strand. But it could still be her attacker's; stabbing involved physical proximity, too. And it being stuck in the blood was encouraging.

'Well, let's keep our fingers crossed,' she said.

When she hung up, she tipped her head back and heard her neck crick. *Come on, think*, she told herself, *what are you missing*?

Suddenly she felt self-conscious, as if there were eyes on her. She turned around but no one was looking at her. Everyone was either chatting to their companions or eating; the only other single table was a woman in her twenties engrossed in her phone. No sign of a looming Martin Engel, ready to pounce.

Dhanesh Gupta. An hour ago, she'd sent a couple of officers round to speak to his would-have-been father-in-law, first to confirm the story, second to ask if he'd prefer to return the thirty-five thousand before or after they referred *his* case to the local CID team. Bastard.

Her scrambled egg arrived aboard two enormous rafts of sourdough toast covered in mashed avocado. Well, technically she *was* a millennial, she thought, even if she felt Gen X to her bones, probably because she'd had Lennie so young. Even though he was two years older, Luke was more millennial in outlook, not in any of the positive ways, obviously, but definitely in his sense of feeling hard done by. Spare her his rants about boomers. Or *her* unfair advantages, whatever they were. She picked up her phone again and rang Dunnington Road. It was answered sooner than she expected and she hard-swallowed her mouthful of toast and coughed.

'Love?' Her mother's voice, sounding surprised.

'Yes, sorry, just choking to death. How are you?'

'I'm all right. Are you?'

Subtext, Robin thought, why the call? 'Fine. I was ringing to see how Luke is.'

'Really?'

'Mum, I'm not a complete monster.'

'Oh, I know, it's not. . . Well, you're busy, aren't you? Anyway, that's kind of you, thank you. He's a bit better – the hangover's gone and Billy's coming this afternoon.'

'Billy as in Hideous Billy?'

Her mother sighed, *And you were doing so well.* 'I wish you wouldn't call him that.'

'Well, he is.'

Billy had been a friend of Luke's since childhood; his parents had lived four houses further along on Dunnington Road until a few years ago when they'd retired to a spot somewhere outside Weston-Super-Mare. Like Luke, Billy had never left Birmingham.

Robin had no idea what he did for work – who'd employ him? – and she knew he wasn't married. Corinna used to say there wasn't a woman desperate enough and while there probably was, somewhere, she hadn't materialized in the years they'd known him. He'd actually had a potent crush on Corinna herself for a while and when she'd finally had to say no in terms he understood, he'd spread a rumour that he'd seen her getting off with someone other than Josh, her boyfriend at the time, later her husband.

'Well, he's being kind today,' her mother said firmly. 'He's coming over and I'm hoping he'll cheer Luke up a bit.'

'I hope so, too.' It would be a good reminder that there were others less fortunate at least. 'Has he spoken to Natalie?'

'Yes.' Her mother's voice dropped. 'They talked last night, she came over.'

'How did it go?'

'Not as well as he'd have liked.' Her voice was barely above a whisper now. 'He wanted to go home but she's asked him to stay here for a bit while she "does some thinking".'

'Really?' Somehow, despite what Nat had said on the phone, she'd assumed they'd patch things up quickly.

'Things have been bad for a while, love.'

'As I'm beginning to realize.' She couldn't quite keep the edge out of her voice.

There was a moment's awkward silence before her mother asked, 'How's my lovely Lennie?'

'Good, as much as I've seen her this week.' She'd texted earlier to ask if she could go round to Asha's again after school. 'Anyway,' she said, 'I was just checking in.'

She hung up feeling strangely melancholy. Why? She tried to parse the feeling. Of course she didn't want Luke and Natalie's marriage to break down. He loved Nat, he always had, and he was better when he was with her, she was definitely a positive influence. For all that Robin had never considered her a potential friend, she respected Nat. She worked hard, she had goals and achieved them – she and Luke owned their house, which was more than *she* could say despite earning a lot more. Nat never forgot a birthday; she was kind to their parents. She had backbone, basically, and she lent Luke some of it.

But the nub of the melancholy, Robin admitted, was personal, that feeling of exclusion again. Natalie was in the Lyons circle of trust; she wasn't.

She went back to her notebook, telling herself to stop being selfish and focus. She started writing quickly, free-associating – *Lara, hair stuck in blood on shirt*. Please let it be the killer's. She paused. If it was, they had another difference in the cases. Obviously there was nothing remarkable about a killer leaving a hair behind – where would forensics be without hairs? – but it *was* worth noting that they hadn't found one on the Gisborne Girl, or any other evidence with DNA potential – a broken nail, saliva, semen – and she'd been stabbed, too, at exactly the same close quarters. He must have been incredibly careful. Added to the debit-card receipt, did it point to less care second time around?

Robin turned to the notes she'd made in her office. The carpet, too. Lara's death was so much more out in the open. There'd been some degree of concealment – she hadn't been killed on the pavement, like poor Kieran Clarke – but being killed and left in an alley between two working businesses on a street facing residential blocks was different from being covered with a carpet deep in a derelict factory traversed only by the dispossessed.

Hm. It was far too tenuous a thread to support any conclusion but it was worth bearing in mind – definitely that.

The other question, then, was how the Gisborne Girl's killer had achieved this meticulousness. Gloves? Had he covered his hair? Maybe he'd worn full-body PPE – there'd been no one to see him, as far as they knew, no one to question why he was dressed for an Ebola ward. Ah – her pen went running across the paper – the lack of CCTV on Warwick Street as well. *Planned – meticulously planned*. She wrote the words and underlined them three times.

Was the same true of Lara's death? They'd had CCTV footage of *her* straight away, plenty of it, and it was only a question of time before they saw her attacker, too – the area was bristling with cameras. If the crime was less meticulous, had the planning been, too? Was it just how the cookie crumbled – the killer happened to lose a hair, he missed the super-soft paper – or had there been less attention to detail? And if so, why?

Robin tapped the biro against the table's edge. This was why she did the mental download and why it helped to get out of the office – a change of scene. And the luck of Malia happening to call when she did with the hair detail. Feeling eyes on her again, she looked up to see the woman at the next table staring pointedly at her tapping pen. 'Sorry.'

The Gisborne Girl's killer must have brought her to the factory. It hadn't happened by chance. Which raised two questions. One they'd asked before: how had he got her in there? The other had to do with Lara. Was it simply bad luck that she'd become his victim? It wasn't her regular routine to walk home at midnight and she hadn't posted her whereabouts on social media. Either she'd been chosen at random or her killer had known where she was going to be.

Her phone buzzed, dragging her out of the thought-bubble. Bugger, just when she was getting somewhere. These moments of crystalline thinking were like dragonflies, beautiful but fleeting, near-impossible to summon; you had to grab them when you could. She was tempted to leave it – even DCIs were allowed to go to the loo from time to time – but when she looked at the screen, she saw *Maggie*. She havered but Maggie had saved Lennie's life. And the damage to her concentration was already done.

'Maggie?'

'Hello, how are you?' Her chatty tone was disorientating after the intensity of the thinking, like standing up from an all-absorbing work session to find oneself thrust into the middle of a cocktail party. 'Am I interrupting something?'

'No, you're fine. What's going on?'

'Well, I thought I'd give you a ring because I've worked out who she reminded me of – your girl at the factory.'

'Really?'

'Oh, don't get too excited, I doubt it's going to help, but I thought I'd let you know anyway. It's an odd one – goes back to when I was married to Trevor.'

Robin felt her enthusiasm evaporate. That had to be twenty years ago.

'It was the last Christmas we were together – that was the straw that broke the camel's back, if I'm honest. We were up in Whitley Bay staying with Trev's mother – God, what a nightmare. The woman meant well, she did, but talk about boring. Don't get me wrong, bar the spectacular outbursts of temper, Trevor was pretty boring himself by that point but compared to his mother, he was Keith Richards. The *routine*, Robin – what's that poem about measuring out your life in teaspoons or something? Up at half past seven. Cup of tea. Tea at breakfast. Tea at eleven with a supermarket digestive – heaven forbid she'd spring the extra few pence for McVities, Christmas or not. Everything so carefully measured out, so . . . tight. I thought I was going to suffocate. Either that or go Incredible Hulk and tear her crocheted doilies to pieces with my bare hands. But we'd had Christmas with my lot for the previous three or four years so I just had to grit my teeth.

'Anyway, you know what those days between Christmas and New Year are like, deathly dull at the best of times, only tell what day it is by what's on the telly. I got hooked on the big local news story, a missing girl. I followed it in the local paper, on the local news. She was fifteen, and she'd vanished without a trace on Boxing Day. Something about being trapped in that house, the grey mist and the grey water and the grey sky when we went for our daily fifteen-minute allowance of fresh air along the sea-front – I don't know, it got under my skin. She felt sort of symbolic: unless I sorted myself out, split up with Trevor, my life was going to vanish into the mist, too.' She paused. 'Maybe literally.'

Robin was startled. Maggie was very open but she never talked about Trevor; thinking back, she could barely remember her speaking his name since he left the scene, which she had the impression he hadn't done quietly. Her mother never mentioned him, either, but from scraps of eavesdropped conversations at the time, she'd come to suspect that Trev had been violent towards Maggie, something that still amazed her. Maggie, the woman who took no prisoners, self-employed and entirely self-governing, her inspiration in many ways, she'd realized last year, the victim of some scumbag not worth the mud off her winkle pickers.

'This girl of yours in the factory,' Maggie was saying, 'she looks like her.'

But it couldn't be her: if she was fifteen back then, she'd be mid-thirties now, and the Gisborne Girl was nowhere near that old. 'Do you remember her name?'

'Well, I didn't so I did a bit of poking round. The Net was up and running twenty years ago, luckily, so I found a few scrips

162

and scraps, including a picture. I'll ping it over to you now. Miriam Chapman, she was called.'

'Was she ever found?'

'Unclear. I couldn't find anything one way or the other – no "local girl reunited with family" but no funeral announcement or "grim discovery", either.'

Robin's phone vibrated with another call. She held it away from her ear to see the screen. 'Look, I'd better go, Maggie, I'm out and the station's ringing, but thank you. Send me the picture and I'll take a look.'

It had been Tark who'd rung, with two bits of news. The first was that Dhanesh Gupta's alibi for Lara's killing checked out: the shop whose entrance he'd been sleeping in had ponied up their CCTV sharpish and on the timestamped tape he could be seen for the entire duration of 10 p.m. until 4.33 a.m., first sitting under his blanket, knees drawn up to his chest, visibly wide-eyed with nerves even in grainy freeze-frame, later conked out on his side, head resting on a 'pillow' contrived by wrapping a bit of clothing round a cardboard packing tube.

Kilmartin would be thrilled.

The second piece of news was that a security camera on a tool-hire shop on Charles Henry Street had picked up a figure walking towards the junction with Vaughton Street in the same two minutes Lara had been approaching Vaughton from Gooch. Robin and Malia stood at Tark's shoulders to watch. 'Here he comes.' He pointed to the left side of his monitor, 'There.'

He was on the opposite pavement, on the side of the street bordered by the area of public space, mown grass and a handful of large trees before the housing developments behind. Tall – very tall – apparently Caucasian, wearing dark trousers, a dark sweatshirt and a cap that obscured his face, he was moving at speed, long strides eating up the pavement, carrying him in and out of the frame in four seconds.

'He's definitely keeping his head down, isn't he?' Malia said. 'He never looks up – his eyes are on his feet the whole time.'

'Is he too tall to be the boyfriend – David Pearce?'

'I'd say yes, but I'll ask tech to give us a height estimate.'

'Yeah.' Robin's phone buzzed, a text from Kev: *How's things? How's Luke today? x* She locked it and slid it back into her pocket. 'It could be the way he holds himself,' she said, 'but I think you're right, he's conscious of the cameras. He might have some other nefarious intent – lots of places to break into along there – but it'd be an unfortunate coincidence as far as he's concerned. Does he look like he's hurrying to you? Let's have another look, Tark.'

They watched again, eyeballs straining for nuance. 'Hard to say whether he's *hurrying*,' Malia said, 'but he's definitely moving quickly.'

'But if he *was*, that would imply he's got a goal, wouldn't it? Something time-limited he's heading for.'

'Like Lara reaching the top of Angelina Street and getting home safe, you mean?'

'Maybe. Which would mean he knows where she is, and how *would* he? He's not *following* her – he's coming the other way. Did he *call* her? She nearly took a cab, didn't she – did he know she didn't?'

Abruptly the balloon of conjecture slipped from her fingers and set off round the room at high speed blowing an extended raspberry before flopping limply on the carpet at her feet. 'But maybe he's just a naturally fast walker. Or he's on his way to a 'bab van that shuts at twelve thirty.'

'Not many that shut that early, to be fair,' said Tark. 'And he's definitely keeping his head down.'

'So where does he go from here? That's the million-dollar question.'

He put a hand on the stack of tapes next to him. 'We'll find out, guv. There's no way this'll be his only appearance. It's not like Warwick Street – we've got stuff coming in from all over the shop on this side.'

'Where are we with her phone records?'

'I was expecting them this afternoon,' Malia said. 'I chased again earlier.'

'God, what about the words "urgent murder enquiry" do these people not understand? Let me know the minute they come in – we need to get straight on that.'

Dhanesh Gupta looked up in alarm when she and Varan entered the interview room. 'Mr Singh?' he said, eyeing the door as if they were thugs in an alleyway and his bodyguard was on a bathroom break.

'There's no need to worry, this isn't an interview,' Robin told him. She watched his face as Varan translated. 'I wanted to tell you a couple of things. First, we've been able to confirm your alibi for the night of Lara Meikle's murder.'

Gupta listened to Varan then nodded emphatically.

'He says yes,' Varan told Robin. 'It wasn't him, he had nothing to do with either of the murders but he doesn't know how to prove it for the girl at the factory.'

'Right, well, he's not the only one.' She nodded at Gupta. 'The second thing is, we sent some officers to talk to your would-have-been father-in-law about stealing your money. He didn't sound very happy about it but eventually he admitted to a "misunderstanding". He'll be returning the payment to your father's account by bank transfer this afternoon.'

Varan translated and Gupta's head fell forward. He covered his face with his hands.

'We're going to check back with him tomorrow to make sure he didn't run into "technical problems" with the transfer or anything similar.'

Gupta's shoulders were shaking.

'Dhanesh?' Varan said gently.

'*Dhanyavaad*,' Gupta said, lifting his face and touching his palms together. 'Thank you.'

Chapter Eighteen

Robin watched her team through the internal window. The figure on Charles Edward Street had boosted morale but the afternoon energy-lull was well underway now. The CCTV lot were slumped in front of their screens like glaze-eyed walruses, Varan was on his second KitKat and even Malia, usually the very poster girl for correct ergonomic furniture use, had her elbows on the desk.

After two nights of little sleep, one way or another, and the early outing to Sparkbrook this morning, she felt so stale she might as well have slept on Stewpot and Martin's old mattresses, drying her eyes over their fire. She opened her drawer and sifted through the detritus for the bottle of Optrex. When she'd finished blinking, she clicked to her inbox. Dozens of emails that needed answering *prontissimo*, plus seven from journalists. They'd been phoning all day, after the story in the *Herald*. She forwarded their messages straight to the press office. As the last one went, Samir's name appeared in bold at the top: *7pm good for update?* Ugh.

Maggie's email had already fallen off the bottom of the screen. Robin scrolled down until she found it. *As discussed*, she'd written. *Doubt it's relevant but see what I mean about similar?*

The link was to an archived story on the *Newcastle Chronicle's* website.

WHITLEY BAY: PARENTS' DESPERATE APPEAL
FOR MISSING MIRIAM, 15

Robin's eyes went to the picture. Like Kieran Clarke's, it was an official school photograph, the same hazy pastel background and unnatural smile, the same awkward now-turn-to-look-at-me-love posture, legs facing one way, torso the other. She was wearing school uniform, too: bottle-green V-neck jumper and green-and-silver striped tie with a grey skirt smoothed to bony knees in grey woollen tights.

If you'd told her it was a picture of the Gisborne Girl, the only things Robin would have questioned at first glance were her age and haircut. The Gisborne Girl was definitely older than fifteen, albeit not by many years, and where her hair had no particular style, Miriam Chapman's had been cut into a long fringe which, though thick, had a slightly unfortunate cowlick that revealed an area of pallid forehead. Robin reached across her desk for a photograph from the scene and held it alongside: the hair wasn't the same shade – the Gisborne Girl's was two or three shades lighter; the word 'burnished' came into her mind for some reason – but it wasn't far off. Their girl had freckles, Miriam didn't, but the faces were strikingly alike otherwise: the same gentle oval shape with a similar lower lip and – she double-clicked on the photo but it wouldn't enlarge – what looked like the same ridged top front teeth. And the nose. Miriam's wasn't quite as Roman nor as large but it was of the same ilk.

She scanned the story. Maggie had obviously read it before she rang so there weren't many new details. As she'd said, Miriam had spent Christmas at home with her parents then gone for a walk on Boxing Day. There'd been one sighting of her a minute or two after she'd left the house, a neighbour who'd said hello at the end of the street, and then – poof! She'd vanished in a puff of smoke.

Further down the piece was a photograph of her parents from the police press conference, distraught and huddled together in front of the Northumbria Police insignia, her father, George Chapman, talking into the microphone as if it were a cobra that might rear up and strike. 'We're terrified,' he was quoted as saying. 'Miriam's just turned fifteen, she's young for her age and very shy. She'd never go off without telling us. Christmas is important to the four of us, me and my wife, Miriam and Judith, her sister, and we'd spent such a happy day together as a family. We love our daughter and all we want is for her to come home. Please, if you know anything, however small or unimportant you think it is, come forward.'

Robin opened HOLMES. Christmas 1999 – it had still been the old version of the software then but they'd been right on the cusp; HOLMES 2, with its hugely improved capacity for linking investigations across forces, hadn't been introduced until 2000. Had Northumbria been one of the first forces to get it? It was one of the biggest, Newcastle being a major city, of course, and one of several on Northumbria's ground. Whitley Bay was a decent-sized town itself.

She typed in Miriam Chapman's name. Yes, she was there, though barely; the entry wasn't much more than her date of birth and address, the date she went missing, and a description of what she'd been wearing – a striped wool dress and leggings, ankle boots. It was a misper record, not a murder investigation, last updated in 2003 by a DC Frazer MacDonald.

She looked at the pictures side by side again then picked up the phone. 'Come and have a look at this.' Seconds later Malia appeared in the doorway.

Robin turned her screen round. 'What do you reckon?'

Malia looked at the picture then looked at her. 'She looks like the Gisborne Girl.'

'Doesn't she? But it can't be. This girl – Miriam Chapman, she's called – disappeared near Newcastle nearly twenty years ago.'

Malia frowned. 'The Gisborne Girl might not even have been born then. What are you thinking? She's a relative?'

'I'm thinking a) it's possible and b) frankly, as far as an ID goes, it's day four and we've got no other leads.'

'How did you hear about her?'

'Maggie. I showed her our girl on the off-chance. She was up there at the time this one disappeared and she remembered her. I've had a quick look at HOLMES but there's not much. My guess is, they had another crack at it in 2003, when the record's last dated, and got nowhere then, either. Can you get in touch with Missing Persons and see what they've got on her? I'll give Northumbria a call.'

There was no Frazer McDonald on the 'Our Team' list at Whitley Bay, and actually no CID based there at all. One of the two stations in the town was closed, she discovered, 'rationalization', no doubt, more swingeing cuts. The website told her that Whitley Bay was covered by their Northern Area Command Unit. She dialled that number and asked to speak to Frazer MacDonald, fully expecting that sixteen years later, he'd be long gone. To her surprise, however, she was put through straight away.

'DI MacDonald,' said a soft Scottish voice.

Robin introduced herself and explained.

'Yes, I remember the case,' he said steadily. How old was he? she wondered. Older than her if he'd already been a DC in 2003, she'd still been at university, but he didn't sound ancient. Mid to late forties, maybe.

'I wasn't on the original team,' he was saying, 'I only came to it later, three or so years after she went missing. Someone thought they'd seen her in Newcastle so I was given it to have a go but I didn't get anywhere. No way of telling if it was her they'd seen or just wishful thinking – well-meaning member of the public wanting to help, you know? It'd be a tough case to forget, though, even coming to it late, with what happened afterwards.'

'What was that?'

'Her dad, George Chapman – Georgie – committed suicide. Gassed himself in the garage in the family Escort.'

'God.'

'It was mostly grief, I think, they were a very close family, old-fashioned in a way, churchgoers, good people, and the strain of never knowing what happened to her wore him down. That, plus people thinking he had something to do with it – he'd abused her and she'd run away, or he'd killed her. Obviously the police had to ask those questions and he knew that but it was the sideways looks in the supermarket, you know, the graffiti on the front wall? The vile letters. His wife told me that about a week before he did away with himself, he'd overheard someone in the corner shop whispering something like "That's him, the one who interfered with his daughter." She reckoned it tipped him over the edge.'

'The poor man.'

'That was 2004, a few months after I had to draw a line under it. Then two or three years after that I heard that the mother had died, too. Cancer in her case, but I wouldn't be surprised if it was sheer grief, you know, that losing them both wore her out. There's only so much the human body can handle.'

His voice was genuinely sad; Robin felt a bit guilty for bringing it all up again. 'I'll be frank,' she told him, 'this could be a complete waste of time, but we haven't got much else to go on. Our girl isn't Miriam but there's a definite likeness.'

'You've got pictures of yours?'

'And a good e-fit. I'll send them now – what's your address?'

She attached the files to an email and a few seconds later heard MacDonald clicking around on the other end. 'Aye, I see what you mean.'

'How old was Miriam's sister? Judith, was that her name?'

'No, it won't be her. She was only a year younger, partly why they were so close. Miriam was fifteen so Judith must have been thirteen, going on fourteen, when she disappeared. She'd be, what, early thirties now, older than this one.'

'Do you know if any DNA samples for Miriam were taken at the time?'

'I can't remember off-hand, I never needed them, but leave it with me. I doubt it, though.'

'Thanks. I know it's a long shot.' It was standard practice these days but twenty years ago, DNA samples hadn't been required in misper cases. 'DI MacDonald,' she said, 'there's not much in the system but when you spoke to the original team, did they have a feeling about what might have happened, even if they couldn't back it up?'

He sighed. 'Honestly? They'd been through the whole thing with a fine-toothed comb, it took me hours on end to go through the files. Georgie, her uncle, a couple of her male teachers, the priest and the other men in their prayer group, boys at school, the bloke who worked at the chippy who was a sandwich short of the full picnic, you know, and had a bit of a soft spot for her, they'd looked at everyone, and they didn't like any of them for it. I think in the end they concluded that she was one of the unlucky ones, one of those poor kids who's in the wrong place at the wrong time, standing on the pavement when the nutter with the van and the nasty appetites happens to be coming through town.'

'They thought she was dead, then?'

'Yes,' he said. 'They did.'

'You want to let Gupta go,' Samir repeated, looking at her over steepled fingers.

'Well, ideally, I'd like him to be our killer but, given that he isn't, yes. We've got clear CCTV images of him elsewhere for the entire window of time of death in Lara's case and a solid reason why he'd be leaving the factory on Bradford Street shortly after the Gisborne Girl's.'

'Which is?'

'He was going to work. Varan checked back with Too Posh to Pick—'

'Who?'

'Tom Peterson, the agricultural college gang-master wannabe. He confirmed that Gupta was on the bus on Sunday morning, said he specifically remembered because he was ten minutes late – big night at the Tipsy Pheasant on Saturday – and Gupta was waiting on the pavement, worried he'd missed him. Nothing remarkable about his behaviour, Peterson said, no agitation positive or negative once he knew he hadn't missed the bus. The man's a bag of nerves – Gupta, I mean – there's no way he's a cold-blooded killer. I doubt he could nick a bar of chocolate without triggering some sort of psychic meltdown.'

'But during the time of death, he *was* in the building next door with access to Gisborne's via this basement level where he could come and go without being seen.'

'As he freely admits. He was asleep, alone, no witnesses. The post mortem didn't find anything and the scene's a bust, too, so far. Frankly, with no forensics, either, I think the only way we'll prove it isn't him is by proving it's someone else. And in the meantime, the clock's ticking. It'll be twenty-four hours at five fifteen tomorrow morning.'

'Unless we apply for an extension, which we can.'

'I honestly don't see the point. It's not him.' She sighed. 'Look, I know I've got form with letting people go, but I've learnt that lesson, Samir. I'm not going rogue here.'

He rolled his eyes. 'Perish the thought. What's the situation with your brother and the Sword of Damocles, by the way?'

'Still over my head if Kilmartin hasn't been on to you breathing hellfire.'

'*He's* not going to like it if we let Gupta go.'

Should have thought of that before announcing we'd got someone. 'T.I.E. Trace. Interview. Eliminate. That's how it works. *You'll* probably catch some more flak from Ben Tyrell and our friendly neighbourhood Neo-Nazis, too, for your rampant desi bias.'

'Sod 'em,' Samir said, eyebrows flicking up. 'It's almost worth letting him go for the pleasure of pissing them off.'

Robin grinned. 'Definitely a happy by-product.' She thought of Gupta in the shop doorway, his eyes round with trepidation. 'Why don't we release him in the morning?' she said. 'Just before the twenty-four-hour mark. He'll get a better night's sleep here than he would on the street, he'll feel secure, and then if word gets out . . .'

'Which it will.'

'Then at least it'll be too late to catch the papers and we'll buy ourselves some time.'

He looked at her. 'You're sure? He's definitely not our man?'

'He's definitely not our man.'

'Then let's do it.'

Chapter Nineteen

There were no spots on Mary Street so Robin was obliged to park around the corner and drag her exhausted carcass the thirty steep yards back uphill. The sitting-room window was warm with lamplight and Robin had a mental image of the sofa, her backside sinking gratefully into it. As she came up the path, however, she noticed that none of the upstairs lights were on. Maybe Len had only been home a couple of minutes, she thought, and hadn't had time to go upstairs yet but as she put her key in the door, she heard music. Surprising: Len never put music on when she was alone, she liked to hear what was going on around her. Then Robin heard her laugh.

She opened the door and dropped her bag. 'Hello?'

'Hi Mum, we're in here.'

She'd expected Asha but when she put her head round the door, it was Austin sitting on the arm of the sofa, Lennie next to him, her hands full of the CDs that Robin hadn't yet – and probably never would – get round to uploading to her computer. They were listening to the Velvet Underground, *All Tomorrow's Parties*. Lennie's cheeks, Robin couldn't help noticing, were a bit pink.

'Hello, Austin, how are you?'

He stood up and came towards her, hand extended. 'I'm well, how are you?'

She shook his hand, thought *Lovely manners*, then felt about a hundred and forty. She didn't remember him being so tall, he had to be six feet, and the height made him look even willowier. He was wearing black jeans, trainers and a white T-shirt that said *Trump for Jail 2020*. 'Nice shirt.'

'We can dream.'

'Austin brought me back, Mum,' Lennie said, as if she needed to explain. 'I was about to call a cab but then he offered to walk with me.'

'That was kind, thank you.' Quite a long walk, she thought; the Appiahs were the other side of Moor Green.

'I was only staying until you got home,' he said.

'Well, don't rush off unless you need to. I'm going to have a glass of wine – long day.' She pointed stagily to the door then beat a retreat to the kitchen.

Interesting, she thought, as she took a glass from the cupboard, *very* interesting. So he liked her as well. Well, of course he did, Len was brilliant and yes, she was biased, but that didn't mean it wasn't true – she was clever and funny and engaged, already a person of character, a million miles from some of these insipid teenage girls who didn't have a word to say for themselves and sloped around with hands hidden inside their sleeves as if to signal their lack of agency in the world. She was lovely-looking, too. Only the other day, she'd noticed a twenty-something bloke ogling her bottom as she leant into the freezer in Tesco. Robin had given him a death-stare and he'd thrown a bag of oven chips into his basket and fled. 'She's fifteen!' she'd only just stopped herself yelling.

But Austin was seventeen, which, at that age, felt like a big developmental leap. A leap over the age of consent. No: she put up a mental hand; don't think about that tonight, enough for one day. But she'd have to think about it soon. Fifteen – Len was a baby. But, Robin reminded herself, she'd only been six years older when she'd got pregnant with her.

Quietly, she moved towards the door. She listened and heard their voices over the music, hers then his, something about Lou Reed and Iggy Pop. She was assailed by a sudden wave of nostalgia, talking about bands and books with Samir when what they were actually saying with their traded snippets about Radiohead and Pulp and *The Cement Garden* was *I like you, I like you, See how we're on the same wavelength? I really like you.*

And now her daughter was the teenager with the rosy cheeks talking about music with the dude she liked. Her turn had been twenty years ago and now she was standing in the kitchen alone.

She gave herself a mental shake and got out her phone where she found a couple of emails from the duty shift which distracted her until she heard footsteps coming down the corridor. They appeared in the doorway, Lennie first, Austin behind her, a good six inches taller.

'We're going to have a quick cup of tea, if that's all right, Mum?'

'Sure, of course.'

Len filled the kettle and Austin hovered nearby. Robin could almost feel the air crackling with their physical awareness of each other, the careful effort never to touch while also never moving too far away. Another pang of nostalgia – no, it wasn't nostalgia, it was jealousy. *She* wanted to feel like that again with someone – well, someone who was actually available. The thought stopped her – what did *that* mean?

'Mum,' Lennie turned the kettle on and leaned against the counter, 'have you heard about these "neighbourhood watch" groups? Not Neighbourhood Watch, Neighbourhood Watch, like the official thing, but these people doing night patrols?'

'Yes. Why?'

'We saw one on our way over, these two guys in reflective vests, "Keeping Your Streets Safe",' said Austin.

His voice was deep, Birmingham-accented to about the same degree as Robin's own was. Having grown up in London, Lennie had lost the accent she'd got from her when she started school and became self-conscious about it but over the past six months, Robin had started to hear traces of it again, a sing-song rise and fall in her sentences.

'Where were they?' she asked.

'Off Russell Road.'

'Hm, I wonder which one that is. The police actually fund some of them, as far as they *are* funded. They're still community volunteers, they're not paid for the work, but they get some financial support and they report anything they see. It's basically a cheap way of giving people a sense that at least someone's keeping an eye.'

'I don't like it,' said Lennie. 'It gave me the creeps – they were all, like, I don't know . . . puffed up with their own importance. Peacocks in high-vis jackets.'

'They mean well,' Robin said. 'People don't feel as safe as they used to.'

'Well, that's definitely true,' Austin picked up the bit of plastic Lennie had pulled from the top of the milk and wrapped it round his index finger. 'Knife crime's out of control.'

Robin nodded.

'That's not all the police's fault, though, is it? There are other reasons. Mrs Appiah's a social worker,' Lennie glanced at Austin, 'and they've had their budgets slashed, too.'

He leant against the counter next to her. 'Some of the groups she worked with had to shut down completely – two of the after-school clubs and her youth group. A lot of kids relied on them and now they've got nowhere else to go so they've started hanging out on the street.'

'Yes, that's definitely a factor. It's not just knives, though, or even physical violence. People want to protect their homes and property.' She thought of Ben Tyrell whipping up his audience with the perceived threat to their PlayStations. Or their 'women-folk', in the case of Manda Pryce's neighbour.

'You've arrested someone for the murders, though, haven't you?' Lennie asked. 'I saw it on Twitter. This morning, when you left so early, you got him.'

'We got *him*, yes, but . . .'

'He didn't do it?'

She shook her head. 'Between us.'

'So the real guy's still out there.'

'We've got other leads, lovely. We'll get him. Or them.' She was glad she sounded so confident.

'I know,' Lennie said. 'And that's why they piss me off.'

'Who?'

'These night-patrol people. I mean, I get what they're trying to do, but it pisses me off when they say the police aren't doing their job. Do they think *you* like it, not having enough staff to do the work? You work all the time, I hardly even see you, and then they say you're not doing your job? Great.'

'It's bound to happen. When people feel threatened, they . . .'

Austin shifted, eyebrows flicking. 'I wonder if it occurs to them that some people might feel threatened by *them*? I'm sure you're right and most of them mean well, but there'll be some who get off on the power and think they're running some kind of, like, vigilante militia. At least with the police there's *some* screening and accountability, and even then you get bent ones

179

and racists . . .' He seemed to remember who he was talking to. 'No offence.'

'None taken. You're right.' She drained her glass and reached for the bottle to pour herself another inch. 'And that's humanity in a nutshell, isn't it? The vast majority of people are decent, or decent enough anyway, and they spend large swathes of their lives dealing with the damage done by the handful who aren't.'

Lennie and Austin managed to eke out their tea until quarter to eleven, at which point Robin called Austin a minicab then went upstairs to clean her teeth while they said goodbye. A moment after the taxi accelerated away, she heard the bolts on the front door and then Lennie came galloping up the stairs, face lit up like Oxford Street at Christmas. She sat on the edge of the bed and bounced. 'What do you think? Do you like him?'

She tried not to laugh. 'I do,' she said. 'And I think he likes you.'

'No, he doesn't!' As if it was the most outrageous suggestion ever voiced.

'Oh, he hangs around drinking tea till the dead of night with all his little sister's friends, does he?'

'*Mum.*' Three syllables.

'Well, you asked what I think.' Robin watched Len trying and failing not to look too delighted. 'But I also think you're fifteen.'

'What does *that* mean?' Alarm and almost immediately the first hint of defiance: You're not going to stop me seeing him! Well, of course she wasn't, she wasn't an idiot. And why would she? She meant it, she did like him.

'It means it's bedtime, my friend,' she said. 'For both of us. Go on, hop it. Go and get your beauty sleep – the love object will be at school tomorrow, you don't want bags under your eyes.'

'The *love object?* Oh. My. God,' Lennie's cringe was all-body. 'When did you get so – *mortifying?*'

'Years ago, but you were too little to realize. And this is just the beginning – I'm only going to get worse.'

She flung her clothes over the back of the chair and got into bed, letting the mattress take the weight of her limbs. Bliss. Down the corridor, Lennie sang 'Sweet Jane' over the sound of running water then padded off to her room. After a few minutes, there was a click as her bedside light went out.

Robin had thought she'd crash the moment her head touched the pillow but instead she left her own light on and lay staring at the ceiling, mind whirring. Lennie and Austin, she and Samir – the generations flicked by so fast, one after another, like frames in a cartoon, carrying the story forward. When you were that age, you thought you always would be; it didn't occur to you that within a couple of decades, you'd be the embarrassing one.

Mortifying – she turned the word over. Killing with embarrassment, presumably, but possibly also killing as in rendering dead. Miriam Chapman had only been Lennie's age when she disappeared, her frame in the cartoon suddenly removed – and the removal had reached back to destroy the frames before, too. But what if Miriam hadn't died? What if she'd just cycled through her time as the youngest generation extra-quickly – more quickly, even, than she had with Len? What if she'd run away and got pregnant – or run away because she'd *been* pregnant? Could the Gisborne Girl be Miriam's daughter? Did the timing work?

On the duvet by her hand, she felt her phone vibrate. She picked it up and saw a message from Kev on the screen: *You awake?*

She hesitated. *Why?*

Look out your window.

If she'd been a hundred and forty earlier, she felt two hundred now – talk about cycling through the generations. She thought with envy of the crane Henry the Eighth used to get out of bed as she hauled herself upright and over to the window. Across the road, she saw the navy Mercedes estate, its dashboard lights glowing green.

Can I come in?

Lennie's here.

I'll be ever so quiet . . .

No, you won't. Stay there, I'll come to you.

She put on jeans and a T-shirt and crept downstairs, careful to avoid the floorboard at the top of the stairs and the step with the Hammer Horror creak midway down. Holding her breath, she drew back the bolts on the front door a millimetre at a time. She might be the older generation, she thought, but look at her sneaking out for teenage kicks.

The street was quiet, even the tortoiseshell cat off duty. Kev leaned over and opened the car door as she approached, and she slipped into the seat next to him. 'Evening.' His smile was audible.

'Evening. Have you any idea what time it is, Mr Young?'

He glanced at the clock. 'Half past eleven. I knew you'd be up. And your bedroom light's on.' He pointed towards the house.

'Fair warning, my days of looking decent on no sleep are fast slipping away.'

'You look pretty good to me.'

She rolled her eyes. 'What are you doing here?'

'You didn't reply to my texts earlier so I came to see if everything was all right. After the other day.'

'Really?'

He frowned. 'Yeah, really.'

'Well, that's kind. Thanks.' She told him what her mother had said on the phone. 'Honestly, though, I haven't had much time to think about Luke today.'

'Saw you got someone. Is it him?'

She shook her head. 'Back to the drawing board.'

'Sorry.'

'Yeah, me, too.'

To her surprise, Kev reached over, took her hand and gave it a squeeze. Rather than letting go afterwards, he held on. Surprised, she looked over to find him looking at her, eyes soft in the semi-darkness. The inches of air between them came alive all of a sudden and as he leaned in, she felt herself leaning, too. Kevin Young, he *was* a sexy kisser – she felt the touch tingle down her body. Gentle at first, tender, even, then increasingly urgent. She tipped her head back into the cup of his hand, breathed in his aftershave and warmth as he shifted closer, seat-leather creaking.

She pulled back and put up a hand. 'Whoa, whoa, whoa. School night.'

He grinned. 'Want to go back to mine? The girls are still at Sasha's.'

She shook her head. 'I can't leave Len on her own.'

'We could make it a quick one . . .'

'Oh, really?' She laughed. 'No. I'd like to' – she would – 'but I can't. I need my brain tomorrow.' Kilmartin would be on the warpath now, sure as God made little apples.

'Worth a try.' He smiled, eyes glinting, but she thought she detected actual disappointment.

'Shall I see if I can sort something out for the weekend? Maybe Mum and Dad could have Len over for movie night – they like doing that, the three of them.' Though she liked movie night with Len, too, and as she'd just pointed out, she'd barely seen her all week.

'That'd be good,' Kev said. 'We could have dinner somewhere nice.'

Robin heard distant alarm bells. 'Oh, we don't have to go anywhere nice.'

He looked at her. 'Why not?'

Was that a real question – a challenge, even? No, she was imagining it, because a moment later, he had on his usual jokey smile. 'And what if *I* want to? What if I want a white tablecloth and ingredients I've never heard of? You can't make me go somewhere crap.'

'All right, Egon Ronay, have it your way. Let me see if I can wangle it. I'll let you know.'

'Good.' He leaned over and kissed her again. 'Off you go then, before I get out of hand.'

She got out, then leaned back into the car. 'Thanks again, Kev. For being so kind.'

'On your way, you daft old bat.'

She closed the door and crossed back to the opposite pavement. Yet again, she had the strange sensation of eyes on her but of course it was only him, waiting to make sure she was safely in the house before he drove off.

Chapter Twenty

The phone rang as she was turning into Rose Road. Her dad's mobile number – odd. Oh Christ – Luke. Had he done something stupid? 'Dad?'

'Robin, is that you?' He said the same every time he called on his mobile, as if he didn't trust it to connect him to the person he wanted.

She normally replied with something ridiculous – 'No, this is the Aga Khan, who's speaking please?' – but he sounded different. Flustered. 'Yes, it's me. Is everything all right?'

'Not really, love, no.' He took a sharp sort of breath. 'Your mother's not well.'

Relief – Luke was still extant – followed quickly by a different alarm: her mother was never ill. In fact, she operated as if feeling 'under the weather' was self-indulgent, a weakness to be mastered by effort of will. 'What kind of "not well"?'

'We don't know for sure yet. Are you driving?'

'Yes, but hold on, I'm almost at the station – ten seconds.' She pulled into the car park and took the first empty spot by the gate. She was aware of her heartbeat all of a sudden. 'Dad?' she said. 'What's going on?'

'I don't know, we're at the hospital. I don't want to panic you, it could be something else, we're waiting to see the doctor again now, but they're worried she's had a stroke.'

'A stroke?'

'Everything was fine last night, we went to bed same as usual, but then your mum woke me up about an hour ago saying she couldn't move her arm.'

Robin felt cold wash over her body.

'Her voice sounded a bit funny,' he said, 'slurred, and when I turned the light on, the left side of her face was drooping.'

'Oh my God.'

'I don't want to panic you, love,' he said again.

'I'm not panicked but of course I'm worried. Really worried. Which hospital are you at?'

'The QE. We're in A&E – I called an ambulance straight away. That's what you're supposed to do with strokes, isn't it? Get help as soon as possible, every minute counts?'

'Yes, you did the right thing. How is she now? Are you with her?'

'No, Luke is – I've stepped out to the lobby to call you, it's no phones once you're through to the bays. She's being brave – you know your mother – but I think she's very frightened.'

'How're her face and arm now? Is there any change?'

'A little better, she says, but I can't see it – she still can't lift her arm. And I can't tell if her face is improving or if I'm over the first shock. Getting used to it.' A tremor in his voice, unmistakable.

'I'll come now.' The Queen Elizabeth was a mile away, if that; even with the morning traffic, she'd be there in twenty minutes. 'Let me know if you move from A&E, otherwise I'll find you there.'

Her dad hesitated. 'Sweetheart, I don't want to sound mean but it might be best to wait.'

'Why?'

'Well, like I said, Luke's here and what your mother needs now is calm. We can't put any stress on her. If you and Luke start squabbling and her blood pressure goes haywire, then . . .'

A flare of disbelief. 'You think I'd come in and pick a fight with Luke and give Mum another stroke? You actually think I'd do that?'

'No, of course not – of course I don't, love.' Mollifying.

'But . . . ?'

'But it's not worth risking, is it? I know it's not all one way, I know Luke provokes you, but . . . It's a stressful situation, no one's at their best . . . You'd never forgive yourself, would you, if things kicked off and something happened to your mum. Why don't I let you know when Luke takes a break – how about that?'

How about Luke gets to be with her and you don't? How about we cut you out even when your mother has a life-threatening emergency – might actually be dying? Robin felt like she'd been punched in the gut.

And yet she couldn't say anything – the last thing her dad needed now was for her to fly off the handle. And he was right, it *wasn't* worth the risk; she could trust herself not to fight with Luke but not the other way round: he was so unpredictable. And on the edge.

'Okay,' she said. 'Let me know. But Dad, please keep me posted. If there's any change, any news, will you tell me?'

She turned the engine on and pulled back out on to the street. She couldn't go in and be professional yet, she needed a few minutes to sort herself out. As she turned onto Park Hill Road, narrowed by parked cars on both sides, a black saloon slowed to let her pass. The driver gesticulated at her and, looking, she saw Samir lowering his window to talk. She pretended not to notice, waved and drove off.

Barely aware of what she was doing, she drove. When she reached Lightwoods Park, she edged the car up on to the pavement behind a row of others. Elbow on the steering wheel, fist clenched, she clamped the soft flesh of her finger between her teeth until it hurt. It felt good to have a physical focus for the pain.

In the terrace across the street, people came and went, going about normal mornings. A woman bumped a pram down her front step on to the pavement then crossed the road and headed over the flat expanse of the park.

Her mother had had a stroke – had *probably* had a stroke. But an arm she couldn't move, one side of her face collapsed . . . What must her dad have felt when he saw that? A numb arm was one thing, maybe she'd slept on it too long, lost sensation, but the face . . . How would her dad cope if anything happened to her? He'd be bereft.

And her poor mother. Robin tried to imagine what it had been like, waking up to discover she suddenly couldn't move her arm – hearing her own voice, seeing her dad's face when he saw hers and realizing something was wrong. Very wrong.

What if she died? She'd never see her again. Strokes often came in multiples, didn't they, like earthquakes, a series of preshocks then the big one. The pain in Robin's chest was back, so sharp that her breath came out like a sob. Cry, she told herself, cry and let some of the tension go. But she couldn't, the tears wouldn't come. God, what was wrong with her?

'Luke's here.' *And you're not.* That wasn't the subtext, she knew the idea hadn't crossed her dad's mind, but it crossed hers. And Luke *was* there – he'd been at Dunnington Road when it happened. But more than that, he'd *always* been there. In the seventeen years that she'd been off in London, he'd been right here in Birmingham, constantly in touch with their parents. He and Natalie had had Sunday dinner with them every week, he popped round all the time, as she'd seen last year. He'd been a much better child to them than she was, she understood now. She might think that her professional success was important but what did it matter to them beyond being something to talk about? Until eighteen months ago, she'd barely been around for years so why now, in a crisis, should things be different? Of course it was right that Luke was there first.

Chapter Twenty-one

Even paused with his mouth unflatteringly half-open, Ben Tyrell had the look of a man with an epic story to tell. Leaning in, shirtsleeves rolled, he was alight with purpose. When Samir hit 'Play', he sprang to life, full of outraged energy.

'Now,' he said, looking directly out of the screen, 'as I said a minute ago, my plan was to talk to you all again this afternoon, same as usual, but then this came to my attention and I thought, no, I'll make time now. Some things, when they happen, *I* think you deserve to know straight away.'

His Venetian blind was open today. Robin looked through the window behind him and saw a dense hedge three or four feet back. No doubt a path ran along there, access between the back and front of the house. He was recording this crap at home.

'Ladies and gents,' he said, 'those of you who've been on this week know that over the past few days I've been talking about the two girls found murdered in our city. Knifed to death. Lara Meikle, just twenty-three, a lovely-looking girl about to start training as a nurse, and, on Saturday night, Sunday morning, the girl whose name the West Midlands Police still don't know. Let that sink in for a minute. It's Thursday now. That poor girl lost her life in the small hours of Sunday morning – if we choose to believe "our" police – and they still don't even know who she is.

'Now,' he shifted in his chair, 'I'm not making any claims for our power here, though I *do* know from traffic to our page that more and more people are finding us and' – he held up a finger for emphasis – '*joining* us, becoming part of our community. We are not alone, folks – far from alone. There's a whole army out there who feel as angry and let down and betrayed as we do. What I also know – and whether it's us or the traditional media, I can't say – what I also know is that the police know we're watching – us, the clued-up part of the public – and they know we know they're screwing up.

'Which brings me to this morning's news. Again, if you've been following the story here or elsewhere – the national papers are getting involved now, it's reached that level – you'll know that yesterday the police told us they'd arrested a suspect. Good news, right? They'd got the guy they were looking for – here he is,' he held up his A4 printout of the CCTV still from Bradford Street, glancing round the edge to make sure it was in focus, 'and we were all supposed to breathe a sigh of relief. Despite their obvious . . . challenges, shall we say, they'd got him.

'Well, let me tell you now that early this morning, they let that suspect go.' He let his body fall back against the chair. 'Can you believe it? *Can* you? Because I've got to tell you, I'm struggling.

'As I see it – and I have racked my brains – there can only be two explanations. One, in order to make themselves look better, they're claiming success when actually they're getting absolutely fucking nowhere. Two – and I think this is more likely – in letting this guy go,' he stabbed at the printout, now on the desk in front of him, 'they've made a big mistake.

'This picture,' he held it up again, 'is from CCTV of the guy leaving the factory where the first girl's body was found *right after she died*. Now let me ask you, what *else* could he bloody well have been doing in there at four-odd in the morning? Those factories on Bradford are wrecks, we've been saying for years that they're eyesores and should be razed to the ground – there's nothing there for anyone any more, nothing even worth nicking. So tell me why a young, able-bodied man – he doesn't look like a druggie to me – would be leaving there in the dark right after she died. Tell me.' He let the challenge hang on the air. 'People, *he was there when she died*. No – when she was *murdered*. He. Was. There.'

Samir stopped it, freezing Tyrell as he opened his mouth to launch in again.

Robin exhaled. 'Jesus.'

'There's more.' He scrolled a couple of posts further down then hit 'Play' again on a wobbly bit of video taken on someone's phone. The angle was awkward – it had been shot from overhead, she guessed a first-floor window – but they were looking at the street where they'd arrested Gupta, Peterson's Ford Transit at the kerb with its rear doors open, Gupta in handcuffs being lifted back to his feet by the arrest team, who in all their gear looked dressed for a riot rather than a single frightened man. She watched herself and Varan appear from the left-hand side and then the camera zoomed right in, lingering on every face it could, one after another, filling the screen: her, Varan, Too Posh to Pick, a couple of the arrest team and then, for a long time, Gupta himself.

The video ended and they looked at each other. 'He needs to take that down,' Robin said. 'Now. All of it.'

'I've called Cyber.' Samir stepped away from the desk to pace in front of his window, moving in and out of silhouette. 'They're on it.'

'Showing his picture like that – bloody hell. How many people have seen it?' She scrolled back to Tyrell's own video, which had a hundred and forty-two views, and nine shares. As she watched, another two views were added. She skimmed the twenty-seven comments, all of them some variant of 'immigrant scum' or 'string him up, the murdering bastard'.

The video from Sparkbrook, which had been posted last night, had been viewed three hundred and twenty times.

Suddenly it occurred to her: 'How does he know already – Tyrell? We let Gupta go at five thirty this morning and this was posted at' – she looked – 'eight twenty-two.'

They looked at each other.

'Is he watching us?' Robin said. 'Has he got some tame creep lurking outside?' She thought of the feeling of eyes on her. Of Martin Engel.

'Or did someone just tell him?' said Samir.

'Who?'

'Is there anyone who *could* know,' he said, 'apart from the team here? Did you tell anyone?'

'Lennie,' she said. 'She asked if we'd caught the guy. She knew about the arrest yesterday morning, I had to tell her I'd be gone when she woke up, and she asked last night if it was him. She knows the drill, though – she'd never talk to anyone about an active case.' Then Robin had another thought. 'Her friend Austin was there last night when we talked about it – he'd walked her home.'

'What's his story?'

'Seventeen, big brother of one of her new best friends, they've got a mutual crush, I think. He's bright, cool – interested in politics.' She remembered what he'd said about bent coppers, racists.

'Interested how?' said Samir. 'And how interested?'

She shook her head. 'Not like that. And there's no way he'd be in with Tyrell's mob – he's black.'

'We don't know yet where Tyrell got the video – it wouldn't need to be one of his mob, necessarily, or even a sympathizer. He could have found it online, on someone else's Facebook page. Maybe the zooming in,' he gestured towards his computer, 'was about police accountability. Either that or it was just something interesting going on outside, something to post and get a few likes.'

Robin felt her face redden. 'I told Kev it wasn't him, too.'

'Kev? Why?'

'He got in touch last night to see how Luke was. Then he asked how the case was going.'

'Did you tell him Gupta was being released this morning?'

'No, of course not, only that we hadn't got a solve.' *Oh yeah*, she was tempted to say, *the precise details of murder cases are pillow talk round my way.*

Samir looked out of his window for a moment then turned back. 'I've asked Cyber to find out where he got the video.'

She sat down heavily in one of the bucket chairs. 'God, man, this case.'

He looked at her sharply. 'Are you still all right with it?'

'What?' She was immediately on guard. 'Yes, of course I bloody am. Why would you even ask that?' Had Kilmartin said something?

'Earlier, when we passed each other in the car, you looked very stressed. I stopped to say hello but you didn't register.'

She thought quickly: should she tell him? If Kilmartin wanted her off the case, she might be playing right into his hands, giving Samir the perfect excuse to hand it over to someone else without embarrassing her. On the other hand, as a matter of pride, she couldn't let him think it was work that was stressing her out.

194

'My dad had called a couple of minutes before that,' she said. 'He's in the QE with Mum; they think she's had a stroke.'

His reaction was instant, eyebrows pulling into a deep V of concern. 'Oh, God, Rob. I'm so sorry. When? How is she?'

She told him what her father had said. 'That's all they know at the moment, as far as *I* know. They're waiting to see the doctor again, and I'm waiting to hear from them.'

'Will you keep me posted?'

She nodded.

'You're going to need time to visit, to be there – do you want me to . . . ?'

'I want to work,' she said. 'I need to. It won't do any good, will it, my hanging around there, winding everyone up?' She saw his puzzlement and remembered that he came from a functional family. 'Luke's with her at the moment and Dad's worried we'll have a fight and the stress of it will finish her off.'

The frown deepened. 'Are you serious?'

'As a heart attack. Or maybe a stroke.' She stood up quickly, embarrassed. He knew better than anyone what Luke was like but even with him – *especially with him*, said a quiet voice – it was embarrassing to admit that her parents still didn't think she could be trusted to behave in a time of crisis. 'Well, I'd best get on. Time and tide wait for no woman.' She gave him a bright smile and legged it.

Back in her office, she found an email from Frazer MacDonald in Newcastle.

DCI Lyons, good to talk yesterday. As you asked, I've checked here whether DNA for Miriam was collected during the initial enquiry and I'm sorry to say that while it was – a sample of hair from her brush – it was apparently

195

destroyed by accident during a departmental clear-out in
2014. Sorry to be the bearer of bad tidings.

Great. She checked her phone yet again; still nothing from her
dad. Why not? Could they still be waiting or had something
happened? Had her mother deteriorated? What if she'd had
another stroke and was dying and . . . Stop, she told herself; just
stop. Even if she did have another stroke, she'd have care immediately, and her dad would send news when there was any. She
knew what hospitals were like, how overworked they were – talk
about budget cuts. They were waiting, that's all. Could they be,
though, another voice asked. It had been an hour and a half
now since her dad rang.

For God's sake, *Robin, stop it.*

Quickly, she reached for the file of the Gisborne Girl's scene
photographs and fanned them out on the desk. There she was
in her blood-soaked T-shirt, her eyelids violet, rich brown hair
fanned out behind her. In Samir's office, she'd felt a stab of
something like panic at the idea of losing the case and not being
able to help her, the same weird protective feeling she'd had
when Varan had suggested putting Lara Meikle on the whiteboard instead. No, no, no, don't worry, she'd wanted to say to
her, I've got you. I'm not going to leave you.

They still *don't even know who she is.* She imagined Tyrell
mocking her – Oh yeah? *You've* got her? God help her!

'I don't know who you are *yet*,' she said to the girl under her
breath, 'but I will. I promise you I will.'

Going back to her email, she sent DI MacDonald a reply,
thanking him and asking if he knew what had become of Miriam's
sister, Judith.

His response arrived in seconds: 'I'm sorry, I don't.'

A whoop came from the incident room. Looking through her

door, she saw that the commotion was coming from the CCTV crew. 'Tark?'

'We've got it, guv.'

She stood and went out there. 'Got what?'

The CCTV team were grouped behind Phil Howell. Over his shoulder she could see his screen, a dark image moving at its centre. They moved aside for her and he played it again. 'Vaughton Street,' he said. 'Further along than yesterday, nearer the turn to Angelina Street.' They were looking at the same figure – tall, white, dark trousers, dark top, cap. He moved with the same hurried walk, eyes never leaving the pavement.

Suddenly another figure appeared at the right of the screen, a woman in a dark skirt and a lighter blouse, her bag pressed tight to her side. 'Lara Meikle,' said Robin, and as if the man onscreen had said the words, Lara looked up. She stopped in her tracks – it was instantaneous. A second, maybe two, then she turned and started running back the way she'd come just as he started running, too, hand outstretched, snatching at the bag-strap as it flew out behind her. Then they were gone, and the film showed the empty street.

Silence – respect for what they'd just witnessed, likely some of the terrified last moments of Lara Meikle's life, the moment her evening out with a friend became the night she died.

Robin spoke first. 'Is that it?'

'I think so,' Howell said. 'I've fast-forwarded through the next twenty minutes and there's no sign of either of them. I'll watch it at normal speed to make sure, obviously.'

'What time is this?' said Malia, who'd joined the group on the other side.

He pointed to the numbers at the bottom right of the screen. 'Twelve twenty-one. Spot on.'

'Do they speak?' Robin said. 'That moment just after she sees him – does she say something?'

Howell went back. The graininess of the tape made it hard to be sure but it did look like Lara's mouth moved. 'Is it a shriek, a cry of alarm, or is it a word? Can you zoom in, Phil?'

He homed right in on Lara's face until the pixels gave her a cubed Lego outline. It was hard to be sure – they'd have to have it technically enhanced to say with any degree of certainty– but it *looked* as if her lips had moved twice, made two sounds, not a scream, then, but a word.

'His name?' said Malia.

'You think she recognizes him?' Tark said.

'I don't know,' Robin looked at the screen. 'Let's see it again.'

'I think she does,' Malia said. 'She's scared straight away, isn't she? Straight away.'

'It's after midnight on an empty street, though, she's a woman on her own,' said Robin. 'Does *he* say anything?'

They watched the man's face in close-up three times. His lips parted, they definitely did, but whether enough to say something, it was impossible to tell.

'Right. Well, I think this answers one question at least: in the first bit of tape, from the tool-hire shop, he *was* hurrying, wasn't he? He knew she was coming. So now we have to figure out how. Tark, we'll need to trace him backwards and forwards. Varan, let's get back on social and make absolutely sure there's no way he could have worked it out from there; we need tape from the pub and the bar if we don't already have it.

'We also need those phone records. Right now. Call your guy at the phone company, Malia, and tell him that unless they're here within the hour, they'll be looking at an obstruction charge.'

'With pleasure.'

'Good work, Phil – guys – this is major. Let's get the best still we can from the tape and also a clip – not the bit where he tries to grab her, that's too distressing. Let's see if any of Lara's people recognize him first – even if we can't see much of his face, his walk's distinctive. Failing that, social media.' Good, she thought, this would stop Tyrell going on about Gupta, brandishing his picture.

'Any sign of this guy around Gisborne's, Tark?'

'No.' He looked at his team, who shook their heads, too.

'How are we doing with footage from Warwick Street now?'

'Not brilliant.' He indicated two tapes in his wire tray. 'That's all we've got left to look at fresh.'

'We're struggling to get any more,' Malia said. 'Apart from the broken cameras, there's nothing like the office building on that side, it's all still industrial. One place had fake cameras for the deterrent value, and the place diagonally opposite tried to tell us that their MD was on his honeymoon and he was the only one who could access it. I've told them that, happily, *we* have people who can access it, too, and we'll be sending them over pronto.'

'Good. Varan, could you call Too Posh Peterson and see if he's heard from Gupta?'

'You think he's gone to work? After spending the night in the nick?'

'It's possible, just about, time-wise. I want to keep an eye on him,' she told them. 'We've got a right-wing bigot flashing his picture round, talking about how we've screwed up by letting him go, so I don't want to take any chances. Let's ask the city centre team to look out for him as well. My feeling is, he'll be back at work tomorrow if he wasn't today. The crooked father-in-law may have paid his dad back the thirty-five thousand but, in the meantime, he's not going to get far on the fourteen pounds he left here with.'

Also, she thought, after what he'd been through, he might need to be with people who spoke his own language. Alone in a foreign country, defrauded, arrested on suspicion of murder by armed police – who wouldn't want the comfort of someone they could talk to?

'A TIA – Transient Ischaemic Attack.' The relief in her dad's voice as it reached her down the line, like a boulder had been lifted off his ribcage. 'A mini-stroke.'

'Is that good? What's the difference?'

'With a stroke-stroke, the blood vessel in the brain's either burst or blocked permanently, the doctor said, but with a mini, it's temporary – the blockage moves on, and the damage isn't permanent.'

'Thank God, Dad.'

'I know. She can move her arm again – not all the way yet, but it's been getting better and better for an hour now, and her speech is much, much clearer. And her lovely face is getting back to normal, too.'

Relief, quickly followed by frustration. An hour? She'd been over here biting her nails *for an hour* and they hadn't thought she might like to know? For Christ's sake – what would it have taken Luke to text her?

'That's really good news,' she said. 'But what now? What are they saying?'

'Well, they don't want us to think we're out of the woods yet, they want us to know it's serious, but now it's about making sure it doesn't happen again.'

'So, what? Blood thinners?'

'Blood thinners, yes, aspirin, warfarin, and after that, diet and exercise, life on the straight and narrow.' The slightly manic laugh of a man newly delivered from the jaws of doom.

'Dad, I know what Mum's like, she'd say she was fine if she'd been hanged, drawn and quartered, but was this really out of the blue? Wasn't there any warning?'

'No, no warning.' He paused. 'Or not really. Her cholesterol, though – her GP's been on at her about that for a while.'

Sticky high-cholesterol blood and sixty-two-year old arteries – decades of roasts and cooked breakfasts and cream sauces exacting their price. Blood money. 'So how long will she be there? Are they keeping her in?'

'Oh no,' said her father breezily. 'Not overnight. They're going to monitor her for a little bit, her blood pressure's a bit high – probably the shock of it all – but then she'll come home and be spoiled rotten there.'

Chapter Twenty-two

Back in the game, Robin thought, mentally rubbing her hands together as she rolled her chair up to her desk. Twenty minutes ago, having drawn a blank among Lara's family and close friends, they'd posted the CCTV clip and they already had a new witness, a taxi driver who said he'd seen him on Upper Highgate Street, shortly after one a.m. on Tuesday. The air in the incident room was static with keyboards and phone conversations, voices full of new determination: *We're going to get you, you cretin, oh yes we are.*

Her mobile rang – Kev. She rejected the call; she'd ring him back in a bit, she needed to capitalize on this energy, her brain was snapping away like a game of Hungry Hippos. Reaching for her notebook, she turned to a blank page and started writing as fast as she could, pen skimming across the paper. From the corner of her eye, she saw her mobile screen light up again. *Kevin Y*, said the screen. She rejected the call again but ten seconds later the screen lit up a third time. She put down her pen.

'Kev, what's up?'

'Have you seen it?'

'What?'

'Mum's just called me – we're all over the *Daily Herald* website.'

'We? Who?'

'You and me. But obviously it's *you* they're . . .' He sounded pained. 'Ugh, you're not going to like it, Rob.'

OUT TO LUNCH: LEAD DETECTIVE RELAXES AS DOUBLE MURDER ROCKS BIRMINGHAM . . . DOWN-TIME ALSO FEATURED TRYST WITH SECRET LOVER

The brutal murders of two young women within 48 hours have shocked the city of Birmingham to its core but at least one person doesn't seem worried: Detective Chief Inspector Robin Lyons – the Senior Investigating Officer on the case.

Tasked with finding the killer responsible for stabbings so vicious a witness described one of the scenes as 'like a horror movie', DCI Lyons responded by taking a lengthy lunchbreak at a chi-chi café in the upscale Harborne area of the city. Later, under cover of darkness, she got hot and heavy in the front seat of her lover's brand-new C-Class Mercedes.

Thanks to an epidemic of knife crime, the UK's second city has a per capita homicide rate higher than London's, with this year's numbers already on track to exceed last year's by a significant margin.

This week's killings, however, have reached to the heart of a city on edge.

In the early hours of Sunday morning, a young woman whom DCI Lyons and her team have yet to identify fell victim to a savage knife attack in one of the many derelict factories that dot the inner city.

On Tuesday, the body of Lara Meikle, 23, was discovered

among weeds and litter in a squalid alleyway between industrial buildings less than half a mile away.

The details of her injuries bear alarming similarities to those of the young woman whose life was cut so tragically short two days earlier but a spokesman for West Midlands Police refused to be drawn on whether the cases are connected.

Local residents are growing understandably frustrated by the lack of progress in the case. And frightened.

'We're scared out of our wits,' said Lynn Tebbit, a resident of the block opposite which Lara Meikle's body was discovered. 'Two lovely young girls have been killed on our doorstep this week. Me and my friends don't feel safe to leave the house after dark when we know there's a vicious killer out there.' Her partner, Neil Daly, said 'We're asking what are the police doing to actually catch this maniac. It feels like they're out of control. Like we've been abandoned.'

Yesterday, the force announced that a suspect had been arrested but this morning, the press office confirmed that he had been released without charge. At time of going to press, no further arrests have been made.

Nevertheless DCI Lyons found time yesterday to relax over smoked salmon and avocado toast (*below, left*) while talking to friends. 'She was chatting away,' said one diner at a table nearby, 'her phone just kept ringing.'

And later, she indulged in a steamy session with her secret lover (*below, right*), whom the *Herald* has identified as Kevin Young, the divorced managing director of one of the city's largest scrap-metal dealers. Young's father, Morris Young, the previous MD, is a colourful figure whose shady business connections resulted in a prison sentence for fencing stolen property.

But DCI Lyons is no stranger to controversy herself. In

2017 she was dismissed from Homicide Command with London's Metropolitan Police for disobeying the orders of a commanding officer to charge a suspect they held in custody. Instead she released Jamie Hinton, a known career criminal – who has not been seen in public since.

Lyons's next stop was Birmingham, her home city, and her current position at Force Homicide. Her move coincided with the murder of her close friend Corinna Legge, whose death was later discovered to have resulted from her own underworld connections in the city.

Whether Lyons will succeed in catching the killer currently terrifying the people of Birmingham remains to be seen – but at least they can be sure that she's not letting the pressure get to her.

*

She had to hand it to Kilmartin: he had a Hitchcock-grade gift for suspense-building. She'd been in front of him for fifteen or twenty seconds now, and he'd yet to utter a word. When Rhona – with a final sympathetic grimace – had opened the door for her, he'd been positioned in his spot in front of the window and he'd stared at her as if he hoped she might just shrivel and die. Then he'd turned his back, repulsed. She'd shot a glance at Samir, who'd shaken his head in warning and looked away.

Silence, apart from the sound of a car on Rose Road and Rhona's typing, barely audible through the firmly closed door. As if calling down the spirits of his ancestors, Kilmartin drew a long, hard breath through his nose and spun around – *Good evening, Wem-ber-leeeeey!* The Freddie Mercury of West Midlands, Robin thought. With tighter trousers.

When – finally – he spoke, his words were staccato, little switch-blade jabs. 'What a shambles. What a complete bloody shambles.'

Robin opened her mouth but was silenced by a glare from Samir.

'Just when we're doing everything we can to reassure the public that the safety of this city is in reliable hands . . . *this*.' He swept a disgusted hand in the direction of Samir's desk, where, presumably, the *Herald* piece was up onscreen. He shook his head, eyes pressed shut, as if words failed him. Freddie would be impressed, Robin thought – what a drama queen.

'With respect, sir,' – *lie* – 'as far as I can tell, the substance of the story is "detective eats sandwich, talks on the phone and has boyfriend". This "information" is presented to make me sound like Nero fiddling while Rome burns when nothing could be further from the truth. The reporting's totally inaccurate. I mean, apart from anything else, I didn't even have the salmon.'

The last bit was a mistake, she saw straight away – Kilmartin was incensed. 'Oh, you think this is amusing in some way, do you? Occasion for some glib humour?'

'Not remotely,' she said. After the initial flood of horror, her first thought had been how Lara's mother would feel when she saw the photographs, as she inevitably would. 'No. I'm mortified by it. Appalled. But as I said, it's inaccurate.'

'Is it?' A flick of the eyebrows.

'Yes. I wasn't "chatting on the phone". I took two calls, one from my DS to tell me a salient detail from the post mortem, another from a private detective with potential information.' She decided to omit the call to Dunnington Road to check on Luke's crazy-level. 'The photograph with Kevin was taken at eleven o'clock at night, and it was a gross invasion of my privacy. It's true that I had lunch but it's also true that I'd been at work for over nine hours by that point yesterday and I'd barely eaten. I went out to get a breath of fresh air and to try to think.'

'I'm not talking about your bloody avocado toast!' Kilmartin roared. 'I'm talking about the fact that you're emblazoned across the Internet in a clinch with the son of a convicted criminal, which information is presented in a consecutive paragraph with the fact that another close friend of yours – now murdered – was also a criminal.'

'Sir, with respect' – Samir's sounded much more convincing – 'Robin and I have both been friends of Kevin's since we were at school and he's completely above board.'

Even his dad was only guilty of buying the odd bit of scrap metal without enquiring too carefully into its origins, Robin was tempted to say; he's hardly Reggie Kray. And what was 'colourful' supposed to mean? Working-class, probably, in *Herald*-speak. As if he knew exactly what she was thinking, Samir shot her another silencing look.

'Even if that *is* the case,' Kilmartin said, 'we all know the story about Corinna Legge *is* true.'

'We also know,' said Samir, 'that it was Robin who *solved* that case, even without being on the team at the time.'

'In fact on *no* team at the time, because she'd been kicked out of the Met.'

'A mistake the Met rectified when the truth about *that* case was discovered,' Samir said calmly. 'DCI Lyons was reinstated in London but chose to accept the offer of a job with us instead.'

'Despite my misgivings due to her having been dragged across the pages of the *Daily Mail* at the time.'

'You demonstrated a faith in my judgement that I've always appreciated in our working relationship, sir. As did she. Robin was one of the youngest DCIs at the Met, her statistics there were impressive to say the least, and yet she chose to join us.' Samir let go of the back of his chair. 'There's no question the piece is highly regrettable – we all agree on that – but as I see it, the important thing here is showing that *we* set the agenda.

We, Force Homicide, West Midlands Police, are running this enquiry, not the *Daily Herald* or any other news outlet.'

'Abso-bloody-lutely,' Kilmartin puffed up his chest.

God, the hypocrisy, Robin thought. It was enough to make you lose your lunch. Had he forgotten that *he* was the one who'd been goaded into announcing they'd arrested someone?

'We can't be told what to do – or be seen to be told – by the media. It's so easy to criticize,' Samir went on. 'Easy for some keyboard-jockey down in London to string together a few salacious-sounding facts and ask why we haven't got someone bang to rights within twenty-four hours. Much, much harder to solve what is beyond doubt a demanding and complicated case.'

'I was right when I said this had the potential to blow up, PR-wise.'

'You were,' Samir nodded. 'Completely right.'

'And I said at the time that I wanted *you* to take this one.'

'It might still be two,' Robin put in.

Wait, Samir's look told her. 'The thing is,' he said, 'if we make a change now, we'll look like we're admitting the *Herald*'s accusations against DCI Lyons have a basis in fact.'

'But—' Kilmartin started.

'And by extension, those accusations imply that the people who put her in the position are incompetent – how could we employ someone who is patently inappropriate, let alone put her in charge of something so important? At DCI level, that reflects badly on all of us, right up the chain of command.' *Not just me, sir: you.*

Robin watched Kilmartin recognize the truth of this, his mouth moving as if he were actually tasting it.

'I have every confidence – I did and I still do – that DCI Lyons is the right person for this job,' Samir said. 'Her record here is exemplary.'

'We've had a significant breakthrough,' said Robin. 'We've now got CCTV of Lara Meikle being pursued by a man two hundred metres from where her body was found, and an eyewitness to him heading away from the scene shortly afterwards. It's a major development.'

Kilmartin looked at her, eyes narrowed. 'And what about this man Gupta?'

'He had nothing to do with either.'

'But, as I understand it, you can't prove he didn't.'

'That's true,' she admitted, 'but we also can't prove he did, and I strongly believe he didn't.'

'Well, it's too late now so let's hope your "strong belief" is correct and he doesn't go and kill someone else, shall we?'

It occurred to Robin suddenly that he was embarrassed – that she'd embarrassed him by not charging Gupta. But that wasn't her fault; he should never have done it. 'Indeed, sir,' she said.

'You will not take matters into your own hands here like you did in London.'

'Sir,' Samir said, 'DCI Lyons consulted me on the decision to let Gupta go, and I agreed with her. We're working closely together and that will continue; she'll keep me informed at every step.'

Robin nodded. 'I will.'

Kilmartin looked between them as if he smelled a rat. 'And you'll keep *me* informed, DCS Jafferi. Every development of note. I will not have this detonating under us – I hope I've made that abundantly clear.'

'Abundantly,' said Robin.

He gave her a final glare, turned on his heel and swept from the room with as much aplomb as someone of his diminutive stature could rustle up. They heard him say a brief goodbye to Rhona – she'd been with West Midlands so long, most of the brass had worked with her – then the solid clunk of the outer door.

Robin exhaled. 'Oof. Is it too early for a drink?'

'What, you'd like the *Herald* to print that picture, too?'

She frowned. 'I'm joking, Samir. Sense of humour?' After the united front, she'd expected some degree of post-battle camaraderie but there was no warmth in his voice at all.

'Humour?' he said. 'It evaporated under the strain of having to kiss his arse to save yours.'

She nodded, chastened. 'I know. Thank you. Really, thank you.'

'Don't make me regret it.'

'I won't.'

'And perhaps you could also do me the favour of conducting your private life in private, at least for the duration?'

She nodded again.

He looked at her, eyes unreadable. 'Did it have to be Kev, Robin?'

Chapter Twenty-three

The new Queen Elizabeth was a behemoth, one of the biggest hospitals in the country. Its main frontage comprised three curved white buildings which, with their bands of lit windows, loomed in the gloaming now like the sterns of three vast ocean-going liners. Leaving, Robin thought, just as she arrived.

When her dad had rung again a little after six o'clock, she'd expected to hear that they were safely back at Dunnington Road, her mum enthroned on the sofa and receiving personal service of a standard Beyoncé might appreciate.

Instead, voice shaking, he'd told her she'd had a stroke.

As they crossed the car park, she looked at Lennie's face, so small and worried, and reached for her hand. Usually this would result in an aggrieved 'Mum, I'm fifteen!' but tonight Len held on as they ran the gauntlet of smokers loitering on the forecourt, a mix of visitors and patients, some in their dressing gowns trailing IV drips on stands. The walking wounded. Hospitals were like pockets of wartime, Robin thought, the life-and-death stakes, the fear, normality suspended for both combatants and those waiting for them at home.

She saw her dad the moment they spun through the revolving

doors. As he crushed Robin's face into the shoulder of his slightly crisp jumper, the scent of Woolite filled her nostrils, summoning an image of her mother rubber-gloved at her tiny utility-room sink pronouncing that while she loved her washing machine, she'd *never* trust it with wool, as if the kind of person who did (Robin) was dangerously unhinged.

'How is she, Dad?'

'I think she's very frightened,' he said, looking very frightened himself. 'She . . .' He stopped and glanced at Lennie.

'It's okay, Grandpa. It's more scary if I think people are keeping stuff back, trying to protect me.'

He looked at Robin for confirmation. 'It's all so sudden,' he said. 'Last night everything was fine and now . . .' He shook his head and she saw a glimpse of him ten or fifteen years into the future, much greyer, weaker. He was almost six foot, her dad, but in this alien setting, surrounded by strangers and powerless to help, he looked small. Vulnerable.

'What are the doctors saying?'

'Not a lot. I don't know how much they *can* say at this point. They've got her blood pressure down a bit, and the nurse keeps coming to see how hard she can hold her hand, whether she's getting any strength back.'

'Is she?'

'*She* says so but . . .'

'You think it's wishful thinking?' Or, more likely, her mum trying to be obliging, hating to be a nuisance.

'I don't know.' He shook his head. 'They keep saying it's early days but her face isn't going back like it did before and it's been nearly four hours.'

'Can she talk, Grandpa?'

'Yes, love, but she's a bit slurred. Like she's been on the sherry.' He tried to smile but faltered.

They'd been getting ready to go home, he'd told Robin on the phone, he'd been talking at the desk when, behind him, he'd heard her mother shriek. He'd spun around as she'd started to throw up, a hand clamped over her eye. Then staff had swarmed from all corners, wheeling in equipment, shunting him and Luke out of the way.

'Seeing you will do her the power of good,' he told Lennie now.

They followed him back through the lobby to the lifts and then along an over-lit corridor lined with double doors. Her mother had still been in A&E when it had happened, but a bed had freed up on the specialist stroke ward a couple of hours later. 'The lady before had been sent home,' her dad told them now, as if it were a good omen.

'Where's Luke? Has he gone?'

'No, he's in the canteen having a bite to eat. Your mother insisted, said the poor lad must be starving.'

So it never stopped, Robin thought, even in here. 'What about you? Have you had anything?'

'Not yet. We could have something together after you've seen her, if you're up for it.'

'I'm up for it,' said Lennie.

They were buzzed through the doors into a long room lined with bays down either side. The patients weren't immediately visible but Robin could feel them, lots of them, breathing and sleeping, zoning out in front of their televisions, lying awake and afraid. The air was over-warm, heavy with layers of disinfectant and the poorly masked human smells underneath. People were ill here, the air told her, very ill.

Her dad introduced them at the nurses' station then led them back through the ward to a bay on the right which held three beds, the first curtained off. Her mother was in the middle and

213

Robin saw her eyes light up the moment Lennie came into view. She'd been lying back against the pillows and tried to push herself upright before remembering that her left arm was useless. Instead, with her right hand, she gripped the metal rail along the side of her bed but she couldn't lift her weight enough to sit up straighter. Her dad was there in a second, one hand supporting her back while the other plumped the pillows and raised the head of the bed with the button.

Lennie went to her first, reaching gingerly around the lines that trailed from the blood-pressure cuff and a cannula in the back of her mother's hand to touch her cheek against hers. 'Oh, Gran, what have you done now?' she said, trying to smile. 'Look at you.'

Robin was grateful she didn't have to talk straight away; the inside of her throat had swollen. Her mother's face. The droop was shocking – the asymmetry of it. It was as if the comedy and tragedy theatre masks had been broken in half and smashed back together with the wrong partner: the right side was unaltered, the eye crinkling, the corner of her mouth lifting as she tried to smile pleasure and reassurance at Lennie, but her left eye was hooded by the soft folds of her fallen eyelid, and beneath it, the corner of her mouth sagged, unresponsive, as if she'd had an anaesthetic at the dentist.

And fenced into the bed, she looked so small. Her upper body disappeared among the pillows; her legs reached barely half the length of the cellular blanket. The lump in Robin's throat wouldn't budge. In reality, her mother was five feet four but to her, she was enormous, a towering pillar of power and energy and scathing judgement. Now the power was disconnected and she was reduced to normal – fragile – human proportions.

Lennie moved away to let her say hello and Robin leaned in to kiss her cheek. She smelled different – no perfume. Of course, she'd woken up having already had the mini-stroke and they'd come straight here: she hadn't had time to shower and dress. Or to put on her make-up – that was missing, too, and shocking in itself. When had her mother last been seen in public without make-up? The Seventies? When had *she* last seen her without make-up, even having lived with her for eight months last year? Every morning before breakfast, without fail, she put on her make-up, her perfume, her earrings. 'Self-discipline!' For her mother, a pyjama day was a sign of moral bankruptcy. Every day was game day. Except this one.

'Mum,' she managed croakily.

'Thanks for coming, love,' her mother said, voice slurred as her father had described but slow, too, as if forming the words took effort.

To her horror, Robin's eyes filled with tears.

'Of course we were going to come!' She blinked hard, sniffing, and looked at her dad across the bed. Had he explained why she hadn't come straight away, the moment he'd called this morning? Did her mum know that?

Movement behind her. She turned to see Lennie carrying a stacking chair. 'Here, Mum.'

'No, you sit nearest to Gran, it's you she wants to see, not me.' She tried to smile.

Lennie gave her a weird look but brought over a second chair then took the first. 'Do you need the bars up, Gran, or can we let them down for a bit?'

'You can let . . .' said the slow, strange voice.

Dennis was on his feet in an instant, cranking the bars up to release them, folding them gently down. Lennie reached for the hand without the line.

'How are you feeling?' Robin managed. She could see saliva shining at the corner of her mother's mouth. She would hate that – was she aware of it? Could she feel it, even?

'All right,' came the response. 'Bit tired.'

Translation: horrendous and exhausted. Robin nodded.

Lennie stood and reached for a tissue from the table across the bed. 'Here, Gran.' She folded it and dabbed the corner of her mouth. Robin saw her mother's look of gratitude. Why hadn't she done that? For very far from the first time, she marvelled that even at fifteen, her daughter was far the superior human being.

'Poor you, it must be so scary.'

'Bit of a shock.' Christine's right eye looked at Lennie, shining with love.

'But they've got you, Gran, the team here. I looked it up on the Net, the stroke ward – everyone was talking about how great they are. They'll look after you and soon you'll be right as rain and you'll come home.'

'Hope so.' The saliva was back and now her eyes were shining with tears.

'You will. I know it.' Lennie squeezed her hand. 'You're tough, Gran. A tough nut. It'd take more than something like this to stop you.'

Her mother attempted a word that came out as a sob. She was trying to stop herself crying in front of Lennie, Robin saw, to hide her fear and pain. Her dad knew it, too, and to aid the effort, he sprung up again and started fiddling about with the scratched plastic jug, adding the barest top-up to the already brimming cup of water on the table.

'Here you are, love.' He picked it up carefully and brought it to her, placing the straw in her mouth beyond the useless lip. It cost her mother effort to swallow and to her dad's visible panic, she choked slightly. She held up her hand, *I'm okay*, and sank back deeper into the pillows. Lennie dabbed some water from her chin then startled as a loud electronic whirr started up behind her.

'The blood-pressure monitor,' her dad said as the cuff on her mother's arm started to inflate. 'It's automatic, takes a reading every fifteen minutes.'

Her mother grimaced as the cuff crushed her arm before slowly deflating. All four of them watched the numbers on the digital display as they clicked down: 174 over 116.

From behind the curtain of the neighbouring bed emerged a nurse whose generous hour-glass shape, accentuated by a wide elasticated belt, spoke of the open tin of Quality Street Robin had seen at the desk rather than the dietary advice they doubt-less dispensed around here. She peered at the machine. 'That's gone up a bit again, love, hasn't it? Nice and calm now, lots of deep breaths. Let me guess – your daughter and granddaughter?'

'Yes,' her dad answered for her.

'I can tell – really strong family resemblance, isn't there?'

'Peas in a pod,' he said.

Were they? Robin was surprised. In photographs of her as a young child, seven or eight, she could see it but as an adult, she didn't think she looked particularly like her mother at all, and she'd always thought Lennie must look more like her own father.

The nurse added the reading to her mother's chart then moved away.

'How's work?' The voice came from the bed, aimed at Robin.

'*My* work? Oh, Mum, don't worry about that – you don't need to be thinking about . . .'

'Tell me.'

Robin glanced round, conscious of the bed behind them and the man she guessed was the husband of the ancient woman lying there, her hair a puff of white smoke against the pillow. Lowering her voice, she told her about the new lead from the CCTV footage. 'It was on *Midlands Today* and the *Post* have it, too, you know, Maggie's friend, Sara?'

Her mother gave a small nod; she didn't know Sara, but Maggie talked about her.

Sweating slightly, Robin undid the second button on her shirt and pushed her cuffs back. On the way over, she'd shown Lennie the *Herald* piece, and told her she was going to keep completely schtum about it because her mother would be mortified. Given the circumstances, maybe she'd finally literally mortify her, kill her with sheer embarrassment. A tart, as her mother had once called her; an unmarried mother far too young and then a third-rate one at that, always at work; bovver-booted, leather-jacketed antithesis of her natural elegance with a job that meant dealing with some of the worst that humanity had to offer – and, in the past couple of years, being publicly shamed in the papers for the privilege. It was fair to say she hadn't made her proud.

'Does Maggie know?' she asked.

'Yes,' her dad nodded. 'I rang her this afternoon. She's going to come and see your mother tomorrow morning.'

'That's good.'

'Will you say hello?' Lennie said. 'You know, you should all come over for dinner at ours when you're out and about, Gran. Mum and I could cook for you for a change.'

Christine smiled crookedly and her hand tightened on Lennie's. 'I'd like that.'

Fifteen minutes later, when the cuff told them that her mother's pressure had risen again, the nurse checked it manually, too. She frowned. 'And you're quite flushed as well, sweetheart,' she told her. 'You need to rest now.'

'We'll go and find Luke,' her dad said. 'Get these girls something to eat.'

Her mum looked at him, good eye wide. 'Will you come back up, Dennis, afterwards?'

'Of course, love. Of course I will.' He leaned over the bed and kissed her forehead. 'I'm here till you tell me otherwise.'

Lennie kissed her goodbye, too, and Robin told her they'd come again tomorrow.

She nodded and Robin thought she saw tears in her eyes. 'Off you go,' she said, lifting her hand off the blanket.

They started to walk away but when they turned near the nurses' station to give her a last wave, her mother called, 'Robin.' They all started to walk back but she said, quite firmly, 'Only Robin.'

'I'll come and find you down there,' she told them.

As she walked back, she was suddenly nervous, a feeling that sharpened when her mother reached for her hand. A fat blue vein ran down her forehead and disappeared beneath her left eyebrow and Robin had the awful idea that it was a worm. An omen. Did *she* think she was going to die? Was that why she wanted to talk to her?

Her mother's one-handed grip tightened, thumb pressing into her palm. Robin felt the hard semi-circle of the nail and her mother's shining eyes locked onto hers. 'Look after your brother.'

The words hit her in the chest, temporarily knocking the wind out of her. 'Look after your brother' – *that* was what she wanted to say to her *in extremis*? Nothing personal, nothing about them and *their* relationship, just look after her sodding brother?

'He's in a state,' her mother said slowly, her nail still cutting into Robin's palm. 'Now this.' She moved her head, indicating the ward. 'He needs your support.'

The lump in her throat was back. Robin blinked and swallowed. She nodded. 'Okay,' she said. 'Okay, yes. I will.'

'Thank you.' Her mother gave her hand a squeeze then let go.

*

She found her dad standing in front of the hot-food counter as if he'd been hypnotized by the tray of cottage pie desiccating under the heat lamps. She put a hand on his back and he jumped.

'Okay, Dad?'

'What? Oh. Yes.'

'Where's Len?'

'Getting some teas.' He pointed to an island in the centre over whose various drink-making machines Robin could see the top of her daughter's head.

'Doesn't look too bad, does it, the food?' she said. 'Better than the canteen at work by a long chalk.' Maybe she should start eating here instead – maybe the *Herald* would like that more.

The woman serving had evidently given up waiting for her dad and moved away to spray the counter at the back. 'Excuse me?' Robin called her.

'Sorry, love.' She put down her cloth and came over. 'What can I get you?'

'The chicken and chips, please.'

'Same for me please,' her dad told her, then to Robin, 'I was thinking about the cottage pie but it wouldn't be a patch on your mother's. I can't believe she's up there, like that, so poorly, while we're . . . I feel sick, Rob. Totally sick. What if . . . ?'

Lennie reappeared holding two beige plastic cups by their rims. 'I'll keep yours on my tray, Grandpa, probably easier. They're thermo-nuclear.' She must have seen how his hands were shaking.

It was dusk, Robin noticed while they were waiting to pay, the brightness of the lights inside making it look much darker than it was. The room was huge and as busy as an airport lounge, almost every table taken even at this time of the evening. She scanned about for her brother. She'd assumed he was alone so it was a moment before she spotted him sitting with someone

220

else. The man had his back to her, more or less, and she could only see part of the side of his face but Luke's posture, hunched forward, elbows on the table, suggested he knew him.

'Who's that, Dad?'

He saw where she was looking. 'Billy.'

'Billy? What – Hideous?'

'Robin.'

'What's *he* doing here?'

'He rang earlier and your brother told him what happened.'

'But why's he *here*?'

'He was nearby, apparently, and he said he'd keep Luke company for a bit while you saw your mother. No fun for him, sitting down here on his own, worrying.'

Bloody hell, she thought, there were toddlers who got less babysitting. What was it like to go through life being so coddled? No one would even ask her how she was. Or Lennie, for that matter, she realized.

They carried their trays over and she borrowed a fifth chair from the next table. 'Hi Len,' Luke said.

'How are you, Billy?' Robin asked, sitting. 'I don't think I've seen you since I went to university.'

It was a genuine observation and the truth but she realized as soon as she said it how it would be interpreted – *since I left you thicko losers in the dust*. Even her dad gave her a warning look.

'Well, *you* haven't changed,' Billy said.

He had, at least physically. He'd always been a squirrelly little thing, modern-day Dickensian, amusement-arcade pale and under-nourished, struggling to fill the jeans that he'd had to strap round his hips with a belt whose excess length she remembered him cutting off at Dunnington Road with her mother's knife. His face was still squirrelly, his eyes a surprisingly dark

221

brown given the rest of his colour scheme, his nose blade-like. The difference was in his upper body which was now beefed up to almost comic proportions. His pecs made clear squares under his tight T-shirt and his arms were so bulky they didn't lie flush against his torso. He caught her looking and gave her a knowing smile, *Yeah? Like what you see?*

'How is she?' Luke asked.

'Her pressure's up.' Their dad picked up his fork and then put it down again.

'What is it?'

'The last one was 172 over 126.'

Luke sucked air in over his teeth, nodding as if he were a cardiologist. 'That's getting back near what it was straight after.'

'The nurse said she needed a break. That's why we're down so soon.'

Luke glared at Robin. 'What did you say to her?'

'Nothing. God, why . . . ?'

'Oh, come on, we all know how you wind her up.'

'Luke, that's not fair,' said her dad.

He huffed. 'Really?' He took a sip from his can of Tango. 'Nice picture of you and lover-boy, by the way – did you show her that?'

'What are you talking about?' asked her dad, frowning. 'What picture?'

Robin gave Luke a what-the-hell-is-wrong-with-you stare. 'I didn't want to tell you, Dad, *I* thought you'd got enough on your plate.' She brought the story up on her phone and handed it to him, watching him frown as he read it.

'It's not true, is it, love?'

'That I'm sitting round twiddling my thumbs while a serial killer stalks Birmingham? No, I'd say not.'

'Camera doesn't lie about Kevin Young, though, does it?' said Luke.

'No,' she admitted, keeping her eyes trained on her plate to avoid meeting Lennie's.

'Couldn't believe my eyes the other day – you and that wide boy.'

What, when we came to bail you out? she barely refrained from saying. *Talk you down from throwing yourself in front of the 6.32 from Birmingham Moor Street?*

'Del Boy!'

Hideous made a kind of snorting sound. 'At least this one's white.'

Robin saw Lennie's mouth literally fall open. She shot an anguished glance at the table next door where a Sikh family were quietly eating.

'Don't,' Robin said in a low voice. 'Just don't, either of you. Keep your disgusting racist views to yourselves and away from my daughter. And for the record, Kev's twice the man either of you is and he always has been.'

'He's a sodding gyppo, Rob,' sneered Luke. 'I mean, we all know you're into your ethnic minorities but—'

'Luke!' Dennis snapped. 'Stop it!'

'He's not a gypsy,' Robin said, 'but even if he was, what difference would it make?' She stood up. 'I'm really sorry, Dad, but we're going to go. I'm at my limit – I can't deal with the poison tonight on top of everything else.'

She expected him to try and talk her down, attempt his usual peace-brokering, but he merely nodded. 'Okay, love.'

'I'll ring you later. Come on, Len.'

Lennie was already standing. She put her arms round Dennis from behind and gave him a kiss on the cheek. 'Bye, Grandpa. Tell Gran I'll be thinking about her all the time.'

They took their trays of barely touched food to the racks for the dishwashers. 'I'm sorry,' Robin said. 'But I couldn't sit there and listen to that. We'll get something to eat at home.'

'No need to say sorry to *me*,' Lennie said hotly. 'If we'd stayed a minute longer, I would have chucked the tea at them. Wankers.'

'Granny and Grandpa really love each other, don't they?' Len said as they pulled out of the car park.

'Yep. Truly, madly, deeply. They always have.'

'It's lovely.' She leaned her head against the window.

'Yes, it is.' Except that if something happened to one of them, the other would be destroyed, ripped up by the roots. *I feel sick, Robin. Totally sick.* She'd been scared by that. Her dad wasn't an emotional basket-case like she was but he never talked to *her* about his feelings. She'd realized then how terrified he was. That was the trouble with loving people: it left you so bloody vulnerable. Much easier to keep your heart ring-fenced, she found. Except that she hadn't, had she, said the voice in her head, because sitting beside her right now was someone on whose safety her entire happiness depended. God, don't think about that now – too much, too much.

'Shall we ring the Lebanese?' she said. 'If we order something easy, it might be ready by the time we get there.'

Lennie trained her eyes on the road. 'Why didn't you tell me about Kev?'

'What?'

'You heard me, Mum.'

Robin signalled left off the roundabout and tried to think. No lies, of course, but . . . Oh, Christ. 'The truth is,' she said, 'I didn't tell you because I don't know how I feel about him and I didn't want you to think . . .' *That I'm a slapper. That I sleep around. That I sleep with people I don't care about. That that's the way things work.* 'You're at the start of it all, Len, and I don't want to be a bad example. I know I haven't been a great example.'

224

Silence from the passenger seat. The spectre of Lennie's father hovered between them, unknown. Unnamed.

'I meant what I said about Kev. He's solid. He's a good person – funny, bright, loyal. He'd do anything for his friends. And he's not a "wide boy" – Luke just can't stand that he's successful.'

'But his dad *did* go to prison. I looked that up on the Net, too.'

'His dad, yes, not him.' *God, Len,* she nearly said, *if people are going to be defined by their parents, you're stuffed.*

'So why don't you?'

'What?'

'Know how you feel about him.' Spelling it out for the hard-of-understanding.

'I don't know.'

'Oh, come on, Mum, don't give me this bullshit!'

'Lennie, please don't talk to me like . . .'

'I know you, remember? You *always* know what you think, you're not all . . . crap and indecisive.'

'Well then, if you want the truth, I think it's because I'd never thought of him like that till it happened. He kissed me one night, and it all . . . It took me by surprise. But I like him. I do.' It was true.

'Right.' *Finally, an answer.* 'But.'

'But what?'

'*But.* You're still being all weird about it, sneaking out of the house. Even when I asked you straight out the other night, you didn't admit it.'

'Because I don't know if it's going anywhere – I didn't want you to think—'

'That's rubbish,' said Lennie. 'It's got nothing to do with me. You can't be straight about it because you're still all hung up about what happened with Samir.'

Robin opened her mouth to remonstrate but she hadn't finished.

'You've got to sort it out, Mum. It was nearly twenty years ago and yes, I know you've had a lot on, but it's time now – *really* time. You've got to move on or you're never going to have a real relationship.' She paused. 'And it's not fair on other people.'

She was talking about Adrian, Robin knew, her last boyfriend back in London. He'd asked her to marry him, and though she'd never told Lennie, he'd wanted to adopt her formally, for the three of them to be a proper family. Len would have loved it, she loved Ade, but Robin hadn't been able to do it. *But.*

'You can't get involved with people only to string them along. It's cruel.'

Cruel? 'I don't get involved only to . . . I would never do that.'

'I think you should talk to someone.'

'*What?*'

'A therapist. A shrink. Being a commitment-phobe doesn't make you all cool and independent, if that's what you think, it turns you into a . . . a human hand-grenade. Anyone gets too close, you blow up in their face.'

For the second time of the evening, Robin felt like she'd been punched.

'I'm not a grenade,' she said ridiculously. 'I don't want to be a grenade.'

'So do something about it. Unless,' Lennie turned her face away, 'you don't want to.'

'What's that supposed to mean?'

'Maybe you don't want to get over what happened.'

'I . . .'

'Because if you *do*, it'll mean you've finally accepted it, won't it? That it's done and dusted. Actually over.'

*

Robin closed her bedroom door and got back into bed. She'd drunk two thirds of a bottle of wine the moment they'd got home, then two large glasses of water to counteract it, and she'd already been up twice to pee. Yet another reason she couldn't get to sleep.

She pulled the duvet around her shoulders and turned on to her side, catching the lingering scent of Kevin's hair from the other pillow. She reached across and laid her hand over the empty space on the mattress. Did she wish he was here? No reason why he couldn't be at this point – that cat was well and truly out of the bag; there was no one to hide it from now. Well, apart from her mother but it wasn't Kev she'd wanted to keep hidden from her, just the embarrassment of the story in the paper. Christine cared so much what other people thought, people she didn't even know; she'd feel the shame at a deep level. And of course, loads of her friends did read the *Herald* so it *would* be people she knew.

No, the hand resting out there where Kev had slept was an apology. It said sorry – sorry you were pulled into this, that they dragged your dad's past up again. And sorry I'm apparently a human hand-grenade. Was she, though? Was that fair? Lennie didn't know she was going to blow up in Kev's face – *she* didn't even know if she was going to. People were allowed time, weren't they, to see how things went, to decide? You couldn't always know straight away.

Streetlight glowed through the curtains. She'd kept her mouth shut because she didn't want to fight with Lennie – and Len had enough to worry about herself, with her grandmother in hospital and her mother splashed across the news snogging her new boyfriend – but alone in the semi-darkness she acknowledged that she was angry with her. She *wasn't* cruel – she'd never consciously gone into something and let someone start liking her while knowing it was doomed. She wouldn't do that.

Maybe not consciously, no, said the small voice in her head. But perhaps not *so* subconsciously, either.

Oh, for God's sake – now she was too hot. She got out of bed again, went to the window and shoved up the sash. Lovely cool air moved around her bare legs and she leaned her forehead against the cold glass before imagining some scrote photographer with a long lens trained on her. She'd checked the street earlier, looking in all the parked cars down both sides, but it didn't mean there was no one there now lying in wait for Kev to roll up for another 'tryst'.

For a moment she wished he would. She'd like that, to go down to the car and chat with the lights of the city as their audience, it would be comforting, and if they came back up here, to bed, they'd have sex and he'd make her forget everything for a little while.

But it would only be for a little while and afterwards, when he fell asleep, she'd be alone again.

Alone. Back in bed, duvet kicked all the way off now, she examined the word as if it was a shell she'd picked up on the beach. She wasn't alone, she was surrounded by people, more now than for years – Lennie, her parents, Luke and Natalie, Kev, Samir, her team at work. Between the lot of them, she barely got a minute's peace.

But when it came down to it, like today, she *was* alone. Her parents were wrapped up in their own fears, of course (though her mother still had the disk-space to worry about Luke) and Samir, whom she'd thought was on her side, had frozen her out the second Kilmartin left the room. Even Lennie thought she was a nutter. A *cruel* nutter. Well, maybe she was right – what did it say about you when your own daughter thought other people needed protecting from you?

But on the other hand, said the voice in her head, there were also people who needed *her* protection and support – Luke, according to her mother; Lennie herself; the women in her case.

God, all this protection, all this care – who protected *her*?

Samir.

His name arrived in her head before she could stop it. She batted it away but it was true. He'd protected her from Kilmartin before, and he'd done it again today, even when he was furious with her. Alongside Maggie, he'd saved Lennie's life, and he'd asked her to apply for her job here *before* he knew the Met had offered her old one back. And, she could see now, if she squinted at it from the right angle, that he'd tried to protect her – albeit moronically – by breaking up with her.

She felt the truth of it glow behind her ribs. Well, they were friends, she told herself briskly, that's what friends did. She was trying to protect *him* from Kilmartin's wrath by solving this case and proving he'd been right to hire her.

And maybe it was why she was fond of Kev, too. Kev was a care-taker – he looked after his parents, he doted on his girls and, she realized, he was taking care of her as well, as far as she'd let him, coming with her to get Luke, checking she was okay when she didn't reply to his texts, trying to take her out to dinner somewhere proper. But if that was what she wanted, protection, *his* protection, why had she felt a chime of guilty recognition when Lennie said she was going to blow up in his face?

Chapter Twenty-four

'Mum!'

She opened her eyes to find Lennie standing over her, shaking her by the shoulder. 'What? What's the matter?' The room was light – shit, what time was it? Had she overslept? She reached for her phone in its spot on the bedside table but it wasn't there. Then, a chill hand round her heart, she remembered her mother.

'Didn't you hear the phone?' Len was saying. 'The landline – it rang twice. I thought you were going to get it. Here.' She thrust the handset at her.

'Who is it?'

'Samir.'

She peered at it – muted, thankfully. 'What time is it?'

'Half past six.'

Robin sat up, cleared her throat then hit 'unmute'. 'Hello?'

'Where are you? I've been calling your mobile but it's going straight to voicemail. Have you turned it off?'

'No, of course not.' But evidently she'd forgotten to plug it in overnight. It must be out of battery. 'What is it? What's going on?'

'Dhanesh Gupta's dead.'

*

Three quarters of an hour later, she let herself into his office. 'Fuck, Samir – fuck, fuck, *fuck*.'

He was at his desk, fingertips pressed against his lips, face expressionless. Nothing was on – the computer was silent, the desk lamp, which he almost always kept on 'for atmosphere' was dark.

'We still made the right decision,' he said.

'What?' She recoiled.

'We questioned a man, believed him to be innocent – had incontrovertible proof of it in one case – then released him. We did the right thing.'

'We released him so that he could be hunted down and killed.'

'No,' he said. 'We released him. What was the alternative? Keep him in custody with no justification? Charge him with something he didn't do? His murder is his killer's fault. It's the fault of Ben Tyrell and his crowd, saying he must have done it.' He hesitated then glanced at the door, making sure it was shut. 'And it's the fault of the person who announced,' he said quietly, 'after we'd published the CCTV picture, that we'd arrested a *suspect*.'

They looked at each other.

'Not that he'll see it like that. In fact, there's a good chance he'll try and throw it back on us – *we* shouldn't have arrested him in the first place, *we* told him he was a suspect—'

'We didn't – we were clear on that. We told him.'

'I know that.'

'We should have offered Gupta *protection*, Samir – *that* was the alternative. We knew Tyrell was firing up his mob, waving his picture around, and who knows how many other maniacs were thinking about it? There could be fifty who'd had the same idea – protect the "womenfolk", the *white* womenfolk, clean the streets yourself because the police are incompetent.'

'I know.'

'I failed him,' she said. 'I hung him out to dry. I knew there was a chance something like this could happen.' She shook her head in despair. 'We had the city centre crew keeping an eye out for him, but he'd gone to ground. I should have done more – we should have had everyone out looking for him.'

Samir rubbed his mouth, looking sick. 'We just don't have that sort of manpower.'

'He must have been terrified.'

Strangely, it had been the rows of men in the gloom of the Ford Transit she'd thought of first when she heard, their eyes wide with fear. They'd seen police and been afraid of being stopped – stopped getting paid peanuts to work twelve hours a day to pick food for a country too lazy to pick its own. Of being deported away from that privilege.

And Gupta's face when the arrest team had lifted him to his feet. He'd definitely been afraid but she'd seen resignation, too. He hadn't been stunned when Varan told him he was being arrested on suspicion of murder: that was the kind of thing that happened to him here. He'd been lied to, defrauded of tens of thousands of pounds, reduced to sleeping in a derelict factory, then in shop doorways; being falsely accused of murder can't have seemed much of a stretch.

And now he'd *been* murdered.

Amit Kapoor had seen it happen from his shop. Gupta had arrived before the van, he'd told Response, and was waiting for it in the usual spot, usual clothes, same cap and rucksack, when a man had calmly walked down the pavement and stopped. At first Kapoor thought he was talking to him, asking him the time or directions, but then he'd guessed they must know each other because Gupta had bent forward as if to hug him. Only several seconds later, when the other man strode away and Gupta collapsed to the pavement had he understood that it had been an attack. He'd raced outside to find Gupta pumping blood from knife wounds in his stomach. He'd died in his arms, before the ambulance could reach them, before Tom Peterson had arrived to pick him up for work.

'I'm giving the case to Webster,' Samir said.

Robin stared. 'You can't. That's—'

'Wait,' he held up his hand. 'Gupta, not the women. Unless – did he say *anything* in his interviews that would give their killer reason to kill *him*? Did he see him at Gisborne's? Could he have identified him?'

She shook her head. 'He had no information at all. He was asleep next door, oblivious. The first time he knew something was wrong was when he got back from work on Sunday and found police there.'

'That's what I thought. Which makes it much more likely it's a separate case. Linked now, after the fact, but separate.'

'Just because he didn't know anything doesn't mean the Gisborne Girl's killer *knew* he didn't. We can't assume that. I want to do it, Samir. Please let me do it. I owe him that – the least I can do for him is—'

'Rob, what you can do for him is give us the best shot of catching his killer, and that is not you.'

'What?'

'How can you give it your full attention?' he demanded. 'How? There's no way. You've got two active murders already, you're being hounded by the media *and* Kilmartin, and on top of all that, your mother's in hospital. Let someone else help him.'

'But—'

'You don't have to do everything, Robin, I thought you'd learned that lesson. In fact,' his eyebrows went up, 'thinking you do is more than slightly arrogant, don't you reckon? You're the only one who can do it? Come on, allow other people some oxygen.'

Smarting, she said nothing.

He sighed. 'Webster has the bandwidth at the moment, that's all I'm saying. If anyone asks much more of you, you're going to combust.'

The Robin of old would have argued but this one knew he was right.

'He'll be SIO on Gupta but obviously we're all in this together. This is going to be teamwork big time, total transparency, every whisker of potentially significant information shared right away.'

She nodded. 'Of course.'

'And we're going to need a united front. Because the media are going to be all over this – all over *you*, given your history. And Kilmartin's going to be breathing fire, so we've got to be ready for that as well. He likes Webster, as we know, another reason for him to handle it.'

Likes him because he's a man, Robin thought, and unchallenging. Webster was good police, reliable, but he was never going to come steaming up the career ladder to threaten him.

'Right now,' said Samir as if he'd read her mind, 'Kilmartin's going to be feeling vulnerable. He's made a big mistake and he'll be pedalling like hell to spin it, not least to himself. I haven't heard from him yet but he'll be on the phone as soon as he's worked out his angle, and we need to be ready. On balance, I don't think he'll have the gall to try to pin it on you and say you told him Gupta was a suspect . . .'

'Wouldn't he love that, though?'

He tipped his head, conceding. 'Probably. But he knows *I* know the truth, so my guess is he'll have "forgotten". I saw him do that once, before you joined – it wasn't as bad as this but he dissociated so thoroughly that, after a while, he literally didn't even remember what had happened. It was kind of impressive in a disturbing way. Trump-like. Anyway, if that's the way it goes – however it goes – we're not going to say anything about what he did. Zero.'

'A man's dead, Samir!'

He held up his hand again. 'We're not going to say anything *yet*. What's done is done, Gupta's dead and beyond help. Our priority is catching his killer, and whoever killed the two women, and for us to do that, I need you to be running the case.'

'We're going to sweep it under the carpet, you mean?' she said, incredulous.

'No.' He shook his head. 'Absolutely not. But much as it'll hurt, for now we're going to keep our mouths shut about Kilmartin's part in it. We'll see what myth we're playing along with and then tolerate it long enough that he'll allow us to catch these bastards.'

'God, Samir.' She shook her head in wonder.

'What?'

'If the policing doesn't work out, you should really consider international diplomacy.'

'Me and Henry Kissinger,' he said, holding up crossed fingers. 'How's your mother this morning? Any word?'

'I called Dad from the car. The same, he says. No improvement.'

Gupta's death had acted on the incident room like a nerve agent through the air-conditioning. People who'd heard the news before arriving carried it in with them; Robin could tell who knew by their posture as they walked through the door, and she watched it act on those who were hearing now, the energy they'd brought from hectic family breakfasts, school runs and commutes disappearing in seconds, as if the carpet were sucking it out through the soles of their shoes.

Local social media accounts were on fire and by nine o'clock, several journalists had managed to weasel their way past the switchboard. 'Anyone gets through, send 'em straight to the press office,' she'd told the team. 'Don't engage, don't even tell them what you're doing; just hit the button.'

They gathered in front of her for the briefing, every face sombre. They'd done nothing wrong, any of them, and yet, like her, they felt responsible. Her chest surged with what she thought was pity until she identified it as empathy and gratitude. They didn't think they'd screwed up or that *she'd* screwed up; they were full of sorrow and they wanted to know how to deal with it. They wanted comfort in the form of action. Direction. *What do we do now? Tell us how we can make this better.*

'We're going to catch the man – or men – who killed Lara Meikle and the Gisborne Girl,' she said. 'We're going to clear Dhanesh Gupta's name beyond any shadow of a doubt. That's what we can do for him now. We are going to channel all the anger – the impotent rage – we feel about what has happened to him into proving his innocence.

'Maybe some of you have strong views about arranged marriages or marrying for a passport – that it's wrong, shouldn't be done. I'm going to ask you to remember that life is compli-cated. Nuanced. Gupta's aim wasn't to sponge off the state or steal jobs. He wanted to make his father proud by making a success of his life, and he thought he could do that here. That was his view of the UK. That was his compliment to us. There's a father in Bangalore who'll have his heart broken today. Let's show him that people like the man who killed his son are not who this country is. We're going to be responsible for proving to Gupta's family that although some elements here *are* full of hate, this is still a place where justice is served. That's in our power. That's what we can and will do.'

Amit Kapoor, Webster told her, was distraught. Robin remembered his excitement at the idea of helping catch a serial killer and wanted to weep for him. 'Yeah, he thinks it's his fault,' Webster told her. 'He keeps saying that if he hadn't tipped us off, it would never have happened. He died right in front of him – *on* him. He'd pulled him up on to his knees, to get him off the pavement. He was drenched in blood when Response got there. His wife went out to see what was going on and she's beside herself, too. Horrific.'

'Will you let me know when you interview Ben Tyrell?' she asked. 'I want to see him.'

'But as you said before, it might not have had anything to do with him. Plenty of other people spitting the same bile, online and otherwise.'

'But the combination of bile and the arrest video – he might as well have put out instructions.'

It was the video, they thought, that must have told Gupta's killer where to find him. In the background behind the van, behind the close-ups of their faces, hers and Varan's and Gupta's, the names of the shops across the road from Kapoor's were clearly visible: a travel agent, a Balti house. Tapping the names into Google was all it would have taken.

'Hard to prove, though,' said Webster. 'If he'd posted the video at the same time, it'd be easier. But because there was an hour between them, and the specifics came first . . .'

'Well, we know he's crafty,' she said. 'Cyber have been saying that from the start.'

Varan hadn't heard the news before he arrived. Robin had seen him come in, early as usual, earbuds in as usual – she had no idea what kind of music he was into but she'd once had the mental image of him pumping himself up in front of the bathroom mirror to 'The Eye of the Tiger' and now she was stuck with it. He'd sat down at his desk, turned on his computer and was peering at a Post-It he'd left for himself when Malia put her hand on his shoulder. He jumped, took out the earbud and gave her a smile which melted off his face in seconds, like snow brought inside.

He'd sat quietly for a couple of minutes, hands in his lap, head bowed, and Robin was on the point of going to make sure he was all right when he stood up suddenly and strode across the room to her office. She thought he was going to do something totally out of character and yell at her, lay the blame at her feet – and personally, at least, she would have been fine with that – but instead he closed her door behind him and without preamble said, 'I want to tell him.'

'Tell who what?'

'Gupta's father.'

It rolled over her, something very close to love, she thought afterwards, a profound appreciation for him mixed with a pride that was undeniably maternal. (God, what was happening to her?) She remembered the first time she'd met him, less than eighteen months ago even now, sitting on her parents' daft aqua-seashell sofa writing down her every word with an earnestness more appropriate to transcribing the tablets from the Ark of the Covenant than her scattered drivel that day and she was proud. He might look like a teenager but he was as grown up as they came.

She shook her head. 'No.'

'Why?' He pulled himself up, ready to argue.

'Because you're here, in Birmingham, and he's in Bangalore. We can't tell him over the phone, Varan, it needs to be done in person. There's a consulate – we're in touch with them now.'

He sagged, recognizing she was right.

'Sit down a minute,' she said.

He did as he was told, taking the chair whose frayed electric-blue fabric exposed the crumbling yellow sponge underneath. 'I wanted to tell him that we liked him,' he said. 'That he wasn't completely on his own here – that he'd made friends in the van, and we liked him. We *saw* him, what he was like. We knew he was a decent bloke.'

Chapter Twenty-five

They were in gear, foot to the floor, engine roaring, with the handbrake stuck on. The collective will was like a generator in the room, she could almost hear it humming, but there was nothing to plug it into, or nothing new.

The frustration was making it hard to sit down. She was prowling the incident room like a panther (*Cougar, you mean*, said the voice in her head unhelpfully) and it was freaking people out. They liked her contained in the glass tank of her office, locatable through the interior window, not looming up behind them every five minutes to see what was going on. Allow people some oxygen, Robin, she told herself. Let them breath. God, it was tough, though.

The problem was, she was deoxygenated herself. They needed another lead. After the CCTV of Lara's attacker yesterday, she'd thought they were full steam ahead but there'd been nothing new since the taxi driver.

The threat of an obstruction charge had galvanized the phone company but when they'd finally arrived, Lara's records hadn't helped them either, or at least not yet. In an ideal world, there would have been a call in the narrow window between her parting ways with Cat Rainsford and appearing on film with her attacker at 12.21, she'd have told her attacker – or he'd have been able to work out – that she was walking home. But the last person she'd spoken to had been her partner, David Pearce, a few minutes before eleven, and he wasn't tall enough to be the man in the tape and he'd been two hundred miles away at the time.

Malia had dispatched people to do another round of house-to-house, re-interview the neighbours. 'Someone must have seen something,' she'd told them. 'Did he disappear into a building somewhere? Get into a car? If he got on a night bus, *someone* must have noticed that he was covered in blood.'

Unless he'd changed his clothes, Robin thought. In the darkness of the alley where he'd killed her, had he also changed into clean clothes, scrubbed his hands and face with baby wipes that he then tucked carefully away in his backpack? Given the attention to detail elsewhere, it didn't seem impossible.

She went back to her desk now, reminding herself that this was what detective work was, the patient building of a picture, brushstroke by brushstroke. People were caught by forensics and the painstaking putting-together of CCTV and ANPR, phone records, bank and witness statements, not opium-fuelled flights of blinding genius.

Some genius was what they needed, though. Or some luck.

Maybe the tape from the place on Warwick Street with the honeymooning boss would come up trumps. It had finally come in, and Tark was on it himself. 'It's decent,' he'd told her, 'in terms of what we can see. Obviously, the focus is on their place, not Gisborne's, but the angle gives us a length of the pavement on that side of the road. I'll keep you posted.'

'Soon as you like,' she'd said.

Clicking in to her inbox, she highlighted another three emails from reporters and deleted them. She opened a red-flagged message from the guy at the CPS, hit 'reply' and typed 'Dear Stephen'. Then she stood up and went back out to the main room.

They'd run out of space on the free-standing board so yesterday she'd asked one of the admins for another to put alongside, and even the new one was a third full already. By contrast, the wall board was still almost empty. Avoiding the picture of Gupta, Robin looked at the Gisborne Girl's deathly-pale face.

Maybe they *would* be lucky, and in finding Lara's killer, which surely they'd do first, they'd also find hers. But the more time passed, the less and less confident she felt about that.

The Gisborne's Girl's killer had given them nothing.

Malia stood up, straightened her jacket and came to join her.

'Not a single person's come forward to say they know who she is,' Robin said. 'Even anonymously. She has to be from overseas, doesn't she? Her picture's been on TV, in the national press. Even if she had no family at all, grew up in care, there'd be people who know who she is.'

'Unless they *do* know who she is and they don't want to get involved.'

True. Though the Gisborne Girl had no police record herself, it didn't mean she wasn't part of a criminal world. They'd thought of it early on, of course, but it had been low on her mental list, she admitted, because she didn't *look* like a gangster's girlfriend, her whole aesthetic was wrong. But, as they'd initially thought, perhaps that was the point. Maybe she'd been making a break for it, incognito, and he or a goon had tracked her down.

They couldn't let themselves *assume* – at this stage, with this lack of progress, they needed to go back and interrogate all their working premises, conscious and otherwise, and make sure they weren't leading themselves down blind alleys. She took a marker from the ledge under the board and wrote *Criminal connections? Player or partner?*

'Let's get in touch with Organized and ask them to put a quiet word out, see if there's anything on the vine,' she said. 'How's the DVI coming on?'

The Disaster Victim Identification form, a.k.a. the pink form, was Interpol's form for identifying victims in mass disasters like the tsunami but it had become their preferred format for single cases like this, too. Pages long, it was exhaustive – and exhaust*ing*, to fill out – but it was recognized internationally and it had the advantage of getting all the details on a single document.

'We're just waiting for Olly to put in all the technical stuff.'

'Right. Will you chase him up? Let's get that off ASAP.'

She went back to her office. *Dear Stephen, thanks for the update*, she typed then stopped. *Had* the Gisborne Girl grown up in care? Or overseas? Or had she been brought up off the grid, leaving no trace in public records? Was that still possible in the UK in this hyper-connected age? And say it *was* – no record of the birth, no doctors, no dentists, no schools – why would someone want that? It would take an enormous amount of effort.

To avoid attention from the state, was one possible answer. Some people wanted no part of it. Travellers, actual Romany gypsies, for example – all they wanted was to live free, outside the lumbering machinery of The Man. But it might be about avoiding police attention specifically. If the mother had been underage, for example, her father older and afraid of prosecution for abusing a minor.

Miriam Chapman had been fifteen when she disappeared – she'd only *just* turned fifteen, had George Chapman said in the newspaper piece? She found Maggie's email, clicked on the link and scanned down. Yes: 'Miriam's just turned fifteen, she's young for her age and very shy.'

243

Robin looked at Miriam's photograph then opened a Google window and typed *Judith Chapman*. Twenty-two million hits – there was an American soap actress with the name. She added 'UK', reducing the number to a mere four million, the top hits being a legal secretary, an HR manager in Ilford, a fundraiser for Cancer Research, a local councillor in Leeds. Leeds – not so far from Newcastle, and you could conceivably be a local councillor in your early to mid-thirties in this politically charged age. She clicked on the link but the picture showed a blonde, blue-eyed woman in her fifties.

If only the Chapmans had gone a bit wilder with their biblical names; a Hepzibah or Bathsheba would make this much easier. And poor Judith, anyway; it was a fusty old name for someone of their generation. She added *Miriam, sister, disappear, missing, Whitley Bay* and *Newcastle* to the search terms and tried again. One of the first hits this time was another article from the *Chronicle* about an event to raise awareness about the long-term missing. Miriam was mentioned but not Judith. There were plenty of links to Victorian Judiths, 1830–1877, 1841–1892, and a loving tribute to a 'Nanna', 86, who'd died the previous year. Robin glanced at the top of the screen – 8,460 results in total. She went back to her email, finished the message to the CPS, then returned.

After three quarters of an hour, she'd drawn a blank and she knew she was wasting time. Her inbox was filling at a frightening rate – every time she looked, another twenty or thirty new messages had arrived. The phone kept ringing, and enough people had stuck their heads round the door with trivia that in the end she'd got up and closed it, despite the competing desire to be completely available to her team today.

Judith Chapman, it would appear, had vanished almost as effectively as her sister.

Fifteen minutes later, Webster rang to say Ben Tyrell was downstairs. She told him she was on her way and then, almost as an afterthought – perhaps to try and justify the wasted time – she gave it a final shot: *Chapman, Whitley Bay, Jude.*

Her eye landed immediately on the third hit down. *Mr and Mrs John and Jude Everleigh (née Chapman).* It was a wedding report from an online parish magazine in a small town Robin had never heard of, a write-up no doubt done from details sent in by the bride and groom. Robin looked at the accompanying photograph, a modest shot taken on the steps outside what looked like a register office. Shallow as she was, her first thought was that John Everleigh was foxy, brown-eyed and tawny-haired – nice one, Jude – and her second was that she approved of her dress, too, a tailored Forties-looking number in a sort of petrol blue-purple with a pencil skirt that reached just below the knee. Blood-red shoes, matching lipstick – she looked cool. She also looked like the Gisborne Girl.

Samir was in the observation room already, watching with such focus that there was a satellite delay in him realizing she'd come in. 'Hey,' he said quietly, shifting over to make room.

Webster was doing the interview himself, Leena Bradley, one of his favourite DCs at the table with him, Tim Horrocks, black, six-four, weekend rock-climbing enthusiast, positioned against the wall behind him and staring at Ben Tyrell as if he'd like to wring his neck with his bare hands. It was kind of a shame he couldn't do it, she thought. She was all about due process, a hundred per cent, no exceptions, but there were certain people who really tested your convictions.

'No solicitor?' she said, amazed.

'He said he didn't need one. Webster tried to tell him he really did but he wasn't having it. Says he's done nothing wrong.'

Both Webster and Bradley were pulled right up to the table but Tyrell was lounging, his chair pushed back, one ankle resting across the opposite knee, brown lace-up shoe bobbing in a way that felt insolent, if you could be insolent in your forties. Cocky was really the word. White shirt, top button undone to reveal the collar of a white T-shirt underneath, khaki trousers stretched by his pose to be slightly too tight across the crotch, perhaps for Leena's benefit. He had his sleeves rolled in a way that reminded Robin of the urban explorer, Jonathan Quinton, but he was much more confident than Quinton, who by comparison she remembered as jumpy and insubstantial. Ben Tyrell was planted; he wouldn't be budged.

'What do you do, Mr Tyrell?' Webster asked.

'I manage a fleet of company vehicles.' The voice Robin recognized from his webcasts, surprisingly deep.

'For who – whose fleet?'

He named a medium-sized budget hotel chain.

'Do they know about your double life as a far-right Internet rabble-rouser? I can't imagine it really fits their corporate image.' Their recent TV ads featured a mixed-race family bouncing on a bed, improbably ecstatic for people who'd found themselves in a hotel at the side of the motorway.

Tyrell shrugged. 'It's still a free country, isn't it? Just about? That's the point of the page – free speech. Everyone's so frightened of the lefty PC brigade that they can't express an opinion any more. My point is, free speech is for *everyone*, not only the people who're going to parrot whatever the "liberal elite" wants them to.' The words dripped with scorn.

'There's a difference between expressing an opinion and spewing racist bile,' said Webster.

'Yeah?' Tyrell said. 'But it's not bile, is it, it's fact. British people are meant to be white, these islands have always been white, and trouble starts when people who've been here since day dot have to shift over and kowtow to frickin' immigrants.'

'Well, happily not everyone sees it like that.'

'Yeah, there's a lot of eager Koolaid drinkers around. Must taste nice, being sure you'll get a pat on the back every time you say the socially acceptable thing. There's a good dog.'

Robin saw Webster take a breath then stop himself. She imagined his inner monologue: don't rise, don't let him wind you up.

'Some of us like to think for ourselves,' Tyrell said, 'and we're man enough to handle a bit of opprobrium from the slathering left up in London.'

Robin would have loved to rap on the glass and ask if he really believed London's slathering left would give him the time of day. The arrogance: *I alone am man enough to be a free thinker, to break free from centuries of earnest political and philosophical enquiry into how best humankind can live.* She thought of Lennie – *Wankers* – and grinned.

But at the same time, she had to admit she could see it. She could see how, if you were feeling lost and directionless and unimportant, unemployed, poor, someone like Tyrell – or even Tyrell himself – might be appealing. The ego was part of it, the self-confidence. The certainty. If you were feeling a bit spineless, he had extra for you.

And maybe you'd look at him and see someone you wanted to be: assured, angry, ready to put his head above the parapet. And charismatic, because he was. Neither she nor Samir had taken their eyes off him since she walked in and they'd barely said a word to each other. Tyrell knew that about himself. He knew he could hold an audience. He had three in the room, hanging on his every word, he'd probably guessed there were others behind the glass, and he was loving it. The very fact that they'd got him in so quickly this morning had let him know they'd been watching him already. He'd like that – people sitting up, paying attention, giving him the limelight.

And much as you'd love to write him off as a troglodyte escaped from a cave, dressed in khakis and somehow holding down a job as commander-in-chief of a bunch of company cars, he had a good brain, as they knew, and as she could tell now by the light in his eyes and his diction. Opprobrium? He hadn't been educated entirely by computer games.

'Mr Tyrell,' said Webster, 'yesterday morning on your site you posted a video in which you told your audience we'd arrested a suspect for the murder in Digbeth.'

'True. On two counts: one) you did arrest a suspect, that was public record, and two) I said it.'

'Right. You then went on to say we'd released him.'

'Yep.'

'And that that had to be for one of two reasons: either we were claiming to have arrested someone in order to look like we were making progress when we weren't or, "more likely", Webster looked down and read from his papers, '"they've made a big mistake" because "*People, he was there when she died.*"'

Tyrell nodded, foot bouncing. 'Yep.'

'Just over an hour before you posted that video of yourself, you posted one of Dhanesh Gupta's arrest in Sparkbrook, taken from an upstairs window by Tariq Abdul, who lives in the street and who started filming when he heard the commotion.'

'He's gutted, apparently,' Samir muttered to Robin. 'He's in the room next door, they had a quick word with him first. We called it – he took the film because when he saw Gupta hit the ground, he thought he'd bear witness to a bit of police brutality. He'd never heard of Tyrell – hadn't even twigged he'd used his footage until he was told a few minutes ago.'

'As I believe you know,' said Webster on the other side of the glass, 'Dhanesh Gupta was killed this morning. Murdered's the more accurate word.'

'I do know,' said Tyrell, 'but only because I saw it online right before you knocked on my door. I didn't know anything about it before then, so don't try and pin it on me.'

'We're not suggesting you personally killed Mr Gupta, though obviously we'll need details of your whereabouts this morning and of anyone who can confirm them.'

Tyrell smirked. 'There's a woman in Barnt Green who'll be happy to oblige you there.'

'Eva Braun, the sequel. I think I'm going to puke,' Robin murmured. Samir frowned, *Sssh*, then grinned to himself.

'Mr Tyrell, how do you think Mr Gupta's assailant – his *murderer* – knew where to find him this morning?'

He shrugged again, *Like I give a shit*. 'Dunno.'

'Mr Abdul's video of the arrest gives a clear view of the shops in the street, in particular a travel agent. Yes?'

'If you say so.'

'I do,' said Webster, and Robin and Samir both heard the tremor of frustration and anger in his voice. 'I do say so. Anyone who saw the video would be able to Google the businesses and find the address in a matter of seconds.'

Another shrug.

'So you broadcast the picture of a man you claimed had killed a young woman and a video that showed where he was picked up for work.'

'First off, I didn't post the two together,' Tyrell said. 'Did I? The arrest video was first – how was I to know that anyone would put the two things together?'

'Oh, give us a break. How stupid do you think we are?'

Tyrell smirked again. 'Also, even if it does tell you where he was picked up, it doesn't say when, does it?'

'It's timestamped, Mr Tyrell,' said Webster, dry. 'It wouldn't be too much of an intellectual leap even for your followers to see that and deduce that a van marked Lissom's Farms might pick up their workers at roughly the same time every day.'

'"Even for my followers",' Tyrell spat back with sudden energy. 'You see, you lot say you want to know why my followers are angry. There's your answer right there.' He stabbed his finger in front of him as Robin had seen him do in the webcasts. 'You call us stupid. You call us uneducated. You treat us like shit on your shoe. You want to know why we're angry? Look at the way we've been treated – look at the way that you've talked to us. No jobs, no services, NHS falling apart and all this while thousands of immigrants pour in, year after year, and you smug lefty pricks laugh at us. You destroy our way of life, call it globalization, then kick us in the nuts and laugh as we lie writhing on the ground.'

'You've got a job, Mr Tyrell,' Webster said evenly. 'A decent job.' *For now.*

'Yeah, well, I'm one of the lucky ones. My brother doesn't, or my best mate. Good working men, both of them, useful, left to rust in the long grass.' He sat back, resuming the foot-bouncing. 'I've done nothing wrong. This is what I think, my opinion, and I should be allowed to express it in the country where I was born and my father was born before me.'

'And Jehosephat begat Jehosephat, who begat Jeremiah . . .' muttered Robin.

'*Ssssh.*'

'I've been in touch with Counter Terrorism this morning,' Webster told Tyrell, straightening his papers.

'Counter terrorism? You going to tell me he was fucking Al Qaeda now?'

'Dhanesh Gupta was a Hindu,' said Webster. 'Not generally known for their membership of Islamic extremist groups. No, I rang them about you.'

'Me?' Incredulity.

'Inciting racial hatred,' Webster glanced at his papers. 'Sending communications with intent to cause distress contrary to Section 1 of the Malicious Communications Act 1988. Both charges that fall under the remit of Counter Terrorism. Both charges,' he said, almost conversational now, 'that can carry significant custodial sentences.'

'What? You're having a laugh.'

'No one round here feels much like laughing today, Mr Tyrell. So there's those two, potentially.' He tapped the papers. 'There's also the question – especially if it turns out that someone who saw your site *is* responsible; especially if we find anything corroborating in your phone or email – of how to deal with what could be incitement to murder.'

Chapter Twenty-six

'Okay, so Webster's awesome,' Robin said when he and Leena took a break, leaving Tyrell to try not to look intimidated by Tim Horrocks while he pondered the idea of jail.

'One of these days,' said Samir, 'you're going to take my word for something.'

'What? I'd never seen him interview anyone before.'

He shook his head.

'Something else occurred to me, though. Webster should have a word with Martin Engel.'

Samir frowned slightly then retrieved Engel from mental storage. 'Victoria Engel's father?'

'Thinking about who might particularly want to hurt someone they thought had killed a girl.' She told Samir about Engel's lurking in the car park, waiting for her. *I follow you. On the news. Social media.* Maybe he'd also been following Tyrell while he'd been taking such a lively interest in their case.

'No one's suggesting Gupta killed Victoria, though,' said Samir. 'I mean, apart from anything else, he'd only been in the country a few weeks and she vanished years ago.'

'No, I'm not saying that. Just, if you'd had years of frustration and not knowing, if you were a bit unbalanced, it might seem like a way of getting some kind of result. Justice for *someone's* daughter, if not your own.'

'You think he *is* unbalanced? *That* unbalanced?'

She considered. 'I don't know. No, maybe not. But it's damaged him, definitely, and the fact that he waited for me in the dark like that, then stood there on the pavement as I drove away . . . I actually thought he was following me in person, watching me, when I was having the bloody avocado on toast and outside my house at night. I kept feeling like there were eyes on me.' She cringed inwardly, remembering the photo of her and Kev in the car.

'Well, at least that worry's been addressed,' said Samir, neutral.

'Anyway, it might be worth having a word with him, that's all I'm saying. Maybe he knows someone who *might* be unhinged enough, someone in a support group who's starting to lose it . . .' She looked at Ben Tyrell through the glass and remembered Austin in her kitchen the other night, his talk of rogue nutters and vigilantes among the neighbourhood watch groups. 'It worries me,' she said, 'it worries me a lot, this trend of people taking matters into their own hands. People losing faith in the system, the law, and deciding to sort things out themselves.'

'Yeah.'

'Which is why I'm hesitating about our next step on Lara Meikle.'

'Which is what, you're thinking?'

She moved away to the table against the wall and pulled herself up on to it. 'I want to release the CCTV of Lara and her attacker to the public. The whole thing.'

'But you're afraid of this happening again. Gupta mark 2.'

'Hm.'

Samir considered. 'We can't worry about that – well, we can and we will – but we can't let fear of this sort of thing' – he gestured at the glass – 'get in the way. It's standard police work. And at least this new guy actually *is* a suspect. You're on solid ground there, aren't you? She's scared and he reaches out to grab her?'

'Yes. And you're right. I don't know, this is going to take some getting over. I know I didn't kill Gupta, but I still feel culpable.'

'But you're not,' he said gently. 'And you're far from alone in feeling like that, believe me.' He tipped his head at Tyrell. 'Ironically, about the only person who *doesn't* seem to feel culpable.'

'There's another element to it, too, though. I really don't want to do a Kilmartin. I don't want to look like we've been forced into releasing it by the media or people weighing in online. I don't want anyone to think they're calling the shots here or that there's some kind of . . . dialogue going on and we're scrambling to justify ourselves. "We might not have got him that time but look, look, we've got a new suspect now!"'

'It's what we were talking about the other day: we need to be seen to lead. *We* call the shots, *we* have the authority.'

'Yes, but not Authority, capital A. Not the state, the iron fist of the law.'

'Moral authority,' said Samir. 'Doing the right thing, in the right way.' He walked back to the glass and looked at Tyrell. 'Integrity.'

Robin clicked on the link in Lennie's email, saw the photograph and let her face drop into her hands. After a few seconds, she took a deep breath and straightened up: her team could see her through the glass.

Corinna had taken the picture, she remembered her doing it. She'd always been the documentarian, the holder-on. She'd been trying to preserve a bit of those last few weeks, stick it in a bottle and put a lid on: she'd known things were about to change. That

254

afternoon, before she and Samir had gone travelling, they were still a gang who'd grown up together and never been apart for longer than a family holiday.

They'd gone to Stratford for the day in Morris's car, an old Bentley that he'd bought a couple of weeks previously at an auction in north Wales. After a significant campaign, Kev had been allowed to borrow it and he'd driven it out of town like Pop Larkin, Samir riding shotgun, she, Josh and Corinna sliding round on the slippery, seatbelt-less back seat.

They'd taken rowing boats out on the river, splashing past in the cool shadow of the theatre balcony, had ice creams from a floating barge, then walked up the road to the Dirty Duck where they'd bought pints served in plastic glasses that they could take across the road to gardens overlooking the river. They'd found a swan-muck-free area of grass big enough for five and settled down for the afternoon. There were three half-empty pint pots in the picture and two packets of Marlboro Lights.

It had been hot, much hotter than they'd expected when they'd set out, and disinhibited after a couple of pints, Robin had taken off the shirt she'd had on top and gone with the white vest top underneath. It had been one with 'in-built support', no bra necessary, but she'd had her doubts about that at the time and as she could see now, she'd been right to: her boobs, albeit eighteen and enviably firm, were all over the place, bulging with the pressure of Samir's arms round her and spilling over the top as if she were an Elizabethan bar-wench.

Samir was sitting behind her, legs bracketing hers, his face buried in the angle between her shoulder and neck. Corinna had called his name just before she'd hit the button and he'd raised his eyes but left his lips on her skin so that he looked like a vampire. 'God, look at you two,' Rin had said when she got the prints back from Boots. 'Dracula Does Dallas.'

BLOODY MAYHEM

Already reeling from the brutal murders of two young women in the city this week, residents of Birmingham received another blow today when a man identified as a suspect in the case was stabbed to death in the street.

The attack on the man, named today by police as Dhanesh Gupta, 32, happened early in the morning in Sparkbrook, an area of the city with a large Asian population. It is believed Gupta was waiting to be collected for casual agricultural work when he was approached by a man in dark clothing. Moments later, he collapsed to the pavement with multiple stab wounds to the abdomen. He died before he could receive medical attention.

News of the death spread quickly in a city increasingly concerned that its police force is losing control. Residents expressed alarm. 'It feels lawless,' said Lynette Barber, 42. 'Like no one's safe.' Mohammed Hussein, 29, who lives on the street where Gupta died, said, 'The police arrested that poor man as a suspect then let him go to be killed on the streets like an animal. There needs to be an official enquiry. Things like this can't be allowed to happen in a country that calls itself civilized.'

DCI Robin Lyons, leading the enquiry into the murders of the two women, was unavailable for comment but some feel her record speaks for itself. She was removed from her previous role as head of a Murder Investigation Team in Homicide Command at the Met after going against orders from a senior officer to release Jamie Hinton, previously arrested for the murder of Jay Farrell. Hinton was cleared of suspicion in the case but has not been seen since his release, leading some to speculate that he, like Gupta, might have fallen victim to someone seeking vengeance.

Going against the orders of her senior officer might not be as much of an issue in her current position, however. It emerged this week that DCI Lyons and the Head of Force Homicide, Detective Chief Superintendent Samir Jafferi, are former lovers (*below, right*). The pair are now said to 'enjoy a close working relationship'.

She picked up the phone and dialled Samir's extension. It was busy so she called Rhona. 'Is he there?' she asked pointlessly.

'He's on the phone to ACC Kilmartin.' She hesitated. 'I'm so sorry, love.'

She felt sick – dirty. It was so . . . sleazy. 'Lovers' – technically they had been, yes, they'd used to sleep together, of course, but they'd been lovers in the non-tabloid sense, too: they'd just loved each other. The piece – with help from the photo – made it sound like they'd met in a strip club and conducted some sordid affair of cheap nylon underwear and by-the-hour hotels round the ring road. In fact, they'd got together when they'd been in the sixth form at their respective single-sex grammar schools and they'd been each other's first loves. Until Luke had got involved, she'd honestly thought they'd be together for ever.

She felt another rush of fury: how dare they? On top of all the innuendo about her professional failures, their sensationalist handling of Gupta's death, how *dare* they pour their dirt over her relationship with Samir? It was over, long gone, but it had been theirs and it was precious.

And what was Liz going to make of their 'enjoying a close working relationship' now? How was she going to feel when she saw the picture of her husband and the father of her children kissing Robin's neck, his body fitted around hers like a sleeve on a coffee cup, her boobs everywhere? She knew there was nothing going on and Samir had been totally straight with her when he'd offered Robin the job – in fact, he'd checked with Liz before he'd even asked her to apply – but seeing this wasn't going to feel good. And it wouldn't only be her who saw it, of course, but her friends and her family, her parents. Harry and Leila might hear about it.

And her team. Though it was common knowledge round Homicide that she and Samir had been together years ago, the photograph was next-level, as was the dig about their current relationship. Well, she thought, not addressing it would only make it worse – it'd make them look guilty. She'd have to bite the bullet, and try to do it with a bit of grace.

She read the piece again. This time it was the bit about Jamie Hinton that incensed her. In the other article they'd made it sound as if Hinton had disappeared off for a life of ease on the Costa del Crime after she'd let him go but today, same facts, she'd released him to be prey for vengeance-seekers, the poor lamb.

Her mobile rang, pulling her out of her own revenge fantasies. *Kevin Y.* Oh God. And then there was what *he* was going to make of all this. She thought about not answering but that was too cowardly.

'Kev?'

'Take it you've seen it?'

'I have.'

'Why can't the bastards leave you alone?' he huffed. 'You're only doing your job. And raking up the past like that, trying to make out there's something going on between you and Samir now . . .'

'I know. Poor Liz. And I'm sorry about . . . you know, you and me.'

'Oh, don't worry about it from my end, I know it's only tabloid muck-racking. A bit of nasty gossip, innit? Like you said that first night we got together, it was eighteen years ago, you two.'

He remembered her saying that? Robin was surprised.

'I just called to check you were all right. Especially with your mum as well. How's she doing today? Any news?'

'I rang Dad about half an hour ago. They're going to give her an MRI but they haven't been able to do it yet. Dad's talking like they've been there for weeks, getting into the lingo – he says her pressure's very *labile*, which seems to mean it swings wildly up and down, so it's really hard to medicate.'

'What are you doing tonight?' he asked.

'Going to see her.'

'Want me to come along? I wouldn't come in, that'd be a bit intrusive for your poor mum, me seeing her in her nightie and all that, but I could sit in the waiting room, be there when you come out?'

Robin felt a rush of affection for him. 'Thanks, that's really good of you. But you don't want to spend your Friday night on the stroke ward, believe me.'

'Yes, I do – if it helps you, I do. Anyway, what else am I going to do? I'm hardly going to go out on the lash while you're in there, am I?'

The warmth of feeling was replaced by an odd guilt. 'Look, I really appreciate it,' she said, 'but shall we try and meet up tomorrow or Sunday? Honestly, it's so depressing in there and we could be hours or five minutes, depending on how she is. I don't want to mess you around.'

She thought he might remonstrate further but he didn't. 'Okay then, tomorrow or Sunday it is, let me know what suits. I don't want you to feel like you have to worry about me as well, concentrate on your mum.' He paused. 'Well, and the three murders.'

'Sorry this is all such a train-wreck.'

'Don't you worry. By the way, I've got to ask, where did they get the photo? I remember that day, out in Dad's old Bentley.'

'I don't know,' she said. 'I mean, I think I do but I hope I'm wrong, let's put it that way.'

'Your brother?'

'I can't see who else. I had that picture, Corinna gave it to me. I thought I'd burnt it when Samir dumped me, though – I burnt all the pictures of us.' She'd taken them out into the back garden at Dunnington Road, dug a hole in one of the flower beds – much to her mother's outrage – and set fire to the lot of them, watched them curl and melt and die. 'Obviously I must have missed that one.'

'Hm. I'm kind of glad you did. In a way. Memory of a nice day. You look so young, both of you.'

'Well, we were, weren't we?'

'I guess so. Feels like a long time ago today.' He laughed a little. 'Nice rack, by the way.'

'God, Kev, please don't make me laugh. If I do, I'll start sobbing and I might never stop.'

The incident-room door opened and she saw Samir come in. He was headed for her office but where she might have come marching across the room, he walked as if it were a normal afternoon, nothing in particular going on, neutral expression, hellos to Malia and Tark and a brief pause to look at some footage onscreen.

'DCI Lyons, have you got a moment?' he said, sticking his head round the door.

'Of course. Come in.'

He shut the door behind him. 'Bloody hell,' he said, face still completely nothing-to-see-here. Her Venetian blinds were open, and from the corner of her eye, Robin could see some very poor efforts at low-key surveillance.

'I think I should step aside,' she said.

'What?' The neutral expression vanished.

'I don't mean resign, just hand this one over to someone else. The *Herald*'s got a bee in their bonnet about me and it's not helping anyone: you, the team, the victims.' She thought of Deborah Harper again and said a silent prayer that anyone who knew her would be kind enough to keep the piece a secret. She'd hear about Gupta, of course, but she really didn't need the boobs or the insinuations. 'It's damaging our work.'

'No, I don't think it is,' Samir said. 'Not the work itself. We'll talk to the team now, together, take the piss out of ourselves a bit and make it clear there's nothing going on between us. Right?'

Their eyes met and for a fleeting moment, in his, Robin saw something – a question. She remembered his look the day of the last article, *Did it have to be Kev?* He broke the eye contact and looked away.

'Right,' she said, slightly unsettled. 'I agree about talking to them but I'm still not convinced it's a good idea for me to carry on as . . .'

He eyeballed her again. 'What were you telling me this morning? *We* call the shots? *We* have the authority? I've just spent twenty minutes convincing Kilmartin of that, drawing on every dark art in my arsenal; please don't tell me it was for nothing. I refuse to be told what to do by the *Daily Herald*. Anyway,' he said, eyebrows up, 'I'm your commanding officer so *I* call the shots.'

'All right, boss man, keep your hair on,' she said, largely to interrupt the weird atmosphere. 'In a professional context, by the way, and only then, to be clear.'

'Good. So take a deep breath and let's go and get this over with.' He opened the door.

261

Robin followed him out, watching the gawpers make a hash of looking as if they hadn't been straining for every syllable. As usual, Samir's presence drew all eyes, no need for any hand-clapping or calling-to-attention. He waited a minute or two for people to finish phone calls. Tark rolled in on his chair.

'Right,' Samir said, looking round. 'It will have come to the attention of the majority of you, I'm sure, that your Senior Investigating Officer here and I have our picture on the *Herald*'s website this afternoon. I'll confess, I was jealous after the last piece but they've done the decent thing and put me in as well this time.' His eyebrows flicked up. 'Robin and I want you all to know that we're deeply embarrassed by our youthful indiscretions . . .'

'I'm considering legal action against the people who sold me that top,' she said, and saw Phil Howell snicker and mutter something to Niall before Malia gave him a laser stare.

'Reports that we were together in our late teens are, as you know, absolutely true,' said Samir. 'However, our teens were a depressingly long time ago, and we've both moved on, sartorially and otherwise, despite the *Herald*'s romantic notion that we're somehow keeping the love alive here at Force Homicide.'

A ripple of respectful laughter.

'Seriously, though, as we're all aware, this kind of piece makes our lives a lot harder, and we can only imagine the effect it might have on the victims' families and their faith in us to do the job as we all want it done. So let's keep up the good work and keep our mouths shut as far as anyone who might conceivably be a journalist is concerned. Loose lips sink ships.'

Chapter Twenty-seven

When they met him at the ward doors, Robin's father looked tired out. She imagined him alone at Dunnington Road last night, her mother's side of the bed empty for the first time in years. When had they last spent a night apart? When her mother was in hospital having her? No, her dad had done occasional trips to Belgium and France for work when they were younger, though he'd been so happy to get home you'd have thought he was returning from the trenches.

'How are you, love?' he said, giving her a tight hug. He held her at arm's length and scrutinized her. 'I heard about that poor chap Gupta,' he said quietly. 'We watched the news on your mother's little telly.' Robin felt Lennie shift beside her. They'd talked about the *Herald*'s piece in the car on the way over and agreed not to say anything about this one unless, of course, he'd already heard about it.

'Yes,' she said. 'It's been quite a difficult day.'

'Well, you're here now,' he said without apparent irony.

Her mother's face had improved slightly, Robin thought when she saw her; her eye looked a little less hooded and the droop at the corner of her mouth less pronounced, unless she was imagining it. Otherwise the only change was her hair. There'd be life on Mars before her mother went without brushing it, but it looked less clean than Robin could ever remember seeing it; usually she washed and styled it every day. If yesterday she'd been frightened, today she seemed subdued. She'd been disappointed, Dennis had told them, because she'd wanted to get out of bed, get dressed and sit in the armchair but the nurse had told her she wasn't allowed yet. 'Lying in bed makes her feel slovenly,' he said, as if Robin couldn't have guessed the exact word. 'And it makes her feel like she's ill. Properly ill.'

She and Lennie had glanced at each other. Did she think she wasn't?

'Have you seen Natalie, Mum?' she asked.

Dennis answered for her. 'This morning. She thought it might be a bit much to bring Jack in here so she left him with her mum – they're back from the Canaries now – and popped in for half an hour, brought your mother some nice hand-cream.'

'That was kind of her. How is she?'

'Hard to say. Preoccupied. Sad. We hope they'll sort it all out but we can't get involved, can we? It's between them.'

With her usual sensitivity, Len had picked up on Christine's unhappiness at being 'out in public' looking less than her best. 'I'll bring you my dry shampoo tomorrow, Gran,' she said. 'Me and Niamh swear by it, not for the cleaning bit, though it does that as well, but because it gives you really good volume. It's the best.'

'Thank you, love.' She gave Lennie's hand a squeeze and Robin felt her own eyes prickle suddenly. She blinked. God, what was wrong with her? Nothing – nothing a quiet couple of hours wouldn't sort out. Nonetheless, now would be a good time to get away from the bed before she started tearing up and really freaked everyone out.

'Where's Luke?'

'He's gone to the break area down the other end of the corridor. We found it earlier.'

'I might go and see how he's doing,' she said. Her father looked alarmed, no doubt remembering last night's canteen blow-up, but her mother nodded, blissfully unaware. 'Thanks, love,' she said, eyes soft.

'You stay here, Len, and chat to Gran. I won't be long.'

She buzzed herself out of the ward and followed the overhead signs down the corridor. A very elderly man rolled by in his bed, escorted by two voluble porters. 'Best Friday night you've had in ages, eh, Jimmy, out and about, eyeing up the ladies?' one of them said, giving Robin a wink as the old man smiled.

Pairs and pairs of double doors to different wards, single ones to technical rooms. It was relatively busy at first, medical staff and visitors on the move, but at the end of the corridor, the signs directed her through a snicket lined with public loos and a maintenance room, and the foot traffic thinned out.

The break area was an alcove full of vending machines off a small glassed atrium filled with tables. Only a handful of people were there, Luke not among them, and she wondered if he'd gone to the loo before spotting him loitering outside on the pavement. He was smoking, which she hadn't seen him do since they were teenagers and Natalie made him stop.

She cranked the door open and stormed over. His usual response to her was an eye-roll, either literal or metaphorical, but he looked a bit frightened now. Good – as well he might.

'What were you *thinking*?' she demanded.

'What?' The fear morphed into poorly concealed guilt.

'Oh, spare me. Giving them the photograph! How could you *do* that? This isn't about you and me, Luke, getting a jab in. People's lives are at stake here.'

'Get over yourself, Robin. No one's going to die 'cause there's a picture of you in the paper with your tits out.'

She felt a nearly overwhelming urge to punch him in the face, and shoved her hands in her pockets.

'No,' she said, voice shaking with anger, 'but have you thought about how the victims' parents might feel, seeing it? What they might think about my ability to find their daughters' killers? And the longer this looks like a juicy story, the longer the media are going to cover it, which puts pressure on us, the police, when frankly, that's the last thing we need. All sorts of nasty people are getting riled up, Luke, stories like that throw fuel on the fire, and I don't want anyone else to die like Gupta did.'

'Oh, come on, there's no connection between a picture in the—'

'There's *every* connection, you just don't know how the world works, and that's because you've never even tried to engage with anything beyond the end of your nose.'

She'd hit a nerve. Rage billowed through him, transforming his posture from vaguely cowering to full-on aggressive; pathetic – at least in her eyes – to scary. The ball of muscle in his jaw was hard as he leaned right into her face, the cigarette heavy on his breath.

'How dare you?' he said. 'How fucking dare you talk to me like that? You want to know why I gave the guy the picture? Ask yourself – you've got all the answers.'

'What answers?' she spat back.

'The way you talk to me – like I'm a moron, like *I* couldn't understand difficult stuff like *you* do, like you're out in the world doing it all while I'm here messing round in the sandpit.'

Aren't you? she nearly said. *Isn't that exactly what you're doing?*

'You've patronized me, made fun of me – you've humiliated me since you were three foot tall. Luke the loser, Luke with his five GCSEs, you with your A stars and your fucking *degree*. How do you think that feels – for me? Or have you ever thought about it?'

'It's got nothing to do with you, Luke. School, uni, my career – it's Not. About. You.'

'*Uni,*' he mocked. 'And yeah, believe it or not, I can understand that you doing it isn't about me but the way you swan around, shoving it in my face, lording it over me . . .'

'I don't do that.'

'You do. You totally do. "*People's lives are at stake here, Luke – all sorts of nasty people are getting riled up.*" Nasty people? I'm not five years old. It's in everything you say, you can't help yourself. You can't even say hello to Billy without reminding him that you went to university.'

'I didn't mean it like that.'

He snorted.

'I didn't!'

'Well, after three and a half decades of your shit, let me tell you, that's what it sounded like to me. And Billy. And Dad.'

'Leave Dad out of it.'

'Why? You think he's on your side?'

Robin stopped. Wasn't he? Her mum was on Luke's side, no doubt about that, but her dad was neutral, Switzerland. Wasn't he?

'I'm his son, Robin. I'm his kid, too. You think he likes it when someone puts his son down all the time, makes him feel small?'

His turn to see that he'd hit a nerve and it seemed to satisfy him. She felt all her own anger desert her, as if Luke had ripped off her shell and it had spilled out on to the pavement. She felt cold and suddenly vulnerable.

'If you want to know why I gave the guy the picture,' he said, 'it's because he offered me money, all right? I don't have any money and he paid me for it.'

She stared at him. 'How much?'

'Four hundred quid.'

'You sold me out for four hundred quid?'

He laughed, a strange empty sound. 'Oh yeah, I forgot. That's small change in your world.'

'How did it happen? Did you contact them, pitch it to them?'

'Yeah, because I'd do that, wouldn't I?'

'I don't know, Luke, wouldn't you?' Probably not, though, she realized – no, of course not: far too enterprising. And he wouldn't know how to navigate it.

'No,' he said. 'They already knew about you and Samir when they knocked on the door at Mum and Dad's. All they wanted was a picture of you together. They offered me the money so I gave it to them.'

'Where did you even get it? I thought I'd burnt them all. After you *lied* to him and made him dump me.'

'Mum's bedside table. She keeps it in there.' He registered her astonishment. 'She saved it that day you nearly set the garden on fire – you dropped it. She says she likes it because for once in your life,' he sneered, 'you actually look happy.'

Chapter Twenty-eight

She'd been afraid she'd lie awake all night but as soon as she got into bed, she'd fallen into a sleep so deep it felt narcotic. Then, just as abruptly, she was awake again, brain whirring. It was five past four, only the streetlight edging the curtains. She lay still for a couple of minutes, hoping to drop back off but when it became clear it wasn't going to happen, she threw back the duvet, knowing the moment her feet hit the carpet that she was going.

She took a two-minute shower while the kettle boiled for a thermos of coffee, crept in to give Lennie a kiss and texted her a message for when she woke up.

The car was cold inside, more March rather than June; she put the heating on before typing in the address she'd emailed herself yesterday. Half a tank of petrol – enough to get her a good way before she had to stop.

The city centre was still asleep, the roads empty apart from a handful of other cars and the first of the morning delivery lorries. She thought of Dhanesh Gupta walking in the quiet to meet the van each morning, and how he'd never walk the streets again, these or any others.

By the time she reached the motorway, she'd slipped into the strange mental state of long-distance driving, that combination of hyper-alertness and dissociated thought. She left the radio off and let the jabbering week start to drain out of her ears. As dawn began to break in earnest the road opened up, the sun rising in shades of peach and gold across fields beyond the opposite carriageway that were packed tight with green wheat. It felt good to be moving, to have a sense of forward motion, and she struggled to keep the car at eighty-five, her foot itching for the floor.

The Great North Road. The words had always held a strange romance, the promise of adventure, albeit quite chilly adventure. The signs advertised coming attractions, Nottingham, Sheffield, Leeds, places she had no personal connection to but felt as if she did. It had to be books: she'd gone through a phase at fifteen and sixteen where she'd hoovered up the Angry Young Men – John Braine, John Osborne, Alan Sillitoe; their sensibilities had suited her teenage angst nicely.

She stopped at the services north of Sheffield to fill up the car, stretch her legs and drink some of the coffee. It was frank daylight now, past six o'clock, but there was still the lovely fresh-washed edge on the light and air, a sense that the day hadn't yet been dirtied by human activity. She shook the last drops from her cup and got back in the car.

It was a good thing they'd gone early to the hospital last night, she thought, because it had taken a long time to calm down after the confrontation with Luke. She'd walked round the car park for ten minutes in an effort to normalize, but on the way back up to the ward, she'd caught sight of herself in a mirrored-glass door and her face had been so crimson, it looked like she'd fallen asleep on a sunbed; she'd hoped none of the nurses wanted to take *her* blood pressure. Len and her parents had looked at her askance but no one had said anything, *Keep the lid on* that *particular can of worms, please.* She wasn't sure but she thought she'd seen entreaty in her mother's eyes and she'd looked quickly away.

It hadn't only been Luke. The bad news had started rolling in before she left the station and it had kept coming all evening, through the trip back to Mary Street to pick up Len, the hospital, the beans on toast they'd had on trays when they got home, one thing after another.

That David Pearce could be solidly ruled out she'd expected, but Lara's stepbrothers were out, too, and her boyfriend before Pearce. 'Same thing,' said Malia, who'd come into her office as Robin was throwing her phone into her bag. 'Rock-solid alibis and they're all too short. Also,' she added, grimacing, 'we've heard from Forensics about the hair found on Lara's body.'

'And?'

'It doesn't belong to any of them.'

'Or, moreover, to anyone else in the system,' Robin had inferred, heart sinking. 'Damn.' That didn't mean it wasn't her killer's but even if it was, it wasn't the fantasy, where the database led them straight to him, address and all.

'She'd come from a bar,' Malia said. 'And a pub before that. The hair could be any old Tom, Dick or Harry's.'

'It might also still be his, in which case it'll help us with a conviction rather than an arrest. How about Interpol? Anything there?' They'd filed the DVI a couple of hours after they'd discussed it (increasingly, Robin had started to notice, Olly could be relied upon to deal swiftly with anything Malia asked of him).

'Three enquiries so far, two of them from the Czech Republic, which is interesting, but none of them look right.'

'Well, it's early days on that front, at least.'

'Yeah,' Malia had replied, but she'd sounded flat.

Tark had called as she and Lennie were pulling out of the hospital car park. 'Thought I'd better give you a quick bell, guv,' he said. 'That tape we got in from the honeymoon place on Warwick?'

'Yes?' *Come on, Tark, no suspense today.*

'They've got two cameras and I've been through both, eight p.m. to eight a.m. The footage gives quite a clear view of the pavement on the Gisborne side, particularly the stuff from the second camera.'

Right . . .

'But there's no sign of her at all, coming or going. Nada.'

Shit. 'How about couples? Did you look at them – people who might have gone in together? Or groups?'

'Of course.' He'd sounded insulted and rightly so.

'Sorry,' she said. 'I'm clutching at straws here.'

'I know, it's all right. I'm sorry I haven't got anything for you. Thing is, we've got tape for all that night now on both blocks, Warwick and Bradford streets, and there's no sign of her. I mean, they're long blocks, aren't they, but we've got tape at all points, no gaps, no *time* gaps now, and there's still nothing, so how the hell did she get in there? Magic? Teleportation?'

Robin remembered the network of underground storage rooms. Could Rafferty and his crew have missed an access point other than the one Gupta had used, one leading not to the buildings either side but *under* either Bradford or Warwick? Was that feasible?

'We need to broaden it out,' she'd told Tark. 'I'll ask Rafferty to take another look at the underground level, and we need to start looking more closely at the streets beyond Warwick and Bradford. We also need to expand the time window. You were looking from eight p.m.?'

'Yes.'

'So let's go further back now, and forward. Start at six p.m. and go to noon on Sunday.'

'Right,' he said but he'd sounded weary. 'I'll come in tomorrow.'

'Thanks, Tark – I appreciate it. But get some rest first, your eyes must be wrecked.'

'They've been less bloodshot, I'll admit.'

Perhaps the final straw in the destruction of all morale last night, however, had been the response to the CCTV of Lara and her attacker. After checking that Deborah Harper and David Pearce were happy for them to do it, they'd put it out on West Midlands' own social media. Sara Kettleborough had got it up on the *Post*'s site at the same time and Robin had recorded an appeal that had gone out on the teatime edition of *Midlands Today*.

In light of the *Herald*'s piece, she'd questioned if it would be better for someone else to do it – 'Someone like you,' she'd said to Samir hopefully. 'Kilmartin would like that, wouldn't he, the Most Senior Foot?'

'Nice try,' he'd said. 'But I'm not letting you hide.'

'I'm not *trying* to hide.'

He'd raised his eyebrows: *Really*? 'You're doing it, Robin.'

So she'd put on the suit she kept in dry-cleaner's plastic on the back of her door and, for the second time in a week, she and Webster had back-to-back TV spots.

'We've gathered a significant amount of information in this case,' she'd told the interviewer, '*very* significant, including, as viewers will see, CCTV of the moment we believe Lara met her attacker. The man who did this *will* be caught – all we're looking for now is the final piece of the puzzle.' She'd turned to look directly into the camera. 'Lara Meikle was a young woman on the brink of her adult life. If you recognize this man or even think you do, get in touch. Please, help us get the final piece and catch her killer.'

The results had been negligible. The comments on social media had been either expressions of horror, calls for the return of hanging, well-intentioned but pointless blithering to the effect of 'Hope the police catch the bastard' or less well-intentioned blithering about their failure as a force. They'd hoped for better from the television but for the most part it had been more of the same, along with the usual smattering of nutjobs and conspiracy theorists. Only two tips had looked at all promising but one of them turned out to have the best alibi going: he'd actually been in police custody in Smethwick at the time of the attack, drunk and disorderly. The other was a man previously convicted of sexual assault who'd recently been released from Winson Green.

'What do you think?' Samir said when he'd called at ten. She'd been stacking the plates in the dishwasher.

'Varan and Niall went to talk to him.'

'Not him?'

'We're doing the due diligence, of course, but it seems unlikely, for the same reason we didn't flag him straight away when we looked to see who'd been released recently.'

'Which is what?'

'He's gay. The three people he attacked before were all men. There was no sexual element to Lara's murder but all his previous was sexual.'

'Right,' he said, and she'd heard hope fade at his end, too.

York, Harrogate, Scarborough: North Yorkshire now, the moors. This was Brontë country, of course, but before them, she'd loved it from *The Secret Garden*. Sallow, spiky little Mary Lennox had been the first fictional character with whom she'd really felt a kinship. It had taken her aback, finding someone like herself in the pages of a book – until then, the female characters she'd read about were naughty at the very worst but always charming and feminine. Mary had felt like a real girl: she'd been tough as well as spiky. She hadn't been scared of Misselthwaite Manor, even alone at night with the wind howling across the moor and a child crying piteously in a hidden room. She'd sorted the lot of them out just as much as they'd sorted her.

Tough. If you were going by national stereotypes, Robin thought, she was much more northern by nature and yet she'd always known that when she finished school, she'd go to 'soft' London because that was where you found out whether or not you could swim with the big fish. London was where you proved yourself, or so she'd thought at the time.

Well, here she was nearly twenty years later, back, and she was *still* trying to prove herself: to her team; to Samir and Kilmartin; to Lara's family; to the public, worried Midlanders and *Daily Herald* readers alike. She wondered now if Freshwater, her old commanding officer at the Met, had heard about all this. If so, he'd be loving every minute. She shuddered at the idea of his ferrety little eyes on the photo of her boobs.

After talking to Samir last night, the ashes of all their efforts so far heaped round her feet, she'd summoned a final ounce of energy and fired up her laptop.

We've gathered a significant amount of information in this case. The man who did this will *be caught.* She'd watched herself again on the *Midlands Today* website and been impressed by how convincing she sounded. She'd said it to scare their killer, if he was watching, or to persuade anyone who might be protecting him to give him up. Was it true, though? Probably. Even if their current lack of progress made her want to tear her hair out, to have this much information and still come up empty-handed would be extremely unlucky.

The Gisborne Girl with her huge, near-empty board, however, was a different matter. Nothing suggested they would catch her killer. Instead, she was slipping further and further out of view by the day.

Chapter Twenty-nine

It was eight thirty by the time she reached Durham. God, it was a long way – more than two hundred miles, according to the satnav. They weren't much shy of Scotland.

She'd only been here once before, on a university open day she'd grudgingly agreed to because her parents had wanted her at least to see other options. She remembered it as being nice, though, and that seemed to be the case. Judging by the elevation and proximity to the castle, which had loomed up ahead before she'd taken the final turn on to this side street, she was in the old part of the city. The architecture said the same: a mixture of styles that ranged across centuries: modern, Victorian, Georgian, some of it much older than that, medieval-looking. All of it was well-maintained; clearly, there was money here.

According to the website, the shop didn't open until nine thirty so she put on her jacket and went to find something to eat. The streets were pedestrianized, a lot of them cobbled, and a surprising number of independent shops and cafés held their own among the usual homogenous Boots and Starbucks. She bought an egg and bacon roll at one of them and sat to eat it on a stone plinth in a square dotted with statuary. The sky was a sheer distant blue.

Church bells struck nine o'clock. She checked her phone but there was still nothing from Lennie. Well, she was probably tired after the week they'd had, and she *was* a teenager. She left a message for her dad asking for a progress report from the hospital then went in search of Jude Everleigh's shop.

She found it easily, near the acute angle of a block that divided two curving streets, one leading uphill, the other downhill towards a stone bridge high over a river. The storefront was narrow but she recognized the leaded bay window immediately from the Instagram pictures – last night she'd thought it looked like the transom of an old pirate galleon. On display were an abundant collection of cushions and make-up bags, oven gloves and tea-towels printed with quirky designs. Jude Everleigh, née Chapman, was a fabric designer.

There was a light on in the room behind the display, and as she squinted past her own reflection in the glass, a figure appeared in an arched doorway at the back, a woman in a dark body-con dress and biker boots who looked up and saw her outside. Robin raised a hand.

The woman hesitated a moment, checking her watch – old-school – then started to move towards her. A bunch of keys rattled against the door.

'Hi,' she said, smiling from the top step, a hint of something herbal in the air that escaped around her. 'I don't open till nine thirty, really,' she indicated a sign in swirling calligraphy, 'but if you're pushed for time . . .' Her accent was Geordie, warm-toned.

In the flesh, at close range, her face was so like Miriam's no one would question they were sisters, and Robin felt a growing sense of rightness: yes, this was right, and she had been right to come.

Jude had coloured her hair a more lustrous chestnut brown and she'd put a single gold streak through a lock at the front that kinked quiff-like before disappearing under a patterned green band knotted on the top like a washerwoman's headscarf. Robin remembered Miriam's difficult cowlick. Her eyes were large and green, liquid-lined in black.

'Jude Everleigh?'

Surprised, she looked Robin up and down, taking in the jeans and boots and the incongruous suit jacket. Robin was almost tempted to apologize for the ensemble, a pitiful effort compared to her biker-rockabilly thing.

'Would you mind if I came in?' she said instead.

Jude hesitated momentarily – What the hell was going on? – then stood back to let her by.

Inside, Robin traced the herbal scent to a lit candle on the stripped wooden counter at the back. The smell matched her first impression of the room as a whole: green – very green – and a little wild. It relied heavily on artificial light, the downside to an old building on a narrow street, she supposed, but there were several healthy-looking plants in big Victorian-looking brass pots. One wall was covered with deep shelves stacked with bolts of cotton fabric. Last night, looking at some of the patterns on the website, Robin had thought 'William Morris on magic mushrooms': at first glance, the designs were traditional-looking but when you looked closer, you saw that the birds perched among swirling foliage had glasses on or pocket-watches tucked into their breast-feathers. Vines, traditional-looking at first, put out tendrils that became slender fingers reaching for bunches of grapes among which nestled tiny imp-like faces.

Jude was waiting for her to say something.

She reached into her pocket for her warrant card. 'I'm sorry to come unannounced like this,' she said. 'But I thought it would be best to come in person. DCI Lyons, West Midlands Police.'

'West Midlands?'

'I've driven up from Birmingham this morning.'

'Why? I mean, what's it about?' Then her expression changed. 'It's Mirry, isn't it?' Instinctively she put a hand on the display table next to her, as if to hold herself steady. 'Have you found her body?'

'No, we haven't.' Robin looked around. 'It's a complicated situation. Is there somewhere we could sit down?'

Visibly shaken, Jude led her through the arch into a second room at the back, this one darker still, the only natural light coming from a small leaded window that overlooked a miniature courtyard. It was part stockroom, part office, part packing-and-dispatch, Robin guessed from a grey mail-sack nearly full of parcels. Jude gestured that she should take the wooden chair at the desk then went back into the shop for another, presumably from behind the counter. 'Would you like something to drink?' she asked, pointing at a kettle on a shelf. 'Coffee? Or tea – I've got quite a few different flavours of fruit, and mint, or . . .'

She was playing for time, terrified of what she was about to hear. 'I'm fine, thank you,' Robin said gently. 'Mrs Everleigh . . .'

'God, Jude, please, that makes me sound ancient.' Her laugh was edged with panic.

'Sorry. Jude, almost a week ago – a week tomorrow, in fact – a body was found in a derelict factory near Birmingham city centre.'

Her eyes were wide open, pupils huge in the weak light. 'But you said you *hadn't* found her.'

'Yes, it isn't her – it can't be. Your sister was fifteen when she disappeared and that was twenty years ago so she'd be thirty-five now if . . .'

'Thirty-four,' Jude said. 'Her birthday's in November.'

'Right. We haven't been able to identify the woman but we

know it's not Miriam because she's significantly younger. She's no more than early twenties at the most.'

Jude sat back heavily, relief written across her face along with something that wasn't disappointment, Robin knew, but resignation: back to the uncertainty and not knowing. The imagining. 'So if it's not her, with respect . . . ?'

'Look, I need to preface this by saying I might be completely wrong – at this point, it's only a theory and I don't have any evidence. It might also come as a shock.'

She shook her head. 'Can't be worse than the pictures I've had in my head for the past nineteen and a half years.'

'Well . . . I think it's possible – only possible – that the woman we found is your sister's daughter.'

Jude stared at her for a moment but then – Robin could almost see the cogs cranking behind her eyes – she worked through the implications of what she was hearing. 'If the woman you found is about twenty . . .'

'Likely younger – eighteen or nineteen.'

'You think Miriam had a baby at fifteen? That *that's* why she disappeared?'

Robin nodded. 'That's my theory.'

Jude shook her head. 'No. It can't be right. She wasn't pregnant when she disappeared.'

'How can you be sure?'

'Because I am.' Emphatic. 'Mirry and I shared everything. We were very close. There's no way she'd be pregnant and not tell me.' An entirely humour-free laugh. 'The idea of it – it's almost funny.'

'What do you mean?'

'She just wasn't like that. I was the feistier one of us, and even I wouldn't have dreamt of . . . I mean, no. No way. Even if that kind of thing had been countenanced in our family. Or even given the opportunity to be countenanced.'

281

'"That kind of thing"?'

'Boys. Sex – any kind of personal interaction with the opposite sex. We were kept on a very tight lead, it wouldn't have been possible – we were accounted for every minute of the day. School, music, church group, home – that was our circuit. I hadn't even kissed anyone when I went to university; I was *twenty* before I saw a man naked.'

She stopped as another realization dawned. '*Oh.*' She sat back, eyes wide. 'If you *are* right, if the girl *is* her daughter, Miriam couldn't have been killed when she was taken – she must have been kept alive. Alive to get pregnant – alive long enough afterwards to give birth to a baby.' She took a sharp in-breath. 'Maybe *still* alive.'

Robin held up her hands: slow down. 'If I'm right, and it's a huge if. I'll be completely honest with you – it's my case, I'm leading this new investigation, and we're struggling. We can't identify the young woman, we're running out of angles to try, and there's a strong possibility I'm clutching at straws here. I'm fully aware of that and I need you to be, too. But it *is* a straw and that's more than we've got anywhere else. If I'm wrong, though, I know I'll have caused you a lot of distress and disappointed hope.'

Jude nodded slowly, absorbing, but the light was still in her eyes. 'It's okay,' she said. 'If there's a chance, we should take it.'

'Thank you.'

'What can I do? What do you need from me?'

'Well, to start with, I have some questions.'

'Okay.'

'In your mind,' Robin said, 'over the years, what have you thought happened? Did you believe Miriam was abducted? Or did you ever think she might have run away?'

Jude shook her head. 'No, I never thought she'd run away.

The police asked me that over and over again. Did my sister have a boyfriend? Did she have a crush on anyone? Had anyone shown an unusual interest in her?'

'And you said no?'

'No to all of it. And yes,' she said, pre-emptively, 'I would have known.'

'How about online? Could someone have found her that way?'

'Groomed her, you mean? No.'

'How so sure?'

'We didn't have a computer. We begged for one but we weren't allowed.'

'It sounds quite strict, your childhood.'

'It was definitely . . . sheltered. There were *some* things that bothered us for sure – we didn't have a television, either, for example, so we never knew what the other kids at school were talking about, that was a pain, and our clothes weren't exactly cutting-edge, shall we say. Later, when I went to college, I did feel incredibly naive. Everyone else was so much more worldly, so much surer of how things worked, more confident. And my alcohol tolerance,' she shook her head. 'I had one glass of sherry at my professor's welcome drinks and I was wasted. But you know, it felt like care. Mirry and I always felt safe. Our parents loved us to bits and they wanted us to be safe.'

'You were churchgoers,' she asked. 'Religious?'

'Yes. Or my parents were, and so we were, too. Back then.'

'Not now?'

'It's hard to keep believing in a benevolent God when your family's picked off one by one.' She pulled her lips in over her teeth and pressed them together for several seconds. 'You're not a believer.' It was a statement.

Robin was surprised. 'No, I'm not,' she said. 'I don't believe in a God, benevolent or otherwise, or any kind of grand scheme.

No one's in charge of all this, there's no plan. It's just . . . chaos, good and bad in a constant state of flux, and I try to weigh in for the good.'

Jude nodded. 'That makes sense to me. When Mirry went, bad definitely had the upper hand for a long time. Things are better now.'

'I'm glad.' Please, Robin thought, don't let this be a disaster. Don't let me have dredged this all up again for nothing.

Jude reached for a tissue from a box next to the kettle then crushed it into a ball in her fist. 'Unless,' she said slowly, 'she *was* pregnant. Or thought she might have been. Maybe that would have been enough.'

'Sorry, I don't follow.'

She took a deep breath. 'If she was attacked. Before she disappeared.'

'Attacked? You mean, raped?' She couldn't say it, Robin thought.

A single nod.

'You don't think she would have told your parents? Or you, given you were close.'

'I don't know.' Now she was struggling to hold back tears. 'I want to say yes, she would have told *me*, but I don't know if it's true. I was younger than her, I was only thirteen, and she would have wanted to protect me. Also . . .' She stopped.

'What?' Robin asked as gently as she could.

'I think she'd have thought it was her fault.' She blinked and a tear slipped down her cheek. 'She would. She would have seen herself as to blame.'

'Why?'

'She was . . . Miriam was really serious about her faith. And our group was quite . . . old-fashioned in how they interpreted the Bible.'

'In what way?'

'Intolerant, really. Homosexuality was all Sodom and Gomorrah, of course, and women . . . Women were difficult for them. Even at thirteen I thought that – like, why did we have to hear about the bad women all the time, Jezebel and Delilah and co? Why emphasize them? Eve and the serpent, Herodias. Why did Mirry and I leave feeling ashamed of ourselves quite often, like we'd done something wrong or at least like we were going to and it was only a matter of time?'

She wiped away two tears, one from each cheek.

'Mirry internalized that idea, I know she did, she internalized everything because she really did want to be good. If something had happened to her, a man, she would have thought she'd done something to make it happen. That she'd tempted him with her evil woman's wiles and she deserved it.'

For a moment neither of them spoke. *I thought your parents wanted to keep you safe?* Robin wanted to say. *They wouldn't let you have a bloody television but they exposed you to* this *vicious bullshit? In your early teens – and presumably before?* She felt furious at their mother in particular: how could she have let this stuff reach her daughters' ears? How self-hating did you have to be? But then, she thought, perhaps their mother had been brought up to believe it, too.

'You haven't told me *why* you formed your theory,' Jude said. 'How did you even know about Miriam?'

Robin explained how she'd shown the scene photos to Maggie and triggered her memory of the news story. She picked her bag off the floor and took out the folder. 'I brought some pictures with me. I've got an e-fit we had done so that we could release it – I'll show you that first and then you can tell me if you think you can manage a photograph from the scene.'

'Okay.' Jude stood and went to the counter along the back

285

wall where she moved a bolt of fabric with a marbled blue pattern and switched on two spotlights clipped to the shelf above. The counter, Robin noticed, was edged with a fixed brass ruler for measuring cloth. She laid the e-fit down and waited.

'It's hard to say,' Jude said, looking at it. 'I mean, objectively I can say, yeah, I see that she's got the same kind of nose as my sister – and me – and the hair's similar, but beyond that . . .'

'Can I show you a photograph?'

She hesitated then nodded.

Robin had been careful to choose the least distressing, a head shot taken at the scene, the closest she could get to their girl looking asleep. She lay on her back, face surrounded by waves of dark hair, her skin so pale under the freckles on a nose that, like Jude said, was very similar to her own. She put it gently down and waited.

Jude was quiet for several seconds. Then she nodded again. 'I can see why you came.'

She looked at the picture for a long time, perhaps fifteen or twenty seconds, and then sat down heavily and was silent for longer. 'I don't know how to feel,' she said eventually, looking at Robin as if she might have the answer. 'I don't know whether to feel horrified – I *am* horrified, that poor, poor girl – but another part of me is . . .' She flung her hands up. 'Because if she *is* her daughter, then Mirry didn't die.'

'At least not immediately,' Robin warned. 'She may have died since. And again, they may not be related.'

'But if she *is* her daughter,' Jude said, 'and if Mirry *is* alive now, then her daughter is dead.'

Into the silence that followed, the church bells struck the half-hour, and almost immediately, someone tried the shop door. Jude jumped and Robin saw relief on her face: thank God,

286

an excuse to step away from this nightmare for a moment. 'Do you mind if I . . . ?'

'No, please.'

Jude went into the front room and she heard her talking to a woman, something about a sister's birthday. Then there were two pairs of feet in the shop, followed by the rustle of tissue paper and the chunter of the card machine. After the bell over the door, Robin heard the keys again. Jude returned a minute later. 'I'm sorry. I've put a note up now.'

'No, *I'm* sorry to have come on a Saturday. It's probably your busiest day.'

'It doesn't really get busy till about eleven, though. She was driving to see her sister in Edinburgh and she knew what she wanted so . . .'

'Do you do well here? I mean, it looks like you must – your designs are great, really unusual, and the shop.' She very much wanted her to be a success, she realized, two fingers to everything she'd had to contend with. She remembered her good-looking husband and was pleased again.

'The shop does pretty well,' Jude said. 'The overheads are quite steep, especially the rent, but it's part of the brand, I use it for social media, and I make most of my profit from the website. We pack up individual things for people who call or email,' she gestured at the mail sack, 'but I have a little warehouse now with a full-time employee who deals with the fabric orders and anything multiple.'

'Good for you.'

'Thanks. I love the shop, even though it's a ton of work. It was always my dream.'

'Really? Not the design part?' She'd gone to Glasgow School of Art, Robin had read on her site, which even she knew was pretty prestigious.

'That, too, but I like the business side. My husband blames it on Barbara Taylor Bradford.'

It took Robin a moment. 'The novelist?'

'I read *A Woman of Substance* as a teenager – world dominion from a single shop in the North.' She smiled.

'That must have been a bit much, as far as your parents were concerned, all those gold letters. Racy!'

Another smile but fainter. 'They didn't know – told you I was the rebellious one. It was probably the title that drew me in, thinking about it – I was probably looking for a counterweight to all those biblical scarlet women. But I *was* rebellious, after Mirry. I was so angry. I was angry at God and I didn't care about the stupid rules any more. What was the point? He wasn't good, and they didn't keep you safe.' She shook her head. 'Also, my parents took their eye off the ball big time – they were broken. And everything else, too – the whole structure of our lives.'

Robin nodded. Trauma seeped.

'The whole community changed, it wasn't only our family. Obviously at school I was an even bigger freak than before, The Girl Whose Sister Was Taken, and the parents – I knew they felt sorry for us but they were also a bit afraid of us, like it might be contagious. I could feel it in our church group, even – like the devil had reached out and touched us personally. No fault of our own, of course, *probably*,' her eyebrows flicked, 'but still *way* too close for comfort.'

'Was it a support to your parents, the group? Their faith?'

'I don't know. Their faith, yes, but not the group, at least not long-term. It broke up a few months afterwards – our leader had a crisis of faith. I think he was like me, struggling to believe in goodness when something like that could happen, and he felt like a fraud. He wanted us to have someone who actually believed the words coming out of his mouth. He ended up going abroad to run a charity eventually, said at least it was something practical. But the group was falling apart anyway. One family had joined another group suddenly, as if they couldn't stand to be around us any more, and another family moved away. Everything just crumbled.'

'And then your father.'

'Yes. That was the worst,' she said simply. 'For people even to have the idea that my lovely dad could . . . It makes me feel actually sick. And then my mum, too. You know about that?'

'I spoke to DI MacDonald at Northumbria – he was DC then, I think. He had another look at the case in 2003.'

Jude nodded. 'I remember him, Frazer, he was kind. I got the impression that he'd been told to cut his losses and stop investigating quite a while before he did, but he stuck his neck out for us. He looked in on us a few times even after he'd had to stop, too.'

'Your mum died of cancer?'

'She did. I think her body gave up, basically – she was so low when she got it, she had no physical reserves left to fight with. It's a terrible thing to say, and I know she felt bad about leaving me, but I think part of her was grateful. She wanted to be done.'

'How old were you?'

'Seventeen when Dad died, nineteen when she did. I deferred university to stay with her.'

'I'm so sorry.'

'Like I said, things are better now. I've got all this going on,' she waved her hand around, 'and I'm married – oh, right, you knew that: Mrs Everleigh.' She smiled. 'John. We met at university, we were in the same year, which we wouldn't have been if I hadn't deferred, so . . . Not evidence of some grand divine plan but definitely a major silver lining. We lived in sin before we got married,' she smiled again. 'I insisted.'

Chapter Thirty

The motorway again, the city exits rolling by in reverse order. Staying under ninety was even harder now – she'd jogged back to the car, bag clamped under her elbow, the DNA swab from Jude's cheek zipped carefully into the interior pocket. She was heading straight to the station to put it in for processing.

Jude had watched her label it. 'If you're right,' she'd asked, 'do you think it means Mirry's in Birmingham?'

Robin heard the hope she was trying to disguise. 'I don't know. There's no evidence one way or the other. Our victim's old enough to have been living there independently.'

And the e-fit was everywhere. If Miriam *was* in Birmingham, she thought as she passed under gantries signposting York and Leeds, why hadn't she come forward? Had she somehow not seen it? Or had she seen it but not recognized her – was that possible? What if she hadn't seen her for years, or even since she was born, if she'd given her up for adoption or her daughter been taken from her, into care? Or illegally. But then, if Maggie had made the connection, twenty years later, having never met either of them, wouldn't the girl's own mother?

Then what if Miriam *had* seen her, had recognized her, but

still hadn't come forward? What if she was scared to contact the police or someone was stopping her?

What if she was dead, too? Murdered.

Among the countless unknowns, one thing seemed certain: if the Gisborne Girl *was* Miriam's daughter, there had to be a chance – a strong chance – that her murder was linked to what had happened to her twenty years ago.

'If your DNA does show a familial link,' she'd told Jude, 'we'll access the files from Miriam's case straight away, but I want to start making some enquiries in the meantime, too.' She'd made some tea and they'd drawn up a list of everyone Jude remembered Miriam knowing. Robin had struggled to hide her hunger for information: she couldn't risk getting Jude's hopes up any further or going off down a blind alley herself and wasting time.

But it didn't feel like a blind alley.

And as the road disappeared between her wheels, another idea was growing, taking on shape and weight.

The Gisborne Girl's killer had been immaculate, leaving no trace of himself at the scene. There was nothing exceptional about that but the pains he'd taken to prevent them identifying the victim were less common. What if, Robin asked herself now, that had been another step in concealing *his own* identity? If they worked out who *she* was, would she lead them to *him*?

Robin pressed her spine against the seat-back, straightened her arms.

Could the Gisborne Girl's killer be her *father*?

There was a service station coming up; she moved into the inside lane. As soon as she stopped, she got out her notebook and started writing, questions and ideas filling a page in a couple of minutes.

It was physical, the sense of being on to something, she felt buzzy and over-caffeinated. To burn some of the energy while she thought, she got out and set off around the car park at a fast walk.

If she was right, where did Lara Meikle fit in? She'd shown Jude three photographs of her – three different hair colours – but she'd looked carefully at each of them then shaken her head. 'No, I don't recognize her.'

'She was only twenty-three, so she'd have been a toddler at the time Miriam went missing, if you knew her back then. Her name's Lara Meikle – does that sound familiar?' Was that why they hadn't been able to find the link between the two women, she wondered; it was twenty years old?

But Jude had shaken her head again. 'No, I'm sorry. I don't think I've ever met anyone called Meikle at all.'

An articulated lorry was pulling out of its bay. Robin stopped on the verge to let it pass and checked her phone: nearly one o'clock. And still nothing from Lennie, which was odd. Even when she did sleep in at weekends, it was rarely later than ten, and she always texted. She thumbed in another message – *All okay? On way back. Dropping in at station v briefly then home, probably four-ish. Pizza Express tonight?* She hit send then remembered she'd told Kev she'd do something with him this weekend, too. She'd text him in a bit, she decided, putting the phone back in her pocket.

After three loops of the car park, she went inside to the food court to buy a sandwich. She sat at a table to eat it, her eyes going to her phone every few seconds, looking for a text from Lennie. When she'd finished and none was forthcoming, she rang her. After last year, her tolerance for suspense where Len was concerned was close to zero.

It rang five times then six and Robin, alarm mounting, was preparing to leave a message when she picked up.

'Mum.' An accurate translation of word plus tone amounted to '*What?*'

'Hello,' she said, a little taken aback. 'Is everything okay?'

'Why?'

Robin heard movement at the other end and TV in the background – or were those voices? 'I hadn't heard from you,' she said. 'You didn't reply to my message this morning.'

'What was there to say?'

The sound of a door closing – yes, she was moving to another room. Robin frowned. 'What do you mean?'

'Well, you'd gone off and I woke up in the house on my own *again* and you were obviously busy so what was the point in texting you? How did I know you'd have time to read a text from me? Or even look at it?'

Robin closed her eyes.

'It's Saturday, Mum, and I've barely seen you since *last* Saturday. Gran's in hospital, you're all over the Net, there's a murderer out there and . . .' She exhaled sharply. 'I suppose I hoped you'd have five minutes this morning for me.'

The guilt was instant. 'Len, I'm sorry,' she said. 'I'm so sorry. I know there's a lot going on, especially with Gran being poorly.' In the usual pattern of their spats, Lennie would now throw a second punch and then, if Robin was conciliatory, she'd start to calm down. This time she said nothing and without her usual cue, Robin flailed. 'Did you get my text?' she asked. 'About Pizza Express?'

'Yeah. It took me by surprise, to be honest. I thought you'd be off with Kev now that *that's* public knowledge.'

Now Robin felt aggrieved. 'No. I wanted to spend time with you.'

'Well, I can't, sorry. I'm busy.'

'Are you?'

293

She sounded more surprised than she'd intended and Lennie took immediate umbrage. 'Yes, I am. Why? Aren't other people allowed to be busy?'

'All I meant was, I didn't know.' Had she forgotten something, she wanted to ask, but if it was important, that'd be another black mark.

'You knew I was coming over to Asha's this afternoon.'

'Right, yes.' Did she?

'The whole of the politics club is here? To make signs for the Brexit protest? It's on the kitchen calendar, Mum, and I was talking about it last night at the hospital.'

'Yes, of course. Of course I knew about that.' It rang a quiet bell. A quiet bell in a large vacuum.

'For God's sake.'

'Len, please, I've got a lot going on at the moment and—'

'You've *always* got a lot going on.'

'Well, this is extreme. We've had four murders in less than a week and I'm SIO on two of them. And one of the others was killed *because* I arrested him—'

'I'm not talking about that,' she cried. 'I get that it's important, *you're* important, I'm not an idiot.'

'Lennie, I'm not saying I'm import—'

'And I even get that you had to go to Durham. My point is, did you really need to go at *four in the morning*? Sneak out under the cover of darkness like you were avoiding me?'

Robin started to answer then stopped: did she?

'You couldn't have waited till six and woken me up? I could have come with you – not for the work bit but for the ride. To spend some time together – road trip? Maybe *I* would have liked to see what Durham looks like. But even if I didn't, I'd like to have been *asked*. To feel like I'm in some way relevant to your life rather than just waking up in an empty house. *Again*. I saw the time on that text – I was on my own for hours, Mum, and I was asleep, I had no idea what was going on. Anything could have happened.'

Robin kept her eyes trained on the tabletop as if Lennie were sitting opposite, burning holes in her. It was true, she could have waited a couple of hours, Len could have come with her if she'd wanted to. She could have done some shopping while she'd been to see Jude; they could have had lunch together. She felt a sharp pang of regret for the day that hadn't been, the wasted opportunity. *To feel like I'm in some way relevant* – God, how could she begin to explain *how* relevant she was?

'I'm sorry,' she said again. 'You're right. It's been a nightmare week but that's not an excuse. Let's do something fun this evening – shall we have our pizza early then go to the cinema?'

'I can't,' Lennie said shortly. 'I'm going to stay at Asha's tonight, she's already invited me. I'll see you tomorrow. If you're available.' She hung up.

Her first impulse had been to phone Lennie back immediately and tell her that she would *not* be spending the night at the Appiahs', regardless of what she'd told Asha: she was fifteen years old, for God's sake, and *she*, Robin, her mother, called the shots until further notice. And how *dare* she hang up on her?

There was also the question of Austin now. The Appiahs seemed to run a tight ship over there from what she'd heard and also seen for herself, but did they know Lennie and Austin liked each other? Would they know to keep an eye on them, listen out for sneaking along the landing in the night? Maybe she should phone them.

No. She was stopped by the memory of Lennie bouncing on her bed after Austin had gone home the other day. Not her question about when she'd become so embarrassing – though that was a consideration as well – but Lennie's excitement. It was completely innocent, nothing had happened between them yet, and even if it did – when it did – she recognized as she began to calm down, Len was sensible, she wasn't going to go wild and start having unprotected sex. They were smart, switched-on young people, both of them, socially aware in a way she'd never been then, and with the age difference, they'd both know how much trouble Austin could get into if anything happened before December, when Lennie turned sixteen.

And – unilateral decision to stay over aside – Lennie was right. Busy as she'd been, she should have been more aware of how Len, with her recent history, would be affected by what was going on. Instead, she'd got so wrapped up in it all, she'd forgotten that her daughter needed her, too.

Why did relationships have to be so bloody hard, she thought, as the North began to fade in her rear-view mirror. Why was it such a struggle to keep things running smoothly even with the people you loved most? Or maybe it wasn't – maybe other people didn't find it hard. Even Luke had managed to be happy with Natalie for twenty years. She, on the other hand, was the human hand-grenade, a crap mother and a disappointment of a daughter not just to her mother (that was a given) but apparently to her dad as well, the person in her family to whom she'd always felt closest. *You think he likes it when someone puts his son down all the time?* She shut off that line of thought quick-sharp: not today.

Anyway, looking on the bright side, at least she didn't have to feel guilty about going to the station this afternoon now. Lennie had turned down her company for the rest of the day so working was the best thing she could do. The sooner she got a resolution on these cases, the sooner normal life could resume.

Yeah, said Len's voice in her head, dry as dust. *For the three days until it happens again.*

Chapter Thirty-one

Robin stopped, her hand on the incident-room door. Through the glass panel she could see not only Tarka, who'd said he'd come in, but Malia and Varan, too, the three of them huddled round his screen. Robin felt a swell of pride and gratitude: it was Saturday afternoon after a week of fourteen-hour days and they must have thought *she* wasn't working but here they were. Her team. Her people.

The moment she pushed the door open, they all turned round, the same light in their eyes she'd seen in her own when she'd got back to the car in Durham. 'We were about to call you,' Malia said, 'but Varan looked out the window and saw your car. It was like we'd summoned you.'

'What's going on?'

'Think we've got him, guv,' Tark grinned, tipping his head at the monitor. 'Finally.'

On the next desk was a tray of coffees, four mugs. 'I didn't know if you'd want one but I made it just in case,' Varan said.

'I definitely do. Thanks.' She put her bag down and joined them at the computer. 'Okay, CCTV maestro, hit me.'

She'd expected one of the streets around Lara's scene but they were looking at Warwick Street. 'Not outside Gisborne's, though,' she said. 'Further along, near the corner with Clyde Street.'

'Exactly. Four lots down, the party-rental people.'

The anticipation was palpable, as if they were waiting for her to open a birthday present. She glanced up and caught Varan watching her face.

Onscreen, it was daylight. The timestamp at the bottom left read 09.06.2019, 15.23. Sunday afternoon? The view was a gated off-street parking area, and Sunday or not, the party-rental people were working: the gates were open and so was the warehouse door, a van parked outside.

'They did a silver wedding anniversary on the Saturday and the clients wanted everything gone the next day, before the marquee damaged the lawn,' Malia said. 'We were there talking to them about an hour and a half after this.'

As they watched, a pair of twenty-something men in jeans and T-shirts emerged from between the van's open back doors with short stacks of dining chairs. They carried them inside the dark mouth of the warehouse.

'And any second now . . .' said Tark.

All of a sudden, a dark shape appeared at the very top right-hand corner of the screen, where the wall of the neighbouring single-storey workshop met the lowest point of its gabled roof. The shape became boots, then legs in black trousers. After a second or two, the legs turned so the toes of the boots were braced against the wall, and the rest of a man's body was lowered into the frame: jeans, a black jacket – lightweight, like an anorak – partially covered by a dark backpack. His baseball cap was pulled right down, hiding his eyes but showing enough of his cheek and neck for them to see that he was white, brown-haired. His feet inched backwards down the wall and his body straightened – he was holding on to something just out of view, the guttering, perhaps, or the edge of the roof.

'Impressive upper-body strength if you ask me,' said Tark, 'cold-blooded killer or not. Another quick look at the warehouse door, make sure the guys aren't coming back, and . . . go.'

The man dropped to the tarmac, paused in a crouch for a split second while the impact reverberated through his knees, then stood and slipped silently – at least on tape – around the front of the van and out of view.

All eyes went to Robin who was quiet for a moment, processing. 'The party-hire place was outside the outer cordon, wasn't it? It was right there, just out of shot. Literally five or six feet away.'

'Yes,' Malia said. 'They did it at the corner so Clyde Street could stay open.'

'The van hides him from view long enough that he'd look as if he'd come round the corner. But it doesn't matter either way – even if they'd seen him straight off, coming out of the little yard here, why would they have suspected? The block had already been secured and searched.'

'This is nearly half past three, guv.' Varan pointed at the timestamp. 'So if it *is* him, he'd been up there for seven and a half hours after it was secured.'

'Time of death's between one and four,' said Malia. 'So again, if it *is* him, he hid more or less in place for *twelve* hours. At least.'

'Clever – very. And self-controlled. He knew it was too risky to leave before the police arrived because we'd be poring over the CCTV, as we have done. He was counting on us not looking at any *after* we had the area secured, and he'd planned to stay hidden until then.'

'Also how to get down without drawing attention. Meticulous

planning – *more* meticulous planning,' said Malia. 'If Ladbrokes were taking bets, I'd put money on that backpack containing full PPE.'

'Meticulous planning on his part and oversight on ours,' said Robin. 'Why didn't Rafferty and his crew check the roof?' And why hadn't *she* checked they had?

'We were talking about that,' Malia said. 'Probably, we reckon, because most of the Gisborne place itself doesn't actually *have* a roof.'

Robin almost laughed – almost. For the love of God.

'And where it does, it's glass. Plus, we were all thinking about the *underground* level,' said Varan.

'Which this guy – if it's him,' Robin said, 'could have used to get next door to Gupta's place and then up to the roof from there.' She clapped Tarka on the shoulder. 'Well done, Tark, that's brilliant work. What made you look this late in the afternoon?'

'Well, that's the not-so-good news, at least so far,' he said. 'Last night you said to start at six the previous evening, go to midday? I did that and nada, either end.'

Oh. 'So still no sign of either of them going in?'

He shook his head. 'I did the evening bit first – nothing. And then, when midday didn't get me anywhere either, I skimmed this next bit just in case. By this point, nearly half past three in the afternoon, I was beginning to think you must have been right about underground access beyond Gisborne's.' He blinked as if his eyeballs were scratchy.

'I've got some drops in my desk,' Robin said.

'Thanks. Left mine at home.'

'On the question of underground access, I had an email from Rafferty an hour ago. He and one of his guys went down there again this morning, and Gupta's is definitely the only way in from outside the factory itself.'

'So either this guy and the Gisborne Girl came in over the roofs during the time frame you've already looked at, Tark,' Malia said, '*or* they were already in there by six p.m. on Saturday evening.'

'Right,' Robin nodded. 'So which is it? And if they *were* in there before six p.m. and she wasn't killed until the early morning, what were they doing in the hours in between?' She thought. 'We haven't had the labs back yet, have we, her blood-work? Varan, could you call and ask when we'll get them? Tomorrow's the week-mark, so they should be imminent. There was no evidence she'd been restrained so was she there willingly or did he drug her?'

'The *other* million-dollar question,' Malia said, 'is, who is he?' She nodded at the computer. 'Tark.'

He started the film again then pulled himself along the desk to the next monitor. The screen woke up on a freeze-frame of the tape of Lara and her attacker.

They watched the films together, side by side. There was no doubt about it: the man striding towards the terrified Lara Meikle was visibly taller than the one lowering himself off the roof, and a good stone or two lighter. Where his gait was loose and loping, this new man's every movement was compactly muscular and – that word again – controlled.

Two completely different physical types. Two different people.

'One thing's bothering me,' Malia said. 'How did he know her body *would* be found?' The four of them were sitting now, perched on the desks. 'I mean, if he killed her then went off to hide until after the police were called, how did he know he wasn't going to be up there for a month? Or indefinitely?'

It was true; one of her first thoughts at the scene, Robin remembered, had been that, unless someone had chanced

301

through, the body could have lain undiscovered amongst the junk for weeks on end. 'He must have known someone *was* going to come,' she said. 'He must have known she'd be found that day.'

'But how would he?'

'Well, we know he knows the building, or he'd studied it – that's clear from how he managed the CCTV. And given this,' she pointed at Tark's computer, 'he must have known he could get through to the place next door.'

'So he's either been there before or had instructions from someone else.'

'Martin and Stewpot knew about the way through,' said Varan, who was scribbling notes as fast as he could. 'And what about Quinton, the urban explorer?'

'But he was *here* at three twenty-three on Sunday afternoon,' said Malia. 'Downstairs, he was here until after five in the end, so it can't have been him.'

Robin looked at her. 'Wasn't he going with someone else, though, originally? His mate – was he a doctor?'

'Yes, that's right,' Malia frowned. 'They were supposed to be going to West Bromwich, he said, but the doctor had to bail at the last minute, for work.'

'Or so he claimed. He's an urban explorer, too, so he could have "done" Gisborne's before, independently.'

'*And* he could have known Quinton was going there so he'd be on hand to find the body, and set up this . . . structure to leave him in the clear, done and dusted,' said Varan.

'Right. Let's get on that ASAP, number one priority. We'll also need to speak to Martin and Stewpot again.' The coffee was tepid now but she took a swig anyway. In the seconds after she swallowed, she heard the rapid movement of Varan's hand across the page. 'You know,' she said, feeling oddly nervous, 'maybe there was another reason he wanted her found.'

At her tone Varan stopped writing and looked up.

'I wasn't here this morning,' she said, all their eyes on her again, 'because I went to Durham. I drove up there first thing, I've just got back.'

'Must have been early; that's got to be a four-hundred-mile round trip,' said Tark. 'What was there?'

'A woman called Jude Everleigh.'

She told them about Miriam Chapman and how Maggie had put her on to the story. 'I looked at it, Malia and I looked at her picture, and she did look similar to the Gisborne Girl. Very similar. The problem was, she'd be too old now, it can't be her, or her sister – formerly Judith Chapman, now Jude Everleigh. *But* the timing works for Miriam to be the Gisborne Girl's *mother*.'

'Whoa.' Varan sat back.

'Last night, when we were drawing blanks everywhere, even after the TV, I went online and discovered that Jude has a shop. I took a punt this morning and went there.'

'And?' said Malia.

Robin unlocked her phone, opened Photos and handed it to her. 'Jude Everleigh.'

Malia looked at the picture then back at Robin. She handed the phone to Tarka, who looked then passed it to Varan.

'I've dropped in a swab downstairs, fast-tracked. Results on Monday morning.'

'What did she say when you told her why you were there?' said Malia.

'She was stunned.'

'I should bloody think so,' Tark said. 'She had no idea about any of this?'

'No.'

'How did she react to your hypothesis?' asked Varan.

'Well, that was interesting. At first she was adamant it couldn't be right, Miriam and she led completely sheltered lives, devout religious family, no interaction with the opposite sex, no way she ran away because she was pregnant, boys weren't even on their mental radar, let alone allowed. But then she looked at it the other way round: if Miriam had been "attacked", as she put it, raped, she'd have been too ashamed to tell anyone.'

'So ashamed that if she'd thought she was pregnant as a result, she might have run away?'

'Yes.'

Varan broke the silence that followed. 'You said there was another reason Roof Guy here might have wanted the body found.'

'Ready for this? I think he might – *might* – be her father.'

'Whoa,' he said again. 'Are you serious?' His look of astonishment was near-comical.

'How? Or rather, why do you think that?' Malia.

'I know it sounds mad, that was my reaction when it first occurred to me, but the more I think about it, the more it makes sense. It makes sense of a *lot* of things, particularly the care he took at the scene to disguise *her* identity – there was literally nothing left to help us work it out except her body and face.'

'You mean, something stopped him going that far – damaging her face? Or her teeth.'

'Even her fingerprints. If he'd really wanted to disguise her, he could have burned them off, God knows that's common enough practice. But he didn't.'

Varan looked sceptical. 'You're saying he couldn't do it because she was his own flesh and blood? Even when he'd stabbed her to death?'

'Or, alternatively,' she said, 'because he knew he didn't need to.'

'Why?'

'Because he knew she'd lived her life off the grid. Look at the official records we've found for her.'

The frown deepened. 'We haven't found any.'

'Exactly. Which, if she's British – and she would be if she was Miriam's daughter, or at least half British – is extraordinary.'

'You think she was purposely kept off the grid,' Malia said. 'Her whole life – nineteen, twenty years – to cover up the crime that led to her being born?'

'I think it's possible.'

'How would you even do that?' Varan asked.

'The easiest way,' Malia said, looking at Robin, 'would be to go overseas.'

She nodded. 'Which would explain why not one person in this entire country has come forward to tell us who she is.'

Chapter Thirty-two

Mark Serra was the name of Jonathan Quinton's urban explorer friend, and he lived in Wake Green with his wife and their two-year-old son. Contrary to Quinton's information, he wasn't, strictly speaking, a doctor, Varan discovered with a bit of online research. 'He's a surgeon. Registrar in orthopaedic surgery. Bones.' The photograph on the hospital website showed a white man with short brown hair.

Robin sent Malia and Varan to talk to him. 'Be careful. If it *is* him, we know he's fit. And strong. First sign of trouble, call for back-up immediately, don't even think about any heroics.'

When they'd gone, she phoned Good Hope on the off-chance of catching someone to take a message for Stewpot and Martin. No one answered, there was no service at dinner time, so she left a message for Daniel Reid on the machine.

She turned to Jude's list of Miriam's contacts and started to put them in order of priority. It was near-impossible to concentrate, however: once Malia and Varan had had enough time to get there, she was checking her phone every twenty seconds. Was this it? Had they found him?

After ten minutes or so, she gave up and went to see if Webster was in next door. He was packing up for the day. 'It's my mother-in-law's birthday and they're coming over for dinner,' he said, pulling his jacket from the back of a chair. 'Sarah's doing a roast.'

'How are you getting on?' She looked at his board, from which Gupta's bulldog-like face gazed mournfully down.

'Making progress,' he said. 'No major breakthroughs, but with CCTV we've been able to track him on foot for about half a mile. Sooner or later he'll get in a car or onto a bus and we'll be off to the races. He's cold, though, I've got to say. After he stabbed Gupta, his T-shirt was covered in blood, obviously, but he'd thought of that. He'd had his jacket open when he accosted him and afterwards he just zipped it up and off he went, strolling along, not a care in the world. At one point, he looks like he's actually whistling.'

'Jesus.' Robin shook her head. 'Did you check in with Martin Engel?'

'Yes, but . . .'

'Let me guess: cast-iron alibi. At quarter past five in the morning.'

'Well, I don't know about cast-iron,' Webster said, 'but yeah. He's got a new girlfriend or more accurately, he's got a girlfriend – first one he's had since his wife left him, apparently. Good luck to him, I say; bloke deserves a bit of happiness after what he's been through.'

'And you haven't found any connection between him and Ben Tyrell and his mob?'

'Engel said he'd never heard of him. Tim went to talk to him after we charged Tyrell and he's confident he's telling the truth.'

'Right.' She felt her phone buzz in her back pocket and pulled it out. Malia.

It's not him.

Robin sagged.

'Bad news?' Webster asked.

'A dead end. Another one.'

An hour later, when Malia and Varan got back, they reported that Serra had been in the garden when they got there, attempting to patch a hole in his son's paddling pool. He'd admitted to his urban exploring straight away and also to having visited the Gisborne works twice on his own.

'He even told us he felt guilty because it was him who recommended Gisborne's to Quinton when he had to flake,' Malia said. 'But he can't be our guy because he, too, has a rock-solid alibi.'

'He wasn't spinning Quinton a line about having to work,' Varan said. 'He was operating all night – a biker on the M42 came off at fifty-five miles an hour around half eleven and he didn't finish pinning his leg and hip back together till half six in the morning. After that, he fell asleep in the staffroom where loads of people saw him at the shift change. He gave us five names off the top of his head, reckons there were probably more if we need them.'

'Can you confirm with the hospital anyway? Get someone to check the theatre records.' It was quarter past seven and she felt hollow-stomached suddenly. 'Is anyone hungry?'

She rang the good Thai place and ordered food for the four of them. 'I can walk round and get it,' Tarka offered.

'Thanks,' she said when she'd recovered from the shock of him voluntarily standing up. She waved off the general movement toward purses and wallets. 'Already paid for. Saturday night – my shout.'

'Something about Mark Serra that made me think.' Malia pinched a piece of chicken panang between her chopsticks and paused. 'His age. He's only thirty-five, right, which means that if the

Gisborne Girl *was* his daughter, he'd have been fifteen when Miriam disappeared. He's ruled out anyway and he grew up in Bristol, nowhere near Whitley Bay, but it made me think: surely he'd have been too young?'

'Plenty of fifteen-year-old rapists,' said Tark through a mouthful of rice.

'Yes, but if we're going by your theory, guv, does it work if Miriam got pregnant by someone that age? The shame part works whatever age, but the practicalities . . . Because if you're right, she had a baby, and could she have done that on her own?'

'Practically, you mean? *How* did she do it, live – *afford* to live – and raise the baby?' Robin thought of her own experience in Lennie's early years, the hellish struggle to make it all work. She'd been older and she'd had help – Corinna, who'd lived with her for the first eighteen months, then Frances, her landlady and resident babysitter in the upstairs flat. Without them, it wouldn't have been possible, practically or otherwise. 'It would have been extremely difficult,' she said. 'A nightmare, probably. But benefits, housing . . .'

'But she never showed up on any of those records,' said Malia.

'Maybe she went under a false name,' Varan suggested.

'Possible but that'd be a challenge in itself. And even if she changed her name, someone could have recognized her.'

'You think the theory's off?' Robin saw Varan and Tark become very focused on their food all of a sudden. She wasn't sure why; she made a point of welcoming all ideas, especially if they didn't fit the current thinking.

'No,' Malia said slowly. 'Not necessarily. I think my point is, if she did have the baby in the UK, someone would know. Much more likely she went overseas, as we said earlier. But how many fifteen-year-olds have the wherewithal to do that, leave home in a state of emotional distress and up sticks abroad to start a new life? Without,' she motioned with her chopstick, 'using a passport at any border.'

'Even *two* fifteen-year-olds,' said Varan. 'Even a Romeo and Juliet situation, nothing criminal. Say you did manage to stow away in a truck over to Europe, where do you go from there? Literally and metaphorically. And if *she* wasn't up for it? Forget it.'

'So if it *is* what happened – Miriam had a baby who turns out to be the Gisborne Girl,' Malia said, 'it's *got* to have been overseas, and to me, that says she had help from someone with means, practical and financial.'

Robin put her fingertips against her lips, a gesture that reminded her of Samir. She moved them away. 'Older, you're saying.'

Malia nodded. 'Older.'

'Which ties into something I was thinking,' said Varan, eyes fixed on his green curry.

'Go on.'

'Well . . . Just, if he killed his *own daughter*, it's got to be really bad, hasn't it, what he's trying to cover up? *Really* bad. If he was fifteen, even if he *had* raped Miriam back then, would he really kill his own child to hide it now, eighteen or twenty years later? I mean, hard enough to get a rape charge to stick at the best of times but twenty years later, with a defendant who was fifteen at the time and the same age as the victim?'

Tark was nodding. 'Yeah, he'd have to be older. If he was worried about being done for sex with a minor, spending years in jail as a nonce, *that* might be enough to kill for.'

'But even then . . . I mean, to *actually kill your own child*?'

'Are you saying he killed Miriam, too, Varan?' Malia asked. 'That *that's* what he was trying to hide?'

'I don't know. That doesn't make sense, either. We know he didn't do it straight away because, if you're right,' a glancing look in Robin's direction, 'Miriam was definitely alive long enough to have a baby. He let her live long enough to have the baby – a baby who could find out the truth years later and come and find him like something out of, I don't know, *Greek tragedy* – and *then* killed her? I mean, I don't want to say I think you're wrong but . . .'

'You think I'm wrong?' Robin smiled.

Varan looked conflicted then smiled – awkwardly – himself. 'I don't know. Maybe. Or if it *is* right – if he *is* her dad – then there's got to be something bigger going on.'

At half past eight, Tark turned off his computer, did another lot of eye drops and gave Robin the bottle back. 'That's me for the day,' he said, blinking. 'Much more and I'm going to do myself long-term damage – I feel like I'm looking through one of those pin-hole cameras.' He patted his pockets for his wallet and keys. 'Anyone fancy a pint?'

Rarely had Robin seen a group of people move so quickly.

'Guv?'

She shook her head. 'Love one, Tark, but better not. Imagine the headlines.'

In her office, she let the 'competent professional' mask drop. She closed her eyes, thought *God, man, this case,* and immediately heard Samir's voice. *Are you still all right with it?* Her answer hadn't changed – of course she bloody was – but as Malia and Varan had diplomatically raised their issues with her theory, she'd actually wondered. It was out there, she knew, and for a moment, she'd struggled to remember how she'd come up with it all. Had she been thinking clearly or had the tiredness and the drive and the stress about Gupta and her mother and Luke and the *Herald* put her into some kind of altered mental state?

Either way, she'd felt her conviction start to ebb away: maybe she *was* making connections where none existed. Okay, so Miriam and the Gisborne Girl happened to look similar – they weren't identical, and some people did look like others, they just did. Was it so unlikely that a girl who'd looked similar to their victim had disappeared twenty years ago? And – bonus – her family had been religious, allowing Robin to spin this whole extra yarn about the shame of a pregnancy and the need to run away.

Go home, said the sensible voice she heard in her ear from time to time these days. *Enough for one day, you're driving yourself nuts.*

She started putting her things in her bag, catching a glimpse of Rose Road through the window as she stood. The sky outside was cerulean, heightened by the contrast with the artificial brightness of her office, the streetlight almost green. Her mind served up the image of Martin Engel standing statue-like by the gate.

She sat back down and opened Facebook on her computer. Cyber had asked them to take For Queen and Country down but they hadn't done it yet. She wasn't on Facebook herself – who'd be interested in what she was doing apart from the people who already knew and people who really shouldn't? – so it took a few seconds to find what she was looking for, and then she was frustrated: she couldn't access either the list of the 137 people who now 'liked' the page or the 178 who followed it.

Avoiding the content of the posts themselves as much as possible, she started scrolling through the comments, looking at the names of the posters. Again she had to credit Tyrell with engaging his audience: some posts had upwards of a hundred comments. She kept going, working down page after page. What she was looking for, she couldn't quite say. Was it still Engel?

Maybe. But definitely something, she could feel it pulling at the corner of her field of vision, almost but not quite visible.

When she found it, she was startled. Startled but not surprised. *Parasites*, he'd written. *Goverment should send em all f*kin' packing!*

It wasn't Martin Engel, it was Billy Torrence. 'Hideous' Billy.

At Mary Street, she let herself into the house, threw her jacket on the peg then went straight to the sofa where she sank gratefully into the cushions.

Some time later, she was woken by the sound of movement in the nook outside the front door. She tensed, instantly on guard. Feet on the tiles, then the lock – a *key* in the lock.

A voice said, 'She must be here, the sitting-room light's on.' Lennie.

Robin felt her shoulders drop. 'Hello,' she called.

Len's head appeared round the door. 'Mum? What's going on? You've only got one light on in the whole house.'

'I conked out here the moment I got home.' She looked at the clock on the TV – more than an hour ago. 'What are you doing back? I thought you were staying at Asha's.'

'Hello,' said Austin, appearing behind Lennie in the doorway, instantly making her look pint-sized. Black Lives Matter was today's T-shirt.

'I changed my mind,' Len said. 'I thought maybe, with everything that's going on, you might like it if I was here.' She shrugged. 'And maybe we could do something together tomorrow instead.'

'Definitely,' Robin said. 'On both counts.'

'Austin walked me home again,' Lennie half-turned, indicating him as if demonstrating on QVC. 'We're just going to have some tea. Do you want some?'

'No, not for me. Wouldn't mind a glass of wine, though.'

'Don't get up,' Len said. 'I'll bring you one.'

She stayed in the sitting room to give them a bit of space, trying not to eavesdrop but inevitably – given the size of the house – hearing some of it as well as frequent laughter. The flirtation had kicked up a notch even since earlier in the week. The level of politesse on display had probably last been witnessed at court – there were multiple solicitations about tea-strength and mug choice from Lennie, and a profoundly unnecessary enquiry from Austin as to whether she was sure about the tea, it being late – but the verbal back-and-forth was quite hilarious; twice Robin had to stop herself laughing out loud and giving herself away. The amount of mental energy going into the apparently throwaway one-liners. She grinned, thinking again about her own early days with Samir, then remembered her brother outside the hospital.

She says she likes it because for once in your life, you actually look happy.

Sodding Luke, she thought, what bollocks. There were hundreds of photographs of her looking happy – thousands of her and Lennie together over the years, the love shining off her face so visibly you could almost feel it with your hand, like heat. What struck her now was that her mum had kept the photo, especially given how much she must have despaired over the bar-wench boobs – in fact, Robin remembered her going on about it at the time and, as a result, of course, her being determined to wear the top all the more, a piece of bolshiness she was now repenting at leisure. Weird, though – had her mum actually been happy for her then? To the extent that she'd wanted to remember it?

Puzzling, she finished her wine and put her head round the

kitchen door to say goodnight. Lennie was leaning against the counter by the oven, Austin at ninety degrees to her against the counter by the sink, his massive trainers almost the length of one of the 12 x 12 floor tiles.

'Thanks for bringing Len back again.'

'No problem. Any time.'

'Lennie, call Austin a cab when you're ready, won't you, it's too late to walk. We've got an account with the firm down the road,' she told him, 'they've got my card details.'

She went upstairs to brush her teeth and a few minutes later – call her the queen of subtext – she heard their voices move up the corridor. The front door opened, there was a bit more chat and then – she couldn't help it, she'd abandoned all pretence now and was listening so hard bats would be jealous – a twenty-second silence. He'd kissed her – or she'd kissed him. Ha!

'See you later,' she heard him say gently, then equally gentle, but full of smile, Lennie's, 'Yeah.'

The door closed and Robin heard his footsteps on the pavement outside her window. She waited, still listening hard, imagining Len looking at herself in the hall mirror, grinning. Had she kissed anyone before or was that the first time? She remembered herself at the same age and shuddered. Her poor mother; she'd led her a merry dance.

Downstairs Lennie went back to the kitchen and put the mugs in the dishwasher. Robin wondered whether she should go and help lock up then thought perhaps Len would like to be alone with her thoughts for a moment; *she* would, in the situation.

Two minutes later, though, Lennie ran up the stairs and appeared at her bedroom door. Yes, he'd definitely kissed her – she was flushed, her eyes shining. Robin kept her expression as neutral as possible. 'Austin go off all right?'

'Yeah.' She came to sit on the edge of the bed and Robin

moved her legs to make room. 'Mum, I'm sorry for shouting earlier.'

'Don't worry about it, you were right.'

'No, I felt bad afterwards. I know you've got a lot going on.'

'That doesn't make it okay for you to wake up here alone this morning. I'm really sorry, and you're right, you should have come with me. Durham's really pretty, quite Harry Potterish – you'd like it.'

'I think some of Harry Potter *was* actually filmed there. Did it help, though? The woman you went to talk to?'

'I don't know. Three hours ago, I would have said yes but I'm not sure any more. But we're making *some* progress. Keep this to yourself, obviously—'

'*Obviously.*'

'Sorry, paranoia. Anyway, we know now that we're looking for two people, not one. The Gisborne Girl and Lara Meikle had different killers.'

Lennie frowned. 'Is that better or worse?'

'How do you mean?'

'Well, it means no serial killer – good – but now you've got to catch *two* people, haven't you?'

Robin started laughing, she couldn't help it, then Lennie started, and they laughed until they were hysterical, eyes streaming.

'So ridiculous,' Robin said, when she was able to. '*Now we've got to catch two people.*'

Lennie laughed, wiped her eyes then fell backwards on to the bed. 'Well, it's true, isn't it?'

'Absolutely true.' She paused. 'Do you want to sleep in here tonight?'

'Can I?'

'Why not? Go and put your PJs on and get in.'

Chapter Thirty-three

'Sod the *Daily Herald*,' Robin said, putting her menu down. 'I actually *am* going to have salmon today. What about you? French toast and orange juice?'

'However did you guess?'

Since they'd moved to Mary Street, The Plough on Harborne High Street had become their favourite place for brunch, but they hadn't been for a month or so – things had been hectic even before the past week, and Len had been spending a lot of time at the Appiahs'. Robin wondered how Asha felt about her and Austin; it must be strange to know something was going on between your brother and one of your best friends. Something *she'd* never had to worry about, at least.

She looked across the table and thought for the millionth time how proud she was of her daughter. *Her daughter* – almost sixteen years later, the phrase still amazed her. It was a source of actual wonderment that she'd had a hand in the production of someone so excellent. Lennie was so sorted. And self-contained. Last night, after they'd turned off the light, she'd wondered if she would tell her about the kiss or at least allude to it – *she'd* been terrible for that, when she was a teenager, wanting to hug things to herself but unable to refrain from incontinently broadcasting hints as subtle as wrecking balls. Lennie, though evidently excited, hadn't breathed a word. Robin respected her for that, even if she was also a bit disappointed.

Len had been in the shower before they came out, and her hair and the tangle of friendship bracelets she never took off were still slightly damp. She was definitely wearing mascara and also some grey eyeliner. Her T-shirt had been an eBay find and she'd declared it perfect when she opened the package, the light-blue material super-soft, the transferred image of California palms crackled and peeling. 'Just the right kind of worn-out, like it's had this cool previous life of, like, surfing in Malibu?' Amazing, Robin had thought – had she even heard of Malibu at fifteen?

'You know,' she said, 'thinking of Durham, we should go there and take a look around when it comes time to choose universities.'

'Okay,' Lennie nodded. She plucked a pack of sugar from the bowl and began folding it, a habit she'd had since she was five. 'I think I want to go to uni in London, though.'

'Really?'

'I mean, I grew up there, and *you* went to UCL . . .'

'Yes, it was what I'd always wanted, too.' She suppressed a pang of anxiety about St Saviour's set-up for university applications. She'd gone to the grammar school, KES, a well-known conduit to the best universities; Savvy's she wasn't sure about. She considered taking the opportunity to suggest – again – that Len apply to the grammar for sixth form then thought better of it. They were having a nice morning; why ruin it? Len had become quite militant recently on the subjects of elitism and privilege; she even complained that Robin had sent her to private school in London, though she'd loved it at the time.

'Any idea what subject you'd do?'

'Not really. English, maybe, or sociology.' She paused. 'Austin'll be doing his applications in the autumn.'

'What's he going to apply for?'

'Politics and/or economics.'

'Good for him. In London?'

Lennie shrugged, avoiding eye contact. 'Maybe.'

Robin nodded. Looking at her, so grown-up, she was reminded of what Malia had said yesterday about fifteen-year-olds and the wherewithal to up sticks overseas. Could Lennie do it? Alone? She was probably practical enough bodily to get overseas somehow but long-term, and financially, Robin couldn't see it. And though she could pass for eighteen in certain lights, a student taking a gap year, people would question it, even with the eye make-up and the artfully distressed surfer get-up. What had Miriam been wearing when she disappeared? A striped woollen dress and leggings, no doubt approved by her in-house woman-censoring moral standards unit. She'd probably looked about twelve.

Two wires connected in Robin's head – she actually jolted. The *Gisborne Girl's* clothes – her whole appearance. Yes, the clothes had been vaguely modern, jeans and a T-shirt, sneakers, but they'd also been completely modest, almost unisex – her jeans hadn't been figure-hugging skinny; the white T-shirt was standard issue with a high round neck, nothing like her own bodacious number in that wretched photograph. No jewellery, though that could have been stolen. But no make-up, and her ears weren't pierced. It was 2019 – what eighteen or twenty-year-old didn't have their ears pierced?

Had the Gisborne Girl been living in the same religious set-up as Miriam?

Her hand itched to text Malia, she actually made a fist in her lap to stop herself reaching for her phone. She'd promised herself she'd give Lennie her undivided attention this morning.

Nevertheless, her brain was flooding with thoughts and ideas – on a scan, it would be flushed with colour, swathes of green and red and blue all madly pulsating. Say the Gisborne Girl *had* grown up in the same sort of environment – what would that mean? That she'd been raised by Miriam to adulthood? That there was a pod of these people elsewhere? Had they helped Miriam when she got pregnant, spirited her away? But no – surely they would have censured her, wouldn't they, this fifteen-year-old scarlet woman, lurer of poor innocent men from the path of righteousness? And her parents had been devastated, there seemed little doubt about that; they couldn't have known.

Their waiter delivered Lennie's orange juice and her cappuccino. Robin took a sip too soon and burnt her tongue.

'Steady there, Eddie.' An inch from her hand on the tabletop, Lennie's phone lit up. 'Asha,' she said, glancing at it, then, 'Oh my God.' Her face was a picture of horror.

'What? What's happened?'

She looked up, eyes huge. 'Austin got beaten up last night. On his way home.' She burst into tears.

They had their food wrapped up and took it with them. 'It's okay, Mum,' Len tried to argue, 'we don't have to leave. Your coffee, and—'

'Lovely, we're not going to sit here and pretend everything's fine. Come on.' She over-tipped to compensate for the drama then led Lennie through the gawping flock of people waiting for a table.

'It's my fault,' Lennie said in the car, tears rolling down her cheeks. 'It's my fault.'

'How on earth's it *your* fault?'

'You told me to call him a cab but he said he wanted to walk. You *said* it was too late. I tried to make him but I didn't try hard enough and now look.'

'That's not your fault, it's mine,' Robin said, stomach sinking. 'I shouldn't have left it to you. I wanted to give the pair of you a bit of autonomy and I didn't want to look like I was throwing Austin out, but I should have just called them myself.'

At Mary Street, they sat on the sofa and Len rang Asha. Austin was at home now, she told her, but overnight he and their dad had spent five hours in A&E, where he'd had stitches for a long cut on his cheekbone. He was concussed, his nose was broken, and the first doctor they'd seen had been worried about internal injuries. Thankfully, in the end, it turned out to be deep bruising, though an X-ray showed that his bottom left rib was cracked. He was sleeping now, dosed up on painkillers.

Robin listened to Asha's tinny voice and longed to grab the phone and demand a detailed description of the assailants and a blow-by-blow account of how it had happened, whether Austin had been able to make out any names, any accents, which direction they'd run in. 'Ask if they've reported it,' she whispered. 'It's assault – it needs to be prosecuted.'

Lennie put her hand over the mouthpiece, slightly impatient. 'They have, Mum – they did it last night.'

When she hung up, she filled in the details Robin hadn't heard. Austin had been three roads from home, apparently, when he'd run into three youths who'd muttered something about his T-shirt then laughed. 'He was wearing his Black Lives Matter shirt,' Lennie said. 'Austin told his dad he knew he shouldn't react but he couldn't stop himself – he'd been in a good mood, happy, and why should they be allowed to ruin that without any comeback?'

He'd turned and asked them what they'd said and from there,

it sounded like, things had escalated quickly, to the point where they'd had Austin on the ground and one of them had booted him in the solar plexus, which was when, thank God, a car came round the corner and they took off. 'Laughing,' said Lennie. 'Ash said they were laughing as they ran away.' The driver had stopped and helped Austin up, called his parents.

'Why are people like this, Mum?' Lennie asked. 'So . . . full of hate?'

'I don't know, lovely,' she said, cuddling her. 'Because they feel threatened. Because they need someone to feel better than because they don't have much going for themselves.'

'But it's *so* bad – it's like it's getting worse and worse. Brexit and Trump and everyone just feeling like they can say and do whatever they want and all this *stuff* – like, a seventeen-year-old can't even walk home without getting beaten up for being black? And that poor man who was *stabbed to actual death*.'

'I know.' She smoothed her hair. 'I know.'

She remembered the comments she'd read on For Queen and Country, that seething pool of bile. Go outside your front door, she thought, and – most of the time – the net of common decency and shared humanity more or less held. It was there, though, the bile, bubbling away millimetres beneath it and rising all the time.

Chapter Thirty-four

When the email arrived on Monday morning – half an hour after she'd been told to expect it, half an hour during which she'd hit refresh at least fifteen times – she stood up and paced the patch of carpet in front of her desk. Then she reached for the phone. 'Have you got a minute?'

Samir looked up from his computer as she shut the door behind her. 'Hi.'

'News,' she said.

'Good morning to you as well. How was your weekend? Mine was good, thanks.' He smiled. 'Go on then.'

'The Gisborne Girl is the daughter of another girl called Miriam Chapman who disappeared in Northumbria in December 1999 aged fifteen.'

'You've got an ID?'

'That's it, though, we haven't. Not beyond that.'

A quizzical look. 'Care to elaborate?'

She told him about Maggie and her own mission to see Jude on Saturday. 'I fast-tracked a cheek swab, and I've just had the analysis – close familial link, consistent with Jude being our victim's aunt, *ergo*, her sister being the Gisborne Girl's mother.'

He nodded slowly. 'Nice work. And nice work Maggie – we owe her a drink.'

'Big time. I can add it to the twenty thousand drinks I already owe her.'

'Going to be quite a bar bill. So where are you going from here?'

'Well . . .' She told him the theory she'd raised with her core team on Saturday afternoon. 'They were pretty sceptical, too,' she admitted, seeing his expression, 'and I can see why – as Varan said, there'd have to be something major going on for someone to kill their own child. I started thinking maybe I was just conjuring stuff out of thin air but yesterday I made a different connection.'

'Which was?'

'The Gisborne Girl's clothes, her whole look – it was so plain, we'd actually discussed whether she was in hiding, trying to stay incognito. But *now* I wonder if she grew up in the same kind of religious environment as Miriam. Yesterday afternoon, I did a bit more research.'

It had taken Len quite a while to calm down enough to eat but then they'd warmed up their food and watched *The Devil Wears Prada*, Lennie's choice. It was one of Robin's father's favourites, and she'd watched it with him so many times, Len knew most of the dialogue by heart. Those memories were probably as comforting to her as the film itself, Robin thought: one of the best things about moving back to Birmingham – especially living at Dunnington Road – was that Lennie had really got to know her grandparents. They'd become very close, the three of them, but part of Lennie – the fatherless part – responded especially to Dennis. He was a substitute dad to her now, a dad-once-removed.

After the film, Robin rang him for a progress report. 'I'm about to go over there,' he'd said. 'She told me not to go this morning, said I looked tired and needed a rest.'

'Can I go with him?' Lennie said.

He'd heard her. 'Of course you can, sweetheart. Great. How about you, Robin? I could come and pick you both up?'

'I was thinking of going later,' she said. 'Around four. There's a few things I need to get done, domestic stuff. The house is falling apart.'

'Right you are. I'll be round to pick up my Lennie in about twenty minutes, then.'

When she'd waved them off, she'd quickly emptied the laundry baskets, put a wash on and unloaded the dishwasher – there you go, she thought; a veritable domestic Goddess – then got out her laptop and the list of names Jude had connected to the Chapmans' church group, seven families in total plus their leader, Brother Philip.

Google found three of the families easily. Two of them were still in Whitley Bay and the third, the Jessops, were in Houghton-le-Spring, south of Newcastle. The next one was more of an effort – their surname was Harris – but based on a triangulation of their children's names, she was fairly confident she'd located them in Chester. They had an asterisk on the list as the family who'd moved away not long after Miriam disappeared.

The other three families were a dead loss. The Evanses and Browns she hadn't been optimistic about to start with, especially as the Browns had moved away later. The Purkiss family – Jane, Jude had thought her name was, and Graeme or Graham, son David – she'd had some hope for, but five different searches had turned up nothing conclusive.

She'd moved on to Brother Philip – Philip Hatton 'in real life', as Jude had put it. Google coughed up seven hits on 'Philip

Hatton Whitley Bay', but there were only two original posts, the rest just the same newspaper articles on different sites. Both dated from the time of Miriam's disappearance and quoted him appealing for her to come home or, if someone was holding her, for them to let her go unharmed.

She'd read the notes she'd scribbled down for him: *crisis of faith after M disappeared, felt like a fraud, went abroad to run charity.*

Abroad.

Google returned more than two million hits for 'Philip Hatton charity'. She scrolled through several pages' worth, a lot of them relating to the same good soul who used his passion for marathon bike rides to raise money for cancer charities. The pictures showed an incredibly fit-looking man in skin-tight Lycra but he was forty, absolute tops, likely mid-thirties: surely too young to have been running a church twenty years ago.

LinkedIn had eighty-plus Philip Hattons and Facebook even more, over half of them abroad – Australia, New Zealand, the US, French Polynesia, for heavens' sake. She looked at twenty-odd profiles before admitting that it was a needle-and-haystack situation: she had no idea what he looked like, how old he was, where in the world he'd gone. She'd texted Jude: *Can I call you?* Jude rang her less than a minute later.

'How old was Brother Philip when you knew him?' she'd asked. If the CCTV did show the killer, could that man – who'd lowered his body so neatly off a roof – really have been a priest twenty years ago?

'I don't know,' Jude said. 'He was an adult-adult, not early twenties, and when you're a teenager, anyone over twenty-five might as well be forty.'

'But he was between twenty-five and forty, you're saying, not fifty or sixty?'

'If I had to guess now, I'd probably say early thirties.'

Well, there was her own prejudice speaking, Robin thought: in her mind, all priest figures were fifty-five and looked like Father Christmas at best, Nigel Farage (ugh) otherwise.

'Is that young, to be a priest?' she'd asked.

'Not wildly. And it was a church *group*, like I said, not a church-church.'

'What was it like, then? What was the set-up?'

'It was simple,' Jude had said after a moment. 'We didn't have a church – it was more like . . . Well, probably the closest thing would be a Quaker Meeting House, in terms of what it looked like. It had been an old community centre, I think, something like that, but he'd renovated it himself, stripped it all back and painted it white. There was a table with a white cloth, a pair of wooden candlesticks. We sat on old wooden school chairs, in a circle. Thinking about it,' she laughed slightly, 'it was quite chic. Minimalist.'

Was that normal? Robin wondered. Did priests usually renovate their own meeting places?

'Your parents can't always have gone there,' she said, 'if he was only in his early thirties?'

'No, none of us did. We used to go to the Catholic church but my parents got frustrated with it.'

'Why?'

'I don't know. The priest was old and a bit doddery, I think. I remember his sermons going on and on – Mirry and I used to joke about getting numb bums.' She'd paused again. 'I was only ten or eleven at the time, most stuff went on out of my earshot, but I think it really boiled down to him not giving them what they wanted. They wanted a bit of strictness, even fire-and-brimstone. I don't remember Father O'Brien doing much of that.'

'Do you know how they found Brother Philip?'

'Though the Jessops – they were friends of ours. They had a son, Gavin, who was "troubled", and Brother Philip was really supportive. He'd met Gavin at this youth group they made him go to, and he'd tried to help him, talking to him, acting as a mediator, you know. It didn't work, eventually he was arrested for something no one would talk about, probably drug-dealing I reckon now. Brother Philip told the Jessops it wasn't their fault and Gavin would find his way back to God. They joined his group then recommended it to us.'

'What were the meetings like?'

'Again, simple. We didn't take the sacrament. Brother Philip gave a long sermon and then there were prayers.'

'The sermons were quite . . . hard-line, though? Based on what you said about Sodom and Gomorrah, the portrayal of women?'

'It's funny, I don't remember it at the beginning – maybe I was too young – but yeah, by the end, definitely. A couple of years ago, Lindsay Harris got in touch again online and we talked about it. The women thing in particular.'

'Did it all come from him?'

She hesitated, as if weighing something up. 'No, I don't think so.' She sighed. 'I don't want to be disloyal but I think it was kind of a consensus among the men that it was a message they didn't mind.'

'How do you mean?'

'It was the Nineties,' she said. 'Lindsay's dad was unemployed – they moved to Chester because he got a job – and one of the others was, too, Mr Burdon. There was a lot of unemployment – the old industries had gone, the shipbuilding on Tyneside, all the stuff associated with that, the old order. They probably felt like they needed a bit of bolstering, being told they were still the alpha dog, at least in their own homes.'

'But your dad wasn't like that, was he?'

'This is what I meant about being disloyal,' she said. 'He was a gentle man, community-minded – he'd do anything to help someone out – but impressionable, if that doesn't sound like a strange thing to say about your own father. Easily led. He wasn't one of the vociferous ones in the group but he allowed himself – and us – to be part of it; he didn't stand up and say, hold on, this is a bit harsh.'

'And none of the women did?'

'No. Not that I know of. I don't think they felt it was their place to.'

'The group broke up three months after Miriam disappeared,' Robin told Samir, perched on the edge of her chair. She'd been halfway through the story when he'd pointed a finger first at her, then at it: *Sit*.

'Where did he go, for this charity work?'

'Jude didn't know. But she rang this other girl from the group, Lindsay, and *she* asked her mother. She couldn't remember exactly, but she said he'd gone to work with street children in South America. He'd visited them in Chester before he left, fundraising, and she'd been horrified because he told her the city he was going to had had a huge problem with children living on the street and some people there – including some rumoured to have links to the police – had seen fit to address it by shooting them.'

'Jesus Christ.'

'I know. Which is true, by the way, because with that and "Philip" and "British", I managed to find a Facebook post from a guy on a gap year who'd volunteered with a charity working with street children in Salvador, Brazil, in 2003, and I *think* the guy he's talking about might be Philip Hatton.'

Samir blew out a long breath then narrowed his eyes. 'Why

do you only *think*? And even if it is him, why do you think he was responsible for what happened to this girl Miriam?'

'Because,' Robin said, 'this charity was founded in the spring of 2000 – May, to be precise – by a British man called John Philips and his seventeen-year-old adopted daughter.'

Chapter Thirty-five

Salvador was four hours behind the UK so it was still only eight a.m. there when Robin phoned. Her first call went to a machine, the only part of whose high-speed message she caught – just about – was the name of the place where the man she wanted now worked.

She waited a few minutes then called again, and this time a woman answered. Robin had looked up how to say good morning, as well as 'I'm sorry, I don't speak Portuguese but I'd like to speak to Luis Abreda,' but her rendering of it was excruciating. Malia was with her, the call on speakerphone; she caught her eye and grimaced.

'Momento,' the woman said, however, and they heard a tap as the handset went down.

Thirty seconds later, a man said in accented but excellent English, 'Good morning, this is Luis Abreda. How can I help?'

His voice matched the picture she'd seen of him online, full of energy and good humour. A handsome man of about forty-five, he'd been dressed in a leaf-green T-shirt, big smile showing a lot of teeth.

Robin introduced herself. 'I'm hoping to talk to you about John Philips.'

'Has something happened to him?' The man was instantly concerned.

'Not as far as I know.'

'Thank God for that.'

'I'd like to speak to him about a case I'm working on. You do know John, then?'

'I did some years ago, yes. He was the director of one of the first places I worked here in Salvador. In fact, I helped him set it up.'

'Lugar Seguro?'

'That's right.' He sounded surprised.

'I'm sorry, I've done a lot of research to find someone who might be able to help me. I found your name on an old Facebook post, and you're the only person I've traced who worked there at all.'

'Yes, it was only small. Apart from me and our head cook, the rest of the staff were volunteers.'

'You say "was" – it's not running any more?' She'd found very little trace of it online but thought perhaps that wasn't unusual. Though the shelter Abreda currently ran had an impressive multi-page website.

Luis Abreda laughed a little, as if she'd said something faintly silly. 'No, it's not running any more. It closed in 2004.'

'Do you know why?'

'He'd done his work there, things were running smoothly. That was his gift, he said, getting things started. He was ready for a new challenge.'

Robin detected a hint of bitterness underneath the bonhomie. 'Right. Do you know what the new challenge was?'

'I'm afraid I don't.'

'Or where? Did he come back to the UK?'

'I'm sorry, I don't know that, either. His gift *wasn't* staying in touch.'

'Do you remember his daughter?'

'Margaret? Yes, of course.'

'She must have been – what, fifteen or sixteen when they arrived in Salvador?'

'A little older – seventeen, I think.'

'If I email you a photograph of her from that time, could you just confirm that we're talking about the same person?' She'd cut-and-paste the one from the *Newcastle Chronicle*'s website.

'Of course,' he said again.

'Thank you, that would be a big help.' Robin met Malia's eye. 'Mr Abreda, did Margaret have a baby?'

'Baby Hannah,' he said. 'Yes, she was born just a few months after they arrived here. My mother could probably tell you exactly when because she was born right there, in the building – my mother was volunteering in the kitchen that day and she helped John deliver her. It all happened very fast, she said,' he laughed, 'no time to get to the hospital.'

I bet, Robin thought. 'Who was the baby's father, do you know?'

He sighed. 'That's a sad story.'

'I'm afraid I don't know it.'

'It wasn't talked about, of course, but John told me Margaret had been assaulted back in the UK, and Baby Hannah was the result. She was the reason they moved to Brazil: a new start for Margaret, a place where she could feel safe. Un Lugar Seguro not just for the street children here but for her. A safe place.'

Varan looked up in mock-outrage as Malia pulled a handful of tissues from the box on his desk. 'Do you really need *all* those?'

'Good cause,' she said, taking them to the whiteboard. Standing on tiptoe, she scrubbed out 'The Gisborne Girl'. Then, marker squeaking, she wrote 'Hannah' in letters twice the size, and underlined it.

Shortly before the afternoon briefing, Robin closed her office door and called Kev. It rang several times before he picked up. 'Sorry about that, I was just talking to one of the guys on the compactor, had to move.' He was still moving, his feet crunching across the lot. 'How are you?'

'Elated, exhausted, baffled, frustrated. You?'

'I'm all right, actually.'

She laughed. 'Good. Kev, look, I'm sorry about the weekend.'

'It's okay, I got your texts yesterday – well, as you know: you replied to my replies.'

'I know, but dinner . . .'

'It's okay, Rob.' There was a finality to the way he said it – end of subject.

In the background now, she heard the crack of glass then the whine of the engine as one of the huge claws grabbed the next car and lifted it to its fate. She'd asked Kev once how he dealt with the noise day in and day out. 'I don't hear it,' he'd said cheerfully. 'Unless I listen for it, which I do from time to time. It's my soundtrack – I've been hearing it my whole life.'

'We've got a name for the girl at Gisborne's,' she said. 'Well, a first name.'

'That's great.' He sounded like he really meant it. 'You know who she is, then?'

'After a fashion.'

'And how's your mum doing?'

She exhaled. 'I don't know.'

'You didn't manage to see her yesterday?'

'No, I did, I just don't know how she's doing. I mean, you know my mum: under normal circumstances she never stops moving. Now she's stuck in that bed surrounded by people on their last legs and they're still not saying when they'll let her go.'

'Decided they like her in there, have they?'

'Something like that.'

From outside in the incident room, she heard a whoop and then clapping. Through the window, she saw Varan make a very uncharacteristic fist and punch the air. 'Hold on a sec, Kev,' she said, 'something's going on here.'

She opened her door. 'Malia?'

Malia grinned. 'DI Webster's got an arrest for Gupta, guv.'

Webster's CCTV crew had traced their man on foot all the way to a muscle gym in Ladywood, where they'd shown photographs to the staff, and learned that his name was Lee Donnelly. When they cut the padlock on his locker, they'd discovered a gym bag with a black T-shirt and jeans in, both stiff with blood. From there, it was an easy hop from his membership file to his home address, and from there to his employers in Great Barr. He was a van driver for a company that delivered top-quality meats direct to home consumers. They'd arrested him as he returned to the depot after his rounds.

'*Is* he one of Ben Tyrell's mob?' she'd asked Webster.

'To be confirmed. We're on that now, scouring the Net and his electronics. The evidence threshold for incitement to murder is so high, though. Even if Donnelly saw the page and got his inspiration from it, it'd be hard to charge Tyrell without corroborating evidence he'd given actual detailed instructions, which, on the basis of what we've found on *his* phone and computer so far, we're not going to get.'

'So, for Tyrell, it'll only be Inciting Racial Hatred and Malicious Communications?'

'Still the potential for a nice long sentence,' he smiled. 'And Lee Donnelly will get murder, of course, pretty much open and shut.'

'Nice work.'

'Thanks. What you asked, by the way, about Varan and Gupta's dad – it's late there, with the time difference, so the guy at the consulate said he'll wait till the morning, but he'll ask Mr Gupta if he'd like to speak to him. I'm sure he will – I would, if it was my son.'

'Thank you, Simon.'

'Any time.'

'So now we need to catch *our* killers,' she told her team. 'Both of them. Tark, do you want to start?'

'Sure. As of about an hour ago,' he said, 'we've got tape that shows Roof Man going down Warwick Street to Moseley Road, where he hangs a right. He crosses Bradford and Cheapside and reaches Highgate Park where,' he paused for dramatic effect, 'unfortunately, he hops the fence and disappears into the trees.'

A collective grunt.

'So, next-level challenge,' said Tark, 'but we're up for it.'

'How about the other end?' Robin asked. 'Any sign of him or Hannah going in yet?'

He shook his head. 'We're back to the same problem: the CCTV blind spot outside Gisborne's itself. We're working on tape from the surrounding streets but going earlier than before, in hour-long tranches. We're back to six p.m. on the Saturday now.'

Subtext, left unspoken so as not to be completely depressing: *and still nothing.* 'Right. How about Lara Meikle?'

'Tape of that guy turning on to Leopold Street but that's it. Most of us are on Roof Man.'

'Okay. Malia?'

'Northumbria are sending the old case files,' she said, 'and I've also spoken to DI MacDonald there about our man "Brother" Philip aka Philip Hatton aka John Philips. Obviously we're all wondering why he wasn't scrutinized back then, and the answer is, he was: they interviewed him several times. DI MacDonald told me there was strong suspicion around the whole of the church group – all the men were interviewed more than once. But "Brother Philip" had a solid alibi for the day of Miriam's disappearance and no one had ever suspected anything odd about his relationship with her.'

'Did no one think the priest thing was weird?' said Niall. 'I mean, this God-squad he'd set up in a community centre?'

'They *did* think it was weird,' said Malia, 'hence the scrutiny. But no one who was actually involved with it said it was weird, and there was no reason to think "Brother Philip" was anything other than a slightly unorthodox God-squadder who liked the sound of his own voice.'

'Plenty of those about, God knows. Ha.'

Robin gave him a watch-it look. 'He had no police record, no one had ever raised any red flags about him. To all appearances, he was a good guy.'

She made it home to Mary Street in time to watch the end of the ten o'clock news with Lennie, and the *Midlands Today* bulletin afterwards. She'd expected Webster to do the interview about Lee Donnelly's arrest but instead, full dress uniform glinting off the camera like a bureaucratic disco ball, Kilmartin appeared.

Robin texted Samir: *??*

"The public," he replied, *"will derive an extra measure of reassurance from hearing it from the top."*

Unbelievable.

And yet, came his response, *always completely predictable.*

Chapter Thirty-six

The day got off to a decent start. She had breakfast with Lennie who reported that Austin was out of bed – 'Eating all the granola and hogging the iPad, Ash says' – and she was still at her desk in time to have an action list ready and waiting when people got in. Standing in front of Hannah's board, which was now half-covered with what they knew about Miriam and "Brother Phil" as the team was calling him with dripping scorn, Robin told her silently, *We're making progress. We're going to get justice for you, too.*

She put five people on calling the church-group families she'd already located and tracing the ones she hadn't. Another seven researched charities in South America and the UK and scoured the Net. Varan had updated the DVI with Interpol, and as soon as the working day started there, they'd put in calls to police in Salvador, Rio and São Paulo.

At about ten thirty, Varan appeared in the doorway, holding a piece of paper. 'She was drugged,' he said.

'Who was?'

'Hannah. The labs are back. Tramadol – enough to keep her knocked out for a couple of days, apparently.'

'But not quite enough,' Robin said, thinking of the hand and its slack fingers, 'to keep her under while she was stabbed to death.'

Some time mid-morning, Malia had disappeared. When she returned, she came straight to Robin's office door, eyes bright.

'What's up?' Robin asked.

'Lara Meikle. I was thinking about the poor response to the CCTV. If there was a local Boo Radley figure who matched the physical description, we would have heard about it, don't you think? We'd have had calls: "You should talk to that lanky oddball who lives two doors down, he's a right weirdo, I bet it's him." His height makes him pretty distinctive.'

'Go on.'

'So I thought what if he *isn't* weird? What if she *did* know him? Remember when she speaks in the tape?'

'We couldn't be sure about that, though, could we? And none of her friends or family recognized him.'

'No, and he's not on her social media, either, I had another look last night. Apart from a couple of Internet celebrity-types, all her friends on there are people she knows in real life, too – childhood friends, school-friends, her boyfriend's friends, etc. But that made me notice something else: she's collected all these people from different areas of her life but there aren't *that* many of her work friends, comparatively. I wondered if it was deliberate – if she wanted some separation.'

'Interesting.'

'So, I've just been back to the insurance company. Her colleagues, desk-mates, they didn't know anything so I spoke to her boss again. He hadn't seen the CCTV so I brought it up on his computer. At first he didn't know him but then he did this kind of startle, like someone had woken him up.'

'So he *did* know him?'

'Not *know* but he said that at the end of last year, November, Lara had gone with him to a conference in London and one of the other delegates had been very friendly with her – flirty – and she'd flirted back. He evidently felt bad about telling me, he knew she was already with David Pearse and he didn't want to hurt him or speak ill of the dead, but he'd thought at the time that she and this guy might have had a bit of a thing, you know, a one-nighter, conference fling? It was the height – the way he walked. He said he remembered thinking he was gangly.'

'So who he is?'

'Well, that's it. Ian – her boss – doesn't know his name or where he worked.'

'Is he local?'

'He doesn't know that either.'

'But he was definitely at this conference?'

'Yes. As a delegate. So I'll get on that now, details of the conference, full list of attendees, etc.'

'Get Niall to help you.'

She nodded and turned to go, already thinking.

'Malia?' Robin called after her. Malia stopped and looked back. 'Brilliant,' Robin said.

Locked up or not, Ben Tyrell was having a day in the sun. Around noon, a handful of poorly punctuated Tweets had demanded West Midlands Police #FreeBenTyrell then #FreeWhiteVoices. The timing corresponded neatly with breakfast on the East Coast of the US, and some prominent American bigot had picked up the story and retweeted three of the posts to his 157,000 followers. A virtual bun-fight ensued, and while sanity prevailed thanks to an answering wave of people pointing out that, in fact, on the evidence available, Tyrell was exactly where he should

340

be, enough momentum had accrued that a man called Steven Taggart had started calling on #TyrellsTribe to gather at five o'clock to protest against West Midlands Police's 'rampant bias against white people and their right to voice an opinion'.

She'd rolled her eyes, envisaging a straggling bunch of losers outside headquarters on Colmore Circus trying to avoid getting mown down by three lanes of rush-hour traffic – should have thought *that* one through – but Varan had corrected her. 'No, guv,' he said, holding up his phone, 'they know Tyrell was brought to Harborne when he was arrested. Taggart's telling them to come here.'

A few minutes before five, they came.

Up in the incident room, the first thing they heard was chanting, quiet to start then suddenly louder – they'd rounded the corner – a call-and-response between a voice on a megaphone, 'We will not be silenced,' and a group of low male voices, 'We will *not* be silenced.' It was restrained, almost monk-like; Robin felt the hairs go up on her arms. She glanced at Malia and Varan who abandoned their desks and went with her to the window, where the rest of the team quickly joined them.

Outside on Rose Road thirty men came to a halt directly outside the station gates and formed ranks around the man with the loudhailer. Was that Taggart? All eyes were trained forward, all their bodies held still. Their ages varied, twenties to fifties, but they were all dressed the same: white T-shirts and combat trousers, Doc Martens.

'We will not be silenced.'

'We will *not* be silenced.'

This wasn't an army put together in a day, that much was obvious. They were organized, disciplined. And fit. Again, in her prejudice, Robin had imagined a group of chubby discontents chiselled off their sofas by a motivated handful but this lot looked like they'd been training at Lee Donnelly's muscle gym. In fact, she realized, some of them probably had. Wherever they'd done it, they'd got results: powerful shoulders, thick necks, big arms.

Shit – Hideous Billy. She scanned the rows of faces but didn't find him. Thank Christ, that was the last thing she needed.

'They're like *Orcs*,' Varan said at her left shoulder.

'Orcs who all go to the same barber,' said someone else behind her, maybe Niall. 'The one with the shaver stuck on "skinhead".'

Robin expected a laugh at that but the response was surprisingly frail. These men *weren't* Orcs, and they could all see it. The power out there wasn't just brute force but mental strength, too, however misguided, and real anger. The joke had been an attempt to minimize it, put it back in its box, and it had failed.

An email had gone round at four to say that, 'to err on the side of caution', the station gates would be locked and Rose Road closed to traffic. From the window now, they could see the backs of the officers stationed along the outside of the fence, some of them eye to eye with protestors only ten feet away. By her earlier assessment, she'd thought full riot gear was a bit of an over-reaction but she saw now that she'd been woefully naive. She didn't envy them stuck out there. Thinking of Austin, she wondered briefly if any of them would rather have been on the opposite side.

'We will *not* be silenced.'

'They're giving me the actual heebie-jeebies,' Malia said, shivering. 'It's like that Bible story – the walls of Jericho. The stillness.'

More people were coming now, in twos and threes, largely men but here and there some women, too. These weren't the crack troops but enthusiastic supporters who surrounded the core squad, quickly taking up the chant and magnifying it. They punched the air with signs that declared #ForQueen&Country, *England 4 the English, White Lives Matter, White Power*.

Robin felt movement and turned to see Samir. Malia gave him room at the window and he took her spot, close enough for Robin to feel his body heat.

'Well, these look like some very fine people,' he said.

'Yes, wouldn't Oswald Mosley be proud?'

The crowd had now doubled in size, and while the base note of the chant was the same, it had grown much louder and cacophonous, far less disciplined. In an upstairs window in a house across the road, Robin saw two children appear, boys, not yet teenage. What could they make of all this? They were probably terrified – she was.

'We will *not* be silenced.'

'And we thought we'd shut this lot down,' said Niall.

'It'll take more than arresting that piece of shit,' Malia told him. 'It's like Medusa – you cut off one snake-head and another two grow in its place.'

More people – more and more. 'How many are down there, do you reckon?'

'At least a hundred,' said Samir. 'A hundred and twenty, maybe.'

Where were they all coming from? And at five on a Tuesday afternoon. Had they taken time off work specially, half-day holiday?

Suddenly, from the other end of the street, came a competing sound, equally loud. Air horns, several of them at once. Thrown off their stride, Tyrell's Tribe hesitated and the horns sounded again, drowning them out.

From behind the wing of the station, a new group came into view. It was about equal in size, a hundred or more people, and judging by their ages and clothes, Robin guessed they were students. Unlike Tyrell's Tribe, white to a man, they were diverse, a mix of black and brown and white, and their leader was a woman, brunette hair in a high topknot, a checked shirt tied round the waist of black jeans. She had a megaphone, too.

'Silence racist voices,' she called, and her crew shouted it back to her: 'Silence racist voices.'

'Stop the hate.'

The air above them was fairly bristling with signs. They were at a ninety-degree angle, facing the original crowd rather than the station, but Robin could make out a few: *Justice for Dhanesh Gupta, Power In Unity, End White Supremacy.*

'We will *not* be silenced.'

'Have they got any other lines, do you think?' Malia asked.

'If they do, I don't want to hear them,' said Varan.

The new crowd was still advancing, and the nearest edge of Tyrell's lot had turned to confront them. Six officers immediately ran into the space between the two groups.

'Stop the hate,' yelled the woman again.

Taggart had pushed his way to the new front. Megaphone in his left hand, he raised his right arm straight out until his hand, palm down, was six inches above shoulder height.

It was lighter fuel, pure incendiary. The two groups surged together like rivers meeting, the officers in the middle instantly swallowed up, visible only here and there when the melee of arms and heads and signs subsided long enough to reveal the rounded shine of a helmet. The officers who'd been lining the gates charged in.

From chanting and shouting to physical fighting in a matter of seconds – shoving, grabbing, hitting. The air above the press of bodies was filled with flailing arms and fists and phones – phones everywhere. And the noise – air horns, shouting, screams, the clatter of signs. Lined with its two facing terraces, the street was an amplifier, the individual sounds bouncing off the walls

344

to become a roar that reminded Robin bizarrely of the piped-in Viking battle sounds at the Yorvik Centre. Even here, two storeys up, behind glass, it drowned out everything else.

One of Tyrell's mob pulled his arm back, fist aimed at a male student's head while another man screamed him on. A woman recorded them on her phone, righting herself every couple of seconds as the crush of bodies nearly pushed her off her feet. The crowd was a thing of its own now, more than the sum of its parts.

Robin watched a young black guy get right in the face of a muscular man in a balaclava, yelling at full volume. The man grabbed him by the neck of his T-shirt, pulled him in and nutted him. Next to her, Samir winced. She'd thought the guy would be out of action but after four or five seconds he came to himself, brought his fist up and punched balaclava man hard in the throat. Balaclava staggered, and the student took aim again but, just in time, Balaclava's mate snatched another man's sign and thrust it at him, the edge straight in his face. The student reeled away, clutching his eyes, and the mate turned to Balaclava, his expression a mix of astonishment – Look what I did! – and horrified disbelief.

In her own horror, it took Robin a moment to understand she was looking at Luke.

'*Look after your brother.*' Her mother's words rang in her ears as she plunged down the stairs, missing steps twice, barely recovering her balance. She heard quick footsteps overhead, the incident-room door. 'Robin!' She ignored him.

On the ground floor, a new group of officers in full gear were getting ready to go. Samir called her name again and she pushed past them to the front door and spun out into the yard.

Two uniforms were posted at the gate. 'Open it,' she ordered.

They looked at each other, uncertain.

She had seconds before Samir caught her up. 'Open it,' she yelled again, 'I'm a fucking DCI.'

As soon as she was through, it clanged shut behind her. She threw herself into the crowd as she heard a final, 'Robin, don't you dare . . .' The rest was lost as a wave of noise closed over her head.

She'd never had to police any serious unrest when she was in uniform and thank God because it was horrendous. As she pushed her way towards where she'd seen Luke, she was fighting every moment to stay on her feet, let alone move forward. Bodies hit her one after the next, knocking the wind out of her, frequently pushing her backwards into the column of sweating, furious human flesh behind. Dodging fists, she fought claustrophobia, understanding viscerally now how people got trampled, how if you got knocked down, you might never get back up through the stamping, kicking feet, the thicket of legs, the press of constantly jostling bodies. 'Luke,' she shouted pointlessly, the word lost even before it reached the man being pushed back against her by a pair of women shoving each other.

Glancing back, she saw Samir three or four people behind her. He saw her, too, and tried to push forward but a man in front turned in outrage. 'Where're you going, fucking Paki!'

Where was Luke? She had to find him. She'd lost track of the man he'd hit with the sign – after he'd reeled away, he'd vanished into the crowd. What if Luke had really hurt him? Blinded him? Sick to her stomach, she pushed on, fearing for her own eyes, trying to shield them and getting her elbow in the snarling face of one of the skinheads. 'The fuck . . . ?' he shouted, breath hot.

She pushed him aside. 'Fuck off! Luke!'

A yell of pain from the far side of the crowd, near the low front walls of the facing terrace – a man's yell. It sounded like her brother – shit, had the other side retaliated? She plunged on, forced more or less over the back of a man who'd stumbled in front of her. On the far side, a collective gasp went up.

'Man down! Man down here!'

Please, Robin was praying now, *please don't let it be him.* Pushing again, she was hit in the face by the corner of a plywood sign and was stunned by the pain above her eye. She opened it to find herself half-blind and in that terrifying moment, she caught sight of a black girl who looked like Asha, her face stretched in horror. Robin blinked, vision smeared and chequering: the girl was gone. She got her hand to her face, saw blood.

People were throwing things now, plastic bottles and cans spinning through the air overhead. She pressed on towards the source of the shout. How could it be so hard to cross a residential street? It was twenty feet wide.

But finally more light, a little more space, and then, as if she'd been spat from the mouth of an enormous beast, she reached the far side. She braced her hands on her knees and took a shuddering breath. Gingerly she touched her face and felt a cut under her eyebrow. She pressed her cuff against it to stop the blood then stood straight.

The man was lying half on the pavement, half up the short length of someone's front path, and it wasn't Luke, thank God – *thank God* – but one of the storm troopers, a bloody gash on the crown of his shaven scalp.

A helmeted officer knelt over him. 'Unconscious,' he yelled, then pointed at her face.

'Just cut.' She turned back to the crowd, trying to focus her good eye on the faces that flashed in front of her then disappeared. Where was he?

In spots here and there, the uniforms had started to get some traction. The four in the middle had found each other again and formed a line to push the students back, making the gap between the two factions wide enough in places that flailing punches missed.

A sudden burst of activity on the side that had belonged to Tyrell's lot then another shout of pain. Robin craned, but then, as quickly as it had started, the fight was over. Word rolled through the crowd, people who moments before had looked like they'd fight to the death scattering as if the street had filled with toxic gas.

She wiped her eye and looked but soon wished she hadn't.

Lying on the tarmac was an officer in riot gear. Standing over him was Lennie.

Chapter Thirty-seven

Her face was white with shock. 'He's hurt, Mum – he's really hurt.'

Robin knelt on the tarmac, her eyes going immediately to the man's groin, where blood was spreading across his assault suit. The material was slashed – a knife had been angled in over the top of his thigh guard, driven hard enough to plunge deep into the flesh underneath. She knew where the wound was but she couldn't see it, there was too much blood. It was throbbing – pulsing: the knife had caught an artery.

His glove was soaking – he'd tried to staunch the bleeding but now he was losing consciousness, his face dazed behind the visor. Robin put her hands on the wound, one over the other, and pressed as hard as she could. He flinched, his whole torso lifting off the tarmac. 'Stay awake,' she yelled at him, 'stay awake.' She raised her head and screamed, 'Ambulance – we need an ambulance here.'

Samir's body blocked the light. 'They're coming. Any second now. You'll be all right, okay? You're going to be all right.'

Blood welled round Robin's fingers. She heard Lennie sob and shook her head: *No, don't show him we're scared.*

Running footsteps and then – thank God – in a blur of bottle-green and high-vis, the paramedics arrived.

Samir gave them his office and when he closed the door behind him, Lennie ran to one of the bucket chairs and curled in on herself, head to her knees. The little of her face that might have been visible was hidden by her hands, which clamped the sides of her head as if she were trying to keep it from bursting apart. Her body heaved as she sobbed, breaths coming faster and faster until she was hyperventilating. Stupidly, Robin scanned the room as if Samir might keep a pile of paper bags lying round.

'Sit up,' she told her. 'Sit straight.'

'Can't,' Len gasped.

'Yes, you can.' Putting her hands under her shoulders, Robin gently pushed backwards until Lennie was sitting upright then prised her hands away from her head. Demonstrating with her own as if Len might have forgotten how, she told her, 'Cup your hands over your mouth and try to breath out – you're breathing in and in and in; you need to breathe out. Out – there you go. And again – try to wait longer before the next one. Okay, and again.'

It was several minutes before her breathing sounded even half right. When it did, Robin knelt so their eyes were on a level. Len met hers briefly then looked away, and Robin was suddenly furious.

'What the *hell* were you doing?' she demanded. 'What were you *doing* out there?'

'Protesting!'

Don't shout, Robin cautioned herself, *don't shout*. 'You should have been doing your homework, for Christ's sake,' she half-shouted, 'not getting involved in something like this. How did you even know about it?'

'Twitter.' Tears poured down her cheeks. 'We saw Ben Tyrell trending and I knew he was involved in your case. Those people and their horrible ideas, and what happened to Austin . . . I just couldn't *stand* it.' Her hands made fists.

'We – you and Asha?' So she *had* seen her.

'We were *all* there, the whole of our politics group. Apart from Austin, because *he* can't even leave the house,' she said savagely. 'It was for him – we were making a stand. I was with Ash but we got separated straight away . . .'

'For God's *sake*, Lennie, do you have any idea how . . . You could have been injured, like he was.' She flung her arm towards the window, as if the officer – Shaun Palmer was his name – were still lying out there in the road. He was long gone, blue-lighted to the hospital the moment the paramedics got him into the ambulance. 'You could have been killed!'

'I know.'

'Anything could have happened.'

'I *know*! Stop, Mum. *Please.*' She was shaking visibly, her skin paper-white.

'Did you see who stabbed him?'

'No. No, I didn't see anything. I wasn't next to him, I was a couple of people away, and it was so mad – all these bodies slamming into me, I was trying to get to the edge but I was trapped, I couldn't move, and . . . Some of those men, the skinheads . . .' She sobbed. 'Then everyone started running and he fell to the ground.'

'You'll have to give a statement.'

A heaving sob. 'Is he going to die?'

The blood pulsing under her fingers, hot and much too fast. 'I don't know.'

Len covered her mouth. She looked so young. No wonder she'd been terrified, Robin thought; *she'd* been terrified and she was thirty-seven and a trained police officer. She wanted to shake Lennie for being so stupid, for even thinking about confronting people like that, but at the same time she was so proud, she was almost tearful herself. Fifteen years old and she'd come to stand up against a bunch of card-carrying white supremacists. And she'd stayed when everyone else had run.

'It'll be okay, love,' she said, crouching again, noticing the sheen of sweat on Len's forehead. 'The paramedics were there so fast, they'll do everything they can for him, and it doesn't matter if you didn't see who did it, we'll work it out.' Steve Taggart evidently didn't have half Ben Tyrell's *nous*. 'I mean,' she almost laughed, 'can you think of anywhere with more cameras than a police station?'

Lennie made a horrible retching sound.

'Len? Are you going to be sick?'

'Don't know.' She retched again; Robin grabbed Samir's bin and put it in front of her. Lennie fixed her eyes on it, swallowing repeatedly. 'Someone else went down.'

'One of the hard-core nutters.'

'He was on the pavement. Is he dead?'

'No, unconscious – knocked out. Someone threw a stone at his head.'

'I know.'

'You saw it?'

She nodded.

'Did you see *who* threw it, Len? Whatever we think about those people, it's still a crime, a violent crime, and someone will be charged for it. We'll get CCTV but if you saw . . .'

'Me.'

Robin didn't understand.

'*Me*, Mum,' Lennie's eyes stayed on the bin. '*I* threw the stone.'

Robin stared.

'I didn't *mean* to,' her voice rose hysterically. 'I mean, I did, but I didn't mean *that* to happen – it was like this one moment, I was so angry and I just wanted . . .'

'*Sssh.*'

Lennie lifted her head, eyes wide.

'Keep your voice down.' Robin gestured frantically around. Could anyone hear them? Samir – had he stayed in Rhona's office? She looked up, made sure the heavy door was closed before whispering, 'Tell me.'

'I was so *angry* – my *body* was angry. I was angry already because of Austin, and then I saw this guy yelling at our friend Mo, really screaming, like he was about to hit him or spit in his face or something, and I . . . I hated him. I saw a stone in the gutter, right by my foot, and I picked it up and threw it. I didn't know it was going to hurt him – not like that.'

'How big was it?'

Lennie made a shape slightly larger than an egg. Then moved her fingers until it was half as large again.

Oh God. 'Did anyone see you do it?'

She nodded, terrified. 'Uncle Luke.'

'*Luke?*'

Another nod. 'I threw it and when I turned round, he was there. Right behind me.'

'I need the loo.' The sweat was starting to bead at Lennie's hairline. 'Now.' She covered her mouth again.

'Want me to come?'

She shook her head and ran, yanking the door open and lurching out into Rhona's office. 'Lennie?' Robin heard Samir say before the outer door was cranked, too, then slammed shut.

Seconds later, he appeared in the doorway. 'Is she okay?'

'She feels sick.' She felt sick herself, and suddenly very cold.

'Are *you* okay?'

'My God, Samir.' She put her face in her hands. 'My family.'

She heard him cross the room and when she looked up, he was standing in front of her. He took a step forward and put his arms round her.

'Your clothes . . .' Robin said. She was covered in blood – her own, Shaun Palmer's.

'Doesn't matter.'

He held her tightly. She turned her head until her ear rested in the hollow between his shoulder and collarbone, her nose a centimetre from his neck. The way he smelled, his clean cotton shirt, the ludicrous Old Spice deodorant, and underneath both, the heat of his body and the scent of his skin, familiar to her now as it had been twenty years ago when she'd used to lie next to him and just inhale it. Abandoning self-restraint, she took a deep breath and let the smell flood her, and as she did, his lips touched the top of her head.

A minute, maybe longer, his arms around her, his nose in her hair, the fabric of his jacket under her fingers. Voices reached in from outside – they were doing the clear-up, bringing in the people they'd managed to lay hands on, starting house-to-house across the street for witnesses. All she wanted, she realized, was to go home, go to sleep and block it all out. And then, when she woke up, to find him there, no barriers between them.

As if he'd read her mind, he let her go and moved sharply away behind his desk. Turning, Robin saw the photographs on the corner. Harry and Leila, and Liz.

'Mad times,' he said, and she had the idea he was explaining for both of them.

Chapter Thirty-eight

She'd delayed and delayed until it was almost too late to come at all, and when she arrived, the ward was powering down for the night. In the bay opposite, a woman pulled the curtains round her bed with a brisk metallic rattle. The nurse behind the desk hesitated, looking for confirmation from a colleague who was locking the medication trolley. 'Okay,' she told Robin, 'but only for a few minutes.'

'Thank you. I'll be quick.' As quick as she could: she needed to get back to Lennie, whom she'd left with her dad at Mary Street. During dinner, a dismal affair of defrosted spaghetti bolognese, Len had barely picked up her fork. Her dad was trying to jolly her along, thinking she was only miserable because of what she'd seen.

As she approached, her mother was lying back against the pillows, eyes shut, hands resting gently on the blanket. Like this, the damage was less visible, her eye normal-looking. Only the slight sag at the corner of her mouth hinted that anything had happened at all. The high colour was gone from her cheeks and her breathing was slow and regular. Was she already asleep?

'Mum?'

Her eyes opened immediately. 'Hello, love.'

'Is it too late?'

Her mother inclined her head, as if she'd asked a larger question. 'No,' she said. 'I was only resting my eyes.'

'You look better.'

'Do I?' One eyebrow went up, the other struggling to follow it. 'I *feel* awful – I hate this, lying here doing nothing.'

Robin was taken aback – her mother, admitting to discomfort? *Weakness*? 'Well, it's not really your scene, is it?' she said, 'There's work to be done, you know, while you're lazing round with your feet up.'

Her mother gave her a crooked smile.

She brought a chair close to the bed, her stomach a knot of nerves. As she sat, her mother lifted her hand off the blanket and extended it to her. Robin hesitated, unsure if she was reading her correctly – apart from the painful grip when she'd asked for her help, she'd probably been eight and crossing the road the last time her mum had held her hand. Awkwardly, she reached over the bed-rail and took it.

'Mum,' she said quietly. 'Did you hear about the protest at the station today?'

Her mother's eyes were locked on her face. 'Yes.'

'Luke was there, with Billy Torrence.' Robin steeled herself, keeping her eyes on their linked hands. 'Not just *there*, Mum, he was in the thick of it, he hurt one of the counter-protestors, a student from the university. Badly hurt him – he's had to have surgery to save the sight in one of his eyes. It'll be okay but that's pure luck.'

She made herself look up. To her amazement, her mother wasn't aghast. Did she understand?

'Mum, Luke's going to face criminal charges. Serious ones –

affray at the very least, and with the violence, it'll mean prison time.'

Her brother in prison – the idea was shocking, almost impossible to grasp. And frightening. How would he survive? *Would* he survive? It would be proper time, too, not a couple of months; the sentencing guideline for affray was up to three years. If the charge was violent disorder, which it might well be, it could be significantly more. He wasn't tough enough.

Her mother nodded, still bizarrely sanguine. Were the drugs clouding her brain or did she not believe it? Maybe she thought there'd been a mistake, her lovely boy would never do such a thing. 'Mum,' she whispered, 'I'm talking about Luke going to *prison*.'

'I know.'

'You understand what I'm telling you?'

'Of course. The stroke hasn't affected my *mind*.'

Robin shook her head, bewildered. 'There's something else: he's gone AWOL, we can't find him – us, the family, I mean, not the police, though they'll be looking for him, too. He's not answering his phone, he's not at home, none of his friends have seen him. Nat's rung everyone she can think of. I'm scared.'

She remembered his desolate face on the railway bridge. If he'd actually felt like ending it then, he had more reason now. His look of horror when he realized how hurt the student was. He'd known he was in real trouble. Would Natalie ever take him back now? And what about Jack? Could Luke stand knowing that his son would grow up like Kev did, with a father who'd done time? And prison would change him fundamentally. Forever.

'He hasn't gone AWOL, Robin,' her mother said quietly. 'He's doing some thinking.'

'What?'

'He came to see me right after it happened. He came straight here and told me.'

'He came . . . So you already knew?'

'Yes. And I know what Lennie did, too.'

Robin stared at her.

Uncle Luke. He was there. Right behind me.

'What a disaster,' her mother said. 'What a complete and utter disaster.'

Robin reeled – she felt actually light-headed. Ridiculously, she'd been holding out a last bit of hope that Luke somehow hadn't seen, that in the madness of the scrum he could have missed it. *Hasn't he done his damage?* No, of course he hadn't. There would always be more.

'I'm sorry, Mum,' she said, 'I'm so sorry.'

'*You* didn't do it – either part.'

'You asked me to look after him and I didn't. I knew he was at the end of his rope but I was thinking about depression. I never thought he'd get involved in something like this.'

But why not? She'd been berating herself with that question whenever she wasn't literally sweating with anxiety about Lennie.

'You know he's easily influenced,' her mother said. 'You've always known.'

'But white supremacists? Taggart gave a *Nazi salute*.'

Walking on to the ward, she'd intended to admit seeing Billy's name on For Queen and Country but now she found she couldn't do it. She was ashamed: she'd seen it and she *still* hadn't put the two together. But then, for her, the idea that anyone she knew, even Billy, would throw in his lot with those people even fleetingly, even *in extremis*, had been unthinkable.

And that had been her mistake.

Naivety.

No, worse than that: it was a lack of understanding of how people – the world – worked. She blinked to stop the prickling in her eyes. She'd fucked up, she wasn't going to cry.

Further down the ward, the nursing staff were plying back and forth between beds, turning off lights for those who couldn't do it themselves, pulling more curtains, but for now, at least, they were leaving her mother and her bay-mates to it. In the silence between them, Robin became aware of snoring from the bed behind, the tiny woman with the puff-of-smoke hair. The sound was oddly reassuring. Life will go on, it seemed to say, mad and mundane.

'You've kept him going,' she said. 'You and Nat – you've kept him on the straight and narrow for years. I was handed the baton for a few days.'

Her mother ran her thumb slowly over the back of Robin's hand. 'There are different ways of taking care of people, you know.'

Oh great, Robin thought, here it came, the extolling of feminine virtues, the detailing of her lack thereof, Robin as Lady Macbeth, too self-absorbed and preoccupied with ambition to keep her own brother out of jail.

'Listen,' her mother said. 'I know you think of yourself as some sort of . . . Tin Woman but you're good at your job because you care. That's *your* caring. I understand it now, since you've been back. We're different in lots of ways, we know that, but we both take care of people, only in different arenas.'

Robin said nothing, completely wrong-footed.

'Sometimes I think that if things had been different,' her mother went on, 'if my parents had ever encouraged me to have a career, maybe *I'd* have liked the police.'

'Really?' She was frankly incredulous now.

'No, maybe not,' another crooked smile, 'maybe something a bit less . . . full on. But I would have liked to do something to help people beyond the family, your dad, you and your brother.'

'You've always cared much more about him than you do about me,' Robin blurted.

'You never needed it as much.'

'But I did. I did need it, I *still* do. You're my mum.'

Her mother breathed out, not quite a sigh. 'You were so self-sufficient, even as a small child. Sometimes I felt . . . redundant. And later, when you had Lennie, you pushed me away. I would have liked to help you but you had your own set-up, you and Corinna, then Frances; you shut me out.'

'I was afraid of your judgement; you were so angry with me.'

Her mother huffed a little. 'You always talk about that. I just thought you'd made it so hard on yourself, having her so young. On your own.'

'But you're tough on me, Mum, you are – much tougher than you've ever been on him. You've got to admit that.'

'Yes, I do. Because my standards are higher for you – because I know you can do more. You're stronger. When you said you were expecting Lennie I was disappointed because I thought you'd messed up your chance of a career, wasted your potential. I was wrong about that, wasn't I? You just did both.'

For a moment Robin didn't trust herself to speak. 'Luke sold a picture of me and Samir to the *Daily Herald*,' she said finally. Well, the gloves were off now. 'The one of us together in Stratford. He said you kept it.'

'He told me.'

'That he *sold* it?'

A small nod. 'Until then, I'd always been glad you dropped it. I liked that picture.'

'What, even with the boobs?'

'Well . . .'

360

Sodding tears, there was no stopping them. 'I'm sorry, Mum,' she said, 'I've got to move my arm, the bar's cutting off my circulation.' She let go of her hand and swiped at her eyes.

'I know he split the two of you up, Robin. You and Samir.'

Robin stared again.

'He told me.'

'When?'

'Today. I was . . . appalled. And it explained a lot of things for me. A lot. And I'm so sorry. I'm sorry now and I'm sorry I didn't know so that I could stop it at the time. It almost broke my heart, seeing how much it hurt you.'

Robin remembered the afternoon, Samir's warmth, his breath in her hair. The sense of loss when he'd moved so abruptly away. *Mad times.*

Her mother glanced around and lowered her voice again. 'What's going on with the man Lennie hurt?'

'I don't know. I asked Samir earlier but he hadn't heard, either.'

'Do the police know it was her?'

'Not yet. Unless they're not telling me.' Which was possible. A CCTV team would be watching the footage even as she spoke. They needed to tell someone, it would look better for Lennie later if they did, but Robin couldn't bring herself to do it, to ruin Len's life over a stupid, spur-of-the-moment mistake driven by righteous anger, an urge to lash out at someone who was filling the world with hatred, who would hate someone she loved.

'Mum,' she said, 'it's not just me in the papers.'

A photographer from the *Post* had got a shot that might well win him prizes. Taken seconds before Taggart raised his arm, it showed him with his megaphone to his lips, surrounded by a bunch of his core nutters, and on the left, brought to the front when they'd turned to face the students, as rage-filled as any of them, Billy Torrence in his balaclava and her brother.

'He's on the *Post*'s website now and I'm sure he'll be on the front of the paper tomorrow. Also,' she could hardly bear to say it, 'the nationals are picking it up; it's on the *Guardian* and *Times*' sites, too. Maybe they'll crop it for the actual papers, cut him off the edge, but . . .'

'There's no way of knowing? Or of stopping them using it?'

'No. Mum, he needs to come forward – it'll be a point in his favour if he does. Will you ring him – keep ringing until you get him? You're the only person he'll listen to.'

When Robin reached home, she had a text from Kev. *Just seen the photo – OMG, your bro, outdone himself this time.*

Certainly has, she replied.

The dots appeared almost at once, then, *Anything I can do? Want me to come over?*

She felt a new strain of melancholy wind itself into the already potent swirl. In another world, she thought. *Lennie's in a bit of a mess,* she typed instead, *needs attention.*

Roger that. Here if you need me.

Thanks, Kev. After some consideration, she added an x. Then deleted it again.

'You're in with me tonight,' she told Lennie after they'd said goodbye to her dad. He'd beckoned her into the kitchen while Len was upstairs. 'She's really upset, love,' he'd whispered. '*Really* upset. I've never seen her like this, even after . . . She's inconsolable.'

'I think the past couple of days have killed what was left of her innocence,' she'd said.

When the light went out, Robin moved across the bed and put her arm around her. She was nearly finished by a memory of doing the same when Len had used to come trotting in from her toddler bed at ungodly hours of the morning, pressing the raised anti-slip pads on her footed suit against Robin's thighs, night-time nappy rustling.

'Are you going to tell them?' Len's voice was low in the dark.

'No.'

'Then I will – we *have* to. They'll find out from CCTV anyway, you said so.'

'They might not.'

'Nice wishful thinking, Mum.' She sounded angry.

'There could be blind spots. In our case, the old factory . . .'

'That's not a *police station*, is it? A *working* police station.'

Robin pressed her eyes shut, glad Len couldn't see her. *No lies to Lennie.* But lies *for* Lennie, evidently that was okay, and *about* her. *Nice moral example, Mum.*

'Just wait,' she said. 'Please, Len.'

It took half an hour but, eventually, physical and emotional exhaustion overtook Lennie's panic and Robin heard her breathing slow.

Her own panic wasn't so easily quashed; she saw two o'clock, then half past. What was she going to do? She couldn't throw her daughter to the wolves, she couldn't, but at the same time, a man was in hospital tonight, unconscious.

But maybe matters would be taken out of her hands. *Uncle Luke. He was there.* When the police caught up with him, he'd be desperate. If he gave Lennie up, could he avoid prison or reduce his sentence? Maybe, if they'd drawn a blank on the stone-thrower otherwise; if, by some miracle, they hadn't got it on CCTV. Would Luke ruin Lennie to save himself? Yes, she knew he would: he'd sold *her* to the *Herald* for four hundred pounds – he'd threatened to dob her in for trying to *help* him.

And if anyone found out she'd known and kept quiet, it would be game over for her police career. Even Samir couldn't get her out of that.

Stomach aching, she searched for mental comfort and found the memory of him in his office again. She inhaled through her nose and tried to imagine his scent. Just tonight, she rationalized; tomorrow she'd get things under control, jam it all safely back down.

Chapter Thirty-nine

She woke to find Lennie gone. She pelted down the landing but she wasn't in her own room or the bathroom. Had she run away? Gone to turn herself in? Heart in her throat, Robin thundered downstairs where she found her sitting at the kitchen table, staring unblinking at a mug of cold tea. 'Everything's changed,' she said. 'Nothing will ever be the same.'

Robin slumped into the chair next to her, heart thudding. 'We'll deal with it, Len.' She wanted to promise but she couldn't. 'Why don't you stay at home today? I'll see if Grandpa's around, if you can . . .'

'No,' she said, vehement. 'I'm going to school, I *have* to. What am I going to do all day, otherwise? Sit here wondering if I've killed someone?'

As she approached the station, Robin's dread magnified. Her own force was actively seeking her brother and, even if they didn't know it yet, her daughter, too.

Only Samir knew her relationship to the snarling bigot on the *Guardian*'s front page today but everyone in the station knew Lennie had stayed with Shaun Palmer and wanted to tell Robin what a great kid she was – Webster put his head round the door, Leena and Tim, Rhona. She thanked them all, feeling sick.

Samir knocked shortly before ten, and closed the door. 'Any sign of him?'

She shook her head then glanced through the internal window: nobody seemed to be watching. 'Samir, what you said last week about him poleaxing my career – compared to this, the drink-driving thing's nothing.'

He frowned. 'But the situation's totally different: you haven't intervened for him.' It wasn't quite a statement.

'No, of course not.'

She felt an urge to tell him about Lennie but she couldn't make him complicit. 'By association, I meant, that's all. Him being involved with those people, almost certainly going to prison . . .' Last night, she'd remembered Kilmartin yelling about her being splashed across the news with the son of a convicted criminal, best friend to a woman who only escaped criminal charges herself by being murdered first. Now this.

'The *Herald* will crucify me.'

'You are not your brother, Robin.' Samir glanced at the window, too. 'Look, you'll get hell from Kilmartin, we probably both will, but we'll handle it, okay?'

Robin was torn between gratitude and grief at the knowledge that if what she wasn't telling him came out, they wouldn't. 'Thanks.'

'In the meantime, I came to give you a bit of *good* news. Shaun Palmer's guv'nor's just rung and it sounds like the surgery was a success. The blood's flowing well to the leg this morning, so as long as that stays the case, he'll make a full recovery.'

'Thank God.' Though he'd survived, the question had remained whether they'd been able to repair the artery well enough to save his leg. 'When I had my hands on him, I really didn't know if he could make it,' she said. 'Do they have a suspect?'

'Yes, they've got it on CCTV, they're about to release the name.'

'How about the other one, the skinhead?' *Careful, careful.*

'He came round last night, apparently, but beyond that, I don't know. He was out for hours and the longer you're unconscious with a head injury . . . They're doing tests.'

Intense relief – he was alive – followed immediately by a new terror: brain damage.

Samir was watching her carefully. There was no way the emotional rollercoaster hadn't shown on her face, and he knew her. After a couple of seconds, he asked, 'How are you getting on with Brother Phil? Any news this morning?'

'Not yet. You'd think they'd just dematerialized, the three of them, when they left Salvador. But we'll find them, I've got everyone on . . .' Another rap on the door; she bodily jumped.

'Sorry to bother you,' Varan said, looking between them as if he were breaking something up, 'but there's a woman downstairs who says she needs to talk to you, guv.'

'Me?' asked Robin.

'She won't talk to anyone else. She says it's urgent.'

The woman sat at the end of the row of plastic chairs, back straight, head up, a pair of polished black court shoes with a sensible inch-and-a-half heel pressed together on the tiled floor. Her navy skirt and pale blue blouse were ironed, a trench coat draped neatly across her lap. A lawyer, Robin wondered, or a paralegal? Was she about to be served a subpoena?

At the sound of the door, the woman's head whipped round. She was in her late fifties, her hair a slightly yellow blonde, probably close to what it had once been naturally. She stood, putting her feet together again quickly, hanging the trench coat over her arm like a butler's towel. No sign of any paperwork, though.

Robin extended a hand. 'DCI Lyons. How can I help?'

'Can we talk privately?' She darted her eyes at the desk staff and the four or five other people waiting.

'May I ask what it's about?'

'I'd really prefer not to talk here.' Her pale eyes were full of entreaty.

Robin took her to the room where she and Malia had spoken to Jonathan Quinton ten days earlier, and she sat in the same spot, looking even jumpier than he had. Robin waited while she appeared to gather herself. After about half a minute, she took a deep breath and met her eye. 'My name's Ann Birch,' she said, 'and you're looking for my son.'

'Your son?'

'For the murder of Lara Meikle.'

Robin looked at her. Yes, she was agitated, but nothing suggested she wasn't in full possession of her faculties. 'What's your son's name, Ann, and why do you think that?'

She looked sick. 'Jeremy Birch. I went round to his flat last week and I smelled bleach. Strong bleach. I found his kitchen knife soaking in a bucket behind the U-bend of the sink.' Her body seemed to deflate, as if the information had been taking up space inside her and she could no longer hold her shape. She gave a single hard sob and her eyes filled with tears.

'How did your son know Lara?' Robin asked carefully. 'Or *did* he know her?'

She frowned as if Robin were being obtuse. 'Of course. Why would he . . . if . . . ?' She wiped her cheeks with her hands, one then the other. 'They met at the end of last year, October or November, at a conference in London. Insurance – he's a broker, she was there with her boss. Jeremy was smitten – I knew he'd met someone as soon as he got back. I teased him till he told me.'

368

Robin couldn't imagine this buttoned-up woman with her trench coat and sensible shoes teasing anyone but it occurred to her that the clothes were protective, a suit of armour she'd put on to come here. To do this.

'He's in Birmingham?'

'Yes. His flat's in Aston.'

'Did they see each other again, after the conference? Here?'

'A lot – two or three times a week for months. Until March. Then, all of a sudden, out of the blue, she broke it off with him.'

'Did your son know she had a boyfriend? Well, a partner, really.'

'Oh, he knew,' she said bitterly. 'She told him from the start. She told him she was in a relationship that was going nowhere, she was just waiting for the right time to end it without causing the other man more pain than she had to. She said they'd be together properly, out in the open, as soon as she did it, but there was always a reason why she couldn't, one thing after another: he's feeling down, his dad's in hospital, it was *her* work, her nursing applications.'

'November till March – four months? Five.'

'She strung him along. She might have cared about not hurting David Pearse but she didn't give a toss how much she hurt my son.'

'He had feelings for her?'

'He *loved* her. That's why he put up with it, being the second string. My son's thirty-four, he wanted to settle down, start a family. Not *all* men want to play the field – Jeremy's always been a homebody. A sweet man. He wanted a house, a wife, children – Sunday lunches, old-fashioned holidays at the seaside, Christmas with the in-laws. A family. And he thought Lara was the one.' More tears, slipping silently down her cheeks like Lennie's in the car when she'd heard about Austin.

'That's why he couldn't accept her ending it,' Ann Birch said.

'He thought she'd felt the same, that she was a kind person, simply too gentle to hurt the other man.'

'What do you mean, he "couldn't accept" it?'

She swiped at her face. 'I told him to let it go, move on, but he wouldn't. "If something's worth having," he said, "you have to fight for it."'

Despite knowing already how the story ended, Robin felt a chill run down her arms. 'And did he? Fight?'

'He tried to persuade her, yes. He phoned her and texted, told her he loved her. That feelings like this came along once in a lifetime – that, for him, she was it.'

'He told you all this?'

'He confided in me, yes. He was in pain, I'm his mother.'

'How did Lara take it, what he was telling her?'

'She answered his calls for a while – good of her – but then, in April, she cut him off. When he rang her number, it was dead. At first he thought something was wrong, that she'd had an accident, so he called her at the office.' The woman drew herself up. 'She told him that if he ever did that again, she'd call the police.'

'Ann,' Robin trod carefully, 'how would you describe your son's mental state at this point?'

She hesitated, searching for the right word. 'Fragile,' she said. 'Vulnerable.'

'Do you think Lara might have thought he was harassing her?'

'I'm sure she would.'

Again the bitterness, the loathing for this woman who had brought her son to this. Even though she was dead, Robin thought; even though he'd killed her.

'And then,' Ann Birch said, 'three weeks ago, he found out she'd moved in with him. Pearce.'

'How did he find out?'

'He followed her. He knew where she worked and he used to follow her.'

Which could explain, Robin thought, how he'd known where Lara was the night she died – she'd gone straight out from work, hadn't she? He could have followed her from there and kept tabs on her all evening, while she was having sausages and mash with Cat Rainsford, the drink afterwards. He could have seen her refuse a taxi and known where she'd be heading when she started walking. How long it would take her to get there.

'Did Lara know he'd been following her?'

She shook her head. 'I don't know.'

Because if she had, she hadn't told anyone, even Cat. But if she'd wanted to make a go of things with David Pearce, as it seemed she had, then that could make sense. It would be uncomfortable forever, having someone who knew you'd cheated on your partner and, if they breathed a word, or accidentally slipped up, it could blow your whole relationship sky-high.

'Ann,' she said, 'if you're right – and I agree, it sounds likely – why are you only coming forward now? You said you went round to his flat last week – which day?'

'Thursday.'

'It's Wednesday – that's six days ago.'

She looked Robin in the eye. 'Do you have children?'

'One.'

'Then you know why.' Her look was a challenge. 'He's the person I love most in the world.' She put her face in her hands and wept, desolate.

You know why.

She waited until Ann Birch had regained a degree of control before asking her again what had finally made her come forward.

'I saw it on the news,' the woman said, 'your Chief Constable talking about that Indian man who was killed.'

'Assistant Chief Constable. Kilmartin.'

'He asked people to come forward so the other man – the dead man—'

'Dhanesh Gupta.'

'To clear his name. For his father's sake.'

One-nil to the patriarchy, Robin thought. Days' worth of appeals on social media and the papers and her own appearances on *Midlands Today* and in the end, it was Kilmartin and his shiny brass buttons that sealed the deal.

'*His* son's dead, killed by someone wanting revenge for the death of the woman that *my* son killed. When I heard that, I knew. I knew I had to say something.'

'Do you know where Jeremy is now, Mrs Birch?'

She raised her head and clasped her hands together to stop them shaking. 'It's Wednesday morning. He's been going to work.'

When Robin got back upstairs, Malia was at her desk, crossing out a name on a sheet covered with two columns of them. 'The conference attendees,' she confirmed. 'I took out the women first, which was the easy bit; now I'm working through brokers' websites, looking at headshots where they exist, ruling out anyone who's obviously too old or too brown. I've got four possibles in the West Midlands so far – Daventry, Leamington, and two here in the city, including this guy who looks about the right age and colouring.' She tapped her mouse to wake up her screen where Robin saw a photograph of a brown-haired man in his mid-thirties. *Jeremy Birch, Senior Broker*, said the name underneath.

'I'll speak to him first, as soon as I've finished.' Malia turned the paper over. 'I'm on the last page but one so . . .'

'You can speak to him now,' Robin told her.

*

372

'They're here,' Varan called when he spotted Malia's car returning, accompanied by the squad car that held Jeremy Birch.

In an echo that turned Robin's stomach, the team crowded at the window to watch as he was brought inside. Charcoal suit, white shirt and tie – he looked smart, all business, especially for a man whose mental balance, if his mother was to be believed, had been so disturbed eight days ago that he'd been driven to kill.

He was six foot five, they knew now, and even with cuffs on, his pace a third of what it was on the Vaughton Street tape, the officers either side of him struggled to match his loping stride. They'd watched the tape again.

'Is that what she's saying? "Jeremy"?' Robin had squinted over Tarka's shoulder.

'Hard to say a hundred per cent, but yeah,' he nodded, 'I'd put money on it.'

The bucket of bleach was gone from beneath Jeremy Birch's sink and it would be Forensics' job to determine if any of his knives revealed traces of Lara's blood. Frankly, Robin doubted it; even if Birch was cold or stupid enough to hold on to the murder weapon, bleach would likely have destroyed any usable DNA. 'But,' said Rafferty, calling from the flat's kitchen, 'one of the guys noticed his tea-towel drawer was catching on something when he tried to open it, so we took a closer look. He had an envelope taped to the bottom and inside? One security pass for a conference at the Excel Centre in London last November.'

'It's hers?'

'Lara Meikle. Her name and a little headshot. Pretty girl, wasn't she?'

The team were live-streaming the interview in the main room but Robin watched at her desk. The breakthrough had been a welcome distraction but the second her mind wandered, it went straight to Lennie. Her anxiety was bordering on paranoia now, to the extent that she thought the team were talking about her in subtext.

'He was asking to be caught, wasn't he?' she'd heard Phil Howell say as he passed her door. 'Keeping the knife when his mum had a key to the flat?'

'Got to hurt, being dobbed in by your mum,' Niall replied.

'Maybe he thought the old bird would cover for him.'

She wrestled her attention back to the screen where Malia, by contrast, was a needle of mental focus. She should be a DI, Robin thought, she needed to get on with that, take the exam. But if she wanted to stay in Homicide at West Midlands, there wasn't much point for now: there was no inspector vacancy and no prospect of one while their budget was so tight.

But maybe there *was* a prospect, said a dark voice: if *she* lost *her* job, Webster could finally move up to DCI and Malia could take his spot.

Physically speaking, Jeremy Birch's height was really the only thing that made him remarkable. He was passably good-looking and yet somehow his face was unmemorable, his features regular, nothing to command a second glance one way or the other, his brown hair cut with no particular flair. He was currently sitting up to the table with the posture and facial expression of a man in front of his bank manager in hopes of arranging a loan both parties knew he'd be good for. Middle class, reliable, surely-there's-been-some-sort-of-mistake-here. Earlier, though, she'd heard he'd been in tears in his cell. Genuine tears or was he hedging his bets, she wondered, seeing which way the wind blew before deciding definitively how he needed to present himself?

His mother's view, that this was a spur-of-the-moment act of passion by someone driven from his right mind, was not widely shared among the team.

'Mr Birch,' Malia said. 'Given the evidence we already have – the CCTV, your mother's account of the knife in bleach, your possession of Lara's security pass and the fact that it was concealed, we think you'll have a hard time convincing a jury it wasn't you who killed Lara Meikle.'

Compelled by guilt at her own treachery, no doubt, Ann Birch had appointed Godfrey Cowper of Seymour Cowper Price, one of the best and most expensive local firms, to represent her son. Cowper was widely disliked in Homicide, a 'pompous git' according to Webster, to the women, the sort of man who'd stand too close at parties and look down your top, maybe stick his card down your bra.

He was at peak condescension today. 'Now let's not leap to any conclusions, shall we?'

Malia ignored him. 'And, as you know, Mr Birch, the search of your flat is only very preliminary so far. Who knows what else forensics might find. Did Lara visit you there?'

'No comment,' instructed Cowper.

'At this point, the question isn't so much whether or not you killed her as under what circumstances – in what state.'

'I don't understand,' said Birch.

'Psychologically speaking.'

He shook his head as if she'd lost him completely. Playing dumb.

'We've started to look at your electronics, too. We're interested that you cleared your search history last week, only,' she made a show of consulting her notes, 'nine hours before Lara died.'

'Of course. I do it every week – more often, if I have a minute.' Though he'd grown up in Birmingham, his voice was only mildly accented. 'Doesn't anyone sensible?'

'So let's say, for the sake of argument, that your clearing your history hours before she died is pure coincidence. How about the fact that she died in exactly the same way as the woman found dead at the former Gisborne works two days previously? That both were stripped – or almost – of anything potentially identifying? Is *that* a coincidence?'

'Until proven otherwise, absolutely,' Cowper's smile was serpentine. 'Moreover, by far the more likely explanation of *that* is that the same man was responsible for both murders *and* as we've discussed, my client has a cast-iron alibi for Saturday evening.'

'But the thing is, Mr Cowper,' Malia said, and Robin heard the pleasure in her voice at outsmarting him, 'we're *not* looking for the same man. We know now that there were two different killers. Mr Birch,' she nodded at him, 'our belief is that, having discovered that Lara had made a mockery of your feelings for her and moved on permanently – to the extent that she threatened you with the police should you contact her again – you learned that a woman of a similar age had been killed within half a mile of Lara's new home and you saw an opportunity.'

Robin peered at the screen, trying to read Birch's face. She wasn't sure but she thought she detected a trace of contempt.

'Pure conjecture. Don't say a word,' barked Cowper at him.

'When we prove it,' Malia said, unperturbed, 'it'll destroy any hope of a loss-of-control defence, I'm afraid. To us, that looks about as premeditated as it gets.'

The entire room, officers and support staff, stood to applaud as Malia came in. She looked embarrassed but then, with her usual poise, she took it in her stride and bowed.

Varan clapped and whistled, Robin noticed, then almost immediately sat back down at his computer.

'What are you doing over there?' Howell asked him. 'Checking your Facebook?'

'Nope,' Varan said. 'Yours. *Three* friends – you've added one. Oh, hang on, it's your mum.'

'Ha ha.'

'Seriously, though, guv,' Varan looked at Robin, 'I think I might have found Miriam Chapman.'

Chapter Forty

The photograph had been taken at a party thrown by an evangelical church in Buenos Aires. On wooden decking outside a white modern bungalow, a group of thirty or so people in summer dresses and blazers stood chatting, holding glasses and plates. A dark-haired boy of about four rode a red tricycle towards a barbecue where a man in a striped apron holding a pair of tongs was waiting, free hand outstretched. Next to him in a short-sleeved yellow dress was a woman who, from what they could see of her face and hair, looked very like Jude Everleigh.

'Mimi Lopez,' said Varan.

'Who?'

'That's her new name – or maybe not so new, I don't know yet how long they've been married.' He pointed at the man with the tongs. 'That's her husband, the vicar of the church – Matias Lopez.' He clicked to a different photograph which showed Lopez in a white shirt and dog collar laughing with another man. Mimi was with them, too, but she'd angled her body towards her husband, showing herself only from the side and bending her head towards his shoulder. 'She appears to be camera-shy,' Varan said. 'There's another two more or less the same, her kind of . . . ducking behind him.'

'But it is her, isn't it?'

'I think so. Yes.' He smiled.

'How did you find this?' Cumulatively, all the people she'd had on it since yesterday had logged a hundred search hours or more and no one had turned up a thing.

'I searched in Images, not Google, Google. Images of Christian groups in South America: churches, missions, charities – mix-and-match, delete-as-applicable. I was going country by country – after Brazil, I tried Guyana because it's English-speaking, then Argentina. I found the church's website first,' he clicked back to the summer party, 'this one, and that gave me their names.'

'What about Brother Phil aka Philip Hatton aka John Philips? Any sign of him?'

Varan shook his head. 'No.'

Robin called the embassy in Buenos Aires and was eventually put through to a man named Toby Bolton, who was blisteringly posh but trying not to sound it. She told him as much as they'd been able to glean about Mimi and Matias Lopez in the interim.

Unsurprisingly, and despite the prevalence of both his names in Argentina, Matias Lopez was proving much easier to research than his wife. The church site alone gave them more than they'd learned from any other source bar Jude in the entire investigation so far; it was almost shockingly helpful by the standards they'd grown used to.

Matias, it said, had been vicar there since 2012, before which he'd been in Patagonia. Before that, *using the language gifted to him by his Brazilian mother not his Argentinian father to spread the good news of Jesus love*, as Google Translate put it, he'd preached in São Paulo, Minas Geras and Salvador.

The wife of Matias, Mimi, has lived in South America for twenty years and shares the mission of her husband and our church to promulgate the Good News of Our Lord along with their children, Hannah, Beatriz and Paulo.

Toby Bolton listened so quietly that twice Robin thought they'd lost their connection. 'We've got familial DNA evidence that the body of the woman we found is Mimi's daughter, Hannah,' she told him. 'Which, unfortunately, I'm sorry, means she'll have to be notified of the death.'

'Understood. My colleague and I will speak to her.'

'Mr Bolton, it's an extremely sensitive situation, but we don't think Matias Lopez is Hannah's biological father. We also need to find out who her real father is and whether he's currently in the UK.'

'Leave it with me,' Bolton said. 'I'll be back in touch as soon as I can.'

'Will that be today, do you think?' The time difference was three hours; it was still early afternoon in Buenos Aires.

'I don't know. If we can find her, if she's in the city, we'll go as soon as possible.'

At seven o'clock, confronted with the news from Forensics that the hair found stuck in her blood matched the DNA sample he'd given them and that Rafferty and his team had found another hair, long and magenta, on the carpet beneath his bed, Jeremy Birch broke down and confessed to the murder of Lara Meikle.

'There's one detail we don't understand, Mr Birch,' Robin told him after he'd been charged formally. 'How did you communicate with Lara, while your relationship was going on? We know you didn't call her at her office and we've been through her phone records for the past year without discovering any trace of your number or any other, in fact, that we haven't been able to identify.'

380

Birch muttered something under his breath.

'I'm sorry?'

'I said, she had a burner phone. So Pearce wouldn't find out. She sold it to me as our "special phone", only for us, but it was him she was protecting. Keeping me at arm's length. When she'd had enough of me, she chucked it away, like she chucked me away.' For a moment his face was transfigured by rage. 'Fucking bitch.'

'I need to tell Deborah Harper we've charged someone,' Robin told Samir in her office. 'I should go over there.'

He shook his head. 'No.'

'But I did the Knock.'

'Someone else can tell her. You can speak to her tomorrow. Go home.'

She was about to argue when her landline rang.

'Chief Inspector? It's Toby Bolton. My colleague Rachel and I are just back from talking to Mimi Lopez.'

Robin sat down and pulled herself in to the desk. Samir raised his hands, palms up: *What was I saying?*

She held up a finger: wait a moment. 'Mr Bolton,' she said, 'I've got Detective Chief Superintendent Samir Jafferi with me here, West Midlands' Head of Homicide. Would you mind if I put you on speaker so we can both hear you?'

'Of course not, go ahead.'

'Thank you. Mr Bolton is at the embassy in Buenos Aires,' she explained to Samir, 'and he's spoken to Mimi Lopez or, as she's better known to us, Miriam Chapman.'

Samir's eyebrows leapt. He came down off the filing cabinet and drew the fraying chair up to the other side of her desk.

'She was at home,' Toby Bolton said. 'When we told her you'd discovered a young woman's body and believed it to be Hannah, she was understandably panicked until I said she'd been found in the UK. Then she relaxed and said it couldn't be her because she was in Santiago, Chile, doing a two-week silent retreat.'

Which explained why they hadn't been looking for her, Robin thought.

'So I showed her the e-fit and the photograph you sent. She was . . . distraught,' he said, delicately.

Robin nodded, looking at Samir, forgetting that Bolton couldn't see her.

'When I told her we needed to notify Hannah's father and asked where he was, she told us he was at the church. Matias Lopez adopted Hannah formally a year after they married, and Mrs Lopez was adamant that he was her "real" father.'

'So she's Hannah Lopez?'

'Yes, and she has been for a long time – they married in 2004.'

Robin looked at Samir again. 'The year the man I think is her biological father left Salvador.'

Robin had asked her dad to meet Lennie from school and stay with her until she could leave work. She'd told them both it would be nine o'clock at the latest but when Samir left, she rang to tell Lennie she had one more call to make. 'I'm sorry.'

'It's okay,' Len mumbled.

'We got one of the two killers.'

'Okay,' she said again, expressionless. Robin remembered their fit of hysterical laughter upstairs on her bed and was filled with despair.

Despite the nearly twenty years Mimi Lopez had lived in South America, Robin heard her Geordie accent straight away. The accent, her timbre – she could have been talking to Jude, except that her voice was thick with crying.

'Mrs Lopez,' she said, 'before anything else, I want to tell you how deeply sorry I am for your loss, and to promise we'll keep doing everything we can to find your daughter's killer.'

The sound of a hard swallow. 'Thank you.'

Robin looked at the note-covered paper in front of her. In a career filled with challenging conversations, this might be the toughest so far. She glanced at the chair opposite and wished Samir was still in it, not for any strategic reason but for the moral support. She took a mental breath. 'I know Toby told you some of the details but you must have a lot of questions. Shall we start there?'

'I need to know,' the woman sobbed, 'whether she suffered. Knife wounds – it's so violent, and . . .' She failed to suppress a sob.

'Mrs Lopez, I—'

'Would you call me Mimi? It would help. Mrs Lopez sounds so . . . distant.'

'I'm sorry. But Mimi, we honestly don't think she did suffer very much. I hope that's a crumb of comfort. The blood loss from her wounds – she would have lost consciousness very quickly, it was one of the first things the pathologist told us. Within a minute or so, most likely. We know she *was* conscious, at least briefly, because she grabbed the blade a single time, but there was no prolonged struggle.'

A sob. 'And nothing . . . sexual?'

'No. Maybe it would also help to know she was found quickly, too.' She knew it would plague *her* to imagine Lennie lying for hours or days on end, all alone. 'She died in the small hours of Sunday morning and she was found shortly before eight a.m.'

A sort of hum came down the line as Mimi tried to contain a long keening sound. 'Why?' she managed after several seconds.

'That's what we're trying to establish,' Robin said carefully. 'I

383

think Toby explained that one of the reasons we've only now been able to notify you is it took us several days to discover Hannah's identity. Her killer left nothing that identified her at all, and because she'd grown up overseas, we had no official records.'

'Then how . . . ?'

'A contact of mine recognized *you*. Miriam.'

Silence on the other end – even the crying had stopped. Robin waited for either confirmation or denial but when neither came, she ploughed on. 'It was a leap, I was going on the physical likeness and Hannah's age, but I took a chance and went to see your sister.'

A small gasp.

'Jude – Judith – gave us a DNA sample and then we started looking for you. You weren't easy to find.'

Still not a word.

'Mimi,' Robin said, 'Toby told me you thought Hannah was in Chile. Do you know why she might have come to the UK instead, without telling you?'

Now she could hear weeping again. She stayed quiet and waited. Eventually Mimi Lopez – Miriam Chapman – cleared her throat. 'She wanted to find her father. Her *biological* father.'

'So he's here? In the UK?'

'I don't know.'

Robin frowned. 'Then . . . ?'

'She knew he was British.'

'But you didn't tell her he was here?'

'I couldn't. I don't know where he is.'

'Your child's father?'

'*Matias* is Hannah's father. He adopted her, he brought her up as his own.'

'But Hannah still wanted to know about her birth father.'

384

'She always knew Matias had adopted her. We didn't talk about it but when she turned eighteen last year, she wanted to know more.'

Again, Robin chose her words with great care. 'When you left the UK in 1999 or the beginning of 2000,' she said, 'you went to Brazil. Salvador – Un Lugar Seguro. You went ahead and, three months later, you were joined by the man you knew first as Brother Philip, Philip Hatton.'

Silence again.

'Mrs Lopez – Mimi – am I right about that?'

A whispered, 'Yes.'

'You had Hannah there in 2000, when you were fifteen,' she said gently. 'Mimi, is Philip Hannah's biological father?'

A long pause then another, 'Yes.'

'Were you and Philip,' she spoke as gently as possible, 'involved with each other when you went to Salvador?'

'We were together. In a relationship. We loved each other.'

'You were fifteen and Philip was how old? Thirty-five? Forty?'

'Thirty-four,' she said, as if Robin had traduced the man. 'And that, what you just said, is *exactly* why we had to leave. He told me at the time and he was right. People wouldn't have understood that it wasn't strange or criminal, that we simply loved each other.'

'But you were a child.'

'Oh, *child*,' she said, dismissive. 'Girls used to get married much earlier than that.'

They used to die of scurvy and smallpox, too, Robin thought; there'd been all sorts of advances. 'So you loved each other. And yet only four years later, you married Matias?'

'You obviously haven't met anyone like Philip,' Mimi said and there was a smile in her voice now, unmistakable, and also, yes, pity. 'To try and keep someone like him for yourself would be selfish, if it was possible.'

'I don't understand. Selfish, how?'

'Philip is a gift. His energy, his light. He should be shared.'

'Shared?'

'He gave me two of the other most important gifts of my life, too: Hannah and Matias.'

'How did he "give" you Matias?'

'He found him for me,' she said simply. 'Matias had come to work at a church in Salvador and once a fortnight, he gave a service in English. Philip went to listen – he missed hearing the Bible in English, he said.'

'Matias speaks English, too?'

'Yes, his mother does and she taught him. Philip and Matias got to know one another, then Matias started to volunteer at Lugar Seguro. One day Philip told me he thought God had sent Matias to Salvador so that he and I would find each other. I didn't know what he was talking about at first, I thought maybe he was trying to get rid of me.' A hint of a laugh, as if even now, in her current situation, the idea were ridiculous enough to be funny. 'But eventually he helped me to see that he was right. Matias is younger than him, closer to my age. Now I think how typical of Philip it was, that self-sacrifice.'

It was incredible, Robin thought. Breathtaking. The sheer brass balls of the man.

'When I understood that Matias and I were right for each other, Philip thought it would be better if he left so we could build our life without distractions.'

'Mimi, did Matias know that Hannah was Philip's child?'

'No,' she said quietly. 'Not until later, when Hannah was eight or nine. When I had our daughter Beatriz I had a crisis about him not knowing the truth and I told him.'

'How did he take it?'

She hesitated. 'Not well. He was very angry with Philip.'

Good, Robin thought, *good*. She desperately wanted Matias to be decent, she realized, to know that, finally, Miriam had found a real safe place in the world.

'Matias wanted to accuse him, involve the police. It took everything I had to persuade him not to – it was only when I said I didn't want Hannah to think she was part of a crime that he stopped.'

'What had you told him until then?'

'The same we told everyone in Brazil: that I was Philip's adopted daughter. We didn't want to have left England and gone all the way to South America only to face the same thing. We kept our relationship private, which was how we liked it anyway.'

'So until then Matias had thought that Hannah was . . . ?'

'Someone else's,' Mimi said, voice back to a whisper.

'Whose?'

'Someone who'd forced himself on me.'

'When you were fourteen. If you had Hannah in May, and you knew you were pregnant when you left, you must have been fourteen.'

Didn't she see it? Did she *still* not see it, now, nearly twenty years later, a mother of three in her thirties? Hadn't it occurred to her when *Hannah* was fourteen?

'Miriam, there's something else I don't understand,' she said. 'Everything you've told me, everything Jude told me about you – your faith, wanting to lead a good life – did you ever think about how your leaving hurt your family here?'

The change in her voice was instantaneous. 'Of course,' she cried. 'Of course I did!'

'Then . . . ?'

'For *Philip*. People wouldn't have understood – he would have gone to *prison*. I had to protect him!' She paused. 'And it was the only way for us to be together.'

For the four years until he got bored of you or you got too old and he palmed you off on Matias and legged it.

'And since then? When you came of age and were happy in your marriage?'

Miriam's voice shifted again, turning colder. 'My father committed suicide. Suicide is a sin, it's against God's will. Philip said that we were right to stay away, that sometimes in life you have to make difficult choices.'

Robin closed her eyes. And Miriam had listened to him. But at that point, she thought, given her situation, perhaps she'd had to, for her own sanity. Because otherwise she'd given up her life, destroyed her family, for – what?

More quietly, Miriam said, 'How could I ever go back when I killed my father?'

'You didn't. You didn't kill him. And you didn't kill your mother, either. They loved you, Miriam. Jude still does.'

There was silence on the line then a wrenching sob. 'How could she forgive me?'

'If you told her what you've told me, I think she would. I really think she would. More than anything, I think she'd just like her sister back.'

Miriam started sobbing so hard, Robin thought it must hurt. Once in the darkest days, when Lennie was tiny and she hadn't been able to see a way forward, she'd cried so hard she'd pulled a muscle in her back. 'It'll get better,' she told her, 'things will get better, I know. I promise.'

A couple of minutes went by before she was able to ask her last questions.

'Where did Philip go after Salvador, Mimi? Do you know?'

'Africa.' She gulped then crooned. 'To travel for a while, then decide. A few years ago, I saw him in a picture online.'

'Where?'

'With a charity in Zimbabwe.'

Robin's heart sank. 'Did he have any connection to Birmingham that you know of?'

'No. I don't think so.'

'Family here – friends? Did he ever mention Birmingham at all?'

'No,' she said. 'Never.'

Chapter Forty-one

Last night, her dad had been clinging to the idea that Luke had merely accompanied Billy to the protest (of course, being a white supremacist's plus-one was *much* better) but he knew the whole story now. When he came to the door at Mary Street, Robin could see it on him, lowering his head, rounding his shoulders. Like them, he was cowering, waiting for the hammer to fall.

That hammer. He still didn't know about the one over Lennie's head, or how Luke might use it.

The powerlessness was excruciating. To see Lennie so frightened and be unable to help her. She couldn't even give her information because there hadn't been any more. People cared about Shaun Palmer and the student but once they knew he'd regained consciousness, no one mentioned the skinhead. She couldn't ask Samir again, especially after the look he'd given her before. Mid-afternoon, she'd thought about calling the investigating team herself but she couldn't risk drawing attention. *Interesting – why do you want to know?* she imagined someone asking, making a note.

Lennie knew she was powerless, and that hurt, too. Robin had assumed she'd sleep in her room again, that she'd want the comfort of being together as much as she did, but she refused. 'No. I need to be on my own.'

'I'm here, Len,' she said. 'You're not alone.'

'I *never* will be, will I,' she said, voice like a slap, 'when I'm in *jail*.'

Though she'd promised herself she wouldn't, when she turned off the light, Robin reached for the sense memories of Samir again. She found, however, that she couldn't quite conjure them. They'd faded, lost their colour, and the slipping away struck her as a parallel for Samir himself. She saw him nearly every day, they talked all the time but, like Lennie at the other end of the landing, he was a thousand miles away, out of reach.

Robin felt a vacuum open up in her middle, an aching sense of loss. Eyes open in the dark, staring at the furniture outlined by the streetlight, she acknowledged what she'd spent eighteen years trying to deny: she still loved him. She'd never stopped.

And it was still over, even if she did know now why he'd ended it. Eighteen years. She'd had a baby, he'd married Liz, and had Harry and Leila. They were friends now – colleagues and friends – and that was that.

Well, *she* might have been in denial, she realized, but other people knew. She remembered Lennie in the car back from the hospital. *Maybe you don't want to get over what happened. Because if you do, it'll mean you've finally accepted it. That it's done and dusted – actually over.*

And Kev, that first night in his room. *You all right? Is it Samir?*

Then she remembered Samir's eyes the day he'd lost his temper. *Did it have to be Kev, Robin?*

Yes, she realized, it *had* had to be, and now she understood that, too. Because Kev belonged to those times, he'd been part of that scene, their friend. Because he was connected to Samir.

Chapter Forty-two

As she swam up towards the light, catastrophic scenarios loomed at her like deep-water fish: Luke was dead; her mother was dead; the white supremacist was dead and the police were coming for Lennie. She opened her eyes to find her heart beating far too fast, her T-shirt soaked. The alarm said 5.07.

She got out of bed too quickly, giving herself a head rush, and went to Lennie's room, afraid that the doom-scenarios had been an unconscious animal awareness of danger but Lennie was curled in a ball under her duvet, asleep and unhurt.

In her own room again, Robin fetched her laptop from the chest of drawers and brought it back to bed. Propping it on her knees, she typed 'Zimbabwe charity Brother Philip Hatton John Philips' into Google. Nearly three million results. She skimmed the first six pages – obituaries, articles from school magazines and various American foundations, nothing that struck her as relevant. Remembering Varan's strategy, she entered the same terms into Google Images and got a single page of bright photographs of children in school uniform, women in a market garden, posters for HIV fundraisers.

Was he still in Zimbabwe? Miriam said she'd seen the

photograph three or four years ago. He'd been in Salvador for four years, Northumbria about the same, as far as they could tell. Maybe he'd moved on. What name was he using these days? And what did he look like? She still had no idea. She'd asked Miriam to email a photograph but she said she'd only ever had a few – Surprise! Brother Phil was camera-shy – and Matias had destroyed them all in his rage when he'd learned the truth about Hannah.

She'd asked her to find the photograph online and send the link but nothing had arrived so far. She'd call her again as soon as she reasonably could but that was hours away – it was too early *here*, and Buenos Aires was hours behind.

Robin ran her eyes down the page. In all the pictures put together, thirty or forty, there were, what, three white people? She knew how old he'd be now: fifty-three. How many photographs of middle-aged white men working at Zimbabwean charities could there be?

Still in Images, she broadened her search to 'Zimbabwe charity' and started scrolling. The answer to her question, she saw almost immediately, was, far more than she'd hoped. Was this him, this guy with his arms around a bunch of schoolboys, doling out food at a buffet? Or this, standing with a group of adults in a nondescript conference room? She had no idea – how could she? He was a continent-hopping, name-changing, camera-avoiding shape-shifter. She kept scrolling anyway – at least while she was doing this, she didn't have to think about Luke or Lennie and whether the light starting to filter through the curtains was the beginning of the day when one or both of them would be arrested.

She reached a picture of a long single-storey building with a corrugated-iron roof, a group of people gathered on the dry grass in front, largely black with a handful of white faces at the back. Robin double-clicked to zoom in and ran her eyes along the row – woman, woman, man in his thirties, girl in her late teens or twenties, probably volunteering on a gap year. She moved on then stopped. Going back, she put her cursor on the girl's face and zoomed in again.

She looked, then looked again to be sure. Yes. Her hair was different, blonder, and she was very tanned, but yes.

It was Victoria Engel.

She texted both Samir and Malia, *Ring me ASAP,* then got out of bed and paced the room. Could it be a coincidence? What were the odds? Long, they had to be – very long.

Her notebook was in her bag in the kitchen. She crept downstairs, skirting the creaking steps. She wanted Lennie to sleep as long as possible before she woke to the nightmare again. She also needed time to think.

Back in bed, she turned to a new page and started scrawling down notes, trying to make sense of how it all fitted together – if it did. Hannah had died in Birmingham; Victoria was *from* here. She'd vanished five years ago, when she, like Miriam, had been fifteen, and now she'd rematerialized in Zimbabwe, in a small town not far from Harare, working for what this new charity's webpage said was a shelter for vulnerable women and teenagers (God, the irony). Zimbabwe, last confirmed whereabouts of Brother Phil.

If he *was* involved in Victoria's disappearance, what did that mean? That he must have been here in Birmingham or nearby at some point five years ago. He'd have been forty-eight then – surely getting towards the end of his days of dazzling teenage girls with his physical charms but maybe not *quite* at the end. One last hurrah? But when Miriam talked about him it hadn't been about physical attraction, had it? She'd thought Brother Phil would help her lead a good life – a moral life.

With a start, Robin remembered Martin Engel outside the station – 'She wanted to be a force for good in the world,' he'd told her. Bloody hell, was that how he did it? Was that how he'd persuaded Victoria to up sticks thousands of miles overseas with a man three times her age: she'd wanted to be good? Good, yes, maybe, but also, Robin thought, it was a powerful thing to be wanted. Wanted a lot. And at that age, by an older, charismatic man who promised you a life in which you made a difference, you mattered? *Teenage earnestness*, Robin wrote, *wanting to change world, awakening sexuality & perceived power over older man = heady, powerful? Drama & excitement, Africa/South America, travel, adventure versus school, exams, powerlessness, being a kid.*

She imagined being able to tell Martin Engel that Victoria was still alive, ending his five years of mental torment. He'd have pictured the worst every single day. If the photograph was anything to go by, she didn't look miserable. But then, like Miriam, if this *was* what had happened to her, she'd been worked on psychologically in some way, convinced that she was in love, that a life of adventure waited where she and this good but older man could be together.

But where had she *met* Brother Phil?

She wanted to be a force for good in the world – Martin had told her that. *She used to volunteer with me.*

Victoria had volunteered. Matias Lopez had volunteered at Un Lugar Seguro, it was how he'd met Miriam.

The Zimbabwean picture was open on her laptop, the long low building with the crowd outside. She clicked over to their website again, then on a link to 'Who We Are'. Tariro Yangu, she read, was a shelter and soup kitchen.

A soup kitchen.

Was it possible? Quickly, as if the idea might slip away, she opened a new window and searched for 'Good Hope Kitchen Birmingham'. A well-designed home-page with a pen-and-ink sketch of the building itself told her about Good Hope's 'mission' to provide warm meals and a sense of community for those in need. She clicked on 'Who We Are'.

The Kitchen, she read, *was opened in 2018 by our Director, Daniel Reid, who was inspired by his decades of charity work in South America and South Africa* – South Africa, nice dodge, she thought – *to give back closer to home in the UK. Funded entirely by donations, he was able to establish Good Hope as a bright spot for the homeless and hungry in inner-city Birmingham.*

Underneath Reid was a list of 'Our Volunteers', voluminous paragraphs about each – partners, hobbies, pets, life goals – accompanying smiling headshots. Reid, at the top of the page, was photo-less.

At half past six she called Samir. It rang five times before he picked up. 'I thought you weren't going to answer,' she said. 'You told me you were up early.'

'I am.'

'I texted you ages ago.'

'You were up *too* early. I got up a minute ago and thought I'd quickly use the bathroom, if that's all right, before getting sucked into whatever new vortex you're about to set spinning. Go on then.'

She told him in the order it had fallen into place for her: Zimbabwe, Victoria, the soup kitchen.

'If I'm right,' she said, 'he's here, in Birmingham, and I know who he is – I've met him. Brother Phil Hatton also known as John Philips is now also known as Daniel Reid of the Good Hope Kitchen.'

'What, is that the soup kitchen in Bordesley?'

'Where Stewpot and Martin go to eat – we've left messages for them there, I asked him, Reid, myself if we could. I reckon that's how he knew about Gisborne's in the first place, from them. He even told me they'd taken food to the homeless at the back, off Warwick Street.'

It occurred to her now that they hadn't heard from Stew and Martin since she left the message for them on Saturday night.

'And you're sure Reid is Brother Phil?'

'Not a hundred per cent, not yet, but . . . There's not a photograph of the man to be had, Samir, anywhere. We need CCTV of him at the factory and I'm going to call Jude.'

'And Martin Engel?'

'Not until we've got Reid in custody and I've spoken to him. Not until I'm sure I won't be raising his hopes only to dash them again.'

Samir was quiet for a moment as he absorbed it. 'Bloody hell, Robin, if you're right . . . Victoria Engel *and* Miriam Chapman.'

Robin remembered Jude in the stockroom behind her shop, her emotional turmoil. *But if she is her daughter, and if Mirry is alive now, then her daughter is dead.*

'But not Hannah,' she said.

'No, not Hannah.' He was quiet but then he said what she'd been thinking, 'Miriam disappeared nearly twenty years ago; Victoria was five years ago. Rob – what if there were others in between? What if there are more girls?'

She texted Jude asking her to call, then emailed Tark to put his entire crew on footage of Warwick and the surrounding streets on Saturday afternoon. She was buttoning her shirt after a fleeting shower when her phone rang. She reached for it, expecting Jude or Malia responding to her earlier message. It was her dad.

'Your mother wants to see you,' he announced. 'Now.'

'Now? I can't, Dad, believe me, I really can't, I—'

'Now,' her father said, brooking no argument. 'Before you go to work. You and Lennie.'

Chapter Forty-three

Malia called as they were leaving the house. Robin looked up and down the street where, as far as she could see, no one from the *Daily Herald* was lurking. Nevertheless, she waited until the car doors were closed before telling her what was going on. 'We need to bring Reid in this morning,' she said, 'Let's get teams to Good Hope and his home address. If we get him, we'll give him two or three hours to sweat then let's interview him together, you and me.'

Lennie was hearing about Reid for the first time, too, and even in the depths of her misery, she was incredulous. When the call ended, she said, 'So all this time, like, *twenty years*, he was going back and forth between the UK and these other places, taking girls away from their families, hiding them and living with them for a bit, then moving on?'

'That's what happened with Miriam, yes; we don't know about Victoria yet.'

'But that's what you think. For God's sake, what's *wrong* with them?' Lennie said. 'These . . . *men*.' Among them, his name never spoken, the one who'd taken *her* from her family, or tried.

'It's a handful, sweetheart, just a handful.'

'It's *enough*.'

For the rest of the ride, Len's responses were monosyllables, and as they waited at the barrier for the hospital car park, Robin looked over and saw that she'd folded in on herself, made herself as small as possible, as if she was expecting physical blows. When she'd gone to wake her up, she'd been lying on her back, eyes open and staring at the ceiling. She hadn't moved and she didn't say a word until Robin told her that her granny wanted to see her. 'Is she okay?' she'd asked quickly and then, when she heard yes, she'd closed her eyes. 'She knows then, doesn't she? About me.'

'Yes, love.'

'You told her.' An accusation.

'No. Uncle Luke did.'

When they arrived on the ward, her mother's bed was empty. Seeing Lennie's face, the nurse at the desk assumed that she'd jumped to the wrong conclusion. 'Oh no, love, don't worry, she's fine,' she smiled. 'In fact, she's doing much better – cup of tea this morning and she was up and out, in the shower. She's in the TV room.'

Her mother had set herself up in a small bay off the main room where, Noël Coward-resplendent in a smart pink paisley dressing gown that Robin hadn't seen before, she'd taken a corner chair with a view of the door like a Mafia don.

Robin kissed her hello – she had her perfume on, too; Dennis must have brought it in – but Lennie hung back.

'Don't I get a kiss, love?'

Len shot Robin a pained look then moved in. Her mother hugged her for a long time then directed them into chairs, one on either side.

'All right,' she said, 'I can't speak loudly so you'll have to listen.' She looked at the door to check no one was coming, then lowered her voice again. 'I spoke to Luke last night.'

Robin opened her mouth but her mother put up a hand. 'As you know, Robin, he's been doing some thinking and now he's made his decisions.' She paused, and cast another look at the door. 'He'll tell the police he threw the stone at that man.'

Lennie's eyes went round. 'What?' she cried. 'No. No way, he—'

'Be quiet,' her grandmother hissed, 'and listen. I know what happened, yes, all of it, and I've thought about it very carefully, as has he. We're agreed: it's the right thing.'

Robin felt momentarily light-headed, as if, like earlier, she'd stood up too quickly. The edges of her vision pixelated. She heard Lennie's voice, an urgent whisper. 'Gran, you can't—'

'Your uncle's actions nearly cost that young man his eyesight, Elena, do you understand?'

'I nearly cost someone his *life*! I might still – we don't know how . . .'

'*Be quiet!*'

Lennie stared. She'd only ever seen the velvet-glove side of her grandmother, Robin realized, coming back to herself. Under normal circumstances, the iron fist was reserved for her.

'He's all over the newspapers with *Nazis*.' Her mother spat the word. 'White supremacists. He chose to go there, he knew what the protest was about – susceptible or not, depressed or not, he *chose*. His grandfather fought in the war to stop people like that – millions of people died. He knows where it leads, that kind of behaviour. There's no excuse.'

Lennie's eyes were bright with tears; her grandmother ignored them. 'The police are looking for him and, as I know from your mother, he'll be charged for what he did to that student and he'll go to prison. So he can add on some time for the stone.'

Len shook her head, and tears spilled down her cheeks.

'Yes, Elena. I'm not having my granddaughter in the slammer

as well as my son, and that's final. You made a mistake, a stupid, *stupid* mistake, but I'm not going to let it mess up your life. Because that is what will happen. If you're charged, if – God forbid – you're sent to a young offender's institute, it will ruin your life. I won't have it.'

'Mum . . .'

'And it's time for Luke to start taking some responsibility for his actions,' her mother said, looking at Robin. 'We can't claim this is a one-off, these views aren't new. We've all heard his comments before, I've spoken to him about it countless times, so has your dad, but I didn't know until this week how much damage they've caused.' She looked back at Lennie. 'If you can't live with Luke taking the blame for you,' she murmured, 'think of it as him finally taking responsibility for what he did to your mother and Samir.'

They were silent in the elevator, silent as they crossed the lobby towards the main entrance, but outside, as they approached the car, Lennie stopped. 'Mum.' Emotions were moving across her face like clouds, grief and fear, guilt then relief. Like the team on the morning of Gupta's death, she was looking for guidance: *What do I do, Mum?* her eyes said. *How am I even supposed to* feel?

Robin pulled her into a tight hug and felt her shaking. 'It's okay,' she said. 'It'll be okay. She's taking care of us, Len. Both of us.'

Lennie had come downstairs in her uniform and when they left the hospital, she was adamant that school was where she needed to be. 'Same as yesterday – what am I going to do otherwise, sit at home with it all whirling round my head?'

'No, I get it,' Robin said. More than she'd ever admit; work had been her refuge for years.

She pulled over in the designated spot around the corner from St Saviour's to protect Lennie's street cred. The rush was over and only the stragglers were left, a couple hurrying, bags banging against their backs, the one she was watching now, a sixth former, dragging his feet as if he were trying to scrape the tread off his trainers.

'How's Austin?' she said. 'Have you been in touch with Asha?'

'Yeah. And him.' The faintest hint of a smile. 'We were texting last night. He says as long as he keeps popping ibuprofen like Smarties, he feels a bit better.'

'Good.'

'Yeah. He's going to try and come back to school next Wednesday or Thursday.' The dashboard clock changed to 8.37. 'I'd better go.' She reached into the footwell for her backpack, pulled it on to her knee. 'I'll see you later. Good luck today – get him, Mum.' She opened the door.

'Len, wait a minute. Are you going to be all right? Really – no bravado?'

She nodded. 'Yeah. I'll be okay.'

Chapter Forty-four

'Anything?'

Tarka looked round only briefly. 'Not yet.' Down the row of desks, and the parallel row behind, his crew were in thrall to their screens, even Phil Howell looking as if he was watching *Game of Thrones* rather than CCTV of a scruffy industrial street on a Saturday afternoon.

'He's got to be here somewhere, Tark,' she said. 'If he got out, he got in.'

'We're on it, guv. We'll find him.'

'Let me know the moment you get something.' As if he wouldn't.

At least she wasn't the only one on edge. The atmosphere had been palpable the moment she'd come through the door, alive with energy. If they touched, she thought, they'd give each other little static shocks. Everyone was waiting; it was like Christmas Eve but with the possibility that Santa might pull a no-show.

She'd missed two calls from Jude while she'd been driving so she went to her office, took a couple of deep breaths then rang her back.

She answered immediately. 'Robin?'

'Hi, sorry for the delay, I was in the car. Are you at the shop?'

'No, I stayed at home.' She sounded a bit breathless. 'When I got your message, I thought maybe something had happened and . . . John's with me.'

'Good. Do you want to sit down?'

Chair legs scraped a wooden floor. 'What is it?' Her voice was full of fear. 'Just tell me.'

'Jude, I spoke to Miriam last night.'

A cry, sharp as if she was hurt, but there was joy in it, too. 'They've found her,' a male voice said in the background. Footsteps then the chair legs again, the rustle of a hug, 'Oh, love.'

Jude was crying when she spoke again. 'I was trying so hard not to hope. After you came, and after we spoke the other day . . . If I hoped, and she hadn't . . . Where is she? Is she all right? Can I see her?'

'She's all right, yes. Devastated to hear about her daughter, but herself, physically, okay.'

'Oh my God, poor Mirry – poor Mirry. Hannah,' she said to John.

Robin told her about the church in Buenos Aires. 'She's married – very happily, I think – she's Mimi Lopez now, and she has two younger children, a girl and a boy.'

'Mimi Lopez? Buenos Aires? Whoa – that's . . . John, she's in *Argentina*.'

'It's a long story,' Robin said, 'but I hope you might hear it from her soon.' At that, Jude started sobbing; Robin waited until she was able to listen again. 'I hope *I'll* be able to tell you more later today. But there's something I need. If I send you a photograph of a man this morning, could you tell me if you recognize him?'

She was distracted by her mobile, a text lighting the screen: Malia.

Got him at Good Hope. On our way.

*

405

While she waited, she began making notes towards an interview strategy. Where to start? She looked through her window at the whiteboard. Mimi was up there now, she'd added her before she left yesterday because she'd wanted Hannah – she knew it was ridiculous – to have her mother with her overnight. None of what she'd worked out this morning was up. She was waiting, holding off for fear that by trying to pin it down too roughly, too fast, she would scare it away. So often this case had felt like a will o' the wisp, now a flickering, tantalizing light, now nothing at all.

From this distance, Hannah's face in the scene photographs was a pallid oval. She'd ask Miriam for new ones today in which she wasn't a victim but a human being, a young woman. Hannah Lopez of Buenos Aires, a young woman on the cusp of her adult life.

Her phone lit up again, not a text this time but a call. *Kevin Y.* She looked at it while it rang three times. Then she picked it up, stood and rounded her desk to close the door.

'Kev?'

'Hello, I was just thinking about you, thought I'd give you a buzz. How are you getting on over there?'

The warmth of his voice was like a blanket round her shoulders and Robin felt a pressing sadness. She would miss these calls – she would miss *him*, his texts and talking in his car, snogging like teenagers, the occasions when they managed a night together. She liked him.

She liked him but she wasn't going to fall in love with him. She couldn't – she wasn't free to.

'Doing okay,' she said. 'Making progress, I think. At last.'

She'd justified their new kind of relationship by thinking he wouldn't fall in love with her, either – he never had before, why now? But he was a man who liked people in his life, a woman to look after as much – no, more than – to look after him, and Sasha's leaving had made him vulnerable. She could see how, because they got on, he might convince himself it was more than it was and find a way to settle for her. He deserved better.

'Glad to hear it,' he said, 'I won't ask details – you can tell me when you've got the bastard. Soon, I hope. Any chance of that dinner *this* weekend, do you reckon?'

'Kev . . .' She closed her eyes for a second. 'Probably not dinner.'

'Sure, whatever you fancy.'

'Can we meet for coffee? Saturday morning? We should talk.'

'Ah,' he said, and it was less a word than a sigh.

Chapter Forty-five

For someone who'd been plucked from work in full view of his staff and clientele, arrested for murder and left to contemplate his fate in a cell for three hours, Daniel Reid was almost preternaturally composed. As she and Malia entered the interview room, he smiled at them not in the supercilious way of a man who believed he was too clever to be undone by the mere legal system but as if he were actually pleased to see them. His body language was relaxed; he sat straight but not bolt upright, his forearms resting lightly on the edge of the table. His blue and white striped shirt looked softened by wear in a way that made Robin think with a pang of Lennie's Malibu T-shirt. The top button was undone, the sleeves rolled to below the elbow, all the better to showcase the dread leather bracelets.

His solicitor, a man called Andrew Evans whom Robin hadn't dealt with before, looked relaxed, too, as if he was confident this would all be easily sortable, and they'd be out, no harm done, in time for a bite of lunch.

Malia started the recording and while she gave their names for the tape, Robin made eye contact with Reid. Like when she'd met him at the soup kitchen, his eyes were warm, the thick

408

lashes adding to an impression of smiling kindness. He was watching her as intently as she was watching him; in other circumstances, she thought, she might have been flattered.

'Mr Reid . . .'

'Please – Daniel.'

Robin nodded but didn't say it. 'You understand that you've been arrested on suspicion of the murder of Hannah Lopez, just turned nineteen, whose body was discovered on the morning of June ninth at the disused Gisborne works in Deritend.'

'I understand *what* you're saying, yes, but not *why*. Why me, I mean. There's been a mistake somewhere along the line.'

'Mr Reid, did you know Hannah Lopez?'

He shook his head. 'No.'

She looked at Malia, who opened her folder and took out a headshot from the scene. She slid it across the table, telling the tape what she was doing. Reid looked at it, his expression one of pity and regret for the stranger who'd met a violent end.

'You don't recognize her?' Robin asked. 'You never met?'

'No. Unless she came to the shelter. She wasn't one of our regulars but she might have come in. There's no way to check that, I'm afraid, no records. We make a point of it.'

'You're familiar with the Gisborne works, though?'

Reid met her eye and smiled again. 'Yes. Not intimately but yes – we talked about it when you came to Good Hope last week.' Again, Robin thought, in different circumstances she might have been charmed that he remembered the minutiae of their conversation. 'Through Stuart and Martin,' he said, turning to his solicitor. 'Two of the homeless men who use us pretty regularly. They're witnesses in the case – the police have left messages with us when they've needed to contact them. I mean, I *say* they're witnesses – I *assume* that's what they are at the moment, given that *I'm* under arrest.' He looked back at her, eyes crinkling. 'I've been with them a couple of times to bring food to a group of homeless who live at the back of the building.'

'On the subject of Stew and Martin, we've been trying to locate them since Saturday. I left a message on your machine.'

'Yes, that's right.'

'So you haven't seen them at all since then? They haven't been in?'

He met her eye again and held her gaze as if challenging her to prove him wrong. 'No.'

'Right.' She let the word hang. 'Where were you on the evening of Saturday the eighth of June, Mr Reid?'

Andrew Davies touched a hand to his arm but it seemed motivated by a desire to look like he was doing his job rather than any real urge to caution.

'Saturday before last? I was at home.'

'All evening?'

'Yes.'

'What about the afternoon?'

'Same. I had a lazy day, pottered around, read a book.'

'Can anyone confirm that?'

He grimaced. 'I'm afraid not, I was on my own. The neighbours would have seen my lights on after it got dark but no.'

'But you definitely weren't out with Hannah Lopez on Saturday afternoon?'

He frown-smiled: *No, you loons, how could I have been when we'd never met?*

'For the tape, Mr Reid.'

'No,' he said. 'I wasn't.'

Robin looked at Malia, who opened the folder again and slid a new image across the table. It was Tark's pièce de résistance, a still from ten seconds of footage from a single camera, found

410

an hour ago. 'At last,' he'd said, letting his forehead rest on his keyboard. '*At last.*'

When the men looked at it, the lawyer jumped infinitesimally before he could stop himself.

'The image is taken from CCTV of Warner Street on the afternoon of June eighth,' Malia said, 'at four twelve in the afternoon. The image, we believe, shows you, Mr Reid, with Hannah Lopez.'

'No,' he said, impressively cool. 'Like I said, there's a mistake. I was at home. I don't know Hannah Lopez.'

'I'm afraid we'd be more comfortable taking your word about that,' said Robin, 'if we didn't know that, in fact, Hannah was your daughter.'

The solicitor looked between them, Robin then Reid. 'What the hell is going on here?'

'Mr Reid is Hannah Lopez's biological father, Mr Davies. Her mother is Miriam Lopez, née Chapman, who disappeared from her home in Whitley Bay on New Year's Eve 1999. Hannah Lopez grew up in South America, where Mr Reid had arranged for Miriam to go on ahead of him, when they learned that she was pregnant by him. Aged fourteen.'

For a moment, Reid's composure seemed to falter. Then he shook his head. 'This is rubbish,' he said. 'I don't know what you're smoking round here. Did you get it from Stew and Martin? They're junkies,' he told Davies, dismissive. 'Hopeless.'

'When Miriam Chapman agreed to run away to Brazil – and she *did* agree, I know that,' Robin nodded at him, 'because I spoke to her last night – she was leaving for a new life with a man she knew as Philip Hatton or Brother Philip, because he was the leader of the church group she attended with her parents and her sister, Judith. I spoke to Judith an hour ago and she identified you by the photographs we took earlier, Mr Reid, as that same man.'

'I'd like time with my client, Detective Chief Inspector.'

'I can imagine. Before you do that, though, so you know the full scope of what we're looking at here – so far – I should tell you that on top of Hannah's case, we're also looking into Mr Reid's – or Mr Hatton's or Mr Philips' – connection to the disappearance of Victoria Engel, aged fifteen, five years ago.'

'Victoria Engel?' Davies looked alarmed. Clearly her father's awareness campaign had worked on him.

'Victoria was volunteering with her father at a charity in Coventry in the months before she disappeared. We've contacted them with your photograph this morning, too, Mr Reid, and they told us you'd been head of fundraising for their group, as well as a weekend volunteer in the same branch as Victoria and her father, between 2012 and 2014. My team have also spoken to staff at a shelter and soup kitchen in Zimbabwe who identified Victoria from a photograph as the young woman who'd volunteered there until last year. As did you, Mr – should I call you Mr Reid? *They* seemed to know you as John Daniels.'

Reid turned to his solicitor. 'This is nuts.'

Robin nodded. 'Isn't it? But it's why Hannah died. As you know, having delivered her yourself, she was born in May 2000 so she came of age last year. She'd started making enquiries about her biological father and – impressive, given the obstacles you'd thrown up – she'd traced you here to Birmingham and got in touch asking to meet. Maybe she did come just to meet you but more likely, we think, given the outcome, she came to confront you with what she'd learned. Your past was threatening to unravel and you couldn't have it. Killing your own child – very tough. But sometimes in life you have to make difficult choices, don't you?'

When they resumed half an hour later, Reid's sangfroid was less convincing, especially when she told him that a tech at the consulate in Buenos Aires would be going through Hannah's computer and email account, including looking for any messages she'd deleted to cover her tracks if Miriam smelled a rat about the Chilean silent retreat.

'Here's the thing,' Robin told him. 'We do know we're going to find messages.'

Reid said nothing but his eyes challenged her again, any warmth gone. *Yeah? How?*

'Hannah's death was immaculately planned. You couldn't have done it unless . . .'

'Again: I *didn't* do it.'

'Unless you'd had significant time to plan – probably weeks. The CCTV cameras – the entire length of Warwick Street without being caught on tape.' She shook her head. 'And the Tramadol you gave her – the levels in her blood were enough to keep her asleep for a couple of days, Forensics said, had the physical shock of being stabbed not woken her up. But you needed that time, didn't you – if you'd killed her earlier and been seen with her body, it would have been a disaster. Hiding on the roof for hours and then coming down *outside* where you'd calculated we might put the cordon, and *outside* the time frame when we would be looking, having been tipped off by Stew and Martin's discovery of the body, or so you hoped, and assuming our killer was long gone.'

Reid's solicitor now had the look of a man several fathoms out of his depth.

'But patience is your thing, isn't it, Mr Reid? It's why you've been able to do this for so long. Meet an underage girl, groom her, pack her off overseas, then wait until the heat's off before quietly sloping off to join her. Most people don't have that degree of self-control. Even when you move on. Attention to detail – if they're happy, why would there be repercussions? Did you find Victoria a Matias?'

'This is harassment,' Davies said limply.

'It's police work, and this is only the start. You've hit the jackpot, Mr Davies. Hundreds of billable hours – thousands. Who knows how many other missing girls we'll find stashed in hidey-holes by the time we've finished?'

Malia had been quiet since they'd come back in. 'Attention to detail is one thing,' she said now, 'but then there's the calculation. The cruelty. One of the things we've been asking from the beginning is how Hannah's killer got her to go into that wreck of a factory. But you'd go in with your dad, wouldn't you? Your charity-worker dad who asked you, his Christian daughter, to help him drop off food to the homeless and desperate? I don't think Hannah *was* coming to unmask you, Mr Reid. I think she came because she wanted to know who you were. And I think she found out.'

Chapter Forty-six

Rhona wasn't at her desk. Before knocking on the internal door, Robin tucked her shirt in and ran a fingertip under her eyes to collect errant mascara. That would be typical Kilmartin: ignore the two murders they'd solved and the two long-standing mispers, one of them famous, to pick up instead on the fact that after multiple nights of appalling sleep and eighteen-hour days, she looked a bit unkempt.

When Samir called her in, however, he was at his desk and alone, the afternoon light free to stream through the long window unimpeded by manspreading.

'Hi. Thanks for coming so quickly. Could you close the door?'

Robin was instantly on alert. 'Thanks for coming' – after all this? And after the last time they were here on their own together?

'I need to show you something,' he said, opening a laptop next to the computer on his desk. Ben Tyrell, she thought at once, but if it was, it couldn't be anything new. Steve Taggart, then – had he taken up the online mantle? But no, of course not, he was in custody, too, where they were throwing the book at him and his Heil Hitler moves.

When they'd watched Tyrell's rants, Samir had called her

around the desk next to him; this time he turned the computer so that she could see from the other side. Not Facebook or a vlog but amateur video, filmed on a phone. When she understood what she was looking at, Robin's heart seemed to stop before it restarted with a single painful beat.

Samir dragged the cursor two thirds of the way along the bar at the bottom then let it play.

The protest, the phone's struggle to keep filming recalling exactly her own experience of being buffeted by the crowd, pushed backwards then forwards, barely an agent of free will. Everything at eye level – faces, shoulders, signs, flying cans and plastic bottles.

The shiny globe of a helmet dominated the picture for several seconds and then, when it moved away, Robin saw her brother's face. Even with the chaos and the poor-quality image, she could tell that he was alarmed, not only by everything that was going on around him, by what he'd just done, but something else. Something specific. In the group of people in front of him, among the thicket of heads and arms and shoulders, he'd seen something.

And then Lennie came into view, as if she'd been hiding and popped up suddenly. Hiding or bending to pick up something from the ground.

Away to the right of the screen, screaming like a Visigoth at the sack of Rome, Robin saw the same skinhead who, a minute later, she'd seen herself in the flesh laid out on the ground.

She thought she might puke as she watched her brother try to push his way through the crowd to reach Lennie, thrust back again and again. At last he managed it but then the crowd swelled behind them, trapping them in place, pinning their arms to their sides like toy soldiers.

Then, rage written across her face, Lennie got her arm free, pulled it back and hurled the stone through the air.

Samir hit 'stop'. 'I've had a call from Marshall, who's running the investigation. Your brother's handed himself in. He's confessed to hurting the student with the sign *and* to throwing the stone.'

Robin waited, hearing her pulse in her head.

'I saw it happen, Rob,' he said. 'I saw her throw it. That's why I've been trawling the Net for these. This is the only one I've found so far that caught it.'

'Has anyone else seen it?'

'Thirty-seven other people according to the page but, Rob, so far, in the comments, no one's made the connection. The stone leaves her hand but this didn't catch him getting hit, we don't see that. Unless you were trying to put it together forensically, you wouldn't necessarily make the connection – there's so much other crap flying through the air.'

She sat down. 'Does he have this? Marshall?'

'No.' Samir lowered his voice. 'And I'm not going to give it to him.'

'But they've got CCTV.'

He smiled – actually grinned. 'No. They haven't – he was lamenting the fact. Apparently, right in front of the camera that would have caught where the stone was coming from, there's a woman with a bloody enormous sign. #ForQueen&Country, no less.'

'You're kidding me.'

'Nope.' His eyes sparkled with amusement.

'Then you've got to give them this. If they find out later you knew about it and . . .'

'They won't – how would they? Are you going to tell them?' He pushed the lid of the laptop gently shut. 'Robin, your brother's going down, stone or no stone – half of Force Homicide were watching from the window when he shoved the sign in that guy's eyes. They might not know he's your

417

brother but there's seven or eight people who could pick him out of a line-up.'

'They don't know *yet*.'

'Like I said before, we can handle that. And if he can handle this for Lennie, let him. Let him and let me. Give her that chance.'

He eyeballed her, refusing to let her look away until she said, 'Yes. All right, yes.'

'Good.'

An awkward silence followed; Robin felt compelled to break it. 'Thank God you're broadly benevolent,' she said, 'because you've definitely got dictatorish tendencies.'

'Oh yeah, drunk on my own limitless power, that's me.'

He looked towards the window where the light caught his eyes and turned their deep brown to golden. 'You know, given Martin Engel's talent for publicity,' he said, 'you'll make it into the papers for the right reasons for a change. And even without Engel. Have you spoken to him yet?'

'Just now.'

'How did he take it?'

'He was . . . I actually don't think there's a word.'

'Joy?'

'To the power of fifty. A hundred.'

He shook his head, smiling. 'This case, man. It's huge. Already huge. Robin – thank you.'

'For what? Putting something in the plus column for a change? Me *and* Webster, by the way. At least when Kilmartin comes rattling his sabre, we'll be ready for him now. For a couple of weeks, anyway. Then he'll be mincing in again, voice two octaves higher due to the spray-on trousers, and . . .'

'Could you stop pissing about for a *moment*?'

She stopped, surprised by his tone: real impatience.

'I'm serious,' he said. 'I'm *trying* to be serious. To say thank

418

you – for all this.' He came around the desk, stopping a couple of feet in front of her. 'When I asked you to apply for the job, I told you I needed you. You've seen that now, graphically. How many days – will it *be* a whole day? – before the next one?' He looked away and his gaze seemed to land momentarily on the photographs on his desk. 'Look, what I'm trying to say . . . I didn't *just* need you. I wanted you here – I *want* you here. Please don't leave again.'

Acknowledgements

I am hugely grateful to Helen Garnons-Williams, whose editorial judgement is second to none, and to Victoria Hobbs, for her deep wisdom and clear-sightedness. I'm privileged to have worked with you both. Thank you.

Anna Kelly, your care and enthusiasm for this book are enormously appreciated, thank you.

I'm grateful to Alex Gingell and Nicola Webb at 4th Estate, and to Alexandra McNicoll, Alex Elam, Vickie Dillon and Gosia Jezierska at AM Heath.

A big thank you to Colin Scott, to Neil Lancaster for his police insight and expertise, and Judith Cutler, doyenne of Birmingham crime-writing, for her local knowledge and support

Written as it largely was in 2020, *Risk of Harm* would not exist without two unorthodox 'writer's residencies', first with my brother- and sister-in-law Paul and Suzy Rosen in Delaware and then with Millie Perry and Andrew MacArthur in Maine. Thank you all for the time and the space, the suppers, the fun and the desk-delivered gimlets. This one's for you.

Joe and Bridget – Captain Logistics and the Leopard Lady – I don't have to tell you that this book would not be finished without all your efforts and sacrifices. Thank you.